RESURGERE

RESURGERE

DAVID CHRISTOPHER PEREZ

ISBN: 978-0-991-56890-1

Cover Design: David C. Perez
Cover Photos: Getty Images / iStockphoto

www.davidcperezwriter.com

RESURGERE

A Love Song

In loathsome hours when the starlings cry,
Boring for ivory grubs with ravenous glee,
A bosom memory of a serpentine lie
Exacts a hoary lesson onto me.

What plague you spat, cajoling my might?
Deftly dancing 'round the world, 'round the world,
  spinning a vertiginous scene?
You choked this blushing neophyte,
  a malingerer of the night,
Drowning in a climactic, oceanic dream.

Laughing and sighing, you stare at the glow
Of another persnickety internet show.

Tell me, dear friend
Do I not speak true?
Do you not long to dance with another
To love and wish anew?

(It's new to me!
Have an upvote, a meme, a bit.ly linked scheme!)

Laughing and sighing, you stare at the glow
Of another persnickety internet show.

Imposter. I shall strike a deal
To reveal an inalienable mystery.
Remember those Stine-tales of chilled zeal?
Tremble. A far deeper, seminal evil will force
  my blind lover to see.

Do I dare? Do I dare? Do I dare? Do I dare?
Of course, said the universe, I long to be disturbed.

Galadriel, lend me your ring!
Ha! Not that one, the one that made my heart sting.
Now three times in a row, say this with me.
Resurgere, Daemon Annuli.

Not static fiction but a whisper that sears
A yearning to gloat or impress its host
Dear, can you hear what spoils your ears?
More odious than the screeching dregs of a
   Rowling bathroom ghost.

(Wiki, wiki, blog. Wiki, wiki, blog, blog.
Research reveals an audio hack. A Wolfram reply.
Or a cheating Cleverbot!)

Let's continue our last temptation of fate.
(OMG, Christ? And I'm the imposter?)
Belief is serially measured and need not complicate.
Sing with me, a-one, a-two, a-three.
Resurgere, Daemon Annuli.

A prickly poke taps your left leg and neck
Silence the world to recapture your breath
Fair chaos has retched the foulest dreck.
Curious still to explore its depth?

(No. The Man with the Yellow Hat is dead.)

Lingua cicuta shall be done by me.
Resurgere, Daemon Annuli.

Crippling night devours the consolation of hope
A somber prophet beckons the demise
Of your True Love, your marvel, your beauty,
   your perfect trope.
One I am not, will never be, and undoubtedly,
   would despise.

Am I a fool continue?
Of course, said Prince Hamlet, you are a proper fool.

Tiptoe, my tulip, tiptoe to me.
Resurgere, Daemon Annuli.

Crouched in a corner or perched on a chair,
Running crooked fingers through your crooked hair,
Spewing needles through your sacred, scarred soul,
The malevolent one has risen.
Throbbing and mocking your own sinister role.

Stop! You shout.
But I cannot! I cannot!
A hundred more times, recited by me:
Resurgere, Daemon Annuli!

Paralyzed.
Pair of eyes.
Bloodied tears and bloodied sighs,
Insufferable pain that only we singed hearts know.
Cruel realization of mistaken trust
Where lonely, lusting fools, fight, wither then rust.

Tell me, Persephone,
Did I not speak true?
Your persistent farming for another
Has triumphantly consumed you.

Is this? Is this? Is this how it ends?
Of course not, I said, but whimper if you must.

(Hear the sirens, sirens, sirens.
How they whirr, whirr, whirr in a 9/11 blur.
To the moaning and the groaning of the sirens.)

Dare I sing the words once a-more,
Letting despair forever ensnare your cancerous core?
No uniformed savior will you be able to find
As my ruins erode your crumbling, mumbling mind.

(It's over. It's been tweeted and repeated and retweeted.)

Yes, it's over. Farewell, old stranger,
I will flee, I will part
With only my celebrated, venerated, broken heart.

(You are not a Tin Man! Everyone knows!)

I am now free.
From sea to shining sea.

(Freedom? Never! Everyone knows!)

Was that a murmur?
A gasp?
As I turned to pass
Through the door?
I shall pause.
And smile.
And mutter the
Cursed words
Once more.

Remember me, sweetly.

Resurgere, Daemon Annuli.

ONE

I met the greatest love of my life, Melinda, during my first year at the University. I feel I have earned the right to say that without hyperbole even though I graduated less than a year ago. We met in our freshman dorm, Perkins Hall, when we were still academic all-stars, simpletons who believed that all arguments were irrational and apocalyptic and all sex was life-affirming and transcendent. We were Google-coached know-it-alls, bloated with grandiose dreams of what amazing things we would accomplish and what remembered people we would become, completely unaware of that austere knowledge that only comes from socially-broadcasted heartbreak and attention-deficit boredom, ironically achieved success and isolating failure. We didn't yet know that there were many things we would never get a chance to try, much less achieve, and we were as cosmetically bland and ordinary as everyone else in the world.

Yes, my greatest love, Melinda, was ordinary. Even though I know full well what caused her death.

But let me go back to vainglorious beginnings. I was two months into my freshman year before I even had the courage to speak to Melinda. At first, my hope saturated ego could only glance at her as we tumbled through the corridors of Perkins Hall, spinning with half-assed solutions on how to maximize productivity and opportunity. Our interactions could be best characterized as indifferent courtesy. Yet we weren't anonymous. Perkins wasn't that large of a dormitory, only the fifth largest housing complex on campus, but it was big on diversity. Out of one hundred and forty two students there were eighty-three females, thirty-four Asian/Pacific Islanders, thirty-one Hispanic/Latinos, sixteen African-Americans, eleven LGBT's, and one paraplegic who was also one-eighth Native American. And, of course, there was one racially-blended coward, an only child, who preferred *The Feynman Lectures* over Netflix and library naps over beer pong, and who each day orchestrated complex, furtive peeks at a blonde-haired, toothy girl from the East Coast whose promise-reflecting eyes had swallowed up his girlfriend-deprived, chemistry lab-loving mind. But most people only knew me as Daniel, the quiet one.

As I said, Perkins was a relatively small space in the University world, and my path crossed often with Melinda. But I had committed to a persona that I called the passive neighbor – the kid who was content to straddle the line between stranger and acquaintance and kept his instant character analyses (assassinations) between himself and his morning coffee. At most, I would give Melinda a sleepy nod as we schlepped out of the dorm's crumbling stone arched entrance, shielding our faces from the 8:00 AM sun as we grabbed our bikes to ride to our respective first classes. Or maybe a groveling smile when I accidentally brushed up against her, pretending to act like a health-conscious scavenger as I weaved through the dining hall chow line to construct a lopsided salad for a ninety second lunch. I hadn't managed to say one word to her aside from a few Unavoidable Salutations and Routine Interjections, but I was seething inside. Swollen with faithful infatuation conceived over a brief encounter with Melinda during Freshman Orientation Week.

It had been my second day at the University. I had already selected my classes for the semester and deemed my roommate, Jose, a calculus *savant*, Acceptable. Acceptable was one notch above Tolerable which is where he stood on Day 1 after I noticed he picked at his nose and crotch far too often, particularly when he unabashedly fawned over the Facebook page of his ex-boyfriend who was stuck going to state college. But on Day 2, Jose unpacked a box of personal books and I spotted one that I owned – *Prisoner's Dilemma* by William Poundstone – and I bumped up his stature. Matching geek aestheticism goes a long way with me.

After another round of touring the campus alone, I had returned to Perkins Hall for lunch, pausing in the dorm's foyer to examine an ornate, wall mounted photo gallery. Inside a redwood framed case, protected by a sheath of tempered, gold-rimmed glass, were portraits of esteemed University alumni who had once resided in our dorm. I didn't recognize half the names listed, but the handwritten, biographical profiles below each 3x5 portrait, swaddled their lives with a reverence that made me feel ashamed of my ignorance.

While I studied the tired, proud faces of each alumnus (some buffed by the soft erosion of the photographic film, others by the overuse of the blur tool in Photoshop), about a dozen students swerved around me like ants avoiding a white chalk line. I didn't care. I continued to stare straight ahead, shifting my focus between the photographs and my own ghostly reflection captured within the casing. My face was an umbral cloud, distorted by fingerprints and dust on the glass surface, and it appeared to engulf the exalted alumni like a Lovecraftian Old One.

A saintly reflection materialized adjacent to my dark one, a glowing vision that dared me to cower from its source – a beautiful girl who had sidled up next to me. The girl didn't seem to mind my presence, saying nothing to me, and she gazed at the rows and columns of glorified success for almost a minute with me, until she got swooped up by a gaggle of newfound girlfriends chirping her name: *Melinda*.

For a few more minutes, I continued standing there, alone, staring at the space where her reflection had been, experiencing a curious sense of loss. It was as if we had been intimately united by a shared experience, a realization that access had been granted to two diametrically opposing souls to enter hallowed ground together. During our time as a couple, I never confirmed this profound experience with

Melinda, but I honestly believe she had been given the same revelation that had instantly crystalized inside my mind during that moment of perfect time:

The University was going to be our kingdom.

But revelations and hope aside, those first two months residing in Perkins Hall were excruciatingly lonely. Not that I disliked my independence, or suddenly grew a craving for social gatherings. And I wasn't completely ignored. Before I was pegged as a non-drinker, I had been recruited to join our dorm's newly established Century Club which consisted of monthly meetings where club members would drink 100 shots of beer in 100 minutes. (Remarkably no one in the club got their stomach pumped or failed a class and one of the club's founders eventually became a Rhodes Scholar.) My issue was that I had zero skill with the opposite sex. To me, it seemed everyone was hooking up and finding mates both inside and outside the dorm. Jose found a new boyfriend by Day 35, a law school student, which kept him out of Perkins most nights and gave me a single room, earning Jose another upgrade to Good. I didn't take advantage of it. I had only talked to seven different girls and only one conversation lasted longer than a couple of minutes (it was to ask for directions to Rico's taco stand off campus and she sent me in the wrong direction). I started to hear whispers. I was becoming tagged as an asexual, as if bumbling, eternal celibacy was a choice I would actually make for myself. I was simply much more comfortable pretending to elevate myself above the competitive sexual game, burying my head in my chemistry textbooks, proclaiming to myself that the only way I would become the world's first and only renowned chemical engineer would be to ignore the pervasive, lustful thoughts that wanted to possess my brain.

My friends in the dorm, all two of them (three if you count Jose), saw through my bullshit and did their best to cheer me up while simultaneously boasting of their own conquests. Laurence, another Perkins resident who had endless internal debates over choosing computer science or mechanical engineering as a major, had somehow landed a fairly attractive girl whom he had met in Physics class and had already deemed his future wife. The only woman I met in my

9

Physics class was a pig-nosed, deGrasse Tyson groupie whose hair smelled like varnish and sent me on the wrong way to Rico's tacos. My other friend, Eddie, whom I met in a misguided attempt to play lacrosse (a sport that I knew nothing about and thankfully most of my teammates didn't either – my body only got pummeled by my own unskilled maneuvers) had christened himself as Master Chief in the art of hooking up. Drunk Girls, Sober Girls, Hot Girls, Cute Girls, Kind-of-Cute Girls, Good-From-Afar-But-Far-From-Good Girls, and I'd-Put-A-Brown-Bag-Over-Her-Face-If-It-Wasn't-So-Cliché Girls – the girl didn't matter to Eddie as long as she was willing. Or rather, if Eddie was willing. He rarely made any kind of first move. Girls were always introducing themselves to him, laughing at his stale jokes, pawing over his bone-thin body, and straddling his lap like he had a battery-operated penis. If he wasn't friends with me, I would've never been friends with him. The girls that went after Eddie were at considerable ease in distancing themselves from me, apparently finding no value in even friend-zoning me. I tried not to care but some nights I couldn't sleep, besieged with cold, engorged thoughts that criticized my lack of effort at talking to Melinda while simultaneously convincing me that the effort wouldn't matter anyway.

Day 64 of my Freshman Year. Midterms had been graded and Melinda sent out an email to all the residents of our dorm pleading for some assistance with her chemistry class. Melinda was apparently not a fan of the hard sciences (*Biology is as techie as my brain wants to go!*), and her email indicated that she was stuck taking Chem 20 in order to fulfill her prerequisites for medical school. Although I was excelling in Chem 100, the uppermost level of chemistry that a freshman could take, provided he or she got the professor's approval, I assumed that she would get dozens of helpful responses and it'd be pointless to offer my assistance. So after reading her email about thirty times, I decided to delete it.

A week passed. The gnawing thought of Melinda needing help, help that I knew I could provide, began to overcome the critic inside of me and I started to undergo a series of small panic attacks. I have had similar, curt shocks throughout my life, stressing out before speaking in public, sweating profusely whenever I've been packed within a large crowd, or hyperventilating when I forgot if I had locked up my bicycle (this fear wasn't without merit – there were bike thieves who roamed the dorm racks and my unscratched Cannondale was my most expensive possession next to my laptop computer). But the attacks regarding Melinda were sharper, like a thin, flexible needle winding its way underneath my skin. I got these attacks at random times. While solving problem sets in my dorm room. Inside the library, while resting my head atop a research paper. At dinner, during mid-bite of a tuna casserole. My wa mind wrangling with itself over who had become her tutor. I only figured out how to calm myself when I realized that he, or even better, she would never be as adept at chemistry as me.

The following Saturday, I entered the dining hall to grab an afternoon snack and spotted Melinda sitting alone with an open chemistry textbook. I swallowed down a rising panic attack and commanded my feet to march over to her. It was no small undertaking. I felt like an unworthy soul walking up to an altar to seek a blessing or a communion wafer. But I needed to find out what imbecile was helping her.

The dining hall was fiendishly dry. And cold. The windows were spotted from a late autumn rain, and the thunderous grey light creeping inside seemed to suck up the heat blasting from the ceiling vents. As I approached Melinda, I tried not to stare directly at her, but my eyes couldn't stop dancing over her face and body. Melinda was a majestically unadorned woman. Like her lips and eyes, the fair skin on her cheeks was only lightly dusted with makeup. Her shoulder length, curl-free blonde hair was tied back into a scattered, lazy ponytail. She had on a pair of tattered, Old Navy-like jeans, a University branded t-shirt, and penny loafers with sun-bleached scuff marks. Before I had gotten halfway to her, she looked up at me and stuck out her toothy smile. I eased a goofy grin out of me. Melinda had a regal smile, not overbearing or mysterious, but inviting – a smile that had enabled her to easily establish a wide range of friends in our dorm. Despite the chill in the air, sweat began to percolate through my skin and I wondered if it was seeping through the white t-shirt I was wearing. I probably looked like an incredibly out of shape person who couldn't even walk thirty feet without generating armpit stains. The thick, ungainly, plastic-framed glasses I was wearing (a high school graduation gift from my mother who said they made me look

11

artistic) began to embarrassingly fog up. I ran my fingers through the uncombed, oily black mess of hair sprouting from my head and tried to ignore the thumping in my ears caused by my accelerated pulse. Thankfully, Melinda's calm voice and casual demeanor were enough to erase some of my tension.

"Hey you! Are you going to be my chem tutor?"

Thick water pellets slammed up against the windows as my head rattled from her surprising question. I glanced over at a dour student sitting at the next table, a coarse bun affixed to top of her head. She was reading a dog-eared copy of *Atlas Shrugged* and mumbling indignations and curses.

Melinda looked back down at her textbook before I could return my attention to her.

"I mean, I hope you'd be able to help me. Heard you were a rock star in chemistry and I'm struggling. I need to pass this class or it's bye-bye Harvard Med. Plus it would be really embarrassing if I were the only blond girl in class to drop the course."

The rain howled against the walls of the dining hall and Melinda's voice grew louder. "So please? Say, yes? I'm really much smarter than I look."

At last my nerves subsided enough for me to regain coherent speech. "Hi, Melinda. I saw your email. I thought someone had already come to your rescue." I averted my eyes realizing how abysmally dorky my response must have sounded.

"Nope. I am completely un-rescued!"

Melinda sat back in her chair, laughing. I chuckled sympathetically while the Ayn Rand critic got up from her chair and left the hall, unspooling the bun from her hair.

Melinda motioned for me to take a seat at her table and I complied. The rain softened in sync with her voice. "No one good applied for the job. A couple of loser dudes in our dorm tried to fake chem knowledge in order to ask me on a date. Guys here have no game – like your friend Eddie – such a liar and a loser. Sucks at lacrosse too. Why do you hang out with him? Anyways, Elsie – do you know her, cute with freckles? She was all lined up, but ended up flaking on me because of some volunteer work. Like the world needs another do-gooder?"

12

I tried laughing at the right places, but I had difficulty keeping up with the speedy flow of her words.

"I would be so happy and thankful if you had the time, but I totally get it if you're too busy."

I caught my breath as if I had been the one speaking rapidly. "No, I have the time. I've got lots of time. I'd be happy to help." It was extraordinary to be able to say such repetitive, trite words.

"Awesome! I'm free tonight if you are?"

"Tonight?"

I was completely free, but grew nervous with the prospect of seeing her again so soon. I needed time to prep, compose some interesting conversation points, triple-check my hygiene. I didn't want to risk disappointing her so quickly.

"Or tomorrow, or this weekend – whatever works best for you."

"No tonight's fine. I can be available."

"Cool. Just swing by my dorm room, two-one-two, around eight. My roommate will be out with her sketchy boyfriend – he keeps putting his hand on my lower back, asking me if I want to join them for a drink. That's sketchy, right?"

I nodded and made a mental note not to accidentally touch her back.

"Thank you, thank you, thank you! I think it's a little late for this, but it's great to finally meet you!"

Melinda held out her hand and I shook it. "Great meeting you too. My name is Daniel, in case you didn't know."

Melinda laughed again. "I already knew that, Danny-boy! How many kids do you think are here at Perkins?" As I got up from the table, forgetting all about grabbing a snack, I jammed my knee into the back of the chair. I walked out of the dining hall without looking back at Melinda to see what her reaction had been. There was no need; I could feel her smile against my back. Smiling not because of my clumsy exit, but because, like me, she knew that our lives were about to drastically change.

That first night tutoring her in chemistry went shockingly smooth, and surprisingly, unbearably short. Typically the longer I remained in company with people, the worse our impressions of each other became. But not with Melinda. As

I left her room, she gave me a hug that was warmer and longer than anything I had received from a woman (who was not a relative) and I had to awkwardly peel away from her and trot back to my own room, fearful that she and every student I passed in the dorm hallways would be able to discern an erection that was at least seven years in the making. That triumphant and overdue success led to my tutoring her three times a week. My teaching ability wasn't amazing, but Melinda listened intently to me, and she started to improve. At the end of the month, she received a B+ on her final exam and thanked me by showing up to my dorm room before dinner and giving me a light kiss on the cheek. Admittedly, I dreamt of a lot more than a kiss, but I was content that it had gone so well, for so long. I decided to ask Melinda the question I had been dreading as Jose gave us some privacy by darting out of room with a Joker grin.

"Looks like you'll pass the course. I guess you won't need me anymore?"

Melinda punched me on the shoulder. "Do you think I was just using you for the stupid class?"

"Yeah."

Melinda punched me again. "Why?"

"I'm not like you, Melinda. You have too many friends. Thought you were being nice because you needed a good grade. You felt sorry for me."

Melinda scoffed. "No. Not at all. So what if you're a little socially inept? You've got a brilliant mind and you're cute with a decent bod. Most girls don't talk to you because they think you're aloof or faking an Asperger's case for techie cred. Most girls around here aren't right for you. Bunch of entitled bitches. Or does that make me the bitch? I am friends with all of them, right? Whatever. I'm talking about you. You're a good guy, Danny-boy. I'm glad we've become friends."

I had cycled through emotions as Melinda spoke. I was a little offended. A little flattered. Confused. Excited. I stopped at disappointment when she said we had become friends. Shit. Was that better than nothing? No, of course not. Still shit.

Melinda's smile disappeared mirroring my own face. "You don't think we're friends?"

I spoke the only words that popped into my head. "No. You're a funny beauty who makes me dream. Hard." I shook my head. I could describe the best practices of PCR optimization, but was God-awful at saying anything meaningful. Worse, I had no clue how to convey passionate interest to a woman.

Melinda let loose with another hearty laugh and raised her hand as if to hit me again. Instead, she draped her arm around my shoulder and gave me another kiss. On the lips.

"Yeah, you're right. I have too many friends already."

A sick kid began coughing in the hallway as Melinda shut the door to my room and kissed me again.

I had always heard that the first few months of a new relationship were the best. It's mostly true. At the beginning of the second semester, Melinda and I had returned from the holiday break, weary of trading phone calls and text messages, and eager to spend all our free time together. Plus a kid in our dorm (Hispanic/Latino #14) had died in a car wreck on New Year's Eve so we needed each other's comfort to dissipate the depressive fog that floated into Perkins Hall and clung to the walls of everyone's dorm room.

When we could, we ate lunch and dinner together, and met up to go on coffee breaks. We took walks to the post office, walks to Rico's tacos, and walks that did nothing more than loop around campus. We biked to classes together (sometimes when they weren't even in the same direction) and we biked along the loping trails that scarred the grassy foothills surrounding campus. I still tutored Melinda occasionally as she continued with her Chem Lab course and told her if she wanted to get through O Chem, I needed to stick around at least through next year. Most of all we got together to kiss.

Kissing begat groping which begat further stages of undress. My confidence about foreplay, romance, and my own body accelerated as if my solitary practice sessions had actually paid off. I grew comfortable with Melinda seeing the heinous birthmark on my upper right thigh and groin that looked like a stray piece of excrement. In eighth grade gym class I was given the nickname "Dickey Shits" and was told I either shit out of my dick or liked sticking my dick in shit. The effectiveness of eight grade mockery was always inversely proportional to its execution. When Melinda lifted the hem of my overly long boxer briefs to explore underneath, I thought she would laugh her repulsion away. Instead she kissed my birthmark, and muttered that there were weird things on everyone's body.

Untrue. Melinda's body was flawless. Every mole, crevice and bump on her skin fascinated me. I grew bolder. I was able to stare and caress her bare breasts without appearing like a greedy, salivating pervert. I converted my initial labored, overly wet kisses on her mouth and neck, into teasing, delicate pecks down her spine, below her navel, or along her hips. And whenever she let me wrap my arms around her smooth legs, I would tickle the soles of her bare feet with the tip of my tongue and she would wiggle her raspberry painted toes against my nose.

Was this the gist of being in a relationship? I had never been in one before and I really didn't know what I was doing. Our companionship was obvious to our fellow dorm mates and I enjoyed deflecting their prying questions about our "status." Aside from physical intimacy, Melinda and I grew closer, sharing our grievances about our dysfunctional parents (mine divorced, hers recovering from bankruptcy), our favorite music (we both loved breezy alternative music from the late 80's and early 90's, we both claimed to have rediscovered *The Ocean Blue* and *The Trashcan Sinatras*) and dumbest fears (Melinda was deathly afraid of the *Matrix* movies – *if you really think about it, Neo stands for neocortex!*). I also connected with her fascination with disease, her acute interest in bizarre and rare disorders that went beyond any typical pre-med student curiosity. She didn't linger on the woeful and cruel physical aspects (we both despised Nature's fuck-ups), but on the painstaking research and medical expertise required for proper diagnoses and treatments. I read her dense textbooks to better understand the academic rigors to which Melinda had committed herself, and began to pick up the doctor's vocabulary, the tongue-twisting medical lingo that Melinda liked to pepper me with.

"You've got an acute ecchymosis of the vastus lateralis! What are you going to do?" I had an ugly bruise on my thigh from lacrosse. I quit the team as soon as it faded.

"Oh my God, you have idiopathic hypersomnia! Snap out of it!" I got overly sleepy during the day for no apparent reason. I told her my circadian clock was broken.

"I have orthostatic hypotension. I inherited it from my mother." Melinda got dizzy when she stood up from her bed too fast. I believed her, but she also said her mother was a hypochondriac.

I admire challenging creatures and Melinda was the closest I had ever been to one, urging me to constantly think and constantly improve. She tolerated my rants on the latest developments in nanoparticles and polymer synthesis, even though she didn't understand the nuances of every reference I made or fully grasped my own specialized jargon. Still, her listening to me was what mattered. She also acknowledged that the zeal for my chosen field invigorated her. Considering I wasn't that passionate about Chemical Engineering, and was only pursuing it because I would be great at it, I found it odd she found so much depth in my words. She was like that in all my interests. Even those interests that I only peripherally understood (like recursion theory or D-brane inflation) and admittedly, only feigned expertise because I knew nobody would ever call me out on it.

But I couldn't pretend to be an expert on sex. My only knowledge was derived from soulless hours of Internet porn (where apparently the only things that mattered were size, speed, and spit), but Melinda, who I pegged as a sexual veteran, having gained technique and ability from a couple of high school ex-boyfriends, took it upon herself to kindly direct me.

The first time I had sex with Melinda I heard a baby screaming. Which made absolutely no sense since we were in my dorm room. Jose was staying with his boyfriend so I had the place to myself. It was a Tuesday, around midnight, and most of our dorm mates were falling asleep. Things had begun smoothly on my bed, thanks to the bottle of wine we had shared (and would regret during our Wednesday morning classes), but once I got to the unwrapping the condom stage, I needed her steady fingers to take command. As Melinda slid the rubber on me and yanked me down on top of her, I heard the first scream, a tinny shriek that I quickly dismissed, chalking it up to the whiny girl in the adjacent room who was always sick. I was more concerned with the struggle for control over my clumsy body and the fact that nature was in no way taking its course. I managed a few monotonous, un-rhythmic thrusts before I heard more screams, the insistent

17

and desperate cries of a baby, and I began to wonder if some student had actually brought his baby brother or sister to the dorm. The screams grew louder and they sounded so close, too close, as if there was a baby lying in a crib right next to me and I started to lose my erection and it felt as if the condom was about to slip off me, which was quite possible since I may have bought the wrong size or wrong brand – Trustee? Trustex? Why didn't I just buy a Trojan? – and the screams grew even louder, even closer, biting into my eardrums as if some unfit mother had dropped her newborn on his head, and the surging needles of another panic attack began to drill into my chest, and I felt the condom completely slipping off me so I ripped my body away from Melinda and rolled off the bed and onto the floor, pawing at the latex covering my penis which was still adequately secured, while the baby continued its deathly screams, crying so horribly that I covered my ears with my hands, and inexplicably, irreparably, I ended up climaxing.

I stared up at the ceiling. My dorm room was silent except for my labored breathing. Melinda had gotten out of bed and was standing over me. I closed my eyes. What was wrong with me? Had I really heard a wailing baby? The only thing I had accomplished was humiliating myself and failing Melinda. I expected to hear the sound of Melinda throwing on her clothes and running out of my room, tears streaming from her eyes from unmitigated disappointment and laughter, and I primed myself to receive the jeers and mockery from everyone in Perkins after they found out.

But Melinda lay down on the floor next to me. Forced me to look at her as she latched her arms across my chest.

"Are you OK?"

"I don't know. I'm sorry. I guess I'll see you around."

"What? This is supposed to be fun, Danny-boy."

"Did you hear the baby?"

"Huh?"

"A baby. Crying."

"Nope. We'll have to do things much better and much worse if we want that to happen."

Melinda squeezed my arms as she kissed me on the neck. Not only did she not care about my bungled amorous moves or ridiculous question, she implied that I would get more than just a second chance to make love to her, and make her happy. My preternatural belief that Melinda was supposed to be with me was emboldened: she had been specifically designed by a benevolent Universe. A universe that wanted to be understood and longed to make sense. I've always been good at convincing myself of self-preserving truths. I never heard the screaming baby ever again.

In reality, the universe is riddled with fractured stars whose historical light obscures their unknowable or ignoble existence.

Melinda used to make up weird stories. She was an amateur writer with no skill or aim to do anything more than amuse herself and her friends, but she did have a fantasy streak corkscrewed inside her brain. Her whimsical tales were sometimes funny, mostly hopeful. She described unique worlds unburdened by classical physics – strange dimensions where light whistled and swirled around like a flying chameleon, changing colors to match the emotional plot points of the story. She wrote about rainbows that sprouted from the ground and flew into the sky to give birth to clouds and rain. She invented mythical animal hybrids – cats with translucent eyes and peacock feathers, horse-sized bats with elephant trunks, and frogs with human legs and long, swirly horns – most of these beasts were friendly, aiding children and unloved folks. The bat creature was actually a guide that led souls into Heaven or Hell depending on the virtuousness of the departed one's friends.

On my birthday, Melinda gave me one of her stories as a present:

Once there was an old speck of a woman who lived alone in an isolated cabin in the Alaskan wilderness. She was tiny like a mouse, but unbearably ugly to look at – her head was shaped like a croissant, with a pointy, crusty forehead beneath a sparsely haired scalp, and a pointy, crusty chin below a cleft lip mouth. Her nose appeared frostbitten, a wrinkled, black mass that resembled a moldy prune, bulging green eyes that were uneven and too wide, and fuzzy, bat-like ears. But she was never lonely; people always came to see her. Visitors from all over the world hiked for miles through the forest and tundra, braving sunless winters and mosquito summers, because she had a miraculous talent. Oil painting. The old woman painted portraits that were astoundingly beautiful. And life-like – skin glowed, nostrils flared, and eyes smiled and wept. Some said the portraits teemed with more vitality than the subjects themselves. The old woman had an uncanny knack of capturing the essence of her subjects, their most admired physical features or most celebrated inner character. Her talent could have made her very wealthy, but she never asked for any money. She only had one request: if they wanted the painting, they needed to kiss her. Despite her ugliness, most paid the price. But some could never bring themselves to touch her, much less kiss her, so the old woman had no choice but to burn their portraits in her fireplace. She also had one final rule: once you received a painting, you could never return. A few tried, but they could never locate her cabin again. Some vain fools even died getting lost in the harsh Alaskan land.

A brutally cold year passed, the coldest Alaska had ever experienced, and the old woman didn't receive too many visitors. Loneliness began to creep into her and she started to become feeble. Her eyesight faded, her hands began to shake, and she could no longer paint as brilliantly as she used to. As word of her condition got out, even less people came to visit her. Her loneliness and weakness increased. She cursed out at God, blaming him for her declining health. Soon, all the knocks at the door ceased, and the old woman plunged into deep despair. She stopped eating and waited for death to arrive.

As she lay on the floor of her cabin, death mere moments away, she heard a soft knock at the door. At first she ignored it, blaming her failing mind for playing a trick on her, but it sounded again. Finding the last remnants of strength inside her, the old woman dragged her body across the floor and crawled over to the door. Her trembling hand reached up and grabbed the door knob, and with one final lunge, she opened the door.

Outside stood a little boy, an Eskimo from the Yupik tribe, no more than five years old, bundled in a traditional sealskin coat. He presented the old woman with a gift – an amazing collage of wildflowers made from the real petals of many different varieties. Chickweed, Dogwood, Mountain Heather, Rockcress, and Northern Yarrow. The old woman was so touched by her gift, her suffering mind was consoled. Joy and gratitude overflowed inside her and she found the strength to rise up to her knees, her soul rejuvenated, and she thanked God for the visitor. The boy smiled and kissed the old woman. Instantly, the woman transformed into a tiny angel, the size of a bee, with wings that matched the radiant flower petals in the boy's gift. As a miniature angel, the woman followed the little boy back to his village. She watched over him, always flying next to his ear to inspire him to be an artist, a painter like she used to be, and to guide his success throughout the years.

When the little boy became an old man, no longer able to paint or take care of himself, the angel realized she could no longer help him. Reluctantly, she flew away, disappearing into the clouds. Alone, the old man grew weak and despondent until a little girl paid him a visit, bestowing her own gift – a watercolor of wild butterflies. Swallowtails, Fritillaries, Sulphurs, and Skippers. The little girl kissed the grateful old man's hand and he too transformed into a miniature angel, with beautifully colored butterfly wings, who guided the artistry of the little girl over her lifetime.

This cycle of artists and angels continued for over three hundred years. Until one day, a little boy presented a gift of birds sculpted out of Jupiter marble to a dying old poet. When the poet transformed into an angel after his kiss, the boy became frightened. He swung at the angel as if it were a repulsive insect, knocking it to the ground, and smashing it with his foot. The angel turned into dust along with his sculpture of the birds. The boy went home, still frightened, and never sculpted again.

It wasn't the best birthday gift. Her story didn't make any sense. At least, I didn't understand it. It ended on the wrong note, in opposition to its "love and magic conquers all" theme. The perplexed look I gave to Melinda after reading it angered her, and she stopped talking to me.

A couple days passed. Melinda wouldn't see me. I decided to ask for help. I got Jose to interpret it for me and I liked his explanation so much, I decided to pawn it off as my own. I intercepted Melinda as she walked out of her Bio lab class. She refused to look at me and started to hop on her bike. I swiped her backpack and took it with me to a nearby bench, an unused resting spot, smeared with pollen dust and needles from an overhanging pine tree. She reluctantly followed me, stomping her feet and demanding her pack. I told her to sit down. She shook her head. I swept the dust and needles away, which caused her to sneeze, and told her again to sit. I had something important to tell her. She looked furious, but complied. I took a seat next to her and told her my stolen interpretation of her story. It was a fable about how the beauty of art, the beauty of creation, depended on its dual nature of immortality and fragility, just like love and magic. I reached out and grabbed Melinda's hand. She interlaced her fingers with mine and for the first time, I told her that I loved her.

Melinda let go of my hand and wrapped her lithe arms around me as tightly as she could. Held onto me silently for a few minutes with her head nestled in my chest. Only when she pulled away did I notice my shirt was damp from the tears that she had let escape.

Her voice was weak. "Why did it take you so long?"

I thought about telling her how my science-laden mind limited my imagination – my creative boundaries were reined by the tight grasp of rote, linear mathematics.

I thought about telling her how I hadn't slept the past two days and I was so desperate to hear her voice, I was starting to feel as if my body was turning to dust.

I thought about telling her that before I met her I could never even conceptualize love, much less recognize it, say it, and give it in return.

Instead I said nothing and let the wind shake and bend the pine branches above us, powdering our bodies with a fresh layer of pollen and needles, causing Melinda to sneeze again.

A later time. Sophomore Year. I was living at Meyer Village Suites on campus – in a four bedroom suite that I shared with Jose and two randomly placed students, Mark and Tobin, who I only talked to when it was absolutely necessary. I saw Laurence and Eddie only about once a month because Melinda and I were going strong, and we spent almost all of our free time together.

One morning, about a half-hour before my alarm was set to go off, I woke up as Melinda playfully teased my naked body. She began whispering clever excuses for ditching our first class (*We can download the class notes from the TA – I think he knows more than the prof anyways!*). I didn't respond to her. Instead, I allowed my mind to wander. It snaked through crooked, dirty alleys, and drifted carelessly around blind, dark corners. I imagined what Melinda would've done if the LASIK surgery performed on me the previous month had actually gone terribly wrong. Even though Melinda had called the square plastic-framed glasses I had worn for several years "erudite chic," and the payment of the procedure by my mother "Oedipally nurturing," she had supported my decision to get my eyes permanently corrected. I suffered no complications, but would she have regretted her support if I had been the 1-5% with complications? What if I had been scarred (<2%)? Suffered a detached retina (<0.5%)? Or Glaucoma (<0.1%)? What if the eye surgeon had been an Oxycontin addict and he fat-fingered the computer controls causing the laser to burn a hole straight into my lens, mutilating me blind (<0.0001%)? Would Melinda have cared for me? Would she have remained my girlfriend?

The alarm went off and Melinda slapped it off. She got out of bed, snapped at me about my being a "lost cause," and began to get dressed. Morbid thoughts continued to intoxicate my mind. What if a random tragedy occurred, like if I got struck by a car as I biked my way to class? *Sorry Melinda, your boyfriend's paralyzed communication skills are now perfectly matched with the gifts of impotence and tetraplegia.* Or what if Melinda was diagnosed with a cancer like leukemia? Spending hours camped out on the toilet as she endured weeks of chemotherapy and radiation. Would we still support each other through pain and misery? What was the ultimate tensile strength of love? Could it even be measured? Was love equal to how much pain one would willingly tolerate on behalf of the other? As Melinda left my room, without as much as a kiss or a word goodbye, I was certain that I could endure any calamity, no matter how horrific, that struck Melinda. But I wasn't at all certain she would do the same for me.

Junior Year. Still living at Meyer Village Suites. Still with Jose, but with two other random students, Joaquim and Ben

23

who did their best to not ever talk to me. When I randomly bumped into Laurence or Eddie, I only spent a few minutes catching up. I was still madly in love, madly spending my free time with Melinda. But a few particulars about her had changed. She cut her hair. Took off several inches which made it too short to tie back in a ponytail. She switched from the Pill to a copper IUD because she said that it made sense for the next ten years and she had to start thinking it terms of decades. She revealed doubts about becoming a doctor. (*It was never a calling. I'm no Mother Theresa – I won't do primary care if that's what's needed.*) And she stopped calling me *Danny-boy*.

"Do you believe in God?" Melinda asked me this one evening while I waited for her to get ready inside her hamster-sized single room at the Kappa sorority house. I had pretended that I didn't care when she had joined the sorority (*entitled bitches* had become *enlivened sisters*) and I had lied when I said I wouldn't mind taking her to a fancy dinner party, hosted by a University (and Kappa) alumnus. At the time, a fancy dinner to me meant going to a place where the bill would be over $50, but in this case, it meant heading to the palatial home of a bubbly woman who had started her own venture capital firm and had somehow made millions off start-up companies that folded within three years. Wasn't she the quintessential definition of *entitled bitch*? At least the main course being served for dinner was a garlic-buttered Rib-Eye for which I was willing to compromise my principles.

"Maybe. Maybe not. I'm agnostic. Haven't I told you this before?"

We never talked much about religion. I was raised Episcopalian, but hadn't gone to church in over five years while she had a Jewish background, but had never once celebrated the High Holy Days or Hanukkah. I had no idea what prompted her question. A few seconds earlier, she had been criticizing my choice of a tie, one with a nerdy pattern of icosahedral fullerenes which she said looked like a bunch of soccer balls.

"Yeah, I know all the rational arguments and obvious causes for doubt. But I want to know what you feel *inside*. Right now. Do you have any kind of faith in God or a higher power? Like you did when you were a kid?"

We had been together for nearly three years and we were already entertaining thoughts of our relationship post-college. I assumed this would be a question we would eventually have to peruse in detail, particularly if we wanted to raise children with religion in their lives, but it was annoying for her to ask this pointed question at this time. I wasn't really in the mood for a deep philosophical discussion, probing my inner psyche for theological underpinnings. I was hungry for a steak dinner. "Do we really need to have this God talk?"

Melinda had a way of looking at me whenever I posed a dumb question to her. A mix of pity and frustration that tapered off into bottled up amusement. But this time there was no hidden jest. Only frustration. And fear. Melinda grabbed her purse and stormed out of her room. I was curiously annoyed, but not overly concerned. Melinda had started to become dramatic whenever she felt I was purposefully being laconic and distant.

Only in hindsight do I realize her question's enormous importance. And despite my ardent belief that I would always be committed to helping Melinda and never causing her any harm, my not answering that question had been a soul-perforating mistake.

Senior Year. Late March. I had finally parted ways with Jose (he moved in with his boyfriend) and had been living in a newly renovated one bedroom apartment off campus, near the downtown commercial district. My mother paid the rent. I only waved at Laurence and Eddie whenever we happened to bike past each other. Melinda had moved out of the Kappa house, but since her plan was to graduate and enter med school before moving in with me, she got her own place – a 310 square foot studio apartment that was tucked up against a freeway overpass and provided no insulation against mold, the neighbor's pot smoke, and ants. It was the best place she could afford. I thought it was a waste of money, especially since she was still sleeping over with me almost every night.

It was a Wednesday morning. Around nine o'clock. I had just stepped outside my apartment to head to class. Late and in a sour mood. The sun was shining clearly and brightly, but the air was frigid and it bit through the wool sweater I was wearing, giving me a headache. Melinda had left my place early to go on a morning jog, which along with a vegan diet and herbal supplements, had become part of her strategy to combat a persistent case of insomnia. She said she had a busy schedule the rest of the day and didn't know when we'd be able to meet up. It was like she didn't want to see me. So when she called my cell phone as I got on my bike, I was taken a bit by surprise.

"Hey. You forget something?"

Her words were incomprehensible. "Going in circles. Spinning and spinning, over and over. I'm spinning out. Stop! I can hear blood! Hear it? Stop it, Danny! Stop the spinning, I'm going to die."

She hung up before I could articulate any sort of response. I tried calling back but was thrown into her voicemail.

Worried, I jumped on my bike and began to trace the looping route through campus that I knew she liked to run. After eleven, angst-ridden minutes I found her. She was lying on her back on a patch of grass near the main Tucker Business School building. I flew off my bike and ran up to her. She was laughing, but not in her usual jovial way. The laughs were slow and mechanical, like a talking doll with a worn-out battery. Melinda's eyes were staring up at the cloudless sky until she noticed me and bounced up to a seated position.

"Can't see this? Every night, every dark night. It burns my ears! Happy? Dreaming of rocks? It's become so dark now, I know things...I know!"

A couple of B-school students sauntered past, barely looking at Melinda. They traded barbs.

"Drunk on weekday?"

"Pathetic."

Next to Melinda on the ground was her cell phone, shattered as if she had smashed it against the concrete sidewalk. There was also a small puddle of brackish vomit next to the broken phone. I tried to reach out to Melinda, but she swatted my hand away.

"Danny! Can you see it? Can you see what it's doing? Little spinning circles. Spinning in my eyes. No! My ears are bleeding! Make it stop, make it stop, make it stop...."

Melinda's body dropped back to the ground and she started whimpering. My heart began to claw its way out of my chest. Her eyes were jumpy and uncertain, as if she knew her speech was unintelligible but she couldn't do anything about it. My throat began to close. Before my voice shut off, I pulled my cell phone out of my pocket and dialed 911.

The day passed as if I were stuck reading the same dreary passage in an arcane textbook even though I felt my fingers turning the pages. The passive act of waiting was a vile terror.

Melinda endured a multitude of prying and invasive tests, scans, and samples and I was bombarded with phone calls and texts to and from family and friends repeating the same questions, same answers, same concerns – all of which were various ways of articulating, *I don't know shit.* While Melinda rested in a hospital bed after receiving a cocktail of sedatives and analgesics, I was battered by waves of insulting, icy worry that overpowered the nausea I had received from lying down on waiting room chairs covered with sticky, buttery plastic that reeked of Pine-Sol. Melinda requested no visitors. I went home and didn't eat or sleep as Melinda spent the night the hospital.

In the evening of the following day, Melinda was released. She had spent thirty-three hours and seventeen minutes in the hospital, and in the end, had been given only a banal diagnosis of temporary delirium brought on by acute stress. Stress supposedly from a lack of sleep, school exams, millennial generation blues – no physician could provide a definitive source – and I felt like the world was awash in ignorance. Knowing the imperfections of science, I have since forgiven the doctors, but my anger never truly subsided. Although every test came back negative, she should have never been released from the hospital. She needed time to let her traumatic confusion pass. But of course, I didn't understand the importance of this until much later.

I waited outside the hospital entrance for her, struggling to breathe in the crisp, brittle air, as Melinda shuffled out the sliding glass doors, wearing the same clothes (jogging shorts and a University sweatshirt) as yesterday. I bolted up to her, slung my arms around her submissive body and blasted her with questions about her well-being. Melinda's arms were folded across her chest and she said only two words back to me: *My place.* I hailed a cab and against my better judgment, instructed him to drive to her squalid studio apartment. On the ride over, Melinda didn't utter another word to me, even after I told her that her parents had managed to grab a cheap cross-country flight and would arrive by mid-morning. She continued her silence as I ushered her inside her apartment, my arm coiled around her waist like a starving python, and told her that I would take care of everything and she would be OK. I helped her take another dose of her prescribed sedative, undressed her and placed her limp body in bed. She shut her eyes as soon as her pillow ingested her head.

I asked Melinda if she wanted me to lie next to her. She appeared to nod slightly, but she may have already fallen asleep. I undressed, turned off the lights, and curled up next to her. It was a little after 7:30 PM and I was exhausted, but I couldn't sleep. I tried to imagine every scenario in which Melinda would wake up in the morning, completely healthy and normal, eager to make love before heading to class. I even imagined an outcome where we both came down with mutual amnesia that wiped out the memory of this entire ordeal from our minds.

"I cursed him."

The words had eked out of Melinda and at first I thought the murmur had only been in my mind. But she repeated, "I cursed him."

Had she not fallen asleep after all? "Are you OK, Melinda? Do you need something?"

She didn't answer me and it took me a moment to detect that her chest was rising in the slow and controlled manner indicative of sleep. Maybe she was dreaming. We both mumbled during sleep at times, nonsense words, sometimes politically incorrect words that we jokingly promised to write down and use as blackmail for any future transgressions. Or maybe she was speaking the same type of nonsense she had uttered yesterday, on the phone and when I'd found her. I rubbed my eyes and resumed staring out into the darkness.

An hour passed. Or maybe two or three. I must have fallen asleep because my eyes flared open from a beam of harsh light. The ceiling light had been turned on. After my eyes adjusted to the invading glare, I noticed that Melinda was not in bed next to me. I assumed she had gotten up to use the bathroom.

I pulled myself out of bed which was more labor intensive than it should've been. It seemed as if I were moving in slow motion – the stereotypical nightmare scenario. But I was wide awake. I jammed my pinkie toe as I accidentally kicked my cell phone which I had carelessly left on the floor by the bed.

I inched over to her bathroom. The door was closed so I knocked. No response. I knocked again and tried the knob. It turned freely so I swung the door open.

Melinda was standing up against the sink, examining her face in a crooked bathroom mirror with deteriorating edges, its glass streaked with rust and lime. The medicine cabinet door to her left was open. Her eyes were sullen and red, but she was smiling. It was a strange smile and it unnerved me.

"Melinda, are you OK? Do you need something?" I repeated the same questions I had asked her back in bed as if stuck on a loop, in the middle of an adolescent nightmare.

"I did this to myself, Danny. I did this."

"No, Melinda. This isn't your fault. Come back to bed and you'll feel better."

"I cursed him. And he made me like this."

"Cursed who?"

Melinda laughed like a petulant, five-year-old girl. "God! But you don't think he exists!" Melinda began scratching at her bare breasts leaving red trails of raised flesh.

"Melinda, you need to rest. You're still not well."

Melinda turned away from the mirror and looked directly at me. She pointed her finger directly at my head. "No, Danny. You're not well."

Her accusation was bewildering, but it still hurt. I struck back, another regrettable mistake. "I'm completely fine, Melinda. This has nothing to do with me."

Melinda laughed again. "Danny, you are completely blind!"

"How am I blind? What are you talking about?"

"You're right. He doesn't exist. You're alone. I'm alone. It wants to be alone."

I tried to fight against my growing frustration. "Stop it, Melinda. You exist. We exist."

"Blind! Blind! Blind!" Melinda giggled again. "And it's staring right at you in the face!"

Melinda was clearly not feeling well at all and I needed to steer her back into bed. But I continued my attempt to maintain a rational discussion with her. "What's staring at me? Are you still talking about God?"

"Does it really matter? If he told me he loved me would it be better if I said it was God?"

"What? Who loves you? Are you saying there's someone else in your life?"

Melinda slammed the medicine cabinet door shut. "Leave, Danny. It's all over."

"No. I want to help you. I will help you!"

"Too late. Help yourself."

"I will not leave you, Melinda."

Melinda crept closer to me. Her body trembled with every step. She was getting weaker. "Leave."

"No!"

"Leave! It wants to be alone!"

"I am not leaving! Not for anything!"

Melinda stood directly in front of me, tears falling from her eyes. Why was I arguing with her? I needed to console her. As I moved closer to her, she slapped me hard across the face and screamed, "Get the fuck away from me!"

I actually stumbled back from the stinging blow and stepped out of the bathroom. I had never been hit by anyone before and couldn't even contemplate that Melinda would do such a thing.

Melinda slammed the bathroom door shut. My mind swarmed with anger and doubt. I no longer wanted to help her. She had crossed a line and I no longer understood the woman I loved. Was all of this about someone else? Some other lover? Ridiculous. I was getting carried away with petty jealousy. But what did she mean? Did she not love me anymore? Or was she just completely out of her mind? I no longer knew what to do. Maybe we were no longer meant to be together. Maybe this was how our relationship would come to end. Maybe this was how all relationships ended. Love was a fraud. Love had no capacity to endure hardship. All it took was for one person to find the other crazy, insufferable, or incomprehensible and that would be enough to extinguish the will of the other.

I hastily got dressed and exited her apartment. I slipped out of her building and started half-walking, half-running, down her residential street in an aimless direction. I had never felt such resentment and fury over Melinda. All I wanted to do was make her happy! Now I wanted to leave her forever. Vanquish her face, her body, her dominating presence out of my life. Rip the resonant memory of love out of my brain that kept ricocheting like an overplayed pop song. I had become a self-indoctrinated fool, captivated by a naïve faith in revelations and miracles.

I had traveled several blocks from her apartment before realizing someone was following me. I glanced to my left and caught a glimpse of a figure walking about twenty feet directly behind me. I was in an area of town where some students had been mugged at gunpoint, but I knew it was Melinda behind me. She had come to apologize. Make amends. Treasure me for all I had done for her over the past forty hours. She probably wasn't even that sick, only testing the resolve of my love.

So I kept walking. I didn't turn around to face her as her footsteps got closer to me. My anger was actually increasing and I felt the sudden urge to yell at everyone in the entire neighborhood who apparently were all sound asleep. Where were the cars? It wasn't that late, was it? No wonder students got robbed – all the residents had air-tight alibis. *I was asleep officer; I didn't see or hear a thing!* Well, wake the fuck up! You're missing out on the latest episode of college students gone amok! The next reality show spectacle coming soon to cable TV! What time was it? I needed to record the time for the next generation of students. This was going to be the moment when the University's Greatest Love Story, the Kingdom of Melinda and Daniel, would reach its pitiful, bottom-of-the-ratings, end.

As I reached into my pocket for my cell to check the time, I realized I had left it at Melinda's. God damn it! Could I do anything right? I decided to turn around. Face the woman I no longer loved. And tell her all I needed was my stupid cell phone back.

But when I turned, there was no one behind me. The street was empty. The air smelled like Melinda – the scent of her hair, her skin, a smidge of her favorite Calvin Klein perfume that she dabbed lightly against her neck every morning. The perfume I had bought for her as a gift on our first Christmas together. That was three years ago and she had worn it ever since. My righteous anger evaporated and I felt very foolish. And terminally alone. What was I doing?

31

What was wrong with me? Melinda needed me. She was significantly ill and I was acting like a mop-headed high school student. A selfish little boy who lost his only toy. There was still time to set things right. I raced back to Melinda's apartment.

When I arrived, I flung open her door and shouted out to her. "Melinda! I'm so sorry. I am blind!"

Melinda didn't answer me. She was lying on the floor next to her bed. Rigid. Pale. A small trickle of blood had seeped from her lip where it appeared she had bitten herself. I threw myself down on the ground next to her, cradled her head and caressed her tenderly. She was breathing, slowly, too slowly, but her eyes, her kind, gentle, lovely eyes, had returned. I started to cry as she strained to focus on my face. How could I ever have thought of not loving her? Of not taking care of her? How could I have left her alone?

She spoke feebly, but I had no problem hearing her words. "I'm sorry. Sorry."

"You have nothing to be sorry about. I shouldn't have left you!"

"Didn't want to hurt you."

"It's OK, Melinda. I'm here. I love you!"

"Already knew that, Danny-boy."

The corners of her mouth tried to turn up as if to smile, but a jarring convulsion ripped through her body. She was having a seizure. I flailed around for a bit, trying to hold her steady until I realized I was being useless and I needed help.

I located my cell phone near Melinda's bed. It was 2:43 AM. Over eight hours had elapsed since I had taken Melinda out of the hospital and I had to dial 911 again to send her back.

The line rang once before my phone cut out. My phone had powered off and I couldn't turn it back on. Did the battery pick this moment to die? How? Why? Melinda's convulsions began to abate, but her skin had turned blue.

Tears were streaming from my eyes and I sat on the floor, motionless. Paralyzed. I needed to do something but my mind was shutting down and I couldn't think. The ceiling light flickered as if the blub was ready to burn out and the quick flashes caused an insulting strobe effect that magnified my witless inertia.

A blast of humid air punched me in the face and I felt a stabbing pain in my stomach and groin. I curled up on the floor into a fetal position, cringing from an intense, burning ache that I had never experienced before. I wanted to shut my eyes, but I couldn't once I saw the figure standing inside Melinda's bathroom, staring into the mirror.

It was a naked woman. She looked like Melinda but she was horrifically gaunt and disfigured as if suffering from polio or some other wasting disease. Her hair wasn't blond, but a greasy shade of black. Wet, graphite strings of hair that clumped together in mats, exposing scattered bald patches that were tinged with fresh blood. It was as if chunks of hair had been ripped out of her scalp. Her crinkled skin matched the color of her hair and there was more blood streaked over her chest and legs. The woman turned away from the mirror and looked directly at me. She opened a toothless mouth and expelled a hollow gasp. I couldn't take my eyes off this foul being, until the woman reached out to the bathroom door and slammed it shut.

My pain abated and I managed to sit myself back up. Melinda, my Melinda, was lying motionless on the floor. I fumbled closer to her and touched her nose and mouth. She wasn't breathing. Her skin was rubbery and cold. She looked like she had been dead for a while. My body began to shake from the enormity of what I was witnessing.

My cell phone rang. It had mockingly come back to life. It rang twice before I numbly answered it.

"This is 911 dispatch. Did you place a call to us?"

"Yes." I glanced around the room. The bathroom door was open and it was empty.

"What is your emergency?"

"My Melinda. My...I think she's...it's too late she's already...."

"Sir, what is your location?"

I might have mumbled out her address but I could no longer tell if I was vocal or coherent. I felt nothing and my ears buzzed with somber, white noise. I looked at Melinda. My Melinda. I tried to stop shaking so I could reach out and caress her. Warm her up. Stroke her shoulders. Her arms. Her sad and pained face. Why? Why did I have to leave Melinda alone? How could I have done such a thing? The future had already been set for us. We were supposed to laugh about this night, at some wondrous moment many years later, like after a tender candlelight kiss during our tenth anniversary dinner or as the dark punch-line of a joke told to our teenage son or daughter....

Instead, my Melinda was gone.

I noticed a small piece of paper resting in Melinda's left hand. I pulled it free and saw that she had managed to scribble a few sentences on it, presumably before she had collapsed to the floor. Why had she used her remaining energy to write out these words?

The answer to my question was simple: because I had left her alone. She should have spoken these words to me. If she had only gotten a chance, I might have understood what was happening to her, and I might've called for help in time. But I was left with only a scrap of paper with three lines of nebulous words, devoid of Melinda's voice and connotation, because I had left her in her greatest time of need. I have never been able to forgive myself for that.

The first written line said:

I always wanted to believe in God.

But I didn't. I couldn't. Not after this night. I couldn't believe in anything anymore.

The next two lines made even less sense.

It wants to kill me, Danny.

And it's coming after you next.

TWO

I had my first of a thousand drinks at Melinda's funeral, sipping brandy from a flask engraved with the initials of the guy who gave it to me – a friend of Melinda's whom I had never met before. I had never been much of a drinker during my time at the University, but I caught up to my binge-drinking peers and surpassed them. I slid easily into the banal character of an inebriated lout not to mute my emotions (it did the opposite), but to give me something simple to accomplish. The alcohol induced haze also made it easier to ascribe Melinda's strange sickness, the worthless hospital stay, the unseemly night of her death, and the crying smiles at her funeral as one big hallucination, a nightmare induced by an onslaught of unchecked emotions. Alcohol had also diffused the disfigured witch I had seen in her apartment's bathroom into an acceptable, clinical explanation. What I had witnessed had only been my own worry manifesting itself into a self-persecuting illusion. A guilt-laden phantom. Unfortunately, alcohol did little to smother the incessant drone of loss and its reproaching refrain: *you should have never let this happen.*

Melinda's autopsy report listed the primary cause of her death was due to natural causes. The secondary cause was anaphylaxis – an acute, allergic reaction caused by the prescribed sedative she received at the hospital in conjunction with a predisposed hypersensitivity to valerian root (which was the herbal supplement she had been taking to help her sleep, thinking it was a healthy alternative). The coroner also noted that she had suffered from abnormal cardiac stress caused by a pre-existing hereditary condition and the disorientation she manifested in the hours prior to her death. In other words, the empirical findings were obfuscated to ensure the hospital would not be held liable in any wrongful death litigation.

I submerged my own cardiac stress with Jameson, Dewar's and whatever cheap beer I could find. I drank almost every night; I was an aimless log during the day, intoxicated kindling after 7 PM. Somehow I managed to graduate from the University despite almost failing two of my last four courses of the semester. My saving grace was that my professors were familiar with not only my strong academic reputation, but also how much Melinda's death had affected me. My Polymer Science Professor, Dr. Rupti, actually paper clipped an AA meeting card onto my C-minus final. I threw the card away along with my final. Group therapy and token assistance was in full opposition to my commitment to self-loathing solitude and affliction.

I was a forgettable ghost during my graduation ceremony which took place in mid-May. I had skipped the pompous commencement exercise reserved for all students and merely slinked through the intimate conferral of degrees given by the Engineering Department. Both my mother and father attended my graduation, but I don't really remember interacting with them. After Melinda's passing, I had seen my parents more often than my previous three years at the University combined. My mother had actually stayed with me at my apartment for a few days during the week Melinda's body was shipped from the morgue to the mortuary. But when Graduation Day arrived, the day that should have been celebrated as another milestone for children of the American Dream, I blew my parents off to sleep away my perpetual hangover. My parents had been divorced for over ten years and had only pasted themselves together for the event –

cordial, but fragmented shadows who staged a proper caricature of familial support and congratulations. I did them a favor by sending them back early to their respective homes.

A few weeks after graduation, after my mother refused to renew the lease on my apartment, I collected my meager belongings, crammed them into a U-Haul mini-truck and moved back into my father's house for no other reason than it was the only coherent future decision I could make. I made no pursuit of a career, no attempt at any gainful employment. I wanted to be an anonymous statistic. I was not going to live the life I had planned. The life I had planned with Melinda. It had only been four months ago when we had argued about all the Big Decisions we needed to decide together. *Where would we live? How would my possible engineering job with Dow or Dupont intersect with her choice of medical school in New York or California? Why shouldn't we take time off to travel the world?* Melinda had convinced herself that a three week South American adventure that would've spanned from the Amazon to Tierra del Fuego would be a "metamorphic experience." She had even wanted to make a t-shirt that said *From Piranhas to Penguins* with a visual morph of the fish warping into the bird. I had told her that her t-shirt idea sounded like it was hatched by an elementary school student who had overdosed on gold stars.

We had Unfinished Arguments. What was the proper time for marriage? (After she finished medical school, but before her residency? Until we were dual-income earners?) How many kids should we raise? (Two? Three? One? None?) And Un-started Arguments. How would we divvy up house cleaning? Who is the better cook? Who pays for this bill? Why can't we share the same toothpaste? Who decided on this fucking brand of toilet paper? I figured all the Arguments and Big Decisions would be quickly tidied up by the agile hands of time and we'd be instantly transported into glowing senescence. I expected to be a seventy-eight-year-old geezer, my grizzled throat gasping with complaints about how the weather affected my prostrate, while Melinda would be chattering me back to sleep, spouting hyperboles about a new healthy recipe for stuffed chicken ricotta and how our oldest grandson got robbed out a Harvard acceptance letter.

Instead, I was regressing. I was going back to live with the fifty-three-year-old man my mother had jettisoned when I was

37

a twelve-year-old middle school colt. The man I had left (and had made a blood vow to never live with again) when I was an eighteen-year-old college-bound stallion. Now, devoid of self-respect, I was crawling back to him as a twenty-two-year-old foal. He didn't protest my decision which wasn't at all surprising. My father was a bad talker, lousy at communicating anything other than accommodation. He rarely voiced displeasure, content to maintain a flaccid state of happiness in his life. My father's art of feigned compromise only exacerbated my mother's own fault of avoiding open conflict and I grew up in state of unnatural calm. It was unbearable. I was extremely saddened when my mother left, but I had empathized with her decision. I would've rather endured a host of fervid arguments between my parents, with a little collateral damage thrown at me, than have existed in the silently buried contempt that haunted my childhood. On the day I left for the University, I whooshed out the door like a deflated balloon. When I returned to my father's house, the pressure rushed back inside me.

"Find a job?"

My father spit these words out at me almost every day after living with him for almost a month, as if getting a job was actually one of my priorities.

"Not yet."

My usual reply. My reticence worried me. It was quite possible that my father's bumbling communication traits had been genetically passed on to me. I had always found weighty conversations difficult but Melinda had stifled the possible malignancy of that behavior. Was cohabiting with my father enabling it to reemerge? Or perhaps even blossom, unleashing repressed genetic expression through some form of contagious nurturing?

I had considered moving in with my mother, but it wasn't feasible. She had embarked on a completely new life when I was still in high school. She had decided to become a travelling photojournalist, never residing in one place for longer than six months, hopscotching across the continents. My mother wasn't hugely successful with her new love and had never remarried, but she was extraordinarily content. For that reason, I forgave her for not being around as often as I would have liked. Melinda had met her a handful of times, including our last Christmas celebration, and they had apparently adored one another. Melinda's death crushed my mother as much as it had crushed me. Even though we shared much of the same pain, we only spoke of Melinda's death once, and I had been so dazed I barely remember her words of condolences.

"Keep checking the want ads."

My father always left me the classified section of my hometown's newspaper. If I were really looking for a job, the classifieds of that small-time rag would be the last place I would look. My father wasn't a dumb man. Just a little uneducated. He never attended college and he was a Luddite, a technophobe. He shied away from computers, smart phones, online connected appliances – anything that had a microprocessor. In high school I had signed him up for Internet service (secretly bundling it with his cable), but he disconnected it once I left for the University. His mind and body were blue collar relics. He read paper newspapers (local only) and paper magazines (sports and cars). He drank Budweiser (rarely) and ate meatloaf (frequently). He was a builder, crafting aromatic furniture out of cedar, ash and pine. Most of the tables in our house were built with his meaty, caveman hands that were bolted to his veiny, inflated forearms. Although he was five inches shorter than me (in work boots he stood 5'6"), he walked with an intimidating swagger that caused most people to move out of his way and shun direct eye contact.

"Already checked them."

I made a point of throwing the classifieds away in front of him, hoping he would get the point. He never did. He seemed disappointed in me, but it was difficult to tell. My father had a perennially haggard face and was also aging badly. Loose folds of skin drooped from his lower jaw and cheeks, and his eyes had sunk back into his balding head. He was a deflated man, still physically strong, but dominated by the prosaic life he had created.

Each day I tried holing myself up in my bedroom like I did when I was a teenager. It should've been easy. My room had been maintained in almost the exact manner as I had left it prior to leaving for the University. A queen size bed with faded plaid sheets and a cracked wooden headboard; a small red cedar work desk that had been built by my father when I was in Kindergarten; a three shelved pine bookcase (built when I was in fourth grade); a black dresser with a broken bottom drawer (built by me in the tenth grade following IKEA instructions), and my poster of Einstein sitting against a rock, wearing an effeminate pair of open-toe sandals that made everyone (even my dad) smile. My room had been preserved as if my father had always been expecting me to return home and resume *B.U.* (Before University) time. Or maybe even *B.M.L.* (Before Mother Left) time. The still life in my room wasn't alone. The master bedroom had been captured in the condition of the day my mother had left. A king-sized bed draped in a rose patterned comforter; a chestnut armoire (another fathered piece of furniture that took him a decade to complete) containing a single wool sweater my mother had left behind; a pair of faux French oil lamps, one atop a chocolate pressboard dresser and the other on a cinnamon pressboard nightstand, both bargain buys from a neighborhood garage sale; mirrored closet doors, and four framed Ansel Adams photographs, one on each wall. I assumed he didn't want to upset the fantasy that my mother might return someday as well.

I hated the fossilized living conditions, but my habits made them bearable. I spent most of my time inside my bedroom sleeping, typically pulling my hung-over body out of bed each day no earlier than 11 AM. It was an existence that only my liver regretted. I drank beer for breakfast after my father left for work. Wolfed down leftovers for lunch. Took a nap or masturbated quickly and pathetically. Slurped down a few more beers while watching TV. Took another nap. Ate a dinner comprised of whatever my father threw over to me, saving some for the next day's lunch. Took a thirty minute shower. Went outside to walk over to a local dive bar, McKinney's, where the friendly bartender would continue to serve me after I was obviously drunk. Stumbled my way back home. Cuddled up with a half empty bottle of whiskey I kept stashed under my bed and milked it until I reached unconscious oblivion.

I paid no rent and leeched cash out of my father for the alcohol. I had begrudgingly sold my Cannondale, but that money only got me two cases of Newcastle and a bottle of Glenlivet, the rest had gone to pay for my U-Haul. I don't know why my father kept giving me money. The mortgage and upkeep on the house couldn't be inexpensive, I had doubled his food budget, and my groveling asks were always accompanied with a sour smile. I guess it amounted to nothing more than I was his son and he loved me. It was his duty to take care of me. Residual love was the most difficult emotion to eliminate even when it was detrimental to both parties. My father couldn't even bring himself to sleep in the master bedroom, relegating himself to one of the other single rooms of his four-bedroom ranch house. His chosen domicile looked worse than my Perkins dorm room, furnished with only a mattress and box spring atop a rolling metal frame, and a TV stand misused as a nightstand. The worst sight of all was the remaining bedroom which was used as my father's storage room. A hoarder's paradise stuffed with his unfinished woodworking projects, broken tools, stacks of family photographs, a pull-up bar, old newspapers, invoices and notices, a cracked mirror, two dead plants, faded books, magazines and CDs, a dozen, taped up cardboard boxes labeled as JUNK, and undisturbed layers of confectioned, decade-old dust.

My routine went uninterrupted for over two months until an old high school friend, Trent, paid me an uninvited visit at my father's house. He had been in the Marines since eschewing college after high school, surviving the latest freedom-loving incursion (central Africa), and returning to our hometown to figure out a life after an unceremonious discharge. We were never particularly close, and it would be more apt to call him a former classmate than a friend, but in high school I wasn't as conservative with semantics. We met during my sophomore year, sharing a one year stint on the soccer team. I had grown bored kicking the ball up and down the field and quit. Trent was kicked off the team for peeing on the field while serving as goalie. We didn't share many classes, but in the few we did, he was smart enough to copy my homework. One time, in our U.S. History class, the teacher caught him scratching out his essay on the Teapot Dome scandal using a copy of my well-researched treatise on President Harding. Our inexpert collusion should have resulted in both of us receiving zeroes on our work. Instead,

Trent said he stole it out of my backpack. I was never sure why he covered for me like that. He never asked for anything else from me in return, and he ended up being suspended and failing that class. After that, I didn't feel so weird referring to him as my friend.

My father opened the front door after Trent's chubby knuckles hammered the wood a dozen times.

"Good afternoon, sir. Do you remember me? My name is Trent. I'm a friend of Danny's from high school. I don't believe he is expecting me, but I'd be happy to catch up with him if he's available."

I overheard Trent's bullshit politeness from the kitchen and almost fled to my room to resume my private indulgences. I was weary of perfunctory small talk, or worse, back-patting condolences. Returning to my father had one unexpected benefit: it muted the din. Jose stopped trying to contact me after two months of not answering his phone calls. Everyone else gave up easier. My other University friends, better known as Melinda's friends, moved on with their lives, their slew of condolences petering out into one sentence messages sent via text and social media. Modern tech provided the most convenient way to slowly ditch someone while still feeling good about yourself. On my Facebook page, one freckled-face Bio major from Melinda's sorority, Amber Stratton (who had sent me a friend request only after she met me at the funeral) had posted on my wall, *Resurgere tento!* I had no clue what that meant and had to Google it. It was a Latin motto meaning *I strive to rise again.* I pegged Amber as an idiot and immediately unfriended her. Did she actually think that an obscure phrase that she didn't even bother to translate or explain would bring happiness back into my life? When I was drunk, I didn't blame Amber or any of these other "friends" for their intentions – who wants to embark on their buoyant adult life reaching out to a muddy anchor? But when sober, my clear-headedness made me a vindictive prick and I wanted their dreams to sink along with mine.

I went to the door to meet Trent, and thankfully his voice changed back into the kid I knew in high school. A know-it-all whose dreams were worse than reality.

"What the hell are you doing back in this shit town? Real world too scary for ya? Happens to a lot of college graduates, drowning in debt and nobody's paying you in gold stars and self-esteem."

Trent's hair was neatly shaven, still in its compliant military style, but if he had gained a sleek soldier's build while on duty, it was now lost. Trent had always been stocky, his limbs compacted together with chunk muscle like a wrestler, but his face was puffy and greasy as if he had been surviving on a diet of fast food for months. He did his best to hide a paunch with a baggy brown t-shirt but when he cast his characteristic lopsided smile, his flabby jowls gave him a double chin. I didn't invite Trent inside my father's house, and he didn't seem to mind as he continued his lecture.

"Danny, you can't be a big failure – everyone had high hopes for you. Never thought you'd be living back here."

I was certain no one in my hometown had more than a passing thought of me, much less pronounced their high expectations of my future. "How did you know I was living back here?"

I let Trent explain that his visit was triggered after he saw me walking away from McKinney's the other night.

I tried not to sound defensive. "Cabs are too expensive and I don't have a car."

"You were shit-faced, bro! Tripping over cracks in the sidewalk. That's why I didn't try talking to you. You probably wouldn't have recognized me and your face was all toasty. Angry red. You an angry drunk?"

"No."

"A lot of people have seen you. This is a small town, you know."

My hometown wasn't small. It was average. An average-sized town with average streets, average homes and average citizens. The town was bisected by a two lane highway that was constructed four decades ago when people still thought it had the potential to be a major hub of commerce. Instead the cars on the highway sped past the city, heading to the more exciting and prosperous cities that lay in both directions. I wasn't average enough to fit in my hometown. It was a place where residents relished their mediocrity, celebrating their polite refusal of ambition and success. If anyone else besides Trent had actually seen me teetering on the sidewalk, maybe they did wonder how I could be so dissatisfied with small-time life, subjecting myself to such debasing inebriation. What

43

they didn't realize was that I didn't deaden my brain to tolerate my hometown – alcohol enabled me to exist in my hometown.

"I've got nothing to be embarrassed about."

Trent laughed and offered to drive me to McKinney's or any other bar around town in his car. I thought the offer was strange, until he revealed that his immediate life plan was in alignment with mine: getting drunk cheaply and easily.

"You know that service that drives your drunk ass home in your own car? I get it for free, because the owner is a fellow vet!"

I finally smiled at Trent because he had instantly transformed into something useful. A chauffeur who wouldn't complain because he thought he was my long lost best friend.

Over the next couple of days and several trips to McKinney's, I began to talk about Melinda with Trent. He listened quietly as I described the absolute wonder. And the damnable end. After hearing me boast about Melinda's beauty at least five times over, Trent bluntly asked me for a photograph of her while we were sitting at the bar.

"I don't have one. I deleted the ones on my phone and I just trashed my Facebook – the posts were nauseous."

"Stupid. Shortsighted too."

"No. I feel better."

"You're so damn selfish. I've keep hearing the same sad shit from you. Is your life over now? Are you never going to move on?

"Whatever."

"You're never going to get laid again with that attitude."

"What the hell is wrong with you?"

Trent chuckled. "Melinda the only woman you ever banged?" The bartender, with half-inch gauges stuck in his ear lobes, was out of earshot of our conversation but he also began to laugh, spittle shooting out of his mouth, and tagging the beer mug of another patron.

I took a long drink to drown my fury. Trent put his hand on my shoulder. I wanted to knock his fingers off me, but that would force me to put down my drink. He squeezed my deltoid as he spoke.

"You need to understand. Melinda wasn't the end all, be all, bro. Never meant to be. You need to accept that she's gone forever. Let your dick have some fun."

"Fuck you."

Trent removed his hand from me. "You think I'm a heartless fucker, don't you? Think I saw too much blood and death and now don't give a shit? It's a stupid game, bro. You gotta adapt! Can't stop playing, and you're only fooling yourself if you think you can."

I finally put down my drink. "A little war doesn't make you a damn expert in life."

"Little? Bodies were flying everywhere, bro. All I'm saying is that you should've kept her photos. If you had those pics now, you could bust 'em out and get any girl in here to pity-fuck you."

"Let it go, Trent."

"What's her last name? Let me Google her and see what pops up."

"Let it go! I don't want to see her!"

"All right, shit! Settle down. You don't like Google or something? Well I got some pics. Want to check out some gory photos I took on my tour?"

I shrugged my shoulders.

Trent continued. "You were supposed to say, *No!* or *Fuck no, bitch!* Then I would have said, *That's cool because I deleted mine too!* Ha! See? Wouldn't that be funny?"

"Not at all."

"Ah, you know it's funny. Truth is I didn't want to take any. I thought the fools taking photos and videos weren't taking their shit seriously. Too caught up in trying to be the soldiers they saw in bullshit war movies. *Let's take a photo with me posing with my M16 like it's my dick! Let's do one of those brothers-in-arms pics and send it to Johnny Purple Heart's mom to show her we loved him! Let's take a pic of the six inch scorpion that crawled inside my boot so we can make the folks back home shit themselves!* I thought they were all in denial. And I was right. Mr. and Ms. Instagram were the first ones who got their heads blown off."

"Really?"

Trent laughed softly. "Nah, bro – I'm joking. Death ain't that picky. I'm just saying that our eyes are all glued to the same program – might as well enjoy watching things circle down the drain when it ain't you that's drowning."

"Your head's screwed up."

"You think I've gone insane? Stared too long into the abyss and can't find the light? Nope. I'm the same as you. Wathcing hundreds of little demons every day, circling around me, nipping at my body, twirling around my eyes, creating the same God damn little heartbreaks, over and over again. We're ths same, Danny. Our days are exactly the same. Shoot at the enemy. Hit some civilians. Apologize. Reload your rifle. Shoot again. Fuck up. Shoot again."

Trent bowed his head and I thought he was about to break down crying but he let out a few grunts instead. "It was a relief when death finally sucked me up."

For a moment, Trent's body began to dematerialize, becoming translucent as if he were becoming a ghost. "You're not dead, Trent."

Trent's head bounced back up. "Metaphor, motherfucker! How did the corporate world miss plucking up a genius like you from the graduation line?" Trent started laughing again and it was giving me a headache.

"I think hanging out with you is a mistake."

"I thought you were sick of all the *I'm so sorry* talk? Only trying to motivate you to turn your life around. Help my bro get laid again."

I turned away from Trent to ignore him, but he continued, oblivious to my writhing misery. "How about that pale redhead over at that table? She got a little pudge, but her tits are holding up. She's been checking you out. Sitting all alone, an eager beaver. You can't say no to eager, bro."

Unfortunately, I directed my disgusted scowl not at Trent's intoxicated face, but at the girl he had referred to – a thirty something with frizzy red hair atop a cantaloupe shaped head. She was starkly fair, her veins shining through her forehead and neck. After spotting my bitter frown, her eyes sunk into her face and she started playing with the wrapper on the empty Newcastle bottle in front of her, tearing off shreds of paper and rolling them into tiny balls.

Trent slapped my back. "Well you creeped that one out. Maybe you need to aim lower. Want to go to a strip club? I've got a coupon."

46

I ordered another beer and began chugging it to see if that made it easier to ignore Trent. He kept babbling about a strip club in the adjacent town that had certain discrete ladies who would be up for more than a dance. He said that I needed to snap out of it, that I had no hope of ever finding love again if I stayed in my despondent condition and didn't at least try to "bang my way to happiness." I finished my beer and stood up from my seat at the bar. I glanced over to the table where the redhead was sitting. She had been replaced by a blonde girl with her back facing me. The blonde's hair was tied back into a loose ponytail, reminding me of Melinda. I stood up and immediately felt dizzy. *(Orthostatic hypotension.)*

"We shouldn't hang anymore. You need help, Trent. Your ignorance is autocatalytic."

"Auto-fucking what?"

"You're damaged." I dropped a twenty onto the bar.

Trent started to laugh uncontrollably as he pocketed my money. I raced out of the bar, his shouts whipping against my back. "Ah, come on, Danny! Damaged people are always the funniest fuckers to be around!"

I felt honorable leaving him so I could return home, drink myself to sleep and dream about Melinda. Trent was too simple and boorish. How could he conceivably believe that I would allow myself to disgrace her memory with an STD-ridden stripper? As I walked home, I passed a couple of raggedy middle school kids kicking a half-dead pigeon down the sidewalk. They stopped and stared at me as I passed them, the pigeon's mouth popping open, grasping for air or death. I felt sorry for the kids. They didn't know that they'd all grow up to be like Trent.

After a month elapsed, Trent showed up at my father's house again. My father was seduced by his overcooked courtesy and allowed him inside, leading him over to my room where I was trying to take a nap. I remained lying in bed with my eyes closed, but I let Trent speak.

"I'm shit-full of sorry, bro. I didn't mean to piss you off. Don't ever know what the fuck I'm talking about. I've never loved anyone in my life. Was supposed to get married once, but she dropped me. I was cool with her cheating, but guess that didn't matter. So yeah, I've never loved anyone. Down to go grab a beer? We don't have to talk. I've got a shit-bricks headache and I just want to watch baseball and zone."

As much as Trent had irritated me, and as content as I was to continue suffering alone, I actually missed our codependent drinking. I missed the neuron-numbing, time consuming nonsense – my go-to websites and TV shows weren't enough. I could only hear the shrewd thoughts of my own jabbering mind. If Trent steered clear of Melinda and my love life, he would provide a needed respite from my father who was still hounding me about finding a job.

I trekked back to McKinney's with Trent and was soothed by his description about the latest viral YouTube video for a 3-D military video game. He said the video reminded him of his worst day in combat. I figured he was about to delve into specifics about a battle or a tremendous loss of life. Instead, he talked about how he lost the photograph of the woman he had intended to marry. Trent had been stuck digging out sleep holes for his battalion. Most Marines dug their own hole, but since Trent had fallen asleep on guard duty, he had been ordered to dig everyone's hole as punishment. Sometime during the digging, the photo of his fiancée had slipped out of his pocket. No one ever found it (or claimed to have found it) and Trent comforted himself by saying he must have wanted to bury it subconsciously.

He didn't elaborate on how his relationship with his girl ended, only burping out minor details of her in between sips of a vodka and soda. I caught that she worked at a grocery store, was half Hawaiian and half Hispanic, had 36C breasts, and had long black hair that swept across the top crack of her ass when he screwed her. But he never mentioned her name. Whenever he came close to revealing it, Trent dropped out of reality. His eyes drifted aimlessly as if he were morbidly drunk, and he lost the ability to delude himself with his purported wisdom. Trent's all-consuming pain lasted for only seconds, but it was enough to secretly delight me each time it occurred.

The benign conversation about his girl didn't last. After a couple of hours, he brought up the topic of the strip club again.

"They let you smash for cash. So I've been told."

I feigned rabid interest in an ESPN highlight show playing on the flat screen above the bar.

Trent continued. "All you're doing is thinking about her. Not healthy, bro."

My health was of no concern to Trent. He goaded me to order more drinks, joking that my tolerance had become higher than an alcoholic's. I suggested we call it a night. He countered by fattening his strip club lure. He offered to chip in for the cost of one of the girl's services. I could at least get a blow job for $30 and he'd pay half for me. I told him to shove his money into another round of drinks for himself and I left him at the bar once again.

When I staggered back to my bed that night, more sober than usual, I couldn't sleep. I was edgy and restless, and didn't know if I should blame the lack of alcohol or Trent. Worse, I didn't get my nightly reprieve. When I closed my eyes, I couldn't see Melinda. Couldn't picture her gorgeous face and body and the more I tried to concentrate on her features, the blurrier her image became until she was replaced by the devilish, emaciated creature I saw at the time of her death, a charred cavernous face staring directly at me as its rotted finger stumps yanked out knots of swamp-thicket hair.

When I got out of bed in the morning, hours earlier than usual, I was disjointed. Uneven. I couldn't drink. I tried to eat, but had to spit out the food before it could turn my stomach. Agitation curdled inside my mind and began to pound against my skull, boring holes, searching for an exit. I should've taken that as a cue to get some help. Some treatment for alcohol addiction.

Instead, I called up Trent and agreed to go with him to the strip club.

The decision calmed me and I got densely drunk with Trent before we popped into a cab that took us to the adjacent town, a haven of cheap commercial real estate offerings and deserted industrial parks. We rolled through streets trimmed with halfhearted recycling plants and oversized, paper-thin warehouses with collapsing For Lease signs, stopping at the appropriately named Wildcat Club. Trent said the club was frequented by a lot of military personnel from the army base ten miles away and that's how he found out about it. However, after he handed a coupon to the doorman in a belly-stretched suit and the two exchanged a well-rehearsed fist bump, I plunged my friend's "never been here before" refrain out of my ears.

We had to take several steps down to get into the cellar-like entrance, and when I stepped inside the club, my eyes adjusting to the muted lighting, I knew this was a mistake. I was too good for this place. The bottle of vodka I had shared with Trent earlier did nothing to abate the shame that began to smother me, and my composure began to blur from self-reproach. The Beastie Boys "So What'cha Want" blared through a myriad of hidden speakers, the bass cranked up to intestine squishing levels. Red and blue LED lights mixed with weeping black lights, creating a psychedelic moonscape better suited for a perverted clown on Ecstasy. Three girls were dancing on a small stage with a mirrored backdrop, each taking turns wheeling their mostly nude bodies around a golden center pole. Their glitter-dusted, fake-baked skin sparkled in sync with an onslaught of swirling, flashing yellow lights bouncing off a massive crystal chandelier above the stage. Although I could tell that each girl was of varying height, hair color, and body shape, I couldn't distinguish their facial features. It was if their faces were incomplete, distorted, drawn by a wannabe artist who never paid for the eyes, nose and mouth lessons. They were robots, bluntly designed so viewers would focus only on their cosmetically enhanced breasts, their gyrating, curvy hips, and their sparse or nonexistent pubic hair which was revealed whenever their programming said to tug their thong underwear down.

The club was practically empty with only eight other patrons, and a dozen non-dancing strippers hovered and circled around them, waiting to splay open the wallets of the rabbit-eyed men. I was ready to leave but instead followed Trent to a row of seats near the stage. We ordered a couple of ten dollar Cokes and watched the dancing girls on stage. Even at close range, their warped faces were featureless. Trent placed a few folded dollars onto the lip of the stage and invited one of the hovering strippers, a blond mannequin wearing a neon green bra and matching boy shorts, to give me a private show. She declined.

I shouted to Trent over the music. "I can't stay here."

He pulled me away from the stage and to another seat in one of the back rows. "Better?"

Before I could tell him he misunderstood me, the blond girl in neon green returned. She slithered up to me and plopped down on my lap with her back in my face and her blond ponytail swaying above my eyes. Her bare skin smelled like strawberries and cigarettes. Trent told her my name was Michael. She turned her head around, her featureless face reflecting my own. I felt trapped as her raspy voice abraded my skin.

"My name is Talia. Did you think I wasn't going to come for you?"

I found the nerve to reply. "I've changed my mind. I have to go."

Talia licked my ear.

"Scared of me, Mikey? I've got something for that."

As an unfamiliar hip-hop song thumped in my ears, Talia grabbed my hand and led me around the stage. An odd flurry of red lights plastered the dancers with bloodlike streaks, and the writhing girls looked like victims from a mass casualty scene. Talia pulled me away from the stage and down a narrow, black painted hallway that left only a couple inches of space on both sides of my shoulders. At the end of the hall was a floor length red velvet curtain. She swept the curtain back revealing another black wall.

Talia pushed against the wall and a panel slid to the side like a hidden closet door and we entered a prison cell sized room. She slid the door closed, muffling the thump from the club music and the room turned almost completely silent. Talia led me to a small twin bed, shaped like an altar, with a long red sheet that appeared to be the same material as the velvet curtain we had parted through earlier. Next to the bed was a wooden TV tray table with two burning yellow candles in glass jars, a cigar box, an unwrapped condom, and a bottle of Moët champagne with two flutes. Aside from the candles, the room was illuminated by a toothpick thin floor lamp tucked into a corner of the room, its light bulb on its last tungsten leg. Talia sat me down on the bed. She teasingly began to lift up my shirt and when she reached inside to caress my chest, I flinched uncontrollably.

"I didn't come here for this."

Talia laughed and exposed her breasts revealing two pierced nipples – two thin silver rings that jiggled more than her silicone did. She pushed me down on my back and

51

reached over to the TV tray, opening the cigar box and shuffling a few of the cigars out of the way to grab a small scarlet crystal vial. She popped off the vial's metallic top and sprinkled a black colored powder from it onto her finger. She licked it clean then sprinkled some more onto her finger and ran it past my nose. It smelled like overcooked fish.

"Lick it. It'll make you feel better. It'll make everything better."

She glided her finger into my mouth and my lips puckered from the bitter substance. Instantly, my heart rate jumped and for a few dreadful seconds I wondered if I was experiencing cardiac arrest. But after a few moments, my heart rate returned to normal and my entire body began to loosen as if my muscles had detached from their ligaments. Talia poured out two glasses of champagne; I sat back up in the bed and we both downed our drinks in a few large gulps. Talia motioned for me to remove my clothes.

My tongue grew numb. I tried to speak. I couldn't. I tried to wiggle my tongue but it felt like it was no longer attached to my mouth. Talia stood up and turned around, removing her shorts. On her lower back was a tattoo featuring two swirling red flowers and the words *hyacinth girl*. She glided to the floor lamp and turned it off. As she crept back to the bed, I saw her face, her features finally coming into view, before she blew out the candles and plunged the room into darkness.

She looked exactly like Melinda.

Melinda's voice echoed inside the room as two fierce hands began pulling off my pants. "This is supposed to be fun, Danny-boy."

My mind froze. I tried to scream but only a strained gasp escaped as the smothering body on top of me began its attack.

The floor lamp clicked back on. The room stunk like boiled eggs. My chest and stomach hurt from several sharp bites. My jaw ached from an elbow punch. I didn't have sex. I had been in a fight and I had lost. I wanted to retch.

Talia stood near the exit door, reattaching her green bikini top. I could see her face clearly. She didn't look anything like Melinda. She was a hideously plain woman. Her skin wasn't tan, but a scaly shade of eel grey. Ruddy stretch marks ran along her waist and down her ass.

"Get dressed and take the rubber with you." Talia exited the room. I lay on the bed for moment, examining every newly formed wound on my body. I had become a miserably weak and puny man.

I dragged myself off the bed and pulled up my pants. I was unsteady, unglued by a frozen blade of reality. The intimacy that I had shared with Melinda was over. It might as well have been a mirage. Was this my life now? A nightmare?

I sped out of the room, slipping my used condom into my pants pocket. I wanted to take it; I didn't want to leave any part of myself in that room.

As I emerged from the hallway and back into the regular part of the club, I turned invisible. The area had become packed with patrons and it seemed as if the club had wrangled in more strippers to accommodate the new guys. No one looked or said a word to me. A few people even callously bumped into me, continuing past as if I didn't exist. I searched for Trent, snaked all around that stifling club, but I couldn't find him. I assumed he had made his way to his own private, secret room. I managed to carve a path through the crowd and reached the exit. Outside, I found an available cab parked nearby and got a ride home.

I took a shower and hopped into bed. My body was still sweaty. And itchy. But once I fell asleep, I didn't wake up. There was no rush to the bathroom to relieve my stomach of its alcohol overindulgence. I slept amazingly sound.

The next morning, I awoke with no residual shame or hangover. I felt relieved. It was very peculiar and I began to think that Trent had been right all along.

The exuberance didn't last long. When I sat up in bed and looked back at my pillow, I saw that a section of the pillowcase was caked in dried blood. My blood. I touched the side of my face near my nose and scraped off flakes of coagulated cells. I smacked my tongue and tasted coppery saliva. It appeared that I had endured a bloody nose during the night and it had bled profusely without my waking up.

I went into my bathroom to wash up, but before I could finish splashing water onto my face, I began to sob. I couldn't contain myself. I fell to the floor and wept quietly, but violently, my chest heaving and jerking. I cried harder than I had during Melinda's funeral.

Later that evening, I got a phone call from Trent. He asked me if I wanted to go out to grab drinks again, but to limit ourselves so that we could actually make it out to the strip club this time.

"Not funny. Shut the hell up." My dismissal came out sounding more like a threat.

"Relax. We'll just look at the girls – you don't have to get with one if you don't want to. I understand you're still not over Melinda, but if you at least looked at them and saw how big their--"

"Come on, Trent! Do I owe you money or something?"

"Dude, what are you are talking about?"

"I don't know how it works! I didn't see you after I left that hidden room in the back of the club. I looked for you all over. Talia didn't ask for any money."

"Who's Talia?"

"Whatever her name is! The ugly stripper you set me up with last night."

"You're losing it, bro. You left me at McKinney's and I had to close the place down by myself. I get it if you're still too pussy to get pussy – just don't bullshit me. You could at least fake your details better. There are no hidden rooms in a strip club. Place would be shut down next day! I heard there's an hour hotel about a block from the Wildcat and--"

"Fuck off, Trent! I made a mistake."

"Whatever. You've given me another headache. Hit me back when you calm down and want to get drunk." Trent hung up.

As soon I pulled my cell away from my ear, the hangover I thought I had avoided all day came roaring into me. Was Trent playing a game with me? Or had he completely forgotten the night in his own drunken haze?

Or maybe it had been a nightmare, after all? I went over to where I had kicked away the pants I wore the previous night. I checked the pockets, searching for the used condom I had been too revolted to throw away.

I couldn't find it. Was it possible that I had once again let my shaken subconscious foul up my sense of reality? Had I just manufactured the entire experience?

I skipped dinner and stayed in bed and stayed sober. After my father fell asleep, I slipped out of the house, and called for a cab. The driver took me along the same winding path through the industrial park but as he pulled into the Wildcat's parking lot, the exterior of the club looked different. It looked smaller. Like a backwoods shack decorated with a stolen neon sign.

I forced myself to enter the club, dishing out twenty dollars to get past the doorman, and saw that it was stuffed with the same strung out elements: the tipsy lights, the rolling music, the slack-jawed patrons. But the stage was empty. Four strippers were milling around and, as before, I couldn't discern their facial features. I couldn't blame my skewed vision on any drunkenness. There was something wrong with this place. I felt exposed. Threatened. I should have raced out of there, but I took a seat and waited. It took only a few minutes before one more stripper arrived. Talia. Wearing a black lace bra and thong with a sheer negligee, a cloud of berries and smokes circling around her. Her face had changed again. Modelesque. Blue-grey eyes. A thin, prim nose. Thick, scarlet lips. Possibly Russian or eastern European.

Talia sat in the open chair next to me and twirled her ponytail as she spoke. "Do you like my hair, Danny-boy?"

I turned away from her. "Don't call me that."

Talia spoke with an overly high-pitched voice. "You asked me to."

"No, I didn't. I didn't ask for anything."

Why was I holding a conversation? I had confirmation that I had been to the place and that Trent was lying. It was time to leave. But I stayed rooted to my seat.

"Danny, I know exactly what you want."

"You don't know me."

"Oh, don't be such a ghost. Ready to take another walk?"

"I don't have any money."

Talia laughed. "I don't want your money! I want you." She extended her hand to me and I grabbed it.

Despite the frightened, begging voices ringing inside my head, I let Talia lead me back to the private, hidden room.

The next three nights, I went back to Talia, returning home with increasingly deeper cuts and bruises from our rank trysts. My back was furrowed by acrylic fingernails and my thighs hammered by bony knees. I had rope burns around my ankles. The worst wound was a circular scab of singed flesh on my left forearm, courtesy of a lit cigar. It was as if I had lost all cognitive and moral control of my actions. I had become enthralled by a series of masochistic therapy sessions that made me feel something I hadn't felt before: resilient. I still drank, but not as much. I slept peacefully. No more bloody noses. No more brutal hangovers.

No more dreams of Melinda. And I didn't feel guilty about it.

I would've slept with Talia for a sixth consecutive night if I hadn't uncovered Melinda's heart notes. On the afternoon of the sixth day, I found the notes underneath my bed while doing some obligatory room cleaning, a chore my father had finally demanded that I perform.

Melinda's heart notes were little irregular scraps of paper that she occasionally left behind for me. Short handwritten thoughts or messages that typically revealed something about her, me, or our time together. I had always saved them in the bottom drawer of the nightstand I had owned throughout my college years.

When packing up my apartment after graduation, I had concealed all these notes in a notebook filled with old lecture papers from my Physics 200 class. I could not bear to look at them and my intention was to stash them in something I would easily forget about, perhaps with the hope I would absentmindedly pack the notebook away in a corner recess of a secluded storage unit. I had forgotten I had slid it underneath my bed, tucked next to some old textbooks, a few high school yearbooks and an iPad that no longer worked. The six inch gap between my bed and the floor was better recognized by my brain as a convenient place to store alcohol.

As I vacuumed the carpet, I shoved the bed aside and one of its legs had kicked open my Physics notebook, revealing the heart notes. It had been over six months since Melinda had died, and it was too soon for this discovery. They were unflawed elements comprised of Melinda's emotional DNA and deserved to be viewed by an untarnished spirit, not the drunk, sexual deviant I had become. Guilt flushed through my veins. What the hell was wrong with me? I shut the vacuum cleaner off and threw the machine out of my room and into the hallway.

Flaxen, autumn light beamed through an open window in my room, warming my skin as I plopped down to my knees and stared at the heart notes. I could see the sloping lines of Melinda's ornate yet clear cursive writing, each gentle arc begging me to ingest the words, her words, and relive the agony of losing her. There were so many of them, at least a hundred, all written during our three and half years together. I had saved them all. Except one. Her final note. The one she had written to me moments before she had died. I had spared myself the torment of that note by tearing it up into unreadable bits.

The door to my bedroom swung shut, and I attributed it to the clammy breeze blowing through my window.

I shifted my body to shield the notes from any further wind gusts and I ran my fingers across the carpet, along the Berber loops and around the pieces of paper, teasing myself with the words as my fingers grazed the notes. I grew bolder. I picked the notes up and let them fall back down like a kid playing with sand.

I focused on one of the notes, unable to stop myself from reading it.

Bubble fighting on the stairwell. Tasty magic?

I traveled back to the birthday party Melinda and I attended for her friend, Kellan Tomajiro, one of Melinda's pre-med classmates, during our sophomore year. It was held in his dorm room, on the fourth floor of Stoyer Hall, and we had grown bored watching the rest of the partygoers' commitment to monotonous drinking games. We snuck out and made camp on the dorm's exterior stairwell that led down to the third floor. Melinda pulled out two Magic Blow mini bubble bottles, two of the dozen or so that Kellan's girlfriend had scattered in his room as party favors. She handed me one and we took turns forming bubbles with our mini-wands, trading jokes about the bottle's brand name which sounded like souped-up cocaine. We quickly dispensed with a contest over who could make the biggest or longest lasting bubble, and commenced a no holds barred bubble fight, laughing and shooting streams of foamy bubbles at one another, darting up and down the stairs like ROTC recruits on a training session. I was breathing so hard, I accidently inhaled the soapy water from my wand and began to choke. Melinda wasted no time and blasted me in the face with her bubble stream, asking me if I enjoyed the taste of defeat. When I finally stopped choking, and the contents of bottles were used up, we returned to the party. Most of the other bubble bottles had ended up spilled on the floor and stomped on like crushed insects. We grabbed a couple of Magic Blow survivors and left Kellan's party without saying goodbye.

I stopped running my hands through the heart notes to pick up another.

Sunlight drips down your face each night, and with that, I find solace.

I couldn't remember receiving that message or what it meant. It may have been one of the poetic renderings she used to write for me or a song lyric from an unremembered band. I had likely blown the note off, oblivious that these notes would eventually come to end. Another heart note was stuck to this one, so I pulled it off to see if it provided supplemental meaning.

Do you hear it? Its daunting voice makes me feel so strong, so radiant, like how I felt when you danced with me at the Moonlight Formal.

The Moonlight Formal was another one of Melinda's sorority functions that I didn't want to attend. Her sisters were giddy over the Senior Year formal dance, stating it symbolized the culmination of all their University years. To me it looked more like an excuse for the sorority to relive their lame high school prom. But I couldn't say no to Melinda. She had saved up money for seven months to purchase a dress for the occasion. A luminous gown, a frictionless, indigo fantasy that effortlessly glided over all of Melinda's curves. Anticipation for the night's end drove me to dance with her. And when she said she wanted to leave early, I began to picture her dress floating over my bed. But I never saw that dress again. We left because she had an argument with her sorority president and she needed to sleep away a foul mood. Alone. I think she returned the dress to the store the following day.

Most likely, I received this particular note a short time after the dance, during the last days of February. Less than a month later she'd be gone forever. The note's complete meaning still eluded me. Had it been a form of apology? Something to improve the memory of that night and the abrupt loveless ending? Had I blown this note off too? I didn't understand what she meant by "its daunting voice" or why something intimidating would make her feel strong. What was *it*? What did she mean by *it*?

(It's coming after you next.)

I had taken these heart notes for granted and all I had left were scraps of contradiction and ambiguity. A hand came to rest on my shoulder and instead of startling me, I was calmed by its touch. Another contradiction. I casually turned my head around to see who was next to me.

No one was beside me. But the air smelled like strawberries and cigarettes.

I stood up. My bedroom door was back open, and the vacuum cleaner stared at me from the hallway. I walked out of my room, calling out "Hello" and my father's name throughout the house, but no one answered. I was alone.

I trotted back to my room to gather up the heart notes and stash them back under my bed. I wasn't sure what was occurring but the notes were the likely cause of it.

My feet pinned themselves to the carpet as soon as I crossed the threshold. Next to my bed was a naked woman, on her hands and knees, hunched over Melinda's heart notes. Blond hair tied back into a ponytail. Tattooed back facing me. Talia. It looked like she was coughing, her back pitching back and forth, in sync with each hack. Repulsion set in as I realized Talia was dry heaving over the heart notes.

"Please leave." I didn't know how she had gotten inside my room, or why I was being so polite.

Talia stopped retching, but remained hunched over the notes.

"Go! Get out of here!"

She still didn't move. I tried to take a step forward with the intent to kick Talia to get her to move away from Melinda's notes, but an instinctual warning wanted my body to flee instead. The mixed message caused my legs to buckle and I fell down to the floor on my back.

59

Talia released a tinny moan and craned her body around to face me. Her eyes were gone. Plucked out. Only bloodless cavities remained. Her mouth curled in a grotesquely carved smile that bubbled with saliva like a festering wound. Talia scattered the notes so they shot off in every direction and she began crawling in my direction.

"Going! Going!" I tried to make the words bolster my nerve, to push myself to get up and get moving, but I could only stare at the stalking entity in terror.

Bile-tinged mucous leaked from Talia's mouth as she drew closer.

"Gone!" A useless word. I still couldn't move.

The vacuum cleaner in the hallway turned on, sending a whirring roar throughout the house. Talia began to scuttle faster to me, vile gasps snorting out of her nose.

The vacuum in the hall seemed to scream louder. I managed one final, guttural scream, "GET THE FUCK OUT OF HERE!" and propped myself up to my elbows.

It was too late. Talia reached me. She grabbed onto my calf and a searing pain shot into my ankle and up my thigh. I tried to yell again but this time only a soft, girlish cry escaped. She crawled her way up my body, each hand hold causing a crushing bolt of intense pain, until our crotches were aligned and her mutilated face and dripping mouth were just inches away from mine. The vacuum cleaner shut off and all I could hear was Talia's beastly breath and my whimpering heart.

Talia extended a finger to my forehead and her jagged nail dug into my skin, slicing a scalpel-precise line that curved down to my right eyelid. She licked my blood off her finger and spoke to me with an agonizingly pleasant voice.

I love the way you taste, Danny-boy.

It was Melinda's voice. How could her loving sound come out of this thing on top of me?

"Melinda?" I eked out her name despite my doubt that her voice was real. Pain splintered my entire body as Talia tightened her grip on me.

She spoke again, still with Melinda's voice.

No. She's gone. I'm the one who devoured her.

"Get away from me."

A garbled, choking noise started to spill out of Talia's mouth and a drop of abhorrent saliva fell from her lips and onto my chin.

60

What's wrong? Don't you want to fuck me now?

Talia slid her hand down my pants and viciously squeezed my testicles. Her voice changed. Deeper. Discordant. And so unlike Melinda's.

Don't worry, Danny. I'll take care of them for you.

The sound of my scream roared throughout the house and I blacked out.

When I awoke, I was outside my father's house lying on the dewy front lawn. It was night. I was sobbing, shivering, whimpering like an injured dog, while my father stood a few feet away shaking his head at me.

He berated me. "Pull yourself together."

The crotch and left leg of my jeans were wet, but not from the grass. I had urinated all over myself.

My father held out his hand. He spoke slower and calmer. "Let me help you inside. Get cleaned up."

I reached out and my father guided me to my feet. He tried to lead me inside the house but I resisted.

"Just keep moving. You'll be OK."

I couldn't answer my father. I was trying to compose myself, focusing on moving my legs and walking, not on what had happened to me.

After a few steps I caught my breath and spoke. Only one word, but it was all I could muster. "Why?"

My dad lowered his head. "I don't know, son. I don't know why your life has turned so bleak. I've been too lenient with you. If this doesn't force you to stop drinking and doing God knows what...."

My legs continued towards the front door. More words tumbled out of my mouth. "What's going to happen?"

"I don't know. Trent will be in the hospital for a while. Then the police will take him into custody."

My mind reeled. I couldn't understand what Trent had to do with anything. "Trent didn't hurt me."

My father snapped at me. "That's not the point, Danny! Don't you understand? It could've been you! I should've never let that fool into the house."

I remained silent as we stepped inside and my father directed me to the bathroom. He undressed me and put me in the shower like a first-time father taking care of his toddler

61

son. I noticed his eyes lingering on the scratches and bruises on my body, but he said nothing and he left me to bathe. I stayed in the shower for quite some time, unable to shake off the confusion that was frothing and overflowing in my mind. I found comfort in the veil of hot water cascading over my rattled body. Until I scrubbed my face, and the soap burned into the scratch etched on my forehead. The soothing water turned to frost as I remembered the monstrous thing that had been on top of me.

I exited the shower and walked around my bedroom in my towel, searching for signs of what I believed had taken place earlier. The room was clean, vacuumed. Where were Melinda's heart notes? I searched the floor underneath my bed. No Physics notebook. No notes. What had happened to them? What had happened to me?

A knock on my bedroom door startled me. I swung around as my father entering my room.

"Feeling better?"

"Yeah. I guess." I picked myself off the floor. I wouldn't feel better until I got an explanation. Nothing was making sense. Had I really been attacked? How did I get outside? Why had so many hours passed since my last memory of the day?

"The police will want to speak with you. I told them I would bring you to the station in the morning. At nine."

"What? What do the police want?"

"To hear your side of the story. Your words will help them with Trent."

"I don't understand."

My father nodded. "Get some sleep. You look better, but I think you're in some sort of shock."

I nodded and he exited, shutting my door behind him. He was right; I was in shock. And my confusion wasn't getting any better. I flung my pillows onto the floor. Ripped off my bed sheets, wadded them into a clumpy ball and threw them next to my pillows. I rolled my body onto the bare mattress, too tired to think, but too stirred up to stop the questions in my head. I started to laugh. Choppy laughs. The kind of low volume, staccato laughter I usually let loose after drinking all night.

It was funny to me. Absolutely funny that the only thing I could rationally decipher was that I was losing my mind.

62

THREE

The next morning, my father jostled me out of an unquenchable sleep and told me he was going to drive me to the police station in an hour. My brain and body complained loudly as they both needed more time to recuperate, but I hauled myself out of bed without voicing any protest.

As I began hunting for some decent clothes to wear, mental snippets of the previous day began to batter me. I couldn't segment the images in my mind between those that were real and those that were fantasies. The stampeding flashbacks were exhausting, but I was cogent enough to get dressed into one of my only ironed shirts (a short sleeved burgundy Oxford) and my nicest pair of slacks (black pleated Dockers). Presentable attire would have to go a long way in concealing my muddied cognitive state.

I joined my father in the kitchen. He had his hands on his hips and was pacing, carving dour tracks in the hardwood floor. My father talked even less when he was nervous, but I could read his mind. He was deeply worried about me.

I was worried about me. Aside from the inexplicable circumstances and visions, I seemed to be missing a large portion of time. I managed to calculate that from the time I was reading through the heart notes in my bedroom to the time I ended up out on the front lawn, approximately eight hours had elapsed. Why could I not remember anything?

"You should eat something. Cereal or oatmeal." My father grabbed a bowl from the cabinet and placed it on the countertop in front of me.

"I'm not hungry."

That was a lie. I was ravenous. I couldn't remember the last thing I had eaten and I was weak and jittery. But I didn't want to reward myself until I had learned more about what had occurred.

"Dad. I don't remember how I got to the front lawn last night."

My father stared at me, posing like a statue that had slipped off its base. He grabbed the bowl and put it back into the cabinet. "You don't want to remember."

My father's face had aged even more overnight. The sagging wrinkles on his forehead and at the corners of his eyes had multiplied, surrounding his dormant skin faults with active micro-fissures. The streaks of black hair that he assiduously combed over his bald crown seemed to have become sparser and grey.

I became impatient. I needed help deciphering the irritable emptiness that was darkening my mind and turning the memories I did have into a swirl of unidentifiable artifacts. I ran my fingers through my hair and a few stands came loose. Hair loss was probably another foible I was at risk of inheriting.

"Can you at least tell me what you know?"

"What do you mean, Danny?"

"Tell me everything that happened from your point of view. It will help with my story to the police." I didn't care at all about helping the police, and was dreading the trip over to the station, but I needed to have some form of preparation.

"Fine."

My father sat down at the dining table and I uneasily took the seat across from him. It had been a long time since we had both sat together at the table. It was my mother who had insisted on eating all our dinners together, as if every night was Thanksgiving. After she left, my father and I usually ate alone – him in front of the living room television and me in my bedroom. Only on the rare occasion when we dined out at a restaurant did my father and I ever sit together.

"I got home from work and the front door was open. Lights weren't on and I heard the vacuum running. I started yelling for you."

My father had worked the same unremarkable job for the past twenty-nine years as a maintenance and operations supervisor at the local community college. The tedious, manual labor job suited him. He thrived as a checklist supervisor, overseeing the tools and tasks necessary for the college's upkeep without being overtaxed by any significant intellectual requirements. Throughout middle school and high school, I was embarrassed by his humble career choice. When classmates asked what my father did for a living, I told them he was retired. None of my fellow students ever cared enough to confirm if my claim was true or not. At the University, I continued the blatant lie until I started dating Melinda. Dumb, ego-preserving bullshit was another weed she had managed to pull out of me.

My father continued with his recap. "You didn't answer me. I saw the vacuum in the middle of the hall and I yanked the damn plug out of the wall. I called for you again."

My father typically arrived back home around seven-thirty, after working from 7 AM to 7 PM. He was only paid for eight hours, but he took his time with prep and clean-up work and that invariably contributed to the security and longevity of his position. I had calculated that my awareness (albeit disoriented) had returned out on the front lawn around eight o'clock. So my father's arrival must have triggered something.

"I walked into your room and saw you on the floor. Curled up like a baby. Like the day when your mother left us."

I didn't remember the day my mother had left. I can clearly recall my twelve-year-old self, distraught and confused in the days leading up to my mother's last day in the house. But on the actual day she left, I could only regenerate a frayed string of sounds and smells.

A television playing too loudly.
The smoky fumes of burnt toast.
My heartbeat pounding in my head.
Gasping, unable to breathe.

I began to wonder if my brain had something akin to an automatic shutoff valve whenever something traumatic occurred in my life. I wasn't sure if that mechanism was a good thing to possess. It meant there were times when my conscious mind wouldn't be in control. Little wonder I experienced horrific visions of unnatural beings and creatures. My subconscious was having a field day casting out unbridled nightmares from some wretched hole in my mind.

My father continued. "Wasn't sure what had happened to you. I rested my hand on your shoulder until you looked up at me. You started to speak, but it took a while for it to make sense. Too shook up, I guess."

"How did I get out on the lawn? Did you take me out there?"

My father shook his head. He pushed his chair away from the table as if he were finished with our conversation. "I'm not sure this is necessary. Just tell the police what you know."

The slow progression of information was becoming unbearable. My voice grew louder. Meaner. "What happened next? I need you to tell me!"

"Yelling! Just like now! Telling me over and over that Trent was gone."

"I don't know what that means."

"You remember."

"No, I don't."

"Damn it, Danny. You said that Trent got drunk and crashed his car. He was gone. Dead."

Did I make up a story to tell my father? Why did I use Trent as a character? "You believed me?"

My father stood up from the table. He looked more uneasy than agitated. "Of course! I called the police and they confirmed that Trent had gotten into a car accident. But it was a woman in his car who was killed."

Woman? Could that have been Talia?

My father didn't look at me. "They said Trent was in the hospital and under arrest for DUI. So I went back into your room to tell you."

My father remained silent and he walked over to a coat rack and grabbed his jacket. I urged him on. "Then what did I do?"

My father put on his jacket, zipping it up to his neck. "You started laughing like some insane fool. Pissed all over yourself. Ran outside and collapsed on the front lawn. Crying."

My father grabbed the keys to his work truck and exited the front door. It signified our conversation was over and it was time to go to the police station.

My father must have felt like disowning me. Hearing him describe my undignified hysteria only amplified my own bewilderment. I started to doubt the veracity of almost everyone and everything, especially myself. Was Talia, the human version, really in my room? And Trent too? What did I do during those eight missing hours? I was weighed down with the disconcerting feeling that I had done something unfathomably wrong and my subconscious had forced me to craft some sort of fabrication in order to protect myself. I could no longer feel Melinda's disappointed eyes gazing down on me. They had turned away. Liars didn't deserve redemption.

I tried to distance myself from my apparent Gigantic Lie as we rode over to the police station. The last thing I needed to do was to continue a pattern of lying to the police. But my honesty needed to be non-specific. Without logical extrapolation. I would confide that I had experienced a series of highly upsetting events and my memory had been affected – I couldn't be certain as to what had happened. I thought about pleading stress-induced amnesia, but was unsure if such a condition actually existed.

When we reached the station, I exited my father's truck with sluggish, deliberate motion, walking in short, shallow steps that matched by breathing. It was as if my guilt was a foregone conclusion and I was trying to delay my processing for incarceration. When I reached the sun-bleached, stone steps that led up to station's entrance, my feet stopped. I turned my head back in the direction of my father's truck, parked in station's rocky, barely used lot, and tried to suppress the urge to bolt.

"If you've nothing to hide, you have nothing to worry about." My father's words were not comforting. I hoisted my legs up the steps after my father put his hand on my back and gave me a firm push.

The police station had once been our hometown's city hall (from 1934 to 1991) so its classical architecture clashed against the surrounding modern glass office buildings like an 80's brick cell phone displayed in an Apple store. The station's entrance featured two Doric columns and matching pilasters that rose out of the earth like resurrected bones, supporting an arched portico engraved with an eagle with flared wings flying above a sulking Demeter, wearing a modius and standing on top a coil of two snakes – the whole thing supposedly symbolized the birth of agriculture, even though there hadn't been a farm in my hometown for years. To me, the police station looked like the inflated, but rarely visited, mausoleum of an affluent misanthrope. The building's eastern wall, shaded by a two overgrown oak trees, was crawling with wild tendrils of ivy and splotches of purplish-black moss. If the town wasn't so frugal with ground maintenance or so afraid that an exterior renovation would tarnish the building's historical landmark designation, the police station might have offered a more pleasant welcome. Instead, I felt like I was walking into a tomb that was a little too eager to accommodate me.

Once my father finished pushing me inside, the scene changed from Solemn Death to Comic Hell. The atmosphere inside the station, in stark contrast with the exterior, emitted a creepy Nickelodeon sitcom vibe. Spotless, snow-white walls and a recently waxed parquet floor cast a made-for-TV shine. Salty enamel reflections gleamed from the ringing smiles of the officers waltzing past me. Two of the traipsing cops looked younger than me, likely can-do rookies with ass-kissing aspirations, while another looked like their mother, a misplaced housewife embarking on a second career after solving too many "Law & Order" episodes.

I checked in at the front desk with an officer whose rhinoceros-sized appearance was more comforting – shaved bulbous head, bloated neck, engorged biceps – a prototypical steroid-infused cop. While his horn (nose) wasn't long and spiky, it was rough and thick, flat like the battered pickle of a heavyweight boxer. The skin on his bald head was brushed with pink indicating it was either sunburnt or flushed, and I assumed the latter since the officer had the immutable, pitiless scowl of someone who hadn't come to terms with how shitty his life had turned out. I liked him instantly.

"Detective Gutierrez will be speaking with you." Officer
Rhino spoke in such a soft, affable tone I couldn't help letting
out a quick chortle. Rhino shook his head at my father who
was standing behind me, and they exchanged similar looks of
chagrin. Officer Rhino told my father to wait in the lobby near
the entrance then informed me that he would escort me to the
interrogation room on the second floor where Detective
Gutierrez would meet with me. I turned back to my father for
any last minute advice, but he had already walked away to
take a seat in the sparsely furnished lobby, pausing only to
select a dusty magazine to read.

Officer Rhino stepped out from behind his desk (he stood
at least six foot six and I apologized for my earlier laugh) and
motioned for me to follow him. I noticed he had a badge that
said his name was Officer Arthur Ledoux – a French surname
that I believed meant "sweet." Another contradictory attribute
that ruined my initial characterization. I didn't like his
increasing multi-dimensionality and I decided to stick with
Officer Rhino. Rhino guided me through a security door, up a
short flight of stairs (passing another two smiling officers
joking about a bungled robbery), and down a yellow-tiled
hallway bordered on both sides with filing cabinets and
tacked posters displaying clichéd, motivational slogans.
Rhino didn't make any further conversation with me and it
saddened me a little.

A thick Plexiglas window claiming a third of the left-side
wall broke up the chain of file cabinets. It provided a
voyeuristic peek into a break room with several plastic tables
and chairs, a refrigerator, a few unopened cupboards, and a
crumb dusted counter top with a microwave, sink and a coffee
pot. Sitting at one of the tables, alone, was a piggish man
with silky, wavy black hair and an overgrown bushy-brown
mustache. He was wearing a wrinkled tan suit that clung too
tightly to the rolls of fat around his armpits and he was
slumped in his seat, cradling a cup of coffee with his stumpy
hands. I stared at him for as long as I could, staring at his
face and his half-closed eyes. His face drooped over his coffee
cup as if it belonged to a man unworthy to ingest the
stimulating contents, a man better suited to sleep away his
life.

Further down the hall, we passed a white door labeled
Interrogation Room #1, and stopped at another white door,

unsurprisingly designated as *Interrogation Room #2*. Officer Rhino opened the door and led me into a claustrophobia-inducing coffin. The room's vanilla eggshell walls had no trimming or painted borders, giving the illusion that the room was circular. The furnishings were meager, but still crowded the room. A brown rectangular folding table with a scratched up particleboard top. A burgundy stacking chair with faded armrests and a torn sitting pad spurting tufts of yellow foam. And two black, unscathed, un-matching folding chairs that had been pushed away from the table like newborn rejects. There wasn't a one-way mirror on the wall (didn't they watch the same TV show & movies?) only a portrait sized, frosted glass window that let in enough outside light to double the illumination created by the single florescent lamp hanging limply from the ceiling. Rhino asked me to take a seat on one of the black folding chairs.

"Sit tight. Detective Gutierrez will be with you shortly." Rhino left and I heard a click on the doorknob that sounded like he had locked me inside. I grabbed one of the black chairs and pulled it up to the table. As I rested the right side of my sweaty head against my arms and the cool table top, I noticed a closed circuit camera in the corner above the door. So they were watching me. I gave the camera a brief wave before turning over to the left side of my head. I didn't want the police to know that the surveillance bothered me.

Five minutes passed before the mustached man from the break room opened the door. His flabby eyes had cracked open and he had crafted a spindly smile, allowing a few yellowed teeth to slip out from underneath his whiskers.

"Hello, Danny. My name is Detective Gutierrez. Would you like some coffee or water?"

I shook my head. I wanted to get this conversation completed as soon as possible. Det. Gutierrez took a seat on the padded chair and a few additional pieces of foam spit out into the air. I wanted to call him Detective Walrus, but decided to be serious so I could gain focus.

"OK. Let me know if you need anything. I can get Officer Ledoux back here if we need him. The chief sanctioned him with office duty again. Poor bastard. Apologize if he was mean with you."

I wanted to tell him that Rhino had been relatively docile with me and that I didn't appreciate the detective's effort to either scare or bond with me. Instead I shrugged my shoulders.

"Terrific. Really appreciate you coming in this morning." There was a coffee stain on the Walrus' jacket lapel – the trainer at Sea World hadn't given him enough cup holding drills. I took a deep breath. Why couldn't I focus? The detective pulled out a writing pad and a pen, and began scribbling out some notes. My eyes fixated on the detective's chubby flippers (hands) as he wrote; his webby, hairy fingers looked like undercooked sausage links.

There was a stranger sight. The detective had one extra finger on his non-writing, left hand. A supplemental digit in between his ring and little fingers. I had seen polydactyly in one of Melinda's medical books, but was surprised to see an actual person possess it. His extra finger was almost fully developed, only a little less straight which caused it to slightly overlap with his ring finger. It tapered at the end with a crooked nail that looked like a small talon.

The detective raised his eyes away from his notepad and looked directly at me. "Are you uncomfortable?"

"No. Not at all." I actually hadn't stopped shifting in my chair since I had first sat down. The folding chair's seat was disproportionately small and I could not find a position that was comfortable for more than a minute.

The detective put down his notepad and asked me a question with a slight sneer. "Are you sure you don't want something to drink?"

"No. I don't want anything." I slunk down a little in my chair to appear relaxed, as well as discover a tolerable posture.

"I heard you've been quite the drinker lately."

A burr of resentment rose up my throat. I sat back up in my chair. "Who told you that?"

"Your father."

I bit down on my tongue, highly perturbed that my father had a deeper conversation with the police than he let me know. This was a redoubtable complication. I wasn't sure what details my father might have shared about me. I needed to counter-attack.

"I've undergone some rather traumatic events recently. I know ethyl alcohol isn't the best coping mechanism, but I haven't let myself get out of control. For example, I've never driven a car after drinking."

I didn't want to have to start incriminating Trent, particularly with the limited information I had, but my instinct to protect myself took precedence.

The detective seemed unfazed. "You were a chemistry major in college correct?"

"Chemical Engineering. There's a difference."

"I took some chem classes back in my college days. Complicated subject. For me, anyways. I'm sure you're an ace. Bet a hundred places want to hire you. Any interesting job prospects?"

My father had probably told the Walrus I was unemployed and this was another attempt to antagonize me. "I'm considering a position with a thermoplastic elastomer toy manufacturer in Las Vegas."

"Sounds important. Is that your dream job?"

I tried to stifle a laugh. "I'm sure it is for some people."

"Something funny, Danny? You do realize that you're in the middle of a serious situation."

Why couldn't I settle myself down? "You're the one asking frivolous questions."

"No. I'm only trying to discover what type of person you are so I can understand what happened. Don't you find that reasonable?"

"If I told you I was working on homogenous post-metallocenes for olefin polymerization to replace traditional Ziegler–Natta catalysis – would that clear things up? Would it even matter?"

"Are you telling me you're employed?"

"No." I slunk back down in my seat. "No point to this."

"I'm upsetting you?"

"I'm not upset."

"Terrific. Let's move forward. How often did you and Trent go out and grab a drink? Once a week? Twice a week?"

"Is my drinking under suspicion or is Trent's?"

"Neither. Your father said that you and Trent were together almost every night. Is that true?"

"More or less."

"How much did you drink yesterday?"

"I have no idea. If this conversation is only going to center around my consumption habits then I'd like to leave."

Detective Gutierrez chuckled and clasped his hands together. The extra finger he had stood up, askew from the rest of his mitt, violating his jolly pinniped appearance. "You sound upset."

"I'm not."

The Walrus thrust his face to me. "Cut the crap, Danny. Are you going to help me put together the chain of events that led to yesterday's tragedy or not? If you need time to think about your choice, I can give you some more time alone."

"No. I want to get through this. I want to help." I wrested control of myself. I had to take a different approach if I wanted to get out of the station before noon.

"Terrific. All I want is for you to answer my questions to the best of your knowledge."

"Zero. I had zero drinks."

"Really? You had no alcoholic beverages yesterday?"

"I don't recall drinking anything."

"Are you unsure or did you forget?"

"I don't recall."

The detective unlaced his fingers and sat back in his chair. He grabbed his notepad and began to write. "Interesting. OK, maybe you can tell me what you were doing at home before Trent arrived."

"I don't recall Trent arriving at my father's house."

"Jesus, Danny. Quit the lawyer-speak. What can you *recall*?"

"Cleaning my room."

"Is that something you usually do?"

"No. My father told me I had to clean my room or move out."

"Sounds fair if you've been living rent free. Did your father's request make you angry?"

"Not at all. Like you said. It was fair."

"Moving forward. Do you remember calling Trent and asking him to come over?"

"No. I doubt I would've called him over to help me clean."

"But you might have called him over for a drink, right?"

"Your question only registers a blank."

"What do you mean?"

"Here's the truth. I don't remember certain things from yesterday – from the time I was cleaning my room to the time my father came home from work." I didn't want to mention

73

Melinda's heart notes and I absolutely wasn't going to describe my vision of the disfigured and sadistic Talia.

"How much time elapsed between cleaning and seeing your father?"

"About eight hours."

"What are you telling me? That you were blacked out for eight hours?"

"No. I'm telling you that I don't remember anything during that time."

"I don't understand why you're being so uncooperative. Don't you care that a woman is dead? Aren't you concerned about that at all?

I gained confidence as the Walrus transformed back into the portly, dejected man I saw in the police break room. "My girlfriend Melinda died just over six months ago. She was everything to me. She was my life. Don't tell me what I should be concerned about!"

Detective Gutierrez nodded. "Your father told me about her. I'm very sorry for your loss. But it might make you feel better if you help us wrap up this investigation. Your friend Trent is in a lot of trouble."

"I'm not lying. Or trying to be difficult. I've tried to remember, but I can't. I only regained awareness when I found myself on the front lawn of my father's house, completely distraught."

The detective started jotting down notes furiously. "Have you ever experienced any memory loss before?"

"Yes. When my mother left my father."

Gutierrez put his notepad down and moved his chair away from the table. He put his hands behind his head before speaking. "Here's the deal, Danny. I'm still not sure you're telling me the complete truth. Your father told me that this is the second time this year you've claimed memory loss. He said you supposedly don't remember being in the hospital for two days after your girlfriend died."

"What else do you know about me?"

Why had my father shared so much with Detective Gutierrez? His openness with the Walrus was doing nothing to better our father-son relationship, and my animosity for him started to enlarge.

"I know your father, Danny. I'm a frequent lecturer for the criminology program at the community college where your father works. We like to chat on occasion."

"You don't really know him."

"Yes, I do."

"My father does not like to chat."

"Have you tried talking with him?"

"About what?"

Gutierrez sat forward in his chair. Something I had said had retriggered his confidence. "Your father told me you've been acting a bit *disturbed* for quite some time." The detective had purposefully lengthened the word *disturbed* to make me as concerned and submissive as possible. I threw a bright smile at the Walrus and he sat back in his seat, confidence evaporating. His extra finger began to quiver, like a nervous tic, and he tried to conceal the tremor by strumming his fingers against the table. "Sometimes when a person suffers from guilt or blame – even when he isn't at fault – he can experience a form of self-inflicted amnesia. Forced forgetfulness to keep away judging eyes. It's not uncommon, and I don't think it's something to be ashamed about."

I answered Gutierrez by staring at his eleventh digit. He noticed my gaze and crossed his arms against his chest, tucking his hands into his armpits. He topped off his spiel with a plea.

"I'm trying to help you, Danny."

"I thought I was here to talk about Trent and a dead girl."

The detective reached down and picked up a portfolio and placed it on the table. I hadn't noticed the briefcase before and assumed he must have brought it in with him. He pulled out a large manila folder and took out several photographs. Four showed Trent's car, taken from different angles, wrecked and mangled up against a tree. Three were gory shots of a girl who had been partially decapitated. Talia. Her hair was still tied back in a ponytail, but it was stained and clumped together with blood. Gutierrez also pulled out a typed report of some sort, stapled to a sheet of handwritten information.

The detective read from the report. "The car crash took place about six blocks from your father's house on Olive Circle around six thirty in the evening. The first officer on the scene found the driver, a male approximately twenty four years of age, trapped in the driver's seat, bleeding from the

75

head and unconscious. A female, approximately thirty years of age was found ten yards from the vehicle, apparently ejected from her seat. She was pronounced dead at the scene." Gutierrez looked up from his report. "At the hospital, Trent was unconscious for a while, but when he awoke, he was eager to talk. Let me tell you what Trent told us. See if that helps jog a memory or two out of your head."

Gutierrez began reading from the handwritten paper which described what had occurred yesterday according to Trent.

Danny called me over to have a few drinks at his father's place. He said he had a full bottle of whiskey to share. When I arrived around 3 PM, the front door was open so I wandered into the house and towards his bedroom after hearing a laugh. Inside his room, I saw Danny and a woman on the floor. She was completely naked. Sweaty and stunning. Danny had his pants down around his ankles, passed out. I figured they had just finished having sex. I was going to leave, but the woman asked me to stay. She said her name was Talia and that she was a stripper from the Wildcat. I really wanted to leave, but Talia begged me to stay for a drink. I'm ashamed to admit it, but I stayed. She was very convincing.

For the next couple of hours I had a couple of drinks but Danny had apparently finished most of the bottle himself. And I started fooling around with Talia. I regretted it immediately and after I finished I got dressed quickly so I could leave. I only had two drinks and I wasn't drunk at all. But Talia asked me for a ride home. She said she took a cab to Danny's house and didn't want to wait for another to take her home. I refused. She got mad and started screaming and hitting me, loud enough to wake up Danny. He was still crazy drunk, laughing and telling me and Talia to shut up and leave. I guess he wanted to clean his room because he started turning a vacuum cleaner in the hallway on and off. I finally agreed to give Talia a ride home to shut everyone up. As we left the house, Danny started screaming, "Going, going, gone!" over and over.

In the car, Talia got angry again. Said I was driving too slow or something like that. She had given me a wicked headache and I tried to tune her out, but she attacked me again. She started hitting me in the face and chest. I swear it

76

was like she became possessed – even her eyes turned red.
She hit me so hard I lost control of my car and it crashed. It
was an accident. But it was her fault. I wasn't drunk. She
made me crash.

After hearing Trent's story I became flushed and ill. Either
Trent was lying or I no longer understood myself. Was it
possible that I had sunk to such a level of dissolute behavior
that I had purged everything from my mind? Had I gotten so
upset from Melinda's heart notes that I had invited Talia to
come over to my house? Plastered myself with sex and
alcohol? Invited Trent to join me only to regret having them
both over in the end?

How did I even contact Talia? I wasn't even sure I had her
phone number. I lowered my head back onto the table as if
despondent, and surreptitiously pulled my cell phone out of
my pocket. I quickly scrolled through my recently dialed
numbers.

I saw that I called Trent yesterday at 2:00 PM. Two hours
earlier was a dialed number listed only as T. T for Talia?
There were dozens of calls to T in the preceding days. I
quickly tucked my phone back into my pocket.

Had my mind been so disgusted with my behavior that I
had even blocked out phone calls? Maybe Det. Gutierrez was
right – self-inflicted amnesia due to guilt. I had even
transformed Talia into some sort of malevolent being. It was
beginning to appear that the only repulsive creature was me.

I hadn't noticed that Detective Gutierrez had pulled his
chair around next to me until he asked me a question.

"Do you remember what happened now? Is it all coming
back?"

He placed a hand on my arm, the one with the extra
finger. I recoiled from his touch. Gutierrez stood up and once
again folded his arms across his chest. His self-conscious
behavior bolstered my acuity. I decided to reveal the truth
about Talia. At least the truth as I knew it. "I can't believe
Talia's dead. I was sleeping with her."

"You had a sexual relationship with the deceased?"

"Yes."

The detective had a puzzled look on his face as if he
doubted my claim. "Is Talia really her name?"

"It's the name she told me."

Gutierrez cleared his throat. "She had no identification on her. We showed her picture to the owners of the Wildcat strip club, but they had never seen her before. Not that they're too eager to share information with us. The club has been under investigation for prostitution for several months. Was Talia a prostitute?"

"I never paid her for sex." I was certain that this was not a lie.

"We are working to get a hold of the club's employment records and security camera footage which should help sort things out. Did you meet her at the Wildcat?"

"Yes."

"When did you meet her?"

"A week ago."

"Did you go to the club looking for her?"

"No. I didn't know her. I went to the club with Trent. It was his idea." I still wasn't sure if Trent had gone with me. If I believed the story he told to police, he had only met her yesterday.

"Are you sure?"

I got defensive in order to counter my doubts. "I never would have gone to a strip club if it wasn't for Trent! I didn't even know it existed!" I sounded more despondent than angry.

"Trent told us that until yesterday, he hadn't hung out with you for over a week." Detective Gutierrez pulled his chair back to its original spot and flopped down on the cushion, causing a few more bits of foam to burst out. He started writing again in his notepad.

I needed to settle down. Get in control of my uncertainty. "Trent knew Talia. He was with me at the club when I first met her a week ago. He may deny it, but he was there."

"OK, I believe you. How often did you see Talia?"

"I saw her every night."

"At the Wildcat?"

"Yes."

"Except for yesterday, of course."

"Right. I mean, if you believe Trent's story. I don't remember her being at my father's house at all." Images of Talia popped into my mind.

Slipping off her neon green bikini top at the club.

Rolling her dancing, naked body on the bed of the secret room.

Burning my arm with a lit cigar.

Crawling on top of me in my bedroom with her revolting, eyeless face as she hissed at me.

I'm the one who devoured her.

An involuntarily spasm ran through my leg and my knee bounced up and hit the underside of the table.

"Take it easy, Danny."

"I'm fine."

"OK. Yesterday. Did you call Talia?"

"I might have called her. But I don't remember any conversation or asking her to come over."

I had to at least admit I contacted her. Gutierrez had been close enough to me that he could've easily seen me pull out my cell phone, scrolling through numbers. Or maybe he already knew I had called Talia repeatedly? How long did it take to access phone records? Talia's cell phone was likely recovered at the accident scene and it probably showed incoming calls from my number dozens of times....

Detective Gutierrez snorted loudly. It had been strong enough to perk up his mustache and had seemed to indicate he knew that I was thinking about the phone calls. "Come on, Danny. What are you hiding from me?"

"I'm not hiding anything."

"I told you. I'm on your side. If you would just open up to me we could be out of here in ten minutes."

"I don't understand."

"Start by being honest. Stop saying you don't remember."

"I really don't."

Gutierrez pointed at one of the photographs of Talia's dead body. Her dissected remains plastered on the street. Her neck torn open, exposing raw, nervy flesh. "Why are you covering for Trent? What did he ever do for you?"

I was genuinely taken aback. "Why would I cover for him?"

"We're very familiar with Trent from his two prior arrests. One more strike and he gets his turkey. Or didn't you know that?"

Trent was a drunkard, but he always seemed in better control of himself than me. "No. I didn't know. Trent never mentioned he'd been arrested."

"Did he have to? Did you not realize the type of person you were hanging out with?" The detective paused as if waiting for an answer. I gave him none, so he continued. "Trent's first arrest was for assault. He had just gotten back in town after his tour of duty when he beat the hell out of his fiancée. Ex-fiancée. He tried to tell us he only hit her in self-defense.

"His second go-around, he rang up multiple charges – public intoxication, solicitation of prostitution, and pandering. His excuse that time? He had been slipped that new designer drug, Night Spice, and didn't know what had happened. Does that sound believable to you?"

"What's Night Spice?"

"It's called other things, Dark Molly, Black Inferno – a black powdery substance that can be inhaled, smoked or ingested. It has stimulant and hallucinogenic effects similar to PCP and MDMA. Are you familiar with it?"

I vigorously shook my head. It wouldn't do me any favors to admit that it sounded like the drug I had ingested when I first slept with Talia. Its chemical properties might cause horrible visions, but I couldn't imagine it would have been potent enough to elicit an effect days later. It also couldn't explain the dreadful vision I had at Melinda's apartment.

"Trent came home from the war with a lot of psych and behavior problems – it's in his military record and described in his general, not honorable, discharge. But let's not fool ourselves by calling him another hard-luck veteran stricken with post-traumatic whatever. That may have worked to keep him out of jail for the prior arrests, but not this time. We need your help, Danny. We found an empty whiskey bottle in Trent's car, but his blood alcohol level was below the legal limit. We need some corroborating evidence to put him away for good."

"Would jail be the best place for him?"

"Come on, Danny. You know as well as we do that Trent's a thug. A drunk, doped thug as well as a liar. A terrible liar."

I decided to remain silent. Maybe I wasn't as bad as I had thought? Maybe this whole episode had been Trent's fault and I had been unfairly harsh with myself. I had always known that hanging out with him had been a mistake.

Detective Gutierrez leaned in closer to me. I could hear his strained breathing whistle through his nose and swirl over his mustache. "Let me tell you what I think happened. Trent hooked you up with this Talia girl and gave you a free sample so to speak. Maybe a few free samples. He then arranged it so she would go to your house, get you nice and drunk then agree to a session that would include payment. You refused, you called Trent for help, but when he arrived they both got mad at you. Probably messed you up a bit – I noticed the bruises on your neck and arms and that cut on your forehead. They rattled you, didn't they? I'll admit that they could've shook you up enough to actually cause a minor mental blackout. But I know you remember the gist of things. Your father said that you kept telling him you wished Trent was dead. A goner. Well you didn't exactly get the wish you wanted did you? They probably continued arguing in the car over the failed deal causing Trent to lose control, crash the car, and kill the girl. Am I close? Or do you not agree with this scenario?"

I didn't know what to say. Was the detective giving me an out? Or was this some clever ruse to get me to admit to some sort of wrong doing? I stayed silent.

"You shouldn't be worried about Trent coming after you. As long as you're willing to make a deposition as to what really occurred yesterday, we can put Trent away for a very long time. You probably wouldn't even have to testify in court."

I had to take him at his word. I nodded my head.

"Terrific. I know this has been difficult for you and I want to tell you again how much I appreciate you coming down here to the station. The assistant DA will be contacting you to schedule a time to record your statement."

Detective Gutierrez stood up. "One final question for you, Danny. Do you love your father?"

Was the detective trying to bond with me again? I wanted to rebuke him, tell him my relationship with my father was none of his concern. Tell him that I only agreed to his scenario so I could leave with some measure of sanity. But I replied humbly and truthfully.

"I don't know. I guess I still do."

"After my own divorce, my mind was in pieces. It wasn't easy for your father either, when your mom left. When you're suffering it's easy to make mistakes."

I nodded.

"Your father is a good man. You need to start listening to him. Jesus, Danny – you're an adult now – do I actually have to tell you that? You graduated from a top notch college. You should have a really bright future. But if you keep drinking and acting like a dumbass kid, your life will continue to go off-track.

"I'm really sorry about your girlfriend, Danny. I'm sure you loved her more than anything in the world. But get your shit together. You might not have cared about this Talia woman, but now she's dead too. If that doesn't scare the hell out of you, nothing will. You won't get better by trying to outsmart the devil, Danny."

Gutierrez reached back into the briefcase and pulled out an item sealed in a plastic bag. It was my Physics notebook.

"This was recovered from Trent's car. It has your name on it. Yours?"

I nodded as he handed it to me. I took the notebook out of the bag and opened it. Melinda's heart notes were still tightly packed inside. A heartbroken smile escaped from my subdued face. Had Trent or Talia taken it? Why?

"I can tell it's important to you. Trent probably took it as a way to extort money out of you."

Gutierrez collected the rest of his things and motioned for me to exit. "Officer Ledoux will escort you to the lobby. Shouldn't be necessary, but we will let you know if we need to speak to you again. Take care of yourself, Danny." Gutierrez patted my back as we walked out of the room together. This time, I didn't mind that he had touched me with his freak hand.

I reconnected with Rhino who was standing in the hallway, looking lost, and he eagerly took me back to lobby. When I arrived, my father didn't seem to notice me. He was trapped in a rapt pose, staring at the floor. Sitting next to my father was a long haired brunette in black slacks, her almond eyes peeking around the edge of a newspaper. When I got close enough to touch my father, the woman buried her face completely into her paper. My father finally looked up at me. His eyes were milky red as if he had been crying. My anger at his sharing my personal details had abated, but I still couldn't bring myself to feel sorry for him. He stood up and told me he needed to get going; he had to get to work.

We hopped back into the truck and headed for home. We remained silent until we crossed Olive Circle, the block where Trent crashed his car. At that moment, I finally found the strength to say a few words to him.

"Do you think I'm lying about my memory loss?"

My father glanced at me and said nothing. I thought he was going to ignore me until he cleared his throat. His voice was dry and reedy.

"No. I don't think you're lying. I don't know what your brain can do."

It was a positive start; I decided to push forward. "I don't remember what happened right after Melinda died. Could you please tell me?"

I don't know how I could've forgotten an entire two days in the hospital after her death. The fact that my father had discussed it with Detective Gutierrez gnawed at me as if there was a disquieting connection that only I was missing. Like the day when my mother left, I could recall only fragments.

My back itchy from stale sweat.

A woman signing the National Anthem.

Steamy, wet hair releasing a sweet and sour scent and tickling my ear.

A brilliant red dot surrounded by a dozen, little, black rings.

My father sighed. "You get overwhelmed. Very easily."

"What do you mean?"

"The paramedics said you hit them when they wanted to take Melinda's body away. Do you remember that?"

"No."

"That's why they took you to the hospital. You were out of control."

"Was I sick?"

"A fever. Pneumonia too, I think. But doctors said you were acting strange. Cursing. Then laughing. Refusing to talk. Kept calling one of the nurses Melinda."

"I don't remember any of that."

"How about leaving the hospital?"

"No. Only Mom with me. Back at my apartment."

"She was also with you at the hospital during your two days there. She stayed with you until you felt better. You didn't want me around. So I came back home."

83

My father's words elicited a tinge of empathy in me. "Mom didn't really do much – got me some food and helped with laundry. Not sure how much that helped."

My father again hesitated before speaking. "I know I messed up, Danny. Messed things up with your mother."

It was the first time I had heard him shoulder blame for the divorce. Had my erratic behavior triggered remorse within my father? Was he shouldering the blame for my actions too?

He cleared his throat again. I saw his eyes turn red like they had been at the police station. "I know I haven't done the best job in taking care of you. It's difficult when you are so much like her. You know how much you look alike. And you're both so smart. Smarter than me. I struggle to talk to both of you. To talk about things that really matter."

My father brusquely wiped his eyes, as if the motion damaged his masculinity. "I want to do better, Danny. I lost your mother, but I don't want to lose you."

Even though these were the most honest words I had ever heard from my father, his most ardent attempt at real communication, I couldn't accept his act of contrition so readily. I thought back to my high school days when I immersed myself in academics and extra-curricular activities such as joining the debate team, playing the trumpet in the school band, and failing at my one season of soccer. I was a standout academically, but in those other activities I had been mediocre, at best. Those preoccupations served only one purpose. It kept the time I had to spend at home with my father very limited. I had never engaged in a significant conversation with him about me or my life, and he certainly had never shared anything about himself. I had always taken this as concrete proof of his ineffectualness as a father.

My father rarely demonstrated any pronounced interest or emotion that would overturn his self-imposed restraint and passivity. Christmastime was the worst. After my mother left, my father plopped down basic holiday decorations around the house: a four-foot Scotch pine, two red stockings with cotton balls as trim, a snow globe of Santa drinking a Coke, and a three-inch wooden manger (he had lost Jesus and the rest of the Nativity scene). Each year he gave me unwrapped, practical presents – bookstore gift cards, toiletries, an occasional box of cookies – things he could buy in less than ten minutes. There were no photos around the tree, no visits to long-lost relatives, no outward signs of affection. At most, he gave me a slight tap on the arm or back, or a weak arm wrap across my shoulders, his hand barely clinging to me like a bargain dryer sheet. Thankfully, my mother always shipped me a pricy present: a digital microscope, a laptop, a cell phone with monthly charges paid, my former Cannondale. I always had things to brag about at school whenever a kid bothered to ask me what I had gotten.

But lackluster holidays with abridged emotions aside, it was my father's unresponsiveness to my mother that upset me the most. When we were still a complete family, my father only managed a hapless smile whenever my mother delivered one of her long-winded stories or shared one of her infrequent jokes. I never knew if my mother's limited humor was due to her own personality or the bland reactions she had received from my father. The safe bet was on the latter.

My father just couldn't express any true love for my mother and that stung my adolescent mind. I actually wanted to be one of the teenage actors who populated TV Land, the wiseass appalled by his parent's giddy behavior (as the audience howled), and pled with them to keep their amorousness away from me (or at least until they were off-camera). Even with my underdeveloped understanding of love, it was obvious to me that their pithy, stunted kisses weren't enough to sustain a marriage.

When I was ten, we had all taken a trip out to the beach for my father's birthday. It was unusual – we had never celebrated his birthday outside the house. Surprisingly, my father didn't protest and the weather was optimum – early October had been blessed with a bout of Indian summer. While at the beach, my mother and I braved the cold, frothy ocean and dried ourselves by playing with a Frisbee on the sand, or more accurately, her attempting to throw it and my attempting to catch it. My mother was usually too busy to play games or entertain me, so I was relishing the rare treat. My father, on the other hand, sat by himself on a half-broken lawn chair, reading the latest *Sports Illustrated*, and wearing jeans, a long-sleeve shirt, an oversized baseball cap, and tennis shoes. His balding head was never going to enjoy the sun (hence the cap) but the rest of his body had no reason to be so shielded; he was used to outdoor work from long summer days at the college. My father ignored us, as he was nose deep in an article (he was an avid college football fan, and of college sports in general, overcompensating for his missed opportunity), but every time I looked at him, the pages in the magazine never flipped. After a couple of hours, my mother seemed to notice this too and she tried to induce my father to join us, wrapping her arms around his neck and spackling him with residual baubles of seawater and sand from her hair and bathing suit. He shook her off with an irritated mumble, a lethargic complaint that said she had gotten his magazine dirty and wet.

My mother was unfazed and kept her enthusiasm intact. "Wait until we get home! I baked you a cake. It's a two tier, chocolate marble fudge, so we can't gorge ourselves during dinner. Did you make up your mind on where you wanted to go yet? Italian or Mexican?"

"Never would have come out here if I knew you were going out in the water." My father was speaking to my mother, but was looking at me as if he wanted my support. "Look." My father extended his *Sports Illustrated* magazine out towards my mother, but kept his eyes focused on me. "It's ruined. Can't turn the page without it tearing. You shouldn't have gone swimming. Right?" My mother also turned to look at me as if she wanted me to be the one to provide a rational response.

Instead I nodded. Agreeing with my father's observation.

"So now you want to leave?" I couldn't tell if my mother was talking to me or my father.

My father answered her. "No, we're here. We might as well stay." He tossed the magazine into the sand and closed his eyes.

My mother's happiness disappeared and it didn't return for the rest of the day. I never went back into the water, choosing to sit next to my father while my mother walked aimlessly along the shoreline. We left the beach early and wolfed down a McDonald's dinner in the car. Later that night, after I thought everyone had gone to sleep, I snuck out of my bedroom to watch some TV. I needed something to calm the worm that was swimming in my stomach ever since I had agreed with my father. Before I reached the living room, I spied my mother in the kitchen, throwing away the untouched birthday cake. I turned around and ran back to bed, pounding my fists into my pillow until I exhausted myself to sleep. The next morning, I vowed to never side with my father again.

As we turned into the driveway of my father's house, the truck's engine remained running.

"Hop out. I got to get to work."

My father had successfully stifled his sobs and I hadn't asked him any more questions. I had never seen him tear up before, and the genuine, intense pain he had released chipped away at my imprisoned sympathy. His claim that I was a lot like my mother was only partially true. I was also like him. We both only displayed true emotion in rare, overwhelming moments.

I took a chance and laid my hand on my father's arm.

"I got to get going, Danny."

"Dad, I need your help."

My father nodded. He took my hand off his arm before he spoke. "I want to help you, Danny. But you also have to help yourself. You can't drink anymore."

"OK."

"You have to start working. I know your brain is made for jobs that I don't understand. But getting one of those jobs might take some time. I might be able to get you some work at the college. Might be able to start next week."

"OK."

"It's not going to be easy. Getting yourself and your mind back together. I know you miss Melinda, but you can't give up on your life. Honor her memory, Danny."

"OK."

"Just because Gutierrez liked my story about what happened to you and Trent yesterday doesn't mean you're in the clear. You could still run into others like that filthy Talia."

I was jolted out of my automatic OKs. Had the scenario of Trent's guilt described by Detective Gutierrez been partially built by my father? And how much did he know about Talia? My father didn't give himself enough credit when it came to his cleverness. I found myself suddenly admiring him.

"What do you mean others?"

My father gripped my hand tightly. "Listen to me, Danny. There are some things that are difficult to explain. Things that don't make sense. Make you wonder if you're losing your mind."

My father's words were starting to sound a bit like my own internal, jumbled ramblings. "Dad, I just need to stop drinking. That will stop me from acting so irresponsible and disgusting."

My father nodded and let go of my hand. I thought he was going to tell me again to get out of the truck, but instead he delivered another verbal blow while gazing out the windshield.

"I know what Talia did with you."

"What?" The idea that my father knew the sordid details of my sex life made my intestines tighten.

"Something similar came to me after your mother left. She looked different, but she was the same underneath."

"I don't understand." My words sounded like a plea but I didn't want him to explain. I didn't need to know any details about what failings my father had from his own bout with loneliness.

"Talia was a demon. Absolute evil."

My father motioned for me to exit the truck. I remained sitting inside, dumbfounded. Did I hear my father correctly? Was he using some sort of antiquated religious notion to scare me into proper behavior and onto the path of improvement? Or was there some definitive, foul truth that lay behind his words? Talia's dead face flashed in my head.

I'm the one who devoured her.

My father pushed my shoulder lightly and I finally found the will to get out of his truck. As I watched him drive away, I decided not to give any credence to his words. He was exaggerating (*Metaphor, motherfucker!*) and I allowed relief to enter and consume my body.

I committed myself to starting anew. I would summon all my inner strength and resolve, embrace my intelligence, and recapture all of my sanity. And more importantly, console my grief-stricken heart with hard work and kindness – the things Melinda would've wanted from me. With help from my father who I was only beginning to appreciate, I figured my life would start to greatly improve from that moment forward. I couldn't believe Melinda's friend Amber had been right all along with her lame Facebook post: *Resurgere tento.* I would strive to rise again. That's exactly what I would do. I would resurrect myself. *Resurgere,* Daniel!

I managed to savor a few drops of happiness even though I really didn't believe in resurrection, and most of my optimistic estimations tended to be either premature or wrong.

FOUR

My first week as a sober individual passed relatively uneventfully, but my energy improved markedly. I had no idea that so much of my strength had been sapped by alcohol. I went for jogs around the neighborhood and realized the surrounding homes were bustling with people my beer-compromised eyes had never seen before. Out of shape football dads mowing their lawns. Underweight soccer moms walking their dogs. Sloth-brained retirees playing with their gnat-brained grandkids. Our next door neighbor, Mrs. Gualia, a bean sprout shaped sixty-year-old widow who always wore a lime Nike sun visor, even waved at me and asked me if I was feeling better. I smiled and waved back but didn't give her an answer. I wasn't sure if she had witnessed my overwrought scene out on the front lawn, or if my newly-tagged chatty father was still oversharing. I made it a habit to check that Mrs. Gualia wasn't around before stepping out of the house.

My relationship with my father continued to grow and we actually sat down at the dining table to eat dinner together one night. We didn't say much as we slurped up bowls of beef and carrot stew, sharing only a few routine delights and annoyances that had occurred during the day, but it was a monumental step. For once, I could envision the path of our becoming the two person family I had never believed would be possible.

I had to acknowledge that I had been suffering from depression over Melinda's death, an illness that alcohol had only exacerbated. Through sobriety, I was learning to manage that illness, and relish the moments when my mood lightened. Best of all, I had no lingering, terrifying visions. I dared to believe that happiness could once again become a dominant attribute of my life.

At the beginning of my second week in my recovered state, I started working at the community college. My father had managed to convince the Facilities Director to approve an *ad hoc* position for me. The tradeoff was that I would be performing essentially menial *ad hoc* work for even more menial *ad hoc* pay. I worked all day on campus, Monday through Friday (but only got paid for 4 hours each day; I wasn't allowed to have more than twenty paid hours per week), and performed a variety of mundane tasks such as scrubbing classroom windows, re-caking urinals and unplugging toilets, fixing broken sprinkler heads, trimming hedgerows and raking leaves, and transporting boxed materials to and from the college's warehouse. It was all manual labor, something I was completely unfamiliar with and my body did stage a minor rebellion with me. I had soreness and aches that never seemed to wane, only shifting from one obscure muscle to another, and I had a pressing need to sleep for more than eight hours each night. I also started getting blisters on both my hands and feet (un-wooly *bullae* as Melinda used to call them), since the used leather gloves I borrowed from the college warehouse were thinner than my skin, and the hand-me-down work boots from my father were half a size too small. The sedentary lifestyle I had been living, only recently burdened by a casual jog, had done nothing to prepare me for work on a community college situated on a series of rolling hills. The students recognized I was out of my element. One baby-faced kid taunted me. "You suck balls at your job. Should've stayed in school." I thanked him for the advice and told him that one day someone would return the favor.

Despite the minor aggravations, I felt a sense of accomplishment at the end of each workday and knew my father had been right to get me the job. The unfamiliar physical pain and grade-school taunts were much better than the mental torture I had recently endured, and I accepted my work as penance for all my misdeeds and self-inflicted sin. It was as if I had vigorously re-embraced my Episcopalian faith.

When I wasn't working, I read voraciously. At first, I read little more than the local newspaper and the magazines my father had around the house (even *Sports Illustrated*) since fatigue limited my mental stamina. But as my strength increased, I began to shop for books on my phone, trying hard not to blow my entire paycheck in one sitting, buying the latest nonfiction works in the areas of astrophysics & cosmology, complex dynamical systems, and artificial intelligence. Loop quantum gravity, evolutionary computation, nonlinear dynamics in dissipative systems – I was smart enough to comprehend the ramifications of these concepts, but also smart enough to know I would never be a prodigy in any of these rigorous disciplines. I had been a scientific bookworm in high school and had received a tremendous intellectual rise from devouring arcane theoretical musings. I wanted to recapture that thrill to help me regain a sense of humility. I wanted to become centered by remembering my infinitesimally minor place in the universe.

I also perused the community college library (my father had check-out privileges) but it was academically woeful, replete with only well-tread novels and coarse research textbooks suitable for the modest scholastic pursuits of the student body. I did check out Dostoyevsky's *Crime and Punishment*. It was mandatory reading in high school and again at the University, but I had only previously grasped it in a strict thematic sense, understanding only the concepts necessary to sufficiently analyze and critique it in class. My early impression was that the murderous Raskolnikov was nothing more than a melodramatic moron. But as I read it for the third time, I let the contemplative, distressed words of Raskolnikov burrow into me – a challenge since some idiot had indiscriminately underlined half of his passages. I felt the man's self-tortured soul resonating with my own, and I discovered that he was one of the most sympathetic characters I had ever read.

Pain and suffering are always inevitable for a large intelligence and a deep heart. The really great men must, I think, have great sadness on earth.

Although I was far from a great man, it seemed that tragedy had always been inevitable for me too. When I reached the familiar end of the novel, I was entranced by the grandiose belief that my own recent renewal and rebirth would've been appreciated by the Russian virtuoso himself.

My reading became salutary therapy, and it gave me the courage to revisit Melinda's heart notes. I could no longer leave them crammed inside my Physics notebook and I was ready to give them the reverence they deserved. I thought I could put them all into some sort of scrapbook or even mount them inside a large picture frame, so I laid them all across the floor in my room and attempted to classify them. At first, I tried to estimate the date for each one and group them in sequential order, but that proved too difficult as I could only associate a few to a particular time. Instead, I read each one aloud, and separated them according to how much meaning and emotion they elicited within me. After reading two that were agonizingly wonderful, I had to stop. I couldn't get through a third note until several days later.

It took me three weeks to go through them all. In the end, I had made only two piles: one with 98 heart notes and the other with 13. The ninety eight were indistinguishable in their effect – each one rattled my core. I decided to place them inside a shoebox-sized pine chest that I salvaged out of the spare bedroom (storage room). The chest was the smallest, and most fragile item that my father had created out of wood. He had given it to my mother to use as a jewelry box, but she owned so few pieces she never used it. And it was another thing she had left behind. Once I filled it with the heart notes, I placed the repurposed chest on top of my nightstand where I could see it every night, allowing me the opportunity to read some of Melinda's words if I felt the need to stew in bittersweet reflection.

The other thirteen notes were a complete mystery. Either the words no longer made any sense to me, or they alluded to events that I could not remember having ever taken place. Included in this group were the two notes that I had rediscovered prior to my ordeal with Talia and Trent – the event which I thereafter referred to as my "Descent." There was the one that mentioned sunshine dripping off my face and the other about a daunting voice making Melinda feel strong. Even with the greater clarity I had recently obtained, these particular notes still meant little to me.

Another one of the thirteen notes read:

Walking alone, desert sand pelting my face, the devil-wind is trying to make me forget your name.

Was that another attempt at a song lyric? Or possibly some abstract or hidden message that she thought I could figure out? Maybe I was so overawed by Melinda's words and love that she could've given me a grocery list and I would've quivered over it. I shuddered realizing it was possible that these thirteen notes were precursors to the meaningless babble she exhibited during her mental breakdown and her last hours alive. Missed warning signs.

I interred that thought. I didn't want to think about Melinda's rapid deterioration. I wanted to let the magic of our relationship stand alone, and stop analyzing a past that I could never change nor recapture. The significance of these notes would have to remain lost along with the thousands of whiskey-fried neurons in my brain.

For that reason, I didn't keep these thirteen notes with the others. I thought about disposing them, but that didn't seem proper either. They were still part of Melinda and a part of me. My solution was to place them in a plastic grocery bag and tuck them back underneath my bed. Maybe these were the ones that would best be left forgotten, and over time would lose their final shreds of admiration.

Three weeks into my recovery, Trent was out of the hospital and into the county jail, awaiting arraignment, and I gave my deposition to the assistant District Attorney. I took an oath to tell the truth and answer all the questions to the best of my knowledge. I retold the story cooked up by Detective Gutierrez and my father, added in a few extraneous details, replied "I'm not certain" a couple of times, dropped several insignificant contradictions, and was out of the assistant DA's office in less than twenty minutes. I was quite proud of myself.

Six weeks into my recovery. My string of uneventful days ended. It was a Sunday, early evening, darker than usual as a storm front rumbled in, and my father and I were at the table eating a spaghetti dinner that I had helped put together. We were discussing my unsuccessful attempt to fix a leaky pipe in the ceiling of the gymnasium when we were interrupted by a knock at the front door.

I peered through the partially open blinds of the dining room window. Standing in the entryway, aglow from a motion-sensor light, was an Asian woman, late forties or early fifties. Her thin, long brown hair was razor-straight, and from my position, I could see only the side profile of her narrow, stork-like face, but she looked vaguely familiar. Modestly attractive despite an elongated nose. A stiff, upright posture with assertively crossed arms. An aristocratic mien. Her clothes were off-the-rack basic, black pants and a yellow blouse, and she wasn't carrying any items with her, not even a purse, that would indicate her purpose for visiting us.

"Did you want me to answer the door?"

My father glanced at me as he twirled a bit of his pasta around his fork. I took that as a "yes" so I stood up from the table.

"No. Sit down."

I remained standing, contemplating what reason he could possibly have for not wanting to show this minor act of courtesy.

"Sit down. There's no reason to answer the door."

The skeptical look I gave my father did nothing to soften the seriousness of his disposition. I retook my seat as the woman knocked on our door again. My father ignored it and shoveled a clump of spaghetti into his mouth. I couldn't think of any logical reason for ignoring the woman.

"Why? Jehovah's Witness or something?"

My father shook his head.

I looked back at the woman through the window. A choppy wind began to develop, and it blew her hair forward, veiling most of her face. From the angled position of the dining table to the window, the blinds shielded us from her view and she wouldn't be able to notice us without turning herself almost completely around and sticking her face up against the glass. I didn't care about being impolite, but I could no longer eat with the woman just standing at the front door. She probably was only trying sell us a newspaper subscription or tickets to a PTA fundraiser.

She knocked again. It was at that moment that I realized that the woman had not moved at all since I started looking at her. She just stood there at our front door. Unwavering. Stringent. Her face focused squarely on the front door, unaffected by the wind slapping her hair against her face. I never saw a casual turning of the head or an impatient shuffling of her legs. I assumed I had missed seeing her arm move each time she had knocked. And even though I wasn't at all close enough to tell, it looked like she wasn't even breathing or blinking.

I returned my gaze to my father and realized he wasn't really eating, just spreading his pasta around with his fork.

"Do you know the woman at the door?" I tried to speak in a hushed tone, but the words came out squeaking instead. I waited for a response from my father, but he didn't look at me and continued toying with his food.

WHUMP. The entire house shook after a thunderclap knock struck the front door. My father dropped his fork and it clattered on the ground. I jumped up out of my seat, the legs of the chair scraping against the floor with a grinding shriek. Had the woman slammed her entire body against the door? My eyes darted back to the window.

She was gone. Vanished. I kept staring at the vacated entryway until the motion-sensor light clicked off.

Even though adrenaline was surging through me, I slumped back into my chair. Why was this happening? I was sober. Doing everything right. And another bizarre episode occurred? My sole consolation was that my father was here with me and I could be certain this wasn't one of my vivid hallucinations coming back to plague me.

"Dad. Who was that?"

My father stood up, grabbing his unfinished plate of food. "I won't let anything hurt you, Danny. We'll get through this together."

My father walked into the kitchen leaving me more upset than relieved. I thought about persisting with my questions for him, but I couldn't bring myself to say anything. Why did he seem relatively unfazed by this encounter? Had something like this happened before? Why would he not even confirm the sighting and settle my agitation?

My body began to visibly tremble. My father either noticed or sensed I was shaken and he walked over to me and put his hand on my shoulder. His strong grip limited my body's tremor. He spoke slowly, but his throat pitched. He wasn't as unfazed as I had thought.

"I told you it would return. But we are stronger and we will outlast it."

I nodded my head and my father released me. He went into the living room and turned on the TV – his easy, preferred escape. Could there actually be some uneasy truth behind the evil vicissitudes that had defined my life this past year? The woman at our door wasn't a personal encounter that I could easily dismiss as an abnormal creation of my own mind. The experience had upset my father as well. I was more secure when I could attribute the unnatural occurrences to some biological disorder of my brain – a synaptic misfire brought on by intense emotion and some fundamental genetic flaws passed down from a schizophrenic great-grandfather. But if such aberrant things actually existed outside of my manufactured perception, it would upend my entire worldview that mysteries exist only because science hadn't yet filled in the gaps. What would the good scientists whose books I'd been reading have to say about this?

I rose up slowly from the dining table, emptied my unfinished plate and washed the dishes. After setting them out to dry, I snuck away to my bedroom. I found an unopened beer can under my bed, took it into the bathroom, and chugged the warm liquid in a series of continuous, hurried gulps. As soon as I emptied the can, I almost threw it all back up. I sat on the toilet for almost twenty minutes until the coiled up nest of misgivings inside my stomach became a bloated tub of indignity.

Later that night, after I had come to terms with my relapse, the pain and fear I thought I had vanquished, cruelly and stealthily returned.

It was around two-thirty in the morning. I was gently awakened by the sound of someone calling my name.

Danny. Danny...I need you.

The voice wasn't my father's. It was Melinda's. Her words had whispered right into my ear as if she were lying in bed next to me, her stomach cuddling against the small of my back. I thought I felt her finger-strokes along the back of my neck, but of course, she wasn't in my room. I was alone.

I considered for a moment that it had only been a leftover figment from another dream, but I heard her voice again.

Where are you, Danny-boy? I'm more than just bits of paper.

I sat up in my bed. The voice now seemed to be coiling around the open crack of my bedroom door, emanating from the hallway.

Come here. I need you. I'm tired of waiting.

I debated whether to jump out of bed, fling open the door, and prove the voice wasn't real, or sneak over and timidly shut the door and pretend I was still asleep.

I did neither. I lay in bed and watched a hand slip through the open crack and grasp the edge of my door. The door began to open, the uneven bottom corner rasping against the carpet. My lungs tightened, forgetting that low compliance made an enemy of air. Sweat sprouted on my back and chest. I was not prepared for the arrival of another dreadful being to shock and torment me.

A head popped out of the shadows and into my room. It was my father. As my lungs relaxed, he said only four words to me.

"Stay in your room."

My father shut my door. I couldn't move, unsure if my father was doing something extremely brave or extremely pointless. Had my father heard Melinda's voice too? Had he seen something? A demon? I refused to believe it, but my father's words had penetrated me. I had seen and endured much worse, but at that moment, sitting up in bed, staring at my closed bedroom door, I felt like a child who has discovered that there were things in the world that were more powerful than his father.

I watched the minutes flick away on my digital clock, straining to detect any further voices or unusual noises, but I didn't hear a thing. Had it left? Had I really heard anything at all?

Fifteen minutes had elapsed. I hopped out of bed. The simple fact that I hadn't heard anything else from outside my room probably meant that I had overblown the entire incident.

My legs moved stubbornly, undoubtedly more cautious than my mind, and I lumbered up to my bedroom door. I turned the knob silently and eased the door open.

The hallway was empty. But not completely dark. A section of the wall was painted in a rhombus of light, a thin beam streaming from my father's room. His bedroom door was open. I crept down the hall.

Keeping my body close to the hallway wall, I peered into my father's open doorway. At the side of the bed with his back to me, was my father, down on his knees, praying. I hadn't seen him formerly pray since the days when he, my mother, and I used to go to church. I never believed my father to be much of a religious man, and figured he had only gone to church to appease my mother, but from the way he reverently bowed his head and clasped his hands together, I knew I must have been mistaken.

I watched him silently pray for a minute then went back to my room. Raindrops began to hammer the roof of the house and pelt my bedroom window. The storm had arrived. The rest of the night passed without any further incident, but I didn't fall back asleep.

Another week passed. There had been no other strange disturbances and I was hopeful that whatever had started to harass me and my father had departed. I started working harder at the college and began sleeping over nine hours. I made sure I had no other cans of beer under my bed and with my father's permission, disposed of any other alcohol I found in the house, including the anniversary gift (25 Year Macallan) he had received from his colleagues at work.

My father had stressed that we would be able to outlast it, even though I was not certain what "it" really was.

(It's coming after you next.)

I needed an explanation. I needed to hear all that my father knew and hadn't been telling me. I needed this lingering "demon" mystery clarified in order for some speck of assurance to germinate within me. I was fine with attributing some of the eerie sights as a product of my frazzled brain staging a revolt with reality. I could accept that I had acted horribly during my Descent and that I shared responsibility (morally, if not legally) for Talia's death and Trent's imprisonment.

But the persistent guilt I felt about Melinda's death was my inexhaustible burden and I would not add anything else to it. My self-persecution could not sustain irrational admonishments. I was committed to reason and strict logic. I needed my father to reconcile the demon as only my colorful personification of sin. I decided to question my father directly, but only when I thought the time was right.

The right time occurred the following Tuesday. My father and I were in his truck, at the beginning of our morning commute to the college. My thoughts were isolated on the troublesome, leaky pipe in the gymnasium that I still hadn't been able to fix. I considered telling my father I was going to give up on it – he had told me not do any other work until I had figured it out – but I was out of ideas and wanted to regain some measure of productivity.

"I'm sorry I'm so terrible at this job, Dad."

I expected my father to batter me with questions about my YouTube taught methods. Instead he gave me one of his characteristic understatements of kindness and support.

"No. You're doing good work. Extremely slow. But good. Keep going."

I smiled broadly. How could such simple words touch me so deeply? I realized the pipe didn't matter. He just didn't want to see me give up. I decided to ask him about the troubling events of last week without any natural segue.

"Dad? Did we outlast it?"

My father pulled the truck off to the side of the road and shut the engine off. Had I misjudged the timing of my question? Tension on his face compacted his wrinkles turning his face into a crumpled up sock. Whatever he had to say to me needed his full attention. I braced myself.

"When your mother left me, things got very dark. I was alone. I didn't care about myself. I didn't care about a lot of things. I know how much you hated me for that."

I thought I should let him know that I no longer hated him. Tell him that I understood the type of agony that he must have endured. But I didn't want to interrupt him.

"I met a woman. Maybe you remember seeing her. I don't know."

I didn't know what woman my father was talking about until disparate images began to merge. The woman I saw nine years ago, on an early Sunday morning, trotting out of our house with her shoes in her hand while I was nibbling cereal out of the box. The woman I saw two months ago, sitting next to my father in the police station lobby, watching us from behind her newspaper. The woman I saw a week ago, the unnaturally still visitor, knocking on our front door during dinner.

"She was nice. At first. I saw her often. Too often – I didn't want you to know. It was too much so I ended it. Didn't matter. She kept showing up. At the house. At the store. Everywhere. I almost lost my job. She wanted to hurt me. Like she hurt you."

I was certain I had never been hurt by this woman and my father must have recognized the incredulity on my face.

"You didn't realize it. She was the one who caused you to crash on your bicycle."

My bicycle accident. I was thirteen at the time, a pupa, inflated with confidence about my place in the world and what I thought the world owed me. I used to boldly ride my bike (a silver Diamondback, my pre-Cannondale days) against the flow of traffic and cross streets in front of passing cars as if I were immortal. The drivers would always stop, and I relished the honks, screeches and curses. Except for one car. As I rode out across a four lane boulevard, a navy Mazda failed to brake. In fact, it sped up and seemed to take aim at me. I managed to swerve out of its path, careening into a parked car, my body catapulting off my bike and onto the asphalt. I received a cratered gash on my left knee and a jagged scrape on my left arm, as well as numerous bruises all over the left side of my body. The parked car I had smashed into had a tire-sized dent on the side door, along with starbursts of chipped, scratched paint. It took six months to rebuild my bike, but I was lucky. I only needed a week of throbbing, bandaged recovery – no broken bones, just eight stitches.

My father, with his usual stoicism, hadn't been angry with me, but he surprisingly nursed me back to health. He changed my bandages, made sure I took my pain medication, and took time off work to drive me to and from school. He also found out who the owner of the parked car was and paid for the damages. Eventually his investment in my well-being dried up and he resumed his normal, unattached parental role. I figured his concern had been a fluke, an unintentional insight of fatherly love, but it appeared there had been a proximate cause behind his interest in me.

"She wouldn't go away. I saw her everywhere. In the shadows. Looking at me. Watching me. I didn't know what to do. It took me a while to recognize what I was dealing with."

Chilled bumps erupted on my skin as if I knew the exact words my father was going to say next. I sensed an underlying, primordial truth that most people, including me, tried their best to either disregard or deride.

"She was a demon. Like that Talia woman that was with you."

My mouth shot out the words rationality demanded me to say. "Bad people exist. Demons don't."

"Yes, they do."

"I can't believe that."

"It doesn't matter what you believe. It only matters what you let them do to you. Your actions invite them into your life. Your actions can get rid of them. Sometimes. Lucky for you, your demon left with Trent. Unlucky for him."

As if it would force understanding, I mixed logic and fantasy. "If my demon left with Trent, why are strange things still happening to me?"

"The woman died. Not the demon."

"Sorry, Dad. I'm never going to believe you." My critical response overwrote the fact that I had never known my father to lie.

"You've made yourself better, Danny. But I'm still worried about you. Don't be careless. The demon will keep trying to come back. God willing, we'll outlast it."

I had one final challenge for him. "Is that why you are praying?"

"I'm praying to keep the house safe. To keep you safe."

"From my demon?"

My father looked away from me. "Our demon." He restarted his truck and drove back onto the road. My father's explanation was ludicrous and didn't eradicate any of the confusion in my mind. In fact, he had made things worse. I wiped the sweat off my palms against my pants, and simultaneously pressed down on my legs to stop them from shaking. When we arrived at the college we went our separate ways to perform our respective tasks.

About two hours into my work on the broken gymnasium pipe, I started to relax, unwind. The physical activity of patching and re-patching the broken pipe gave my body a chance to release and process the pent up stress. The repetitive job allowed my mind to fall into a gentle, unfettered rhythm and remarkably, I managed to finally fix the leak. I let loose with a celebratory howl that bounced off the urethane floor of the empty gym.

Before breaking for lunch, my father asked me to assist him with moving a load of boxes from the warehouse to the college's communications building. The boxes were filled with books, audio/visual equipment and other supplies – a generous donation from a local radio DJ that essentially would keep the cash-strapped department afloat at the college.

In the warehouse, I told my father about my success with the pipe, but he made no comment. Instead, he directed me to a stack of twelve, various sized boxes, each one stamped with a garish sticker that read, "Courtesy of DJ Slim Sanchez! 107.9 – the Rhythm." My father retrieved the forklift while I plastic wrapped the boxes onto a wooden pallet to secure them for transport. The plan was to carry the items on the pallet directly to the communications building, snaking along a service road and up the adjacent sidewalk. It wasn't customary to use the forklift to carry goods across campus, but the building was only about two hundred yards away so my father didn't see any issue with using it in this one-off instance. Also, the campus denizens had thinned out since most students and half the teachers had already wrapped up their semester before the start of the December holiday break; my father didn't foresee any bystander interference.

My father maneuvered the forklift, picking up the pallet and raising it about three feet in the air. He spun the machine around 180 degrees, like it was a dressage horse or a Westminster show dog, and I followed the lift on foot as my father drove it out the warehouse and along the curved path that led to the communications building. Another one of the warehouse workers, Bernard Barton, was supposed to assist with the unloading process since we had to get all the boxes stacked into the building's supply room which meant hand carrying the boxes inside the building and up a small flight of stairs, as well as stacking them neatly in accordance with the fire code. But Bernie couldn't be located and he wasn't responding to our calls to his cell phone. My Dad was upset that this particular task would run longer and be more strenuous than it needed to be. He told me that if he fired Bernie, it might mean there would be an open position for me to take. I was honestly appreciative, but I kept redialing Bernie's number on my phone.

I was lagging behind my father by about fifty yards, my fingers fumbling over the QWERTY screen, when the lift reached the halfway point to the com building. Bernie was not responding and it made sense for me to conserve some energy by deliberately slowing my pace. As my father crested a small hill in the path, I saw someone approaching him, a student, casually walking down the recently mowed grass of the hill. My feet shuffled to a stop. The student looked exactly like Trent. I had to be mistaken, especially since Trent did not post bail after his arraignment. I continued walking. It was just a kid who looked like Trent. Fake Trent. With the same buzz haircut. And chunky build.

My father noticed Fake Trent and he stopped the forklift. Fake Trent continued his gradual approach down to the curved path, but started weaving and swaying like he was intoxicated. That's when I noticed the look-alike's lopsided grin. Trent's defining characteristic. I picked my pace up to a jog so I could get close enough to prove that this was Fake Trent, not my former friend.

But as I got closer, it was unmistakable. It was Trent. How the hell had he gotten out of jail?

I heard my father shout something out. His gravelly voice was loud, but it sounded like he had spoken Spanish or Italian. I did discern two words: *God* and *help*.

Trent stopped walking. His legs started to shake and it appeared as if they were going to fail and drag his entire body to the ground. Trent's smile grew wider. He exploded off the grass and onto the path, lunging forward, springing onto the forklift and on top of my father, and began pummeling my father's body with his fists. I tore off in a sprint, determined to help the man I had come to love and respect more than I had ever thought possible.

Inundated with rage, I jumped onto the forklift to dig my hands into Trent and rip him off of my father. But my added weight and momentum caused the machine and its load to become unbalanced. The lift toppled over and crashed onto its side, flinging me and Trent onto the curved path.

My chin and palms skidded against the concrete, burning off chunks of my skin. The impact knocked the wind out of me, and I tried to stave off a panic attack as I struggled to recapture oxygen. Trent's familiar voice teased my ears.

I got tired of waiting for you, Danny-boy.

I lifted my head. Trent's smiling face was a foot away from mine as he bent down to meet my prone body. I still couldn't breathe as Trent backed up and stood fully upright, showcasing a grotesquely broken left leg. His bone had snapped below his knee and his shin and foot dangled loosely to the right at an acute angle. Words spewed out of his mouth again.

I missed you so much. Do you still love me? Don't you want to fuck me? I'm shit-full of sorry, but take what you can get!

Trent arched the upper part of his body above his waist ninety degrees to the right. He dropped his right arm to the ground and used it as a replacement for his broken leg. He started walking towards the communications building, dragging mangled flesh behind him, and leaving a cottony trail of skin and blood.

At that moment, I vanquished all my uncertainty about the existence of demons. Air finally filled my lungs and my grisly scream frightened me more than my acknowledgement.

The demon turned its head to me and spoke again.

The deeper the grief, the closer is me! Won't be much longer now…it's still coming for you, Danny.

The demon continued with its unearthly gait until it passed out of my view behind the com building.

I fought back against my fear and tried to stand up, but a searing pain shot through my left calf. I couldn't put my full weight on my foot and it appeared I had either sprained or broken my ankle. A terrible groan sounded but it didn't come from me. I turned around to its source – my father.

The forklift had pinned my father to the ground with its front wheels and carriage. His legs were free, but his upper body was trapped. Ruptured boxes were scattered around him, electronic guts shooting out at all angles. I fought through the sharp pain in my ankle and limped over to my father.

He was conscious, but it looked like the forklift had crushed part of his right arm. I crouched down and tried to comfort him, but knew he needed immediate emergency treatment. I spun my head around – four students were running up to us.

"We called for help," said one female Asian student who looked more excited than worried.

"Are you OK?" said a short Hispanic male who had put his hand on my shoulder.

I shrugged off his hand and stood back up. I felt woozy, my ankle was pulsating like it wanted to break free. Snap off like the demon's left leg.

I scanned my eyes past the crowd, searching for the demon. I had been too passive, too disbelieving, and look what the result had been. I needed to fight back! I needed to confront the demon. I spotted its trail of blood.

I summoned all my reserve energy. *Resurgere Daniel.* I dragged myself away from the crowd and limped painfully towards the back of the com building, following the gruesome trail.

The Hispanic student reached out to me again, "Where are you going? You're hurt!"

I ignored him and kept moving, trying to block out my increasing agony and the continued protests from the students in the crowd. I gnashed my teeth together, channeling the fire ripping into my foot into an unstoppable desire to throttle the demon and strangle its existence.

When I reached the back of building, there was no demon, only a man reaching for the building's back door. Bernie. He stopped short of grabbing the door's handle and bent over, placing his hands on his knees. He opened and closed his mouth as if he were forcing himself to throw up.

I used the remaining joules in my body to yell out to him. "Bernie! Did you see it? Where did it go?"

Bernie craned his neck to look at me. He shook his head, but didn't alter his awkward, bent-over position.

"How did you not see it? What's wrong with you?"

A brownish-black stain formed in the back of his tan corduroy pants and streaked down his right leg. Bernie had just defecated on himself.

My eyes started to water. The demon had eluded me. My left ankle finally gave out and my body collapsed to the ground.

My father spent a week recuperating in the hospital. His humerus had broken in three places and he suffered a dislocated shoulder and a torn rotator cuff. He also had two broken ribs and a bruised spleen that almost required extraction surgery. While he was admitted, I stayed at his house alone, hobbling on crutches from a broken ankle, and barely left my bedroom. I expected another attack. Nothing occurred.

Once my father came home, I exchanged parent-child roles with him as I helped him get dressed, prepared his meals, and filled out the necessary paperwork for him to collect disability. The story the college administration surmised was that I had foolishly jumped onto the forklift, causing it to topple over. The crowd of students were useless. Not one of the bystanders had witnessed the accident or seen the demon. Bernie was worse. Although I was positive his traumatized state was due to some sort of interaction with the demon, he stated that he saw nothing. He resigned a week after the incident, claiming occupational stress. With only my unbelievable explanation as an alternative, the administration had no choice but to terminate me. I readily accepted it as long as no blame went to my father for driving the forklift on campus or for hiring me in the first place. The administration thankfully agreed and chose to not punish my father, realizing that he had suffered enough.

My father had been home for several days and hadn't said anything about the demon. Not that I was eager to discuss it. I had no idea what would happen next, what troubles the demon could possibly further inflict on us. Was it possible that the demon had gotten the upper hand?

Christmas came and went without any celebration or muted decorations. My mother's pricy gift never arrived in the

107

mail. And the approaching New Year was looking like it would be a replay of my current *annus horribilis*.

New Year's Eve. I was sitting in the living room next to my father on the faux leather sofa, watching an afternoon college football game on TV. We had been doing a lot of TV watching as it was the only activity that we could do together that didn't require much effort for either of us.

I had started to doze while the game was playing, and only became fully awake when my father turned the TV off. I thought he had wanted some silence to take his own nap, but he started talking instead.

"I spoke with your mother. She agreed that you should live with her for a while."

I was stunned. They had actually come to an agreement on something and that was the result? I couldn't live with her. My injured father couldn't take care of himself. And what if the demon returned? Would he try and face it alone? I started telling him how foolish it would be for me to leave him now, but he cut me off.

"Danny. I can't have you taking care of me. I am supposed to take care of you. Even if I wasn't hurt, it would still be impossible for you to stay."

I pleaded with him. "You don't mean that. You'll be healthy again soon and you'll go back to work. I'll look for another job. I'm not leaving you alone."

My father closed his eyes. "I'll be fine, Danny. But if you stay in this house, neither of us will be."

"I don't understand."

My father opened his eyes. "Your mother helped me in my fight against the demon. She told me what I needed to do. She can do the same for you."

It appeared that my father wasn't the only one who held a belief in demons. But I didn't want to see my mother. I had grown so close to my father and I didn't want her to know about our newly formed relationship. I didn't want my time with my father to end. "OK. I'll call Mom and talk to her. Doesn't mean I have to leave you."

My father struggled to sit up in his seat. I moved to assist him, but he shook his head at me.

"I love you Danny, but I cannot have you in my house any longer."

I grew indignant. "When do you expect me to leave?"

"Tomorrow morning. There's a plane ticket on your bed – it's your mother's Christmas gift. I know you probably didn't want to spend the first day of the year on a plane, but you need to leave as soon as possible. You can keep most of your things here. I'm not sure how much room she has."

I stood up to leave. If he wanted me out of the house then I would oblige. Maybe he was correct to blame me for everything that had happened, but that wasn't what was upsetting me. The confidence and resolve he had shown to help me, to protect me, had completely evaporated.

"I thought we would outlast it. Together."

My father raised his voice. "Danny! The demon's in the house right now!" He pointed through me, towards the kitchen.

I scanned the kitchen but saw nothing. I was unsure if my father actually did see something or if he was just trying some last ditch tactic in order to get me to leave. I didn't matter. I grabbed my crutches and limped off to my room.

I shut the door, threw my gimp sticks to the floor and flopped down on my bed, knocking the plane ticket to the ground. I felt like cursing but I couldn't utter a sound. Maybe this was all complete bullshit. There was no actual demon. My father and I were suffering from some sort of inherited or shared psychotic disorder and we needed psychological help. Strong medication. Intensive therapy. That would be the proper course and undoubtedly would be the recommendation of any rational human being. Maybe that's what my mother had done. Maybe she had helped my father by signing him up to see a psychiatrist.

I reached over to the wooden chest on my nightstand. I wanted to be reassured with Melinda's words. I missed her love so much.

I opened up the chest. It was empty.

I bounced up on my bed. What had happened to her heart notes? Had my father thrown them out? No. He would never do such a thing. Would he?

I hopped down onto the floor, ignoring the hot blast jamming my ankle, and looked inside my garbage bin. It was empty. Maybe they were under my bed? Maybe I had never separated them at all?

I dropped to my knees and looked under my bed. I found the plastic bag that contained Melinda's segregated notes. I still had the enigmas. I grabbed one and read it.

My cells lyse and regenerate over and over and I can't stop laughing.

I threw the note back into the bag. These were the ones I had managed to safeguard? The other heart notes, the beautiful ones, couldn't have just disappeared. I thought back to the last time I had read through her notes. It was prior to my hearing Melinda's voice in my room.

(Where are you, Danny-boy? I'm more than just bits of paper.)

Had the demon taken them?

I needed to stop reinforcing that concept in my head. Enough with the supernatural schlock.

I got up from my bed, and chucked the plastic bag with the undecipherable notes into the garbage.

Demon or disease, Melinda had crumbled and paid the ultimate price. Was the same thing happening to me? I wanted to live. Recapture some semblance of an optimistic life. Mold my mind into a blissful state where demons existed only in fiction and vital memories always remained intact.

I picked the plane ticket off the floor and put it on my nightstand. My recovery had been a failure, but I wasn't ready to give up. I would find another way for my confusion to end. I would go see my mother. Listen to her advice. Submit to any of her treatments or medications. I would go to her absolutely determined to accomplish one thing.

I was going to rid this God damn demon from my life once and for all.

FIVE

My two hour flight south to my mother's apartment could be summed up by three undesirable elements: an inappropriate hug, a noxious odor, and another sighting of Trent.

Still impaired on crutches, I had relied on a cab driver's help in getting up to the curbside check-in at the airport terminal. Once inside, I was given a wheelchair and an attendant to push me, making it easier to get around, but still burdensome to pass through the TSA checkpoint.

The attendant wheeling me around was an employee of my flight's airline. He was a gaunt, African American with an impish eye roll suitable for a smart-ass teenager but not for the forty-something man he was. And every time he rolled his eyes he would say: *Washin' my shit.* Even in the context of the stories he shared the line didn't make sense. He told me about his own broken ankle injury after he fell off a ladder. *Should've said it happened at work – missed out on my comp checks! (eye roll) Washin' my shit.* And how he never visited his mother because of her persistent hounding on his lack of a wife. *I've got two baby girls – what more does she want? (eye roll) Washin' my shit.* He laughed a lot which made both

111

of our pathetic conditions bearable, but when it came time for him to leave me at the boarding gate, he surprised me with a lingering bear hug. His articulated rationale didn't help.

"You'll make it, man. Don't be too disappointed – you ain't dead yet."

I expected the eye roll and catchphrase but it didn't happen.

Once I got onboard the plane, a fifty year old flight attendant stowed my crutches and escorted me to my assigned seat. I was in the first row of economy and had the aisle, but the two adjacent seats were taken up by a slug – a gum-chewing middle-aged man wearing bright blue sweatpants and a t-shirt pockmarked with holes. He wasn't obese, but had positioned his top-heavy body in between the middle and the window seats. Before I sat down, the slob shouted at me.

"These two are mine! I paid for both! These two are mine."

I tried not to look at him as I stowed my carry-on, a backpack, but his filthy appearance grew larger with every glance. The uneven strands of his Guinness-colored hair stuck together as if they hadn't been washed in months and had been cut with his own imbalanced eyes. Overgrown, bristled eyebrows and a half-shaven mustache were pasted onto his taut, acne-scarred skin – he looked like a Scottish terrier with mange. Worst of all, he had marinated himself with a sluggish, balsamic-scented cologne (ostensibly to mask an underlying body odor) so that I and half of the cabin were enveloped with the smell of honey and musky sweat. The obdurate aroma stuck to the hairs in my nostrils, but the stink didn't seem to be bothering anyone else. Either the other passengers near me had a lack of olfactory cells or they were too generously polite to utter a complaint. I tried burying my nose and mouth inside the neck of my sweater while I took my seat. He spoke to me again.

"You're strange. Do you know that? Do you comprehend that observation? You're odd. An odd little duck."

I wasn't sure if being called odd by a derelict lunatic lent credence to my sanity or revealed that I was in worse shape than I had thought. I looked down at the magazine he was reading. *Fortune*. The cover title: *More Stagnation? Or The Rebirth of Innovation?*

I decided to prick him back. "You must work at Goldman Sachs."

"Ha! I was once a king! A high-frequency master, caught in a singularity of shit. You know so little. So little, so little. Little lost brain inside a little lost duck. Quack, quack little duck! Quack!" The man let out a giggle that sounded like a fart. He rolled away from me, exposing his butt crack as his sweatpants slipped down. His skin tone had the shade and texture of leftover bits of berries floating in cheap champagne. As the plane took off, he buckled up in the middle seat, closed his eyes and released a few more flatulent giggles as his right arm and leg invaded my space.

During the flight, I asked every flight attendant on the plane if there was another seat that I could take – the plane was not completely full – but they all rebuffed me. With a well-trained smile, they said my assigned seat was well-suited for someone in my condition. Aside from my flight companion's odor, the constant view of his bare ass trying to escape its blue elastic binding was making me ill. About an hour into the flight, my uncomfortable situation became intolerable. Despite being so immobile, I took a few extra trips to the restroom, to both the front and rear lavatories, trying not to arouse unwarranted suspicion. The last thing I wanted was to be mistaken for a passenger who had health, or worse, terrorism issues.

The plane thankfully landed on time, we disembarked, and I stood at the gate on my crutches, waiting to be picked up by another wheelchair. I checked my cell phone for any messages from my mother. Nothing. But I had received an email from my father with a subject line that simply read: *It's over.*

The message itself contained only a link to a newspaper article. Clicking on it took me to a mug shot of Trent with an accompanying blurb stating that his trial would occur in two weeks. It noted that he had been charged with DUI second degree murder along with vehicular manslaughter and faced fifteen years to life in prison. It said little about Talia, only mentioning that Trent had been in an accident resulting in the death of a still unidentified female. There was no mention of Trent's military career, and the article ended with a quick recap of his previous arrests.

In his photo, Trent looked scared. Too aware of his fate. I took my father's email to mean that this entire situation – Trent, Talia, and whatever he had meant by the word "demon" – would soon be behind me. Distance would make me feel better. Maybe that's why I had seen Trent as a demon. I had let him get too close to me.

I wasn't sure what to expect from my mother. Was she some sort of expert on a demon-haunted mind? In college, my mother had been a social psychology major, but I doubted she had much hands-on experience to go with her classroom work. She once told me she had plans to go on to grad school and earn her Ph.D., but changed her mind after the thought of aging amidst a perpetual cycle of college kids derailed her ambition.

Had she learned something during her undergrad years that could be applicable to my current troubles? She could've maintained a trusted connection, a psychologist or mental health professional, who would provide assistance as a favor to my mother. My father didn't bother elucidating how she had been able to assist him, and I suspected he considered it strictly personal.

Via another attendant (an older man not nearly as hands-on or loquacious as my previous escort) I was wheeled down to baggage claim. I spotted my mother near one of the sliding glass door exits. She was only a couple years younger than my father, but she appeared to be at least fifteen years his junior and could almost pass as my older sister. Her young looks were exaggerated by a pixie haircut that I hadn't seen before – her thick black hair was usually shoulder length, and curled in long, placid waves.

My mother was a puree of ethnicities and her age-defying genes could've been attributed to a number of ancestors. I didn't know much about her parents, my grandparents (they had died before I was born – my grandmother from ovarian cancer and my grandfather from a heart attack), but I knew her father had Scandinavian and Russian roots while her mother had bits of Irish, German, and Cuban DNA. My mother's winter tan reflected the Cuban lineage that had seeped to the surface and it was one of the major physical traits I didn't share with her. (I always thought my lighter skin took after my father and his singular Anglo-Saxon forebears.) I did have my mother's oval, near-sighted eyes (she had hers laser-corrected a long time ago), and her genuinely symmetrical nose, but I did not have her irresistible toothy smile, something that only fully revealed itself after she had left my father. She was grinning at everyone in the airport, touching off reciprocal smiles and even a few hand waves from otherwise indifferent strangers. Although she was wearing a frumpy, white blouse and a pair of faded mom-jeans, she had the presence of someone noteworthy and familiar, similar to an actress who had once been popular, but whose name and starring work could no longer be remembered.

As the attendant whisked me up to her, I threw my own smile and wave at her and tried to smooth out the wrinkles in my shirt and slacks, the same outfit I had worn when I visited the police station. She frowned. Before I could say hello or ask what was wrong, she scolded me for using the wheelchair. She sent the sheepish attendant away, forced me to return to the crutches I held across my lap, and made me shuffle alone to the carousel to pick up my single suitcase. She did carry my suitcase for me as we headed to her car, though it was a fifteen minute struggle for me to exit the terminal, hobble across three busy lanes of airport traffic to the parking garage, inch up a flight of stairs (the elevator was out of service) and reach her Prius that was parked on the second level.

As we drove to my mother's apartment, we spent about five minutes chatting politely about the unusually mild weather, my father's condition, and the infuriating traffic within the city that my mother was calling home, at least for this moment in her life. She spoke with a tone that was a bit more reserved than the effusive manner I usually experienced and had taken for granted. I didn't know how much she knew about what had happened to me, or what my father had shared with her (likely everything), but I wanted our conversation to be more authentic, more urgent. I needed her help, some answers, so I could ignite a plan that would get me back to my normal, constructive self. So I decided to initiate things by asking her the question whose answer I had always wanted to know, but had been too afraid to acknowledge during much of my life.

115

"Why did you have to leave me?"

My mother glanced at me before responding. "I've been in my latest apartment for five months. It's small – there's only one bedroom. I've put a pillow and blanket on the couch and I think it will work for you. The floor is another option. I should've told you to bring a sleeping bag."

"You don't have one?"

"No."

"I don't have one either."

"The couch it is."

My mother turned on the radio and didn't say another word to me until we drove into her apartment complex.

"We're here. It's enough to call home. For now."

She lived in a dated, 400-unit complex that my mother said hadn't been renovated since the early 90's, except for the carpeting and a few appliances. Four, two-story buildings were sprawled over two blocks and were nestled next to a run-down shopping center that housed a Walmart, a payday loan center, and the county unemployment office. The apartment complex adequately reflected the city which had never been the most prosperous locale, and housed (according to my mother's progressive heart) hardworking people who lived for small joys and continually searched for the one decent, break that would take their children out of their current reality. I had told her that some of the bystanders we passed along the road looked like freeloaders, even a bit dangerous. She admitted that there were always a handful of struggling fools who settled for anything, but she never had a problem with feeling unsafe or unwelcome.

Stepping inside her apartment, I was transfixed by the dozens of framed photographs mounted to her walls. My mother's passion. Some of the photos had a corporate logo or watermark – *National Geographic, Time Magazine, Associated Press* – but they all appeared to be prize winners to my untrained eye. Her photos were blatant liberal social statements. One featured dusty, doe-eyed children sitting on a dirt floor schoolroom, being taught basic math by a woman in a *hijab*. Another depicted a shriveled, dark-skinned elderly man, his turnip head bandaged and bloodied, exiting a mortar shelled hospital with a toothless smile, arm in arm with a tender-eyed, young male soldier in an IDF uniform. My mother seemed to aim her lens on gruff snippets of human concern and courage in worlds saddled with conflict and hopelessness.

There were also a couple of personal photographs on the walls. One showed my mother when she must have been around twenty years old, barefoot in a white sundress, sitting on a multi-colored, postage stamp quilt on a soccer field, covering her mouth as she stared into an open book on her lap like she had just read a fantastic dirty joke. Another photo showed me as a toddler, wearing only a diaper and standing in between a pair of soiled work boots, my hands and arms being pulled up by a pair of fingers. The boots and fingers had to belong to my father and I'm sure he had been cut out of the photo on purpose. My mother had managed to capture an unnaturally pensive look on my ten month old face as if I were trying to calculate the necessary force to stay upright (assuming a body mass of nine kilograms) and push myself forward on the floor (assuming a friction coefficient of 0.17 and a constant velocity of 0.08 m/s).

One other personal photograph, not on a wall but in a silver frame, rested on top of a sparsely filled three foot high bookshelf. A black and white close-up of Melinda's face. She wasn't smiling. She had struck a contemplative, borderline-depressed pose, but the vivid beauty that I had treasured was unmistakable. I didn't know this photo existed and I wanted to dive over to it, press it against my chest, and try to imagine the warmth radiating from her cheeks. But I couldn't look at her photo for more than a few seconds. I turned to gaze at a sepia filtered photo that was on the wall by the entryway. It showed a rusted and broken tractor sitting in an overgrown wheat pasture with an abandoned farmhouse in the background. I forced myself to stare at this maudlin photo until I thought I could hear the wheat cracking from a blanket of humid air that had settled over the neglected stalks like a hospital bed sheet draped over a soon to be forgotten body.

"The bathroom is on the left, first door. You can put your things in that closet. I emptied it out." She pointed to the closed door next to the front door. I dropped my suitcase and backpack on the floor next to it. I also propped my crutches against the closet door since the apartment was small enough to hop through. I wasn't sure how long I would be staying here so I had followed my father's advice and didn't pack a lot of clothes. Aside from what I was wearing, I had brought only enough clothes to wear for four days before laundry would be necessary for a repeat cycle. My backpack just contained an extra jacket along with the science books I wanted to read. It also held the plastic bag with the remaining thirteen heart notes. Before I had left my father's house, I had pulled the bag out of my trashcan and stuffed it into my pack. I decided I couldn't part with them, especially if I had lost the others. I thought they might actually warrant a use if I showed them to my mother. If she could help me understand what was happening to me, maybe she could help me understand what happened to Melinda.

Aside from the photos, the apartment's light green walls were otherwise bare and the only furnishings other than the bookcase were a frumpy tan couch with a floral pattern, a small discount end table made of thin, unvarnished wood that held my mother's car keys and a black ceramic desk lamp, and an elliptical throw rug with a green and brown hexagon design. The adjacent kitchen seemed even more threadbare with only a stocky refrigerator, an electric range and oven, and a two slice toaster (and strangely, no microwave). Although there was only one window in the living room area and it was covered with tacky white plastic blinds, rolled up halfway at an uneven angle, the apartment wasn't overly dark thanks to the green walls and an overhead kitchen light. My mother had managed to create a friendly, rather than a reclusive atmosphere, despite her commitment to a no-frills lifestyle that was greater than my father's. I didn't like it, but I would have to abide by it.

I limped over to the window and ducked under the blinds to scan the neighboring units. There were three apartments in the building next to us – two upstairs and one downstairs. The entryway of the downstairs apartment was surrounded by five male teenagers wearing black knit ski hats and baggy black jeans. Although sunset was still over an hour away, and it wasn't that cold outside, all five had their hats pulled down tightly, partially concealing their eyes. One of them, a shaggy, blond-haired kid, spotted me with a passing glance. Without turning to directly face me, he flung his middle finger out at me. I had a feeling my mother gave these "struggling fools" too much credit.

I dragged myself to the couch and flopped down on the stiff cushions, bouncing the pillow and blanket my mother

118

had left for me onto the floor. I tried to stretch out to give my broken ankle a rest, but the couch was too short and my feet hung over the edge of the armrest, causing my ankle to throb. I closed my eyes as regrets about my decision to stay with my mother started to formulate. I wasn't sure why she had completely blown off my question about why she had left me. I didn't expect her to ramble on with a trite explanation about how the decision had nothing to do with me and in the long run was actually in my best interest – how if she had to do it all over again, she would only change the amount of times we saw each other (which had been sixteen times, an average of 1.6 a year). Or succumb to a histrionic breakdown, apologizing for all the precious moments we never shared and the missed opportunities to swaddle my ears with motherly advice, and, if it was any consolation, how she would never be rid of the bombardment of nightmares symbolizing her inadequacy and remorse. It was likely my question was too presumptuous and inappropriately timed, or even too cornball and not worthy of a response. Still, it would have been nice if she had simply deferred her response to an unspecified future date. I needed her to understand, even if she had heard already, that my relationship with my father, her ex-husband, had greatly improved over the past few months. I was no longer the boy who wouldn't have hesitated to sleep on the floor of my mother's apartment if that was my only option to spend time with her. I had a new understanding of what family meant to me and she needed to know that it had changed. And the thought of sleeping on this reject-from-the-Goodwill couch was making me more than just physically uncomfortable.

My mother called out to me from her kitchen. "Daniel, do you want anything to eat?"

I struggled to stand up. If my ankle had been plastered in a cast it would've elicited more sympathy for my injury, even from myself. Instead, the doctor had told me I suffered only a hairline fracture and a cast wouldn't do much good. I hadn't been able to tolerate the prosthetic boot the doctor had given me for more than a week and I had been wearing a regular, untied shoe over an Ace-bandaged ankle for quite some time. So I appeared to be a psychosomatic weakling who exacerbated things by complaining.

On a positive note, my injury served as a physical reminder of what I had been through and needed to overcome, and that was reason enough to give living with my mother a chance. I stifled my go-to curse words as I ambled to my mother who was preparing a sandwich from toasted bread. Turkey and tomato on toast. My favorite when I was ten years old. Couldn't remember the last time I had eaten it.

I glanced over at the bookshelf to allow myself another glimpse of Melinda. Her photo was gone.

My mother had a smile on her face, the first one since the airport. "You still like this, right? I didn't get a chance to go food shopping."

I nodded and my mother passed the sandwich over to me. I took a bite and before I had finished swallowing, mumbled out a few words to her. "Where's her photo?"

"Really, Daniel? Finish chewing. Don't need to regress on manners." The toaster popped and my mother started to prepare another sandwich.

I took the time to clear my mouth completely before speaking again. "I'm sorry. Melinda's photo. Where did it go?"

"I thought it might bother you. I saw the look on your face when you walked in the door so I put it away."

"Put it back. Please. I want to see it."

My mother nodded. She finished the second sandwich and slid it over to me. I wanted to protest that I didn't want it, but I had almost finished inhaling the first one she had given me.

She poured me a glass of water and a glass of milk – another vestige of my childhood. I had always drunk the combination at our family dinner around the dining table. I didn't like milk anymore and I forced some of it down to be polite. My mother spoke while she poured herself the same drink combo. "I love seeing you, Daniel. I miss you all the time. I miss your father too. I still love him very much."

It sounded like she was ready to give me her explanation on leaving. I decided to let my mother dictate the pace of her reveal so I said nothing.

"I was never going to feed you a sob story to explain away my decision. I have no excuses."

"That's not what I was looking for."

"I was never going to be the mother that your father wanted or the mother that you needed. My only option was to leave."

I couldn't drink anymore of the milk so I poured the remainder into the sink. "Things change."

"I'd like to believe it. I let you blame your father for what happened for so long and I was fine with that. He was fine with that. I do regret letting that happen, but I still don't regret leaving."

I countered. "Dad admitted he messed up. That he lost you."

My mother started making a third sandwich. "Your father, the savior! I did love his messiah complex. I think he truly believed that everything would work out on God's terms – that I would settle down and we'd walk together on the same well-worn path, hand in hand, one heavenly step at a time. I've got selfish blood, Daniel. Wickedly selfish blood. Your life would not be better if I had stuck around."

I wouldn't allow my mother to completely blame herself for the collapsed marriage. She was talking as if she were a remorseful spouse who had been caught in multiple acts of adultery or addiction. I knew my father's faults and how that had precipitated their collapsed marriage, but I had been wrong to pelt him with unmitigated scorn. I wasn't going to make the same mistake with my mother.

"Mom, you're a good person. You're a good mother. You're the reason I got into the University."

Aside from any inherited intelligence, my mother had given me every intellectual benefit an overly doting mother could provide. Starting from my birth, I was generously given instructive toys, computer games, videos, and cultural outings – all to stimulate maximum brain development. In second grade, when most kids were into the *Power Rangers* and *Toy Story*, I was flipping through *Wired* and *Encarta '95*. At age eight, I watched all six hours of *Stephen Hawking's Universe* in one night and wrote out my own algebraic equation that described the universe (it didn't make any mathematical sense, but that wasn't the point). By the end of fifth grade, I had visited every major museum in a five hundred mile radius from my father's house.

For schooling, I was placed in a selection of top private institutions from preschool through middle school – only my high school was public and that's because *US News* had rated it as the number one high school in the state. Even after the divorce, my mother continued her support. She funded all my high school extra-curricular activities, my book purchases, and any other academic pursuits that would look good on a college application. I took for granted how easy it had been for me to impress my overworked teachers, earn lazy A grades, knock out the highest score on rote standardized tests, and manufacture a diverse profile of interests – all of which added up to an acceptance letter from the University. I even took for granted how easily my mother covered my four years of tuition. Despite hearing the constant "I'm broke" complaints from my University peers, it was only when Melinda shared her family's financial struggles, and the difficulty she had in securing funding to attend college (a last minute Jewish Federation scholarship greatly mitigated her toxic loan burden), that I realized how extraordinarily stupid I had been.

"I'm proud of what you've accomplished. But even before the divorce, I was never there for you."

Before photojournalism, during *B.M.L.* (Before Mother Left) time, my mother was a real estate professional, one of the top female brokers in our county. It was a career that had typically kept her preoccupied for sixteen of every twenty-four hours (most of it outside of my father's house; it wasn't until college that I realized I had modeled my high school extra-curricular activity on her family-escaping behavior). It was a career that had been chosen based on nothing more than the advice of an ex-boyfriend who thought she had a great face for selling houses. It was a career that had made her an intense amount of money in commissions. Her timing had been propitious; she entered at the bottom of the market in the early 1990's and dropped out of the game before it had reached its terminal phase of exponential growth. Before I understood the black magic of interest rates and the Federal Reserve, I once asked my mother her selling strategy. She mentioned detailed research, extensive networking, honing her closing skills, and several other by the book tactics, until my dubious, bored face made her tell me the truth. She said she used fear. Every buyer and seller believed their lives needed to be in another place – so she found a way to capitalize on the fear that their belief was wrong. She didn't elaborate on "how" she performed her manipulation, segueing instead into the "why." As her hot, dry hands squeezed my overly-responsive cheeks, she said that she was doing it all for me.

My mother picked up the third sandwich to peck at it while she continued her explanation.

"I mastered the art of overcompensation. I really enjoyed playing Santa Claus with you. I wanted nothing more than a successful life for you and that's still possible. Your father thinks so too, and that's why you're here. This is my second chance with you, Daniel! Despite the past, and all our disagreements, your father knows that I'm the best person to help you now."

Was my father trying to win back my mother? He was stubborn enough to believe that Sisyphus was a hero. My father had met my mother at the community college. She had been taking a class in real estate finance, still mulling over a possible broker license as well as the boyfriend who had suggested her career path. One evening after class, he spotted her in the parking lot, pacing. Stuck. Her decade-old Civic refused to start. My father was on his final check of the grounds, about to head home, but decided to approach her and offer his help. My mother rebuffed him, stating her boyfriend was coming to get her. Undeterred, my father said he would take a look at her car, that he was good at fixing things. My mother told him it wasn't worth the effort – she would be fine if her car turned into scrap. My father persisted. Reluctantly, she handed him the car keys and he popped the hood and started tinkering with the engine.

He kept tinkering after the boyfriend picked up my mother, kept tinkering after all the students and faculty had left campus, and only stopped tinkering when a security guard told him the car couldn't remain in the parking lot overnight. My father didn't give up. He got the guard to help him push the car to the back of the warehouse so he could work on it the following day. The day turned into a month. During that time, as my mother continued with her class (and her boyfriend, the chauffeur), my father hustled for spare parts and spent most of his free time working on the Civic. He even failed to recognize my mother's diminishing efforts to dissuade him. When my mother's finance course neared its end, my father at last handed her back her car keys. Told her it was a piece of shit he couldn't fix. She had the Civic towed to the junkyard the next day.

His exercise in futility turned out to be his most fruitful experience. In the ensuing weeks, my mother dumped her boyfriend, bought a new car, and started dating my father. Six months later they were married at the City Hall. Two months after that I was born. This was the PG-rated love story that both of them had shared with me, but I knew the truth to their quick courtship had to be a lot more complicated. A lot more complicated than falling asleep in love with a stranger, and waking up ten years later with just the stranger.

"Dad's just trying to make you happy. That's all he's ever tried to do."

My mother waved her hand at me as if I had disgraced her name. "Your father never had a problem making me happy! I've always been the one who's made him miserable."

"That's not how I saw it."

"Your father and I lived very measured lives, Daniel. We were very deliberate in what we did. You know that."

Despite my father's decent salary and my mother's growing one, my parents lived very frugally. The house (purchased when I was a newborn) had been their biggest asset. Furniture was either built by my father or purchased on discount. They shunned consumerism, except of course, when it applied to me.

"If you're going to buy me off with something, I'll go ahead and take it now."

"I deserve that. I've done plenty of wrong things."

I was becoming disappointed. My mother wasn't making anything clearer. Or better. "What wrong things?"

"You don't need to know every detail, Daniel."

I understood my father's frustration. "Vagueness is better? I've done wrong things too. Some very recently."

"Your father told me what you've been going through. I'm very sorry for what's happened."

"I don't need your condolences. I need help!"

"That's what I want to focus on. Not my past mistakes. This is about helping you understand how special you are and figuring out a path forward."

"An intervention? I'm sorry I don't have any friends you could've called. It could've been a huge play."

My mother walked past me and into her bedroom. She came back with Melinda's photo and placed it gently back on the bookshelf. She looked at the photo for a moment and I could tell she missed her as much as I did. She didn't look at me while she spoke.

"Better?"

I said nothing. My mother walked back into the kitchen.

"Melinda didn't understand that you were special. She wasn't the right one for you."

"What? You didn't know her that well. Only met her a few times."

"I'm glad I got the chance to talk with her this past Christmas. Didn't know how important it would be. That's when I took the photo. She burst out laughing after this pose. Can you tell? She was good at pretending, Daniel. She was a lot like me."

Pretending? Melinda had abhorred fake people. Had she really gotten along with my mother after all? They did have some similar qualities, namely an innate eagerness to embrace life with passion and creativity, but they were completely different people. Melinda had gorged on whimsy and humor. My mother had given up on laughter. Melinda had a sense of gratitude for small, simple possessions. My mother had chosen to live simply because she was selfish, acting like she had attained some sort of ascetic enlightenment that elevated her above everyone else. Melinda was a planner. My mother made up and lost things as she went along. Most of all, Melinda would never describe herself as "wickedly selfish."

The sandwich and a half inside my stomach began to bubble. "You barely knew Melinda. You barely know me."

"She had a difficult life growing up. It changed her."

"I know that."

The economic woes Melinda's family faced did have a bruising effect on Melinda. Her father's house painting business had failed when Melinda was fourteen. Painting was the only work her father had known and it devastated him. He fluctuated between misdirected anger and gloomy indifference (neither of which was conducive to earning an income) and his behavior battered Melinda and the rest of her family. Melinda never said her father had been physically abusive, only that he had primed her to take bullying with a smile. When her friends ridiculed her with: *How can a Jewish family be broke?* Melinda would always laugh the loudest.

Melinda's mother scrounged for part-time administrative work, but it wasn't enough to stave off bankruptcy. The family lost their house to foreclosure and were forced to move into a one bedroom apartment where she and her asthmatic six-year-old brother traded places sleeping on a leaky air mattress and a sweat-stained couch. SNAP coupons did not stretch far enough to fill everyone's plate (with most going to her sickly brother) and Melinda's weakened body was often misinterpreted as suffering from an eating disorder.

Despite the hardship, Melinda managed to excel in high school. She was voted onto the Homecoming court (10th grade) the ASB student council (12th). She earned local renown as a captain on the academic decathlon team (11th and 12th). She volunteered at a hospice and had a part-time job scanning patient files for a medical group (her earnings going back to the family, of course). All that coupled with her stellar grades got her accepted to every school she applied to as well as that last-minute scholarship to the University.

"It made her a master at showcasing her emotions – the ones she wanted everyone to see. I think you know what I'm talking about."

"Stop. This is not helping me."

"It's OK to admit that she was not a strong person."

"No. You're wrong."

I admired Melinda's survivor skills so much. I despised her family. Her parents had congratulated her University admittance by co-signing student loans with mafia interest rates because of their jacked up credit rating. Worse, her parents and brother had pulled a no-show at a good luck/farewell party sponsored by one of Melinda's high school teachers. Melinda didn't talk about her family much to others. She covered for them, revealing only tidbits of her adolescence to her University friends and sorority sisters, coming of age anecdotes that were framed as if her family were boringly perfect and prototypically middle-class. I met her family a few times and each time Melinda had to apologize. It was clear her parents, and her younger brother who had grown into a wheezing, teenage misfit, never liked me. They never once called me by my name, preferring "your University friend" or simply "your guest." At Melinda's funeral they refused to speak to me or even exchange silent condolences. The only positive aspect to her funeral was that it would be the last time I would ever see her family.

"It doesn't mean Melinda didn't love you."

"What are you talking about?"

"I'm talking about the kind of person Melinda was...she wasn't like us, Daniel."

"Will you stop? That's enough!" I limped out of the kitchen.

"We should've had a deeper conversation about Melinda when you were in the hospital. Your health improved so I didn't think it was necessary. I was wrong."

I wanted to storm out of her apartment in overdramatic fashion, but my feeble ankle would've only gotten me to the doorway. So I skittered over to the couch and collapsed. My mother had exhausted me.

"Why start now, mom? We never talk."

My mother came closer to me, taking a seat on the rug next to the couch. I didn't look at her. I stared at the rug's hexagonal pattern and imagined that my mother was sitting on a bee hive. I could hear the rising buzz of the harried insects, getting poised to sting the meddling intruder.

"Do you remember anything I said to you at the hospital?"

The buzzing intensified. "No. I don't even remember being there."

"Your father believes you forget things intentionally."

I could barely hear my mother over the din of the angry hive. "What do you think?"

"He also said you don't remember the day I left. Is that true?"

The buzzing stopped. I smelled something burning. "Check your toaster. Smells like you left it on."

"You're remembering."

"What?"

"I wanted to make you lunch before I left."

"Are you going somewhere?"

"You wouldn't talk to me. As stubborn as your father, even at twelve years old."

"I don't understand."

"You wouldn't even look at me. Your face was two feet away from the television. Volume cranked up too high. I kept trying to talk to you but you wouldn't turn around. You wouldn't look at me. I kept calling your name, again and again, and I forgot about the bread in the toaster. It started to burn."

I closed my eyes as my brain began to defragment a disorganized, closeted memory.

Daniel.
I punched up the volume on the TV remote.
Daniel!
I'm sitting on the living room floor. Dad went to work, but it's Saturday. He said he had things to do. I think he didn't want to be home when....
When she left.
Daniel. Please!
I'm mindlessly watching the X-Men movie on DVD. Mystique fighting against Wolverine.
Please don't do this. This is difficult for me too.
The room is cold and dry, but I'm sweating.
Daniel!
I sense someone walking up behind me. I won't turn around. I don't want to look at her.
A hand falls on top of my head. Doesn't she understand! I refuse to move. I hate this house so much.
The hand is large. Strong. It's not her – it's not her hand. Father? Did he come home?
I try to turn my head. But the hand won't let me move.
Long fingers creep down onto my forehead. Over my ears. Against my neck. It's not my father standing behind me. It's something else. Something bad. Fingers cannot possibly be this long. Or this sharp. They can't be fingers. They're not fingers. They're blades. Adamantium claws like Wolverine. Indestructible. The thumping, over-pumping of my heart echoes inside my head.
I can't move. Can't get away.
The clawed hand tightens its grip around my head. Squeezing my skull. It feels like the blades are going to slice my skin and carve their way into my brain.
Mom! Are you there? Help me. Mom! Please, help me!
I can't breathe. I'm gasping for air. I smell smoke. Burnt toast. The smell trickles into my nose and rains down my throat.
I'm choking. Gasping. Falling.

"It's OK, Daniel. It's OK to let it go and remember."

I opened my eyes. My mother was now standing up, looking down at me with concern and kindness. Like the mother I had always believed she wanted to be.

"I remember the day you left."

"I knew you could. Memory suppression is under your conscious control."

I remembered my mother consoling me after "Wolverine" had disappeared. Hugging and kissing me. Telling me there was nothing to fear. Telling me that she'd see me again soon. I clung onto her as she walked out of my father's house, dragging me and a second-hand suitcase behind her. As she got into a rental car, I let go, unable to tolerate the citrus odor of the vinyl interior. As she began to drive away, I waved at her, weakly, like she was going out to run an errand and my waving was a mistake, an overreaction. She didn't wave back.

I didn't see my mother again until almost a year had elapsed.

"Before you left. What happened to me? In the living room?"

"I didn't know how to explain things at the time. I thought it wasn't necessary. I thought I soothed you. But this past week your father finally told me. He called it a replay. Lying on your bedroom floor. Curled up and crying. I wish I would've known, Daniel. I wish I would've known how to help you years ago. You never would've have had the same thing happen to you again. You deserve an explanation about what you are."

"What do you mean?"

"You are an Incarnator."

"What?"

"You can generate incarnations. Visual manifestations that embody your emotions and fears."

"Is that some psych definition I'm unfamiliar with?"

My mother took a seat next to me on the couch. "You can create demons."

Demons? Would it always come back to that? Were we the Demon Family? Was there any hope of embracing normal, skeptical sanity for us?

"You believe in demons? Actual demons? Like dad?"

"Of course not. I don't have his antiquated beliefs. But I do believe in the language. It was the only benefit I got out of

129

your father's religion. I can't think of a better word than demon to illustrate the distress that haunts our minds."

A rational definition. "I always thought Dad was religious because of you."

My mother chuckled. "I'm an atheist, Daniel. We only went to church because your father insisted on all of us going."

"You fooled me."

Did my mother have an affinity for tortured souls? Why else would she force herself to endure an Episcopalian service? The attraction was evident in all the photographs that lined her walls. And in my father. And in me. But if that were true, she should never had left us.

"I was never trying to fool you. I was fooling myself."

"The more you talk to me, the more alien you become." What else was a farce? Family dinner? The expensive gifts? This moment, here at her apartment?

"Let me make up for it. Let me help you."

"How? By telling me that I generate incarnations? Stop with the religious terms – I don't believe in God either."

"I use the word because the things you have created appear to be very real. Very powerful. And originiate from the most primal center of your mind."

"How is this supposed to help me?"

"Because incarnations can be controlled."

So I did have a mental illness. My mother was simply trying to sugar-coat another one of my defects. I was an amalgamation of latent, repressed horror, born out of emotional pain. My brain was spinning grotesque, schizophrenic nonsense, trying to rid itself of the loss and grief that kept lodging itself within the membranes of its cells. Would my mother recommend medication or therapy? Perhaps both.

"I've been hallucinating."

"No. You are not mentally ill. Not you."

"Then what am I?"

"You are an Incarnator. Like me."

I stood up from the couch. A sudden swoon of vertigo rolled through me as if I were a suicide jumper having second thoughts. I swallowed down regurgitated acid and trekked back into the kitchen. The fire in my throat was matched by the choleric jolts biting into my ankle on each step. My mother. My father. And me. We all had our feet entombed in a foundation of madness.

"Is father one too?"

"No. The harassing woman that he called his demon was a real person, though her stalking frequency was a bit exaggerated. And I don't believe she tried to run you over in her car. You've got to understand, Daniel. Your father wants to be like us. But he doesn't understand. He's too superstitious. He can only frame things in terms of demons and prayers, and believes God can fix anything. Your father's perspective is much different from our own."

"No, you're wrong. She's still around. The woman. She came back to the house while Dad and I were eating dinner."

"That's not true, Daniel. That woman left town as soon as I came back to help your father. She didn't care about--"

"No! I saw her! Multiple times."

It was an incarnation – your incarnation. Your father didn't see anything. He knew you were only reacting to your manufactured visions. One night, he even heard you talking in a strange voice. He thought you were asleep and it surprised him when he saw that you were awake."

"I didn't--"

"Don't be upset with him. He was only trying to fix you like he tried to fix me. It was bound to fail. We don't need fixing."

On the kitchen counter, my half-eaten sandwich had transformed. The bread had turned black from overgrown mold. Yellow, fetid juices were seeping out from the remaining innards and flowing onto the counter top, forming gooey pools and rivulets that slithered their way off the Formica and down to the linoleum kitchen floor. My mother and father were manipulating me with my own mind. I covered my eyes with my hands.

"Coming here was a mistake."

"I know what you're going through, Daniel. I had the same confusion." I dropped my hands. My mother had somehow crept up next to me. "I want to help you control your incarnations so you can use them as a tool to conquer your fears." She reached out and grabbed the rotten sandwich with her bare hand and tossed it into the trashcan under the sink. "I don't want your fears to control you."

"We are already past that point."

"No, we're not. Come on, Daniel – let's sit back down on the couch and we'll talk everything through. Including Melinda." She placed her hand, the one that had picked up the rotten sandwich, on my arm. On top of my burn scar. I pulled away from her. I found it more difficult to believe my mother's words than the physical existence of demonic creatures.

"You've only made things worse."

My mother retook her seat on the couch alone. She seemed to shrivel in size. She bowed her head and lurched forward onto the edge of the cushions, causing her back to curl over like a senior citizen whose vertebrae were deteriorating. She spoke to the rug on the floor.

"Four years ago, I was in Rio de Janeiro trying to photograph three teenage brothers from the *Rocinha favela*. I wanted to capture their faces because they were very well-known as *os meninos de olhos verdes* – the green-eyed boys. Their eyes were so striking, so unusual, that a host of wild stories about them emerged. Rumors about how they were not completely human. How they were possessed by jungle spirits and had the ability to become invisible and sneak into homes without being noticed.

"As I traveled through the slum with a local translator, asking more questions about the boys, their exploits became less mythical. More grim. Residents were eager to confirm stories about how they were actually murderous criminals, accused of rape, muggings, and the vicious torture of a toddler. After several days of searching, a relative finally met me and agreed to set up a meeting.

"I never got a chance to photograph them. I didn't realize the police had been trailing me and the boys were brutally gunned down as I walked into the meeting house."

I was aware of my mother's flirtation with danger. I knew she was emboldened to travel and take risks for her job, but this far surpassed what I had imagined had occurred during her photographic journeys. I suspected it wasn't true.

"Was that your incarnation? Three boys getting shot?"

"No. Unfortunately, they were killed. The horrible stories about them – those were my incarnations. I kept seeing them in the slum, performing atrocious acts, running away with blood covered faces. When I mentioned what I saw to the residents, they confirmed my visualizations as truth. Those three boys were just poor kids who had only committed petty crimes. I had been so keyed up for this photo shoot, I had let my incarnations get out of control. When that happens, incarnations can unintentionally affect other people. I allowed my fear to be channeled into the creation of artificial memories of a reality that never existed for those people."

My mother spoke with such earnest conviction I was almost sold on her borderline psychotic story. "Sounds more like collective obsessional behavior. Mass hysteria. I know your psych background, mother. I'm not sure what type of corrective therapy you are attempting to perform with me, but it's not working."

My mother sat up straight on the couch. "Fine. Go to the front door."

Was she kicking me out? Maybe I had taken my dismissive remarks too far. I still needed a way to get back to my father's house. Reluctantly, I limped over to the door.

"Open it."

A cold shiver rolled up my neck. She was deliberately trying to unnerve me. I didn't move.

Her voice grew louder. "Do it, Daniel. Open it."

I opened the door.

One of the black ski hat wearing teenagers I had noticed earlier was standing in my mother's entryway. The shaggy haired blond who had flipped me off. Wet, straw hair sprouting out from under his hat, sticking to cadaverous skin that was streaked with bluish veins. His eyes were closed, but his mouth was agape, exposing a top row of crooked teeth.

"What do you see, Daniel?" My mother's muted voice sounded as if she were speaking with a pillow over her mouth.

The kid opened his eyes. They were a luminous green. An enthralling set of irises that gleamed like props from a sci-fi movie set. He smiled at me and spoke clearly. In my father's voice.

Hello, again. Miss me?

His hand shot out and grabbed my neck.

"Daniel." My mother's voice grew fainter.

My instinct to survive, fight back, did not materialize. I was weak. Growing weaker as my oxygen flow dwindled. The kid tightened his grip, throttling my life.

It's coming for you, Daniel. And there's nothing that woman can do to help you.

"Daniel!"

My mother's voice finally reached my ears and I felt her arms wrap around me. My life was not going to end! The teenager relinquished his grip and the door shut solidly in my face.

Words and saliva dribbled out of my mouth. "A green-eyed kid. I saw one of the green-eyed kids."

My mother spoke into the middle of my back. "Do you believe me now? Let me help you!"

"He attacked me."

"That's impossible, Daniel. What you see can't hurt you."

"OK." I didn't know what to believe. But I wanted my mother to let me go so I could lie down. I could still feel the kid's crushing fingers against the side of my throat. That wasn't a hallucination, or a self-generated visualization of bottled-up fears. I had been attacked. But my mother had seen nothing. Unease dug its claws into my gut.

My mother let go of me and I dragged myself to the couch. "I want to rest."

"It's not real, Daniel. Always remember that. Can I get you something? A glass of water?"

"No." I flung my shaken body onto the couch. I bumped my ankle against the arm rest, and another searing bolt shot through my leg, but I was learning how to stifle the pain.

"How about something out of your backpack?" My mother zipped open my bag. "It looks like you brought some books – do you want one to read?"

"No."

"What are these?" My mother was holding up the plastic bag containing the thirteen heart notes. What was she doing? I wanted our conversation to end.

"Notes from Melinda. Please. I need rest."

She dropped the notes back into my backpack. "It's your intelligence that makes them so powerful. But your intelligence will also allow you to gain control."

I didn't respond. My head became the latest body part to ache as my thoughts began to convulse, swirling with ambiguous beliefs and frustrated constructs of truth. My mother was punching craters in my mind, and the tenuous strands of rationality that I thought I could cling onto began to unravel. Why did no one, including myself, make sense anymore?

"This will be my second chance, Daniel. I love you and I will make you feel better."

I closed my eyes and turned my head into the back of the couch. I needed to figure out how to get out of this apartment and away from a woman whose delusions were greater than my own.

"You'll find happiness soon. And strength. Then you can leave here and never have to see me ever again."

Before I could spin around to mockingly agree with her last statement, my mother hurried past me and went into her bedroom, shutting her door.

I sat up. Turned to stare at Melinda's photograph on the bookshelf. Kept staring at her face, feeling her arms around my waist, hearing her jocular laugh against my ears, dreaming of a normal, mundane existence where I would grow happy and grow old with the woman I loved....

I was ripped awake. Awakened by the glaring, incontrovertible fact that she was gone forever.

I detected another unwelcome pronouncement from my mother. Through the wall that separated the living room and my mother's bedroom, I could hear her hushed sobbing. I had heard my mother cry before, most recently at Melinda's funeral. Most notably, at my father's house, a week before she had left.

It had been around midnight, and I had woken up in a highly alert state, possibly sensing something was awry. I had slipped quietly out of my room and into the hallway. I heard my mother's elongated sobs pour out from the living room. She sounded so exasperated. Drained of hope. Animalistic. I crept closer to her.

She was alone in the unlit room, lying down on the floor next to the sofa. Flat on her back, her hands covering most of her face. As I stood still, watching her, I was certain she saw me. She lifted an arm as if to reach out to me. I should've been riddled with concern. I was her son; I should've sat down next to her and provided some form of comfort. But I was angry. I wanted her to stop. To shut up. I couldn't stand hearing her wails and I didn't want to be that close to her. So I ran back to my bed and buried my head under the covers, hoping to smother out the remnants of her cries. It didn't work. I continued to hear her crying for another hour until I finally drifted back to sleep. That desperate mourning had been the most dreadful sound I had ever heard from my mother.

Until this moment. The hushed cries coming through the wall sounded nothing like that previous agonized weeping. Nor did it sound like any of the other times I had heard her cry. Her sobbing at this particular moment oozed into me and strangled my heart because it sounded very much like laughter.

SIX

As night deepened, the apartment was quiet except for outside noise seeping into the apartment. Shrieks and howls from boorish neighbors, restless honking and engine revving from passing cars, and the occasional squeal of wind slicing through the walls of the unit buildings. My mother had remained in her bedroom, and I assumed she'd fallen asleep. Around eight o'clock, I tried forcing myself to do the same on the floor since sitting and lying on the couch had become interminable. I didn't have an alternative. There was no television and my head was swirling too much to read or search for any worthwhile entertainment on my cell phone's browser. I eked out little rest. I could find no comfortable position on the floor without adding strain to my back, shoulders and neck, and a rickety stand-alone gas furnace, located in the short hallway space between the living room and my mother's bedroom, kept clicking on. The one thing my mother's selfish blood never skimped on was the heating bill. Thankfully, despite my solitary confinement, I had no visualizations, attacks, or any other abnormal phenomena that was either internally or metaphysically created.

A couple of hours before sunrise, my fitful sleep was quashed when my mother finally reappeared, flicking on an overhead light in the hallway. She was fully dressed and getting ready to leave the apartment with a camera bag and suitcase.

"Sorry for waking you. I got a call for a photo shoot at the state capitol – a union protest. I'll be gone for two or three days. You can use my bed while I'm gone."

I sat myself up, wiping my eyes. I started to feel better. Her leaving might give me enough time to formulate my next steps.

"I've left you some money for food on the table as well as a list of things to do that I think will help you."

I glanced at the end table next to the couch. I had placed my cell phone in between the lamp and my mother keys. The keys were gone, replaced with two twenty dollar bills and a piece of paper. When did she leave these items? Had I been more asleep then I realized?

"I'm taking Melinda's notes to read. I'll let you know what I think they mean when I return."

My internal thoughts snapped off. "Why did you take those? I never said I wanted to give them to you."

"You didn't? Try to get some more sleep. I love you, Daniel." My mother clicked off the hallway light and exited the apartment.

Was she trying to intentionally unnerve me? Or had I told her my purpose for bringing the notes? Maybe I had been talking in my sleep again and had mentioned them. But that meant I had slept through her sneaking into the living room, listening to my muttered speech, fumbling through my backpack, and tiptoeing around me to leave me money and a to-do list, all in the pitch dark, early morning hours. That was even more unnerving.

I tried to settle my mind and return to sleep. I was exhausted and still wearing the same uncomfortable clothes I had worn on the airplane. I rolled around on the carpet, as if I could still discover a possible position of comfort, until the sun rose. I pulled myself off the floor and sat up on the couch. It was the second day of January and it felt like the year had already gone on too long.

I grabbed my mother's to-do list. How would a list of chores would help me? I was handwritten and bulleted:

- READ DAWKINS' *THE ANCESTOR'S TALE*
- STEP OUTSIDE ONLY WITH AN AGREEABLE SKY
- LISTEN TO THE FLOW OF TIME
- DON'T RUMINATE ON MELINDA

The first one made sense if she had rummaged through my backpack. Dawkins' account of evolutionary history was one of the five books I had brought with me, and she possibly emphasized it because she felt a kinship with a fellow atheist. I was intrigued to learn more from Dawkins after reading *The Selfish Gene* and a book of his essays, and I readily accepted his description of cultural evolution. But I had selected the book because he was a dogged supporter of rational thinking and it would serve as a solid counterweight to everything I was experiencing, including my mother. I had to be sure to thank her for her self-defeating suggestion.

The second and third items were vague or overly metaphoric, reminiscent of the remaining heart notes that my mother had absconded with. It was as if she had purposefully written these two points in the same style to illustrate a supposed connection between herself and Melinda, showing that my mother could be as poetically enigmatic as my girlfriend had been. Or maybe it was a confession? Could my mother have been the source of Melinda's strange words? I never knew what my mother and Melinda had conversed about when they briefly saw each other. I had always given them private time to bond, thinking it would facilitate Melinda becoming part of my family. Regrettably, I hadn't given my father the same accommodation. I had always kept the interaction between Melinda and my father at a minimum. Why was I always too late to realize my bad decisions?

The last item was trite and condescending. As if I could simply erase the memory of her alabaster skin against mine, or turn off my addictive, molecular desire that no longer had a release. I shifted my eyes back to the bookshelf and Melinda's photograph.

Vertigo returned, fierce and vindictive. Melinda's portrait had been desecrated. Her eyes had been blackened out as if someone had blotted them with a marker and jagged scratches stretched across the rest of her face. The frame's glass cover was shattered.

I teetered over to her photo and cradled it in my hands. I ran my index finger over the broken glass, and a jagged shard scratched open my skin. This was no hallucination. The photo slipped out of my hands and hit the floor. Blood rose to the surface of my finger and ran down to my palm. Was this my mother's doing? Was this what she meant by asking me not to think about Melinda? If so, she was the demon and I had been foolish to believe my mother would be the one to lead me out of darkness.

It was over. I was lost. Every step I had taken since Melinda's death had been a wrong one. I had meandered into the decadent depths of my ego with profuse alcohol and sex, leading to disastrous consequences. I tried embracing rationality and living with purpose only to be walloped by an irrational scourge that almost cost my father his life. Now my last attempt, seeking my mother's comfort and wisdom, had only enlarged the foulness crawling inside me, and her diagnosis of incarnated fear had left my sanity lurching and my love for her depleted. Nothing had worked. Fate had been pulling me towards failure all along.

The will to move forward, to prevail, had left me.

My body surrendered to the ground and I began to howl in misery. Wails emanated from the fractal recesses of my lungs and expunged not fury and phlegm, but trifling puffs of forlorn air. My stomach pitched and my spine cracked; my prone torso curled into the shape of a dying fetus. I focused my remaining strength into my hands, clenching them and pounding the floor in humiliation and defeat.

I no longer feared death or chaos.

A series of rapid-fire knocks on the apartment's front door interrupted my anguish. I was able to formulate a thought that was stout enough to break through my incoherence. It had to be a neighbor. Ready to voice a complaint about my desolate cries that were upsetting the sanctity of his morning crap. Or a more fitting scenario, the green-eyed boy had returned, ready to finish his job. In either case, I longed for the violent action against me that would likely ensue after I opened the door.

I struggled to stand. My energy had been almost entirely depleted but I willed my body to the door. The knocking remained constant until I turned the doorknob and pulled.

A short, young brunette stood outside. She looked close to my age, maybe younger, and I would've considered her attractive if her nostrils were smaller and her chin wasn't so square. Her most appealing feature was a curly mop of brown hair, a few web-like strands dangling over her mascara rimmed, brown eyes and her rectangular, tortoise-shell glasses. She was dressed in an oversized blue sweatshirt with a state college emblem, black tights and flip-flops. Her toe nails were painted bright purple and she had a small tattoo of Snoopy reading a book on her right ankle. All she needed to do was drop the small red purse she was holding and pick up a rolled up rubber mat to complete a picture of a trendy college girl heading to yoga class.

The girl pinched me with a wary grin. "Daniel? Wow. You look like shit. If you didn't look so much like your mother I'd run away. Are you doing OK? Look like you need help. Do you need help? Your finger's bleeding. Aren't you gonna do something about that?"

I only got a chance to lightly nod in response to her first question before she pelted me with the rest of her words. The girl pulled out a tissue from her purse and stuck it out to me. She looked benign, but her intensity flustered me like the lecture of a castigating teacher. For a complete stranger, she was too familiar with me. I wanted her to leave but a small part of me was thankful for her critical words. I accepted the tissue and wrapped it around my cut finger.

"Who are you?"

"Sorry, rudeness runs in my family. I'm Sky. I'm good friends with your mother. She told me to swing by and introduce myself to you."

Sky held out her hand. I briefly shook it with my unbloodied left hand then started to retreat back into the apartment. I didn't feel any relief deducing that the SKY from the second item on my mother's to-do list referred to an actual person.

"I need to be alone."

"Bullshit. That's the last thing you need, Daniel."

"Don't call me Daniel. Only my mother calls me Daniel."

Sky was oblivious to my dismissiveness. "From what your mother has told me, you've gone through hell lately. I get it. No one wants to share their personal shit-storm with some random visitor. But in my own smacked up, magical way, I know what you're going through. Your mom stressed it was important for me to meet you this morning."

"OK. We've met."

Sky nodded. "Wow. OK, I'll fuck off. I guess you can figure things out on your own. But if you feel like you need someone to talk to – I don't know – about *incarnations*, here's my cell number."

Had my mother brainwashed this courtesy-challenged girl with her stories too?

Sky handed me a business card. Below her name read "Owner and Manager – Skyward Books" as well as a street address, an office number, a cell number, a website URL, and three different social media profile pages.

"Don't be too impressed. It's a dumpy little bookstore and the books don't sell worth a damn, but I make up for it by selling herbal supplements and healing candles. Older women really eat the alternative healing stuff up. Makes them feel hip. My father owns the building to my store so my rent kicks ass – he'd do anything for me. Wish I could say the same. Anyways, I got lucky. I'm not that smart – I didn't finish college. This fatty sweatshirt was a gift. I live in a tiny apartment, much smaller than this one, with my adorable fatty beagle, Mr. Rogers. I named him that because after I adopted him, he waddled around the neighborhood acting all friendly to everyone. Don't look at me like that – it's not like I make him wear a fucking sweater or anything."

I could barely process all the information Sky had blurted out and I was unsure how to respond. "My mother should be back soon."

"Really? You never know with her. Sometimes she says she'll be gone for a week – next thing you know she's traveled to Morocco for a month to take photos of babies on camels. This apartment is the third one she's rented in this town – she loves to bounce. For some reason this city appeals to her. OK, I'm really smellin' the shitty look you're throwing at me so I'll leave. Lemme give you one bit of advice, Daniel. When you can't tell what's what, just remember – you're the one thing that will always be fucking real."

142

"Thanks for the tissue." I started to close the door. Sky put her hand out to block it.

"It's good advice. And put some peroxide on that finger. Looks like it could get infected."

Sky let go of the door and turned to walk away. I didn't turn back inside right away. I let my eyes linger, watching her hop down the stone step pathway and into the unit parking lot until she was out of my sight. I hadn't met someone who shared so much, so quickly before, and she should've only aggravated my condition. Yet her presence had caused my anguish to fade. She had been a good distraction.

I walked over to the couch and my eyes drifted to Melinda's photograph to the ground. The glass covering was still cracked, but the photo itself was unmarred. I picked it up. It had been a hallucination after all. An *incarnation*. Was my mother's explanation true?

I placed her photo back onto the bookshelf. If my brain was the source of all that had happened to me, there had to be a way for me to make it stop.

I rubbed the remaining sorrow out of my blurred eyes. I pulled the tissue off my finger and went into the bathroom to wash my finger. I found some peroxide in the medicine cabinet and used it to foam away bits of tissue paper and dried blood. It cleaned up nice – Sky's advice might actually be prudent. I walked back to the entryway, grabbed my backpack by the closet and dropped it on the couch. I flopped down on the floor, pulled out Dawkins' book from my bag, and began to read.

I didn't move from the floor until I had finished the entire book. I had persisted through a spate of thirst and hunger cramps and had even minimized my calls to the restroom. When I put the book down, I felt like I had just woken up from a recuperative sleep. I jumped up, but tumbled backwards, careening into the couch. Aside from my hurt ankle, my right leg had fallen asleep. I stretched my stiff body on the couch until I managed to limber myself up enough for another trip to the bathroom.

When I returned to the living room area, there was another knock at the door. I considered ignoring it, but since I was already up, I went to answer it.

Sky was at the door again, this time she was wearing a light blue, long sleeve t-shirt, faded jeans and a pair of black

Converse low tops. She also was no longer wearing her glasses.

"Damn. Even with my contacts on you still don't look better. Have you even taken a shower?"

"Why did you come back?"

"So I guess I'm not only rude, but presumptuous. Thought you might be feeling better than yesterday and would want to talk. I guess you need another Daniel day. If you're not going to shower at least change your clothes and comb your greasy hair. How much are you sleeping? Do you feel sick?"

"Yesterday?" I cut off my own perplexed state when I spotted a kid walking up the pathway, donning a black ski hat. The green glint of his eyes flashed right at me.

"Sky. See it? Can you see him?" I reached out and grabbed her arm.

"Whoa, picadillo. Don't be grabbin' me."

I quickly let her go and Sky turned to follow my gaze. It was just a normal kid. No green eyes. Puny and listless. A grating teenage delinquent. The kid bobbed his head at Sky.

"Hey, 'sup girl?" The kid's leering grin was as subtle as the genital repositioning he did with his hand.

"My standards. Shit – I'm sorry. That probably went way over your head – looks like you just learned how to adjust your big boy Pull-ups. I'll let ya get back to your Play-Doh and paste party." Sky turned back to me. "What did you see?"

Sky skipped past me and inside the apartment before I had a chance to answer or move out of the way. As I closed the door, Sky plopped down on the couch.

"You saw something else, right? Not that pocket playing genius." Sky pulled out a lime colored cell phone from the back pocket of her jeans and placed it face down on the end table, next to my own phone. "You've got my undivided attention. My Adderall and Strattera doses have kicked in."

I stared at her like she was another figment of my imagination. An incarnation of harlequinesque proportions.

"Come on – quit creepin' at me. Are you gonna say something or not?"

"I lost a day."

"Huh?"

"Since your last visit, it seems like only a few hours have passed. I've just been reading my book."

"That's not good. Have you eaten anything?"

"You believe me? Just like that?"

Sky bounced off the couch. "This neighborhood is probably like a foreign country for you. Ghettosburg, USA, right? Your mother must have wanted you to be alone for a very good reason. Otherwise it just seems cruel."

Sky wandered into the kitchen and continued speaking to me while she opened and closed a few cupboards and the refrigerator.

"When my brain gets carried away, my body doesn't realize what it needs. I forget to eat all the time. Did she leave you anything? I see nothing. So pathetic! There's nothing here but milk, bread, a few slices of cold cuts – oh, a bruised apple – this is prison food! What did you do to her? Did you deserve this treatment?"

I took Sky's seat on the couch. "I saw the kid but he was different. Looked like someone from one of my mother's stories."

Sky's voiced jumped up an octave. "Mioten?"

"What?"

"Nevermind." Her voice flattened and she walked up to me. "I haven't had lunch yet. Do you want to order pizza? Spavaldo's will deliver over here."

"Why are you doing this?"

"We both need something to eat."

"No. Why are you here?"

"Because I'm like you, Daniel. I'm an Incarnator."

Was she serious? Could I trust her? "I'm not hungry."

"Do you like olives?"

I shrugged my shoulders.

"That's another thing we have in common. Olive apathy." Sky picked up her phone and took a seat next to me as she called in an order for a large pepperoni pizza. In between us on the couch, sat Dawkins' book. It was almost 700 pages but it wouldn't have taken me an entire day to read it. I checked my cell: 2:14 PM. Closer than thirty hours must have elapsed since I started reading it. An even greater amount than my Descent with Trent and Talia. Had I not even noticed the change from day to night? Was the time lapse caused by another possible incarnation?

Sky hung up the phone and picked up my Dawkins book. "A day's not too bad. I would've lost a whole year reading this."

"Why are you here? This isn't funny."

"You probably fell asleep without realizing it. You haven't been sleeping well, right? Passed out like a narcoleptic dog."

"Advocacy – is that why you're here? To bolster my mother's claims? I guess that's why you're on the list."

"What list?"

I pointed at my mother's to-do list. She picked it up and read it, knocking her hair away from her eyes several times like she was swatting a pesky fly.

"Who's Melinda?"

"Not important."

"Sure she's not. You read the book she wrote down. I stepped inside so you didn't have to face the world, although I'm becoming less agreeable by the minute. And you told me you lost track of time, so I'm assuming you're going to start paying better attention or 'listening' to time as it flies by your face. Your mother wrote in this style to make you think. And to be clever – she's like that. But she put down Melinda for a reason. Probably because she hasn't been good to you."

"Brilliant. You figured it all out. Thanks for saving my life."

Sky bolted off the couch as if I had pushed her. "Ass. I don't need to be here! I don't have to help you. I've got a bookstore to mismanage. Enjoy your fucking pizza."

"I didn't want pizza! I'm not hungry; I'm not feeling normal! I don't know what normal is anymore. I don't know what's happening to me and I don't know what to do."

Sky had opened the door, but paused at the threshold. "Laugh. I have to."

"At me?"

"At everything. Do you think I go around telling everyone I create incarnations? I know what it's like to be alone, stuck inside your mind."

"Are you going to stay?"

Sky turned back inside to face me and closed the door. She probed my beaten face, my neglected body, searching for insights into my faltering mind. Looking for a confirmation or a denial about my hopelessness.

"What the hell is that on your arm?" Sky pointed at my cigar burn scar.

"Nothing. An old burn."

"It's gross. I don't think it healed right. Hope you're taking better care of your finger."

"Was it my mother? The one who said you were an Incarnator?"

Sky shuffled closer to me and took a seat on the floor. "Yeah. It's not the word I used to use."

"It's difficult to believe."

"Why would it? I can barely make sense of it. I used to call my incarnations *Brain Droppings* – you know, from the old George Carlin book?"

"Who?"

"Who? Really? That's your fucking problem, right there."

"How did she explain it to you?"

I didn't believe Sky would provide any huge illuminations, but I wanted her to keep talking to me. She made me feel like I still had some sense. Some worth.

"I don't remember her exact words...." Sky tapped on the sides of her head with her hands like she was playing the bongos until she tapped something into place. "OK! Have you ever read a story or watched a movie that was either so cool or interesting that you had no problem believing the characters or situations that occurred?"

"Suspension of disbelief."

"No, not that. I mean what if there's an exciting or sad scene, something that really shakes you to the core, and you actually start cheering or crying or peeing your pants. You go home and without even trying, you start acting like the character you just read or watched. You actually start to become that character."

I remembered Dostoevsky's Raskolnikov, a man near my own age, exhibiting erratic behavior, and consumed by internal conversations of madness. It eerily mirrored my own recent experiences. "I know when it's my imagination. I would know if I was reenacting a scene from a movie or--"

"Let me finish! Haven't you ever had an event happen in real life that is very similar to something in a story? Something impactful?"

I hadn't murdered anyone as in *Crime and Punishment*, but there had been a death of a woman as a result of my actions. Was Sky trying to formulate some additional parallel between fiction and real life?

"Instead of art imitating life, life imitating art?"

"Yeah, yeah. Your brain makes up a story to deal with certain fears and emotions and then acts it out for you."

"So incarnations have purpose?"

"Exactly. Hallucinations are random. Incarnations are not."

"Still sounds like a mental defect. Mental illness."

"It's not – it's a normal process. Everyone does it. Except you, me, your mother – we all do it better."

"Or worse."

"Yeah, it depends on your perspective. I suck at science, but one of the brain books in my store that I read – OK, skimmed through – said that at the smallest level of reality, quantum something-something, objects exist in every possible way. Alive, dead, here, there, everywhere. And an object in one place can be connected to a distance object. Spooky action or something like that."

"Superposition. Entanglement. Wave function collapse. Basic properties of quantum mechanics. All possible configuration states exist simultaneously, and only collapse into a definite state once an external measurement is made. Paired particles whose state depends on the other demonstrate a correlated collapse even if separated by a significant distance."

"That made no fucking sense. But I think that's what I meant. Our brains cause things to collapse."

I laughed. My first real laugh in months.

Sky was offended. "No, that's what I read! The quantum stuff happens in our brains."

My laughter stopped. "Decoherence at the neuronal level? Quantum activity is only relevant at the Plank scale of existence. You're essentially rehashing unproven arguments of explaining consciousness by Roger Penrose and Stuart Hameroff. You haven't explained anything."

Sky's face turned sour. "Like I know who fucking Roger Penrose is?"

I remained pedantic. "Did my mother tell you that science appeals to me? Is that why you're dropping scientific terms?"

"You're the one having the nerdgasm. Fuck science. And fucking get over yourself. You won't even tell me who Melinda is."

I lowered my head. I was expecting too much from Sky. "She was my girlfriend at the University. She's dead."

Sky got up from the floor. "I get it. I'm sorry, Daniel. You've been having a lot of incarnations since then, right?"

I didn't respond as she retook her seat next to me on the couch.

Sky continued. Softer. "Let me tell you what happened to me. How incarnations affected my life."

I settled into silence as Sky began to detail how she met my mother on a photo shoot where the subject had been Sky's mother, Daisy.

"Daisy grew up in this town and never left. I fucking hate it when I realize I haven't done much different. People who knew my mother growing up said she was pretty enough to be popular, but she never was. She was poor and vain and no one wanted to put up with that screwed up combo. Until she met my dad. I don't know what she did to him, but he took care of her poor problem. He's a successful commercial real estate developer. His claim to fame was leading the revitalization project downtown – that's where my bookstore is – and he shoveled money right into her. She hit the life jackpot. Popped me out, probably on accident, then became a stay-at-home mom who never stayed home. Fifteen years later, what does she do? Files for divorce. I guess she thought alimony checks and minimal visitation rights with me would be heaven enough. Last check, she's now fifty thousand dollars in debt. Total dumbass. She still gets her hair styled at an out of town boutique – the sixth of every month unless the sixth falls on a Sunday then it's the fifth. Still shops like it's 2006. Is that an Escada? Buy it. Jimmy Choos? Buy it. Her fucking Hermès scarves are the worst – she always has one wrapped tightly around her neck like it's keeping her head attached. Wish that brick brain could float away. Some people have the nerve to tell me I look like her. I wanna hit those people."

I couldn't tell if Sky was getting angrier or relieving stress. "I've been told I look my mother." Melinda never had. "You said so yourself."

"Shut up. You know your mother's a beaut. Anyways, a few months into the divorce, Daisy gets her worst idea yet. She wants to become a teacher. Said she was inspired by some documentary, but I think it was a side effect of her new anti-depressant. So Daisy goes back to school, somehow gets her credential and applies for teaching jobs. Only one place offered her a gig. Arrowstone Elementary. Worst school in town. Even the kids there made fun of themselves: *No money, no smart, no problem!"*

Sky said that Daisy was two weeks into the new job, still mispronouncing and forgetting her students' names, and on the verge of quitting, when my mother first saw her. My mother had been interviewing the school's principal, inquiring about the possibility of shooting some of the teachers for an "education in crisis" photo exposé, when she spotted a woman wearing designer label clothes, crying and prattling that a student had intentionally thrown up on her.

"Daisy didn't realize that your mother wanted to use her as an example of a shitty teacher. She actually called me up to boast about the shoot. So I pried the time and location out of her and crashed the party."

Sky revealed it was a quick shoot, taking place at a park playground on an early Saturday morning before any kids arrived, and my mother spent more time chatting with Sky than taking photographs. Sky connected with my mother, admiring the vivid tales about her camera-toting, world travels.

"My parents never took me anywhere. Had couples vacations when they were married. Singles vacations after the divorce. I told your mother I wanted to save up and use my own money to travel. But since my savings account only had eleven dollars in it, I asked your mother to lunch so I could hear more of her stories. For inspiration."

There was a loud knock at the apartment door. I tensed up.

Sky stood up. "Relax. It's the pizza."

I handed Sky one of the twenties my mother had left me and she went to greet the pizza delivery man whom she apparently knew. She dropped the pizza on the floor, and put the twenty back on the table.

"Spav's is next to my bookstore. I see Marcos, the delivery guy all the time. I don't think he saw you or this probably wouldn't have been free."

Sky grabbed some paper towels from the kitchen, and I dropped to the floor to begin eating straight from the box. I was hungry after all.

Sky sat down next to me and picked up a slice. "It's kind of greasy, but it's always quick."

"It's fine." Gummy crust. Charred pepperonis. But my greedy, empty stomach wanted Sky to limit herself to one slice.

I asked her a question before she could take a second bite. "I thought you were going to tell me about your incarnations?"

"I'm getting there." Sky dropped her quarter-eaten slice of pizza back in the box and started talking again.

"I met up with your mother for lunch or coffee, whenever she was available. We learned that we both loved Neil Gaiman, turmeric tea, and making fun of Daisy. Your mother never used any of her photos, said Daisy's face came out looking too 'plastic,' and was glad that I had been at the shoot so it hadn't been a complete waste of time.

"I started opening up to her. About the klepto phase I faked in high school. About the string of women that my father called 'development associates' who always treated me better than Daisy. And I talked about the spiders. When I was little, I only saw them occasionally and thought they were another fucked up thing the town was breeding, but I would see them everywhere. At school. At home. In between the pages of closed books, completely unharmed. Sometimes in my food. No one else saw them and when I tried telling my dad, he just laughed and bought me some bug bombs. But I told your mother the sightings had grown worse. They were scaring the shit out of me. I saw dozens bunched together under my bed sheets. Big, fat, hairy ones in my pockets. I even saw once crawling over Daisy's face. I was actually OK with that one. Your mother told me not to worry – that the spiders weren't real, and that I wasn't crazy. She said I had a special ability. At the time, I didn't believe her and I thought she was dicking me around so I didn't bring up the subject again.

"A few weeks later we got together and I told her about Alan – the guy I was seeing. A divorced father of two, same age as my mother. Aside from his Jared Leto eyes, his age was the only reason I was dating him. He said he went to high school with Daisy. Made me laugh so hard."

For some reason I had the urge to roll my eyes and say, *washin' my shit.* I only got to the eye roll before Sky cut me off.

"I'm not cruel. It's not like I wanted Daisy to see me with him. I just enjoyed the power it gave me over her. Your mother said it was disgusting and told me to break it off with him immediately. I told her I had tried, but it hadn't stuck. She warned me that I needed to be careful. That humiliating a childish man was a dangerous thing."

"Did she call my dad, childish?"

"Never talked about your dad. Can I go on?"

I nodded.

"Your mother asked me if I was still seeing spiders. When I said yes, she got really quiet. Called me an Incarnator for the first time. I asked her to explain and she said she wanted to share a story about Costa Rica first."

"Not Brazil?"

Sky shook her head and said that my mother had segued into a story about a trip she took to an indigenous village on the coast of Costa Rica. The village hadn't been her choice. It was an assignment for a spread in an eco-magazine, one that my mother had earned by overpromising on the delivery deadline. The job was doomed to fail; the village was a tourist trap, seething with manufactured photo ops unsuitable for publication. The only thing that wasn't commercialized was the cockroach infested grass hut she slept in. As she searched for an underappreciated photo subject, my mother was constantly followed by a teenage boy. He didn't wear the traditional dress that most of the other villagers pasted on to cater to the tourists. Instead, the boy wore tattered pants and a t-shirt, and appeared to be as downcast and frustrated as my mother. Whenever my mother approached him, he would point to himself, say the word, "Mioten," and run away. My mother asked several villagers about him, but no one knew who she was talking about. When she mentioned the word Mioten, they told her it was an indigenous phrase that meant "my name is."

She considered him a minor curiosity until one night she woke up in her hut and saw Mioten. Standing in the dark, a few feet away from her. Playing with himself. Her scream scared him away, but during the onrush of confused people who had come to her aid, her camera was stolen. My mother packed up her remaining items and left the village at daybreak.

But she saw Mioten again. At the San José airport, watching her as he stood behind a crowd of tourists. She saw him when she arrived back home, crouching behind a row of parked cars near her Prius. And she saw him at her apartment complex, standing on the second floor of the adjacent unit building. My mother didn't sleep well that first night home and she became ill. Doctors worried she might have Dengue Fever because of the dozen mosquito bites on her arms and legs. Luckily, the blood test came back negative, and as she recovered, she stopped seeing Mioten. Unfortunately, since the job was a bust, she failed to deliver any photos and her reputation took a significant hit.

About a month later, she received a package in the mail. No return address, but with postage originating from Costa Rica. Enclosed were developed photos from her camera. All were throwaway shots that she had taken. Except one. It was a shot of Mioten, sitting inside a grass hut, similar to the one she had been in. He was holding up a piece of paper with words written in English. It read: *I still see you.*

Sky closed up the pizza box and kicked it aside. Half of the pizza still remained because I had stopped eating during the Costa Rican story.

"Your mother started explaining everything. She explained that Mioten was an incarnation, the product of the emotions and fear that had been spawned during her the trip. She said even the photograph was an incarnation – an aftereffect as she struggled to find an opportunity to reestablish her credibility. I guess the rest of pics were real – she said she found out they had been sent by a tribal chief when her recovered camera showed up on his doorstep."

"Her story was enough to convince you?"

"Not at all. I tried to listen, tried to understand her explanation, but it still sounded like bullshit and I was starting not to trust her. So I made up an excuse and told her I had to leave. She wasn't offended. Gave me a hug, told me she hoped to catch up in a couple of weeks when she got back from New Mexico." Sky tucked her legs up to her chest and wrapped her arms around her knees. I mimicked her childlike posture even though it made me very uncomfortable and my stomach started to moan from the bad pizza.

Sky's voice became brittle like an early morning recap of a fading dream. "While your mother was gone, I broke up with Alan. It finally looked like it was going to stick. I felt good – wasn't seeing any spiders and books were actually selling at my bookstore. Then I started seeing him. A scrawny Hispanic-looking kid with a sad face and dirty clothes. Hanging around the entrance to my store. I pointed him out to people in the store, but nobody else saw him." She had started to rock her body; she wanted to go back to sleep and dream of something else.

"Mioten."

"It was fucking ridiculous. I kept seeing him. Every day, in front of the store. I started cursing your mother. Did she do something to me? Get into my head? I hated her. After four days I couldn't take it anymore. I stayed home. Didn't open the store. It was Sunday and the weekends were always the best days, but all I could do was lie in bed with my dog. I was so tired. So fucking tired. I had almost fallen asleep when Mr. Rogers woke me up. Growling at something in my apartment."

"Can't believe my mother told you that story." Actually I could believe it.

"It wasn't Mioten. It was Alan. I forgot he still had a spare key to my place. I told him to leave. He said we needed each other. I said it was over and to give me back his key. He smiled and sat down on my bed. Mr. Rogers, the chicken shit, ran away. I yelled at Alan to get the fuck out. Instead he climbed into bed with me. Told me he loved me. I felt sick. Confused. And still so damn tired! I yelled at him again, but it came out like a whisper. Alan got on top of me. I saw spiders, falling out of his hair, landing on my body. I started slapping him. Slapping at the spiders. Slapping myself. I had no energy and my fighting was worthless. Alan didn't stop. So I stopped fighting and closed my eyes."

Sky got up from the floor and went into the kitchen. She poured herself a glass a water and continued her story, standing by the sink.

"I went numb. Stayed that way even after he left. I couldn't move. Didn't want to. Until my dog started growling again and I finally opened my eyes.

"Mioten was back. Standing in my room. Spiders were crawling all over his body.

"It was too much. Energy returned and I jumped out of bed. Grabbed Mr. Rogers and ran half-naked to my car. Started driving – didn't know where I was going – just trying to get the fuck away. I drove in circles – absolutely losing my shit – I didn't know what was real! If Alan had been real. If what he did to me had been real. If Mioten was real. So I kept driving and driving until somehow I ended up at Daisy's house.

"I ran up and banged on her front door. She answered but wouldn't let me inside. I told her everything that happened to me. She still didn't let me inside. Said she knew about Alan all along. Said my guilty conscience wasn't her problem. Her door slammed in my face. My mother shooed me away like a fucking stray cat!"

"I'm so sorry that happened." My words failed to match the sympathy I wanted to convey to her. I wanted to comfort her somehow, but didn't know what to do.

"I fell into a hole after that. A big fucking hole. Blamed myself for everything that happened. I was giving up. I gave up. Then I got a text from your mother. As if she knew what had happened and what I wanted to do to myself. I didn't want to text her back. But I did. I wrote: *I hate you*. Turned off my phone so I wouldn't hear from her again. It felt good to do that to her. Good enough to give me the strength to go back home. When I arrived back at my apartment, your mother was at my door. She had apparently flown in an hour earlier and had driven straight to my place after my text. She tried to get details out of me, but I wouldn't answer. She tried to hug me and I slapped her. It didn't faze her and she hugged me anyways. I kept hitting her, and hitting her, but she wouldn't let me go. I was crying and everything hurt so much – I had given up! I shouldn't have even fucking been alive!"

Sky sped out of the kitchen. I thought she was heading for the door, but she darted into the bathroom. Her story had generated such a concussive impression on me that my legs had started to tremble. It was only hours earlier when I felt I

155

had lost all hope. If she had found a way to overcome such a tremendous ordeal than it was possible I could find a way to recover from my own self-imposed delusions (demons).

When Sky returned from the restroom, she grabbed my cell phone and began scrolling through it, her glassy, swollen eyes squinting until she realized her mistake. She put it back and picked up her own phone and punched away on it as she spoke.

"I had to take my contacts out. I need to get going. Shared way too fucking much with you"

"How did my mother help you?"

"By taking care of me! She took me to the hospital. Took me to the police station – though lot of good that did. She stayed with me, explained incarnations, explained how I was strong enough to control my fears, and explained how I could overcome them. Most of all, she mothered me. She wants to do the same with you. Fucking let her." Sky left my mother's apartment without saying goodbye.

I tried to process all the events that had occurred since my mother had left the apartment. My to-do list. Melinda's photograph. My breakdown. Sky's visits. Reading my Dawkins book and an entire day elapsing without my recognition. The green-eyed kid and Mioten. Quantum mechanics.

Sky's story.

She didn't even know me and she shared the most traumatic episode she had ever endured. She wanted to help me. That was real. Sky's pain was real. I was real. *I am fucking real.* I repeated those four words as if they had become my new mantra, and I did reach a steady state. Her advice was true. I could regain my confidence by simply trusting in my own existence.

I finally felt that if I could just piece everything together, I would understand not only what was happening to me, but what I needed to do.

That evening I showered for the first time since I had left my father's house, and put on a clean t-shirt and a pair of boxers. I ate the rest of the pizza for dinner and started reading a second book, *Phi* by Giulio Tononi. It was an artful narrative that used Galileo as a fictional character to describe a theory of consciousness based on integrated information. I hoped I would connect with Galileo the way Sky had explained a person could become enraptured by a character in a story. Maybe Sky's fuzzy understanding of science wasn't too far from the truth.

I dozed off reading the book on the couch. It was night when I awoke, but I had left the end table lamp on as well as the kitchen light and I was certain I didn't lose another day. My cell phone confirmed the date and showed that it was 11:35 PM. I closed the book, turned off the lights, and tried once again to make myself comfortable enough to sleep on the floor.

When I woke up once again, I was shivering. Why was it so cold? Hadn't the heater turned on? I could see my expelled breath forming as I reached up to the end table, fumbling for my cell phone. I immediately stopped reaching for my phone once I discovered the reason for the chill.

The front door to the apartment was wide open.

I activated my wits. I needed to close the door, flip on the lights and confirm that nothing was amiss in the apartment. I wasn't sure if my mother had anything worth stealing, but who knew what a neighborhood thug would do? Carelessly, I bounced up off the floor to put my thoughts into action, forgetting about my ankle. The pain shot up into my spine and I had to let myself fall back down on the couch to recover. I checked the time on my phone: 1:13 AM. No missed calls. Mo missed messages.

A childlike laugh drifted into the apartment from outside. Had someone seen me? I fought through my lingering pain, and limped over to the door to close it.

Before closing it, I peered outside. Walking along the pathway, with his back to me, was Mioten. He would take a few steps, laugh, make a small pirouette, and continue walking.

He continued the pattern for a couple of yards, moving further away from my mother's apartment, until he suddenly stopped. He stood perfectly still, underneath the feathery glow of one of the walkway lamps that revealed ragged haloes in the back of his torn shirt and pants, and glittery dust trapped in his tangled and tousled hair. A deep, static-filled voice, too resonant and artificial to come out of a human boy's larynx, split the cold, night air.

I still see you.

Mioten spun his head around to look at me. He did not possess the face of a forsaken child. He was a ravenous animal with flaring eyes and an eager, snarling mouth, dripping with foul anticipation. We stared at each other for an eternal second before he broke out into a wild sprint, laughing and bounding towards me, while I struggled to close and lock the door.

WHUMP! The wood in the apartment walls cracked as Mioten banged against the door as I shut it. I applied the chain lock even though its latch looked like it would snap off from the slightest gust of wind. I decided to rest my back against the door as extra support.

WHUMP! WHUMP! The latch to the chain lock broke loose and fell to the floor. Devilish laughter sounded on the other side of the door as well as the sound of desperate scratching – claws trying to eat through the paneling near my feet.

No! This wasn't real! It was only an incarnation. Only a product of my frightened brain. I needed to gain control of myself!

WHUMP! My back bounced off the door from the impact. The scratching intensified. I had to take control. This was not real! Only I was real.

I am fucking real! I am fucking real!

The scratching stopped. I stood motionless against the door for a full minute, counting every quiet second, before I pulled myself back into the living room. I wasn't going to open the door to confirm if Mioten had vanished. I flicked on the end table lamp, and skittered into the kitchen to turn on its overhead light.

As I walked back into the living room, I saw the door to my mother's bedroom snap shut. For a moment, reasonable explanations popped into my head. It might have closed due to a lingering breeze or a slight pressure differential in the apartment. It wouldn't take much to seal a door that had been left ajar.

However, I remembered that my mother had left her bedroom door wide open in case I had wanted to sleep on her bed.

I walked towards my mother's bedroom, flipping on the hallway light. I passed the furnace – the thermostat dial was

158

turned down to the lowest setting. I cranked it back up, but the heater didn't click on – was it broken? I returned my attention to the closed bedroom door. Maybe I had been mistaken – my mother had left it closed. No, I had walked past the open door several times. This was ridiculous. What did it matter if it had been open or closed? I simply needed to reopen the door and look around inside the room – I could use some extra blankets if the furnace wasn't working.

Still, I hesitated. My neurons began firing off a stream of paranoid suppositions. What if there really had been an intruder, someone who was now lurking inside my mother's bedroom? The incarnation of Mioten had been a mental misdirection, a phantom to obscure the fact that there was someone, *something*, behind the closed door.

I was losing control. I harvested more illogical thoughts. Mioten was real. He was keeping me inside the apartment. He knew what was waiting for me....

(It's coming after you next.)

I repeated my mantra again. *I am fucking real. I am fucking real.* It was only an incarnation. Mioten didn't exist. There was nothing inside the bedroom. Open the door, Daniel! You are in control!

My jittery hand pushed open the door, and I stepped inside.

Standing atop a wooden chair next to a small desk at the far end of the room, was a toddler, a little boy no more than one-year-old, wearing only a diaper. His hands were resting against a computer keyboard on the desk. He was fixated on the screen of a bulky, decade-old monitor that displayed a child's game with penguins. The boy spanked the keyboard with his hands and the penguins began bouncing around on the screen. The monitor illuminated the entire bedroom, but I still turned on the light switch by the door. As a floor lamp next to the bed flickered to life, the toddler spun away from the monitor and glanced in my direction before tumbling off the chair, falling hard to the floor.

I rushed over to the boy, almost stumbling to the floor myself. The toddler had landed on his back. His body was motionless. His unblinking eyes stared up at the ceiling. One of his doll-like arms was bent backwards underneath his head, clearly broken.

Worst of all, I recognized him. Recognized where I had seen him. Recognized the birthmark on his inner thigh.

It was me. He looked exactly as I did in my mother's photograph on the living room wall.

This had to be another incarnation. Why couldn't I control myself? I fought the urge to touch the boy. Check to see if he had any life remaining. Check to see if his skin was real. If I touched him on the thigh, would I feel a poke on my own leg?

Before I gave in to the urge, the toddler flipped over and with inhuman speed, crawled between my legs. I spun around and watched as he scooted across the floor on two knees and one hand – his broken arm was still bent back behind his head – and he slipped out the bedroom door.

I began to follow him, but was stopped by the daunting force of my own voice.

Poor Danny. Are you afraid of yourself?

The sound had come from my mother's bed where a body lay, completely draped by a single white sheet. The body hadn't been there when I had first entered the room. The bed had been neatly made.

I heard my voice again as air expelled from the body's mouth, billowing up the sheet covering up its face.

You're not a very good playmate. It won't like that. It won't be happy when it comes for you.

An arm jutted out from under the sheet. It was withered and slimy, emitting a gooey shimmer like the leftover mucous trail of a snail. The skeletal arm pulled the sheet off the rest of its body.

Lying in bed was a naked, decrepit man. His splintering bones poked through his muculent, paper-thin skin giving him the appearance of a rotting, skinned deer discarded by a callous hunter. A deep wound had partially split open his abdomen, exposing a segment of his bowels surrounded by dark ichor. And next to his shriveled, grey haired penis was a birthmark on his thigh.

The old man was another version of me. A ghastly incarnation of my future self.

The dying man's bald head began to shake, his eyes rolled in their sockets, and his toothless mouth gaped open. A rust-colored tongue licked the air as he (or I?) continued the conversation.

You're a wretched lump in the Universe. Look at yourself! Darwin would deem you unfit. Science cannot help you. You're only a fool who wants to be captured by a lovely Sky.

A loud buzzing noise came from the computer desk. The monitor's screen was flashing with a blue DOS error message, indicating a system crash.

Help yourself, Danny. Accept who you are – you are different!

The old man sprung up from the bed, and his silky, dying hand reached out and locked onto my forearm, twisting my tendons. As I struggled to pull away, his rotting flesh sloughed off, leaving gelatinous driblets stuck to my own skin.

Is this fucking real enough for you!

With several gut-wrenching pulls, I managed to break myself free. The force shot my body backwards, and I tumbled out of the room and into the hallway. As I scrambled up to my feet, trying to dampen the flurries of panic cascading inside me, the computer monitor and the bedroom floor lamp shut off, and the room returned to the darkened, empty space I had wanted to see all along.

I looked at my arm. It hurt but was unmarked. I gently rubbed it until the hum of the furnace caused me to jump. The heater had finally decided to click on.

I took a step back inside my mother's room and turned the floor lamp back on with the switch. The bed was crisply made. The room was clear. Normal.

I lumbered back into the hallway; my ankle and arm were throbbing, and my mind was depleted. As I entered the living room, I saw that the front door was once again wide open. I moved as quickly as I could to shut and lock it without taking a glance outside, but couldn't help noticing the broken latch on the floor. I kicked it away from me.

With both my head and ankle ready to give out, I made my way back to the couch and let my body drop onto the cushions. I thought about using the final bits of my resolve to call Sky, so I picked up my phone and her business card. Before punching in her number, I checked the time on my cell: 1:15 AM.

Either my cell phone wasn't working correctly or only two minutes had elapsed since I had first woken up and checked the time. Time was behaving differently. LISTEN TO THE FLOW OF TIME. My mother knew things would be different.

161

(Accept who you are – you are different!)

It was too late to call Sky. It'd be better to wait until tomorrow before reaching out to her.

Before I put my phone down, I saw that I had a new text message. I opened it up. It was a draft, directed to my own number. It read: *the souls of the mind are functions of phi.* A meaningless derivative from the book I had been reading. Had I written it? When? The last time I checked there had been no messages. It didn't matter. I deleted it and put my phone back onto the table.

I was drained. Something had eaten away at me, ingesting chunks of my life and my identity. Something that was *different*. I closed my eyes, and my soreness began to abate. My legs grew heavy and my muscles relaxed, as Fight or Flight gave way to Nestle and Recuperate. I succumbed to my fatigue and fell asleep on the couch, leaving almost every light in the apartment on.

I was awakened by the sound of my phone ringing. It was late morning. I answered the call even though I didn't recognize the number.

"Hey Daniel. It's Sky. Hope you don't mind – I grabbed your number off your phone so I could recognize it if you called. Actually I'm kidding. I wanted to call you. Thought it'd be nice if I changed up my stalking approach."

Sky's voice soothed me. "Can you come over?"

"What's wrong?"

"Something happened last night. Something different."

"Shit. OK. Let me see if I can get Gayle to cover for me again at the store. I could be there in an hour?"

"Thanks, Sky."

I hung up the phone as a tickle rose up in my throat, causing me to have a minor coughing fit. I used the blanket on the couch to cover my mouth, more out of involuntary polite habit than any actual benefit.

When I pulled the blanket away I noticed a few tiny specks of blood. I didn't feel sick so I thought little of it. I took a quick shower, and put on the vintage 90's outfit (a twentieth birthday gift from Melinda) that I had brought with me – a long-sleeve *R.E.M.* t-shirt and matching stone-washed Levi's – and waited patiently for my new friend's arrival.

Sky arrived about an hour and half later, bringing a couple of hoagies to eat that I ravenously enjoyed, and I relayed to her the events of the preceding night. She listened without interrupting and several times I caught glimpses of both sadness and uncertainty in her eyes.

My phone chimed. A text message from my mother. It read that she would be returning around five o'clock. I told Sky and her eyes perked up.

"Good. She got my messages. I'll wait here with you until she returns."

"Do you think something else will happen before she gets here?"

"No. I don't think so."

"I'm glad you're here, Sky. You've helped me a lot."

Sky remained silent. Her face grew more somber. I started to become nervous. "Is something wrong?"

"I thought we were so much alike."

"I think there's some truth to that."

Sky shook her head and took a deep breath. "You need to tell your mother exactly what happened last night. The same things you told me."

"What aren't you telling me, Sky?"

"Daniel, I don't think we're anything at all alike."

Sky got up from the couch and took the leftover half of her sandwich to the kitchen. She had stopped eating again. She was upset, either for me or about me. The swagger, the boldness I saw in her when we first met had vanished. I needed that back. Sky had given me the only sense of progress that had the potential to be sustainable. I wanted to believe that things had not gotten worse last night. I was ready to learn more about my incarnations. I wanted Sky to teach me.

Or was I too far gone, too intertwined with the pain that had invaded me, and had become someone beyond Sky's help? Was it too late for me?

Maybe there was something else happening to me. Something beyond Sky's expectations. An aberration in the equations of quantum physics.

Maybe I really was *different*.

SEVEN

My mother arrived around five-thirty in the evening. Sky was sitting on the couch, leafing through my Tononi book, while I was splayed out on the floor drifting in and out of sleep. In the hours prior, we had spent some time in my mother's bedroom, examining the computer (which we couldn't even boot up) and searching for any possible sign of a disturbance (the bed sheets were dark blue, not white). My casual acceptance of my mother's room, contrary to the description of my incarnation, seemed to relax Sky and that calmed me. I spent the rest of the afternoon trying to ease Sky's mind further. I opened up as much as I could about the good things in my life, my rekindled relationship with my father and my best memories of Melinda. Sky listened uncritically. When I glossed over Melinda's death, she didn't probe or express any warmed-over sympathy. She simply decried the unjustness of life and disclosed a bit of selfish envy over a description of love that she had yet to experience.

As soon as my mother entered the apartment, she dropped her belongings to the floor and without saying a word, gave me an enveloping hug. The same hug she had likely given Sky after her own life-altering event. I didn't find it reassuring. I felt like a stage prop, or a MacGuffin popping back up in the denouement of a movie that I had wasted my time watching. I pulled away from her.

My mother went to Sky and gave her a similar, prefab hug. I thought I overheard a whisper from Sky. "He's gotten worse."

My mother seemed to nod in response. She broke away from Sky and flashed me one of her patented smiles. "Were you going to close up the bookstore?"

Although she was looking at me, it was question for Sky. Sky appeared as annoyed as I was by her demeanor. "You need to hear what Daniel experienced."

My mother picked up her bags and carted them off to her bedroom. "I'm starving. Have you two eaten?"

Sky remained silent while I shrugged my shoulders.

My mother continued from her room. "How about we all head to Sky's bookstore? We can grab a pizza at Spav's and eat in the backroom. It'll give the three of us a chance to talk things over."

Sky looked at me. "Does that sound like it would help you?"

I gave another shoulder shrug. "We had pizza yesterday."

I didn't know whether my mother wanted a serious meeting or a lighthearted pow-wow, but it would only be a frustrating waste of time if I ended up getting no further clarification on my experiences. My mother returned from her bedroom.

"Well, Daniel? How about it?"

I was still looking at Sky. I wanted to go back a few hours and relive the moments before my mother had returned. Sky had been slowly returning to her old self, demonstrating resilient strength and an ability to chisel out sanity from her petrified layers of dismay.

Sky shuffled towards the front door. "Pizza is fine. The quicker I get back to the store the better. Mr. Rogers is with Gayle and he gets sick when she forgets to fill up his water bowl." My mother nodded and excused herself to the bathroom.

Sky opened the door. "I'll meet you two there."

"Who's Gayle?" Truthfully, I didn't need an answer. I was only trying to stall. I didn't want to go anywhere; I wanted to stay in the apartment with Sky.

165

"She's my part-time help, though this week she'll probably hit forty hours. She's about sixty years old. Semi-retired. Horrible eyesight too, but got some hops left in her. She hooked me up with her cousin who's become one of my main suppliers of herbal supplements." Sky started edging out the door. "Thinking about getting rid of her. She misplaces books all the time and keeps tripping over Mr. Rogers. Could easily get someone better who's just as cheap. But that makes me the shit ass, right?"

"No. I think you'll do what's best."

"For who?"

I left her question unanswered as my mother came out of the bathroom. Sky darted out the door.

My mother and I exited the apartment, jumped into her Prius, and followed Sky who was behind the wheel of a cherry colored Jeep Wrangler. I was a bit jealous as Sky was driving the type of vehicle I had wanted to own since high school. It was surprising that such pettiness could arise in me after all the whipsawing emotions I had experienced. I'd be happy to accept any vehicle – I had never owned a car since I didn't really need one at the University. Maybe if everything worked out, one would make its way onto my mother's gift list. But I doubted it.

My mother maintained a quiet, directionless glower as we lost sight of Sky's Jeep, zigzagging along surface streets until we reached Downtown, the section of the city that had been revitalized by Sky's father. The downtown blocks did look inviting, with trash-free streets coated with fresh tar and paint, un-cracked sidewalks dotted with precisely trimmed, pink-flowered, Dogwood trees, and advertisement-free, century old buildings treated with reinforced Mansard roofs and renovated brick façades. But there were plenty of unoccupied or closed storefronts which gave the area a cracked gleam as if the glaze of runny utopian drippings had been almost entirely licked away.

Sky's shop, *Skyward Books*, was situated along the main, central artery running through Downtown, aptly named Center Street. Pedestrians near her store were scarce. Scavenger pigeons and crows mainly crossed her storefront along with a handful of wandering unemployed folk. Only two of the downtrodden (a middle-aged man and woman) fit the pervasive homeless stereotype with their haggard, soiled clothes and overflowing bags stuffed in shopping carts. The rest looked like typical working class individuals, and if they hadn't been holding signs asking for spare change or work, I never would have guessed they were so in need. Sky's bookstore was indistinctly crammed between Spavaldo's Pizza and a Christian gift shop, and I would have easily missed it if my mother hadn't parked directly in front of the entrance.

As I clumsily exited the Prius, still encumbered by the crutches I had brought along, Sky stepped out of the shop's entrance, holding open the door. Sky's presence didn't make the shop any more eye-catching. There was only one narrow display window that was filled with a few prosaic novels and a selection of healing candles. The name of the store was written above the door in dark, block letters that matched the color of the walnut door – probably someone had been too cheap or lazy to stain the sign a different color than the door.

"Pretty obvious I'm gonna put Barnes & Noble out of business."

I stifled a chuckle over Sky's dumb joke and ended up coughing and choking on my own saliva. Sky whacked me on the back as my mother pushed past us and into the store. Sky stuck her tongue out at my mother either in protest over her rudeness, or the fact that coming down here was a mistake. Regardless, we dutifully followed my mother inside.

The undersized shop had its inventory divided in half – one side promoting books and the other, herbal supplements and holistic health supplies. In the center of the store were two black leather couches, presumably for customers to use for reading and loitering. The walnut planks on the walls of the bookstore matched the rustic condition of the front door, but clashed with the waxed sandalwood floor. The bookcases were a hodgepodge mix of unfinished wood and stainless steel and were likely castaways, rescued from flea markets and shuttered libraries. The store had a roomy, vaulted ceiling that was painted a parched shade of yellow, blanched further by the jarring glare spewing from the overhead tracks of florescent lights. The shop had an odd, pseudo-technical feel to it as if we had entered the training library of an osteopathic medicine hospital.

Behind the checkout counter, to the right of the entrance, stood an older woman, looking more like seventy years of age, wearing a plain, eggshell-colored, floor-length dress with a conservative neckline – I assumed this was Gayle. She was chatting with the only customers in the store, a female couple, both around Gayle's age, with matching silver-dyed hair and green polo shirts. While she talked, Gayle was staring at the center of the couple as if she couldn't see either one clearly and was splitting the difference. Gayle's face was tanned and sun-aged, and her long, blond hair with streaks of red and grey was tied into two tightly braided ponytails. She looked like a 1950's spinster librarian or a 1960's hippie, depending on what angle you chose. On the floor behind the counter was an overweight beagle, lying next to a half-filled water bowl. He barely raised his head at our entrance, and he didn't seem at all friendly like I figured a dog called Mr. Rogers would be.

The couple exited the store hand in hand and Gayle stepped out from behind the counter to warmly greet Sky. "Disgusting ladies, but they left us six hundred and fifty dollars!"

Sky raised up her arms as if she were praising God in church then lowered them as if she had been merely stretching. "I'm going to close up now, Gayle. Thanks for watching Mr. Rogers for so long. You made it another day without killing him."

Gayle graciously accepted the off-color compliment and walked briskly past me to greet my mother, giving her a very amiable embrace. My mother whispered something back in Gayle's ear. Gayle looked at me strangely, then nodded her head at me as if accepting an apology. Sky walked Gayle to the door.

I queried my mother. "What did you say to her?"

My mother snapped at me. "She didn't see you. I had to tell her you were standing there."

Sky hurried over to me and placed her hand at the small of my back. Her touch caused me to momentarily squelch thoughts about Gayle's impertinent behavior. "I'm going to give Daniel a quick tour of the place. Were you going to grab the pizza?"

My mother rummaged inside her purse. "A medium veggie OK for everyone?"

We agreed and while my mother exited, Sky led me to a seat on one of the couches in the center of the shop. "This concludes our tour."

I appreciated Sky's lightheartedness, but I felt like I was being set up for an ambush. "Gayle couldn't see me? Is she really that blind?"

"No, she saw you. She's not that blind or I would be robbed every day. She was making a point to your mother. That you don't give off any aura. Gayle is really sensitive to them. You probably think auras are like six layers of bullshit, right?"

"More like ten."

"Hah, well I can see auras too. And Gayle's wrong. Your aura is clearly a thick cloud of black smoke swirling around you."

I started choking on spit again. (*Metaphor, motherfucker!*) "Facetious?"

"You talk too smart. Need to cut that shit out." Sky turned away from me. "I'm gonna clean up the backroom so we can eat there. I have a science section – there on your left." Sky pointed over to a small bookshelf with a meagre selection. "But I don't know if I have anything brilliant enough for you."

"I'm not that smart, Sky."

"Don't kid yourself. You're not that modest."

I took a seat on one of the couches (its tufted cushions were quite comfortable), trying to fathom how Sky saw me. An arrogant freak? A willing victim? A maladjusted Incarnator? "I'm fine sitting here."

Sky was already walking away from me. "Whatever. Feel free to say hi to Mr. Rogers. He won't bite, but he'll probably fart on you."

Sky walked to the back of the store and disappeared as she turned a corner behind a row of empty bookcases. I assumed she went through a door that was hidden from the general public. I felt a bit antsy sitting in the store alone. I tried closing my eyes, but it made things worse. It felt like I was back in the hospital waiting room. Waiting for an update on Melinda's condition. Waiting to take her home. As I stood up to go distract myself with Sky's wares, I became dumbfounded. Amazed. My ankle felt strong, almost healed. It was extremely peculiar, but I relished it. I left my crutches against the couch and walked, with a normal gait, to the bookcases that housed herbal supplements. The top shelves were devoted to some of the more well-known varieties:

169

Echinacea, Ginkgo, and Ginseng. The bottom shelves were arrayed with a selection of scented oils and incense, and lesser known remedies. I picked up one of the oils marked for healing and optimum well-being. Its label read: *TerraVolga – a pure essential lavender oil, free of synthetic compounds and contaminants. Excellent as a natural pain and stress reliever – recapture your native state of bliss. For external use only.* I started to believe that there really were healing elements in the shop, possibly some rehabilitative oil flowing through the air that was infusing my ankle with renewed energy. Either that or the placebo effect it elicited in me was prodigious. My thoughts about alternative medicine faded, however, when I noticed a shelf devoted to sleep remedies. Kava. Melatonin. Valerian root – the bilge that had contributed to Melinda's death. My ankle twitched but held. I quickly pushed the Valerian supplements behind the other options and walked over to the other side of the store where the science books were located.

I perused the science books with little interest, skimming old mainstream copies written by Sagan, Greene and Bryson – books I had already breezed through years ago. Based on the condition of the books, it appeared a lot of Sky's inventory was used. I considered donating some of my old books that I had stored at my father's house to her cause, and raise the quality bar up a few notches. Provided, of course, that Sky and I remained in touch or even became good friends. I let the thought of a prolonged friendship with Sky dance in my head until it was invaded by a strange beeping noise. Coming from behind the checkout counter. Gayle had returned and was punching keys on the cash register.

I walked over to her since I wanted another chance at a more welcoming introduction. I strongly doubted she had some sort of special vision which could detect my "aura" (or lack thereof), but I felt I needed to at least hear Gayle explain her impression of me. As I walked over to her, it felt outstanding not having to limp and I put my full weight on my left foot. I picked up my pace, excited to feel normal again.

Gayle ignored my approach. She didn't waver from her focused key punching and the beeps of the register began to grow insistent. I had no idea what she was trying to accomplish and felt a bit guilty thinking that she was too blind to operate the machine. But as Sky had said, if Gayle regularly minded the store, her vision had to be acute enough to conduct customer transactions. Was she trying to access it improperly? I considered getting Sky, but I terminated any thoughts that Gayle was doing something wrong. She couldn't possibly be that corrupt or inane.

Even when I was only a few feet away from her, Gayle still didn't acknowledge my presence. I decided there was no way to minimize the surprise so I called out to her.

"Hey, Gayle. What are you doing?"

Gayle stopped pressing the register's buttons, but didn't look up at me. She kept her head pointed at the keys. Something was wrong. Down on the floor, Mr. Rogers picked up his head. He started growling.

"Gayle. Did you need something? Let me go get Sky."

Before I could pivot to grab Sky, Gayle lifted up her head like a mechanical doll.

"No, you won't."

I was taken aback by her uneven demeanor and my resolve to get Sky increased. "I don't know what's wrong with you. I'm getting Sky."

"You need to leave! You've made me sick." Gayle lurched away from the cash register and spit a gob of mucus onto the counter. The stringy mucus was tinged with blood.

I hustled to the back of the store where Sky had disappeared. Mr. Rogers let out a few more shallow growls in my wake. When I reached the area behind the empty bookcases, I saw two doors. One was unmarked, the other had a sign with big red letters: EMPLOYEES ONLY. I opened that one.

It was an empty restroom.

I tried the other door, but it was locked. Before I could knock, a hand touched my shoulder. I flipped around and saw Gayle's diseased face staring back at me. Her tan complexion had turned pallid. Her eyes were bloodshot. Cloudy mucous dripped from one of her nostrils.

Her words came out hoarse and the scent of vomit steamed from her mouth. "Get out of here!"

I yanked my arm away from her and pounded on the locked door. It took only two hits with my fist before Sky flung open the door. She pummeled me back with worry. "What the hell? Are you sick?"

"No, it's Gayle." I turned around expecting to see the genuine sick person, but the store was empty. Sky ushered me into the adjacent bathroom.

"Go clean yourself up."

My body clicked on the automatic light and I walked over to the bathroom sink. My reflection in the oval mirror above the sink startled me. A crusty white film ran along the side of my nose to my mouth and some soppy excess had stained the front of my shirt. My eyes were rimmed with tears and my forehead lacerated with sweat. I looked as if I had a severe case of the flu.

But I felt fine. The only explanation I could formulate was that Gayle was an incarnation and somehow I had assumed the characteristics of her visualized illness. I quickly cleaned myself up and exited the restroom.

I scanned the bookstore looking for Sky, but all I saw was Mr. Rogers lumbering over to me, dragging his belly across the floor as he waddled to the couches in the center of the store.

"Daniel."

My mother's voice. I turned around and saw her and Sky in the backroom adjacent to the bathroom sitting in plastic chairs around a small card table that had a box of pizza on top.

I stepped into a makeshift break room, with a small cube refrigerator tucked into a corner, and a budget microwave and a two-cup coffee maker crammed together on a counter top that was actually a slat of plywood resting across a rusty utility sink. Storage racks filled with book-sized boxes lined one of the walls, and a hand dolly rested in the corner opposite the fridge. The room was better suited for storage than eating.

My mother got up from her chair and escorted me to an open seat at the table. Her voice gurgled with mushy concern. "How are you feeling, Daniel?"

"I feel fine. Not sure why it happened, but I had another incarnation – I saw Gayle. She was horribly sick."

Sky piped up. "You were in the bathroom for a while. Are you sure you're not sick? Don't want you to puke in here."

My mother didn't wait for me to answer Sky. "I think I made a mistake, Daniel. You do look physically ill." Was my mother admitting that her handcrafted healing process for me had gone awry?

"I'm telling you both. I feel fine! Look." I got up from the chair and jumped up and down, hopping from one foot to the other in an almost comical fashion. "My ankle doesn't hurt anymore."

During my boast of agility, I managed to step on the handle of a broom lying on the floor and I fell solidly onto one knee. The scream from my patella jangled nerves all the way up to my pelvis. Sky jumped up from her chair and helped me back up. I reluctantly let her guide my pompous ass to my seat. Worst of all, as I sat down, rubbing my knee, my injured ankle started crowing again.

"Really. I'm OK. Just uncoordinated." I grabbed a slice of pizza and stuffed it into my mouth even though I wasn't hungry.

My mother and Sky exchanged a wary glance before grabbing their own slices of pizza. As they began to pick at their dinner, I decided to disclose my interpretation of what had occurred. My voice rose an octave, heckling the seriousness of my case.

"I visualized a demonic entity once again. It took the form of Gayle who appeared to have the flu or something worse and she was acting strange at the cash register. As I interacted with that vision of her, some of the foul illness I ascribed to her must have been adopted by me, but only in appearance because I feel healthier than I have in a long time. I don't know why I would create this particular type of incarnation, or how I would mimic flu-like symptoms, so please – educate me. I'm eagerly awaiting an explanation on how this episode relates to my underlying fears and emotions and how I can go about controlling it."

I smiled at Sky, but she didn't smile back. "Are you trying to sound like your mother?" Sky looked away from me and stared at her pizza. "I think something different is happening."

That word again. *Different.* My mother shook her head and pushed her uneaten slice of pizza away. "No, it's the same thing. He just doesn't manifest consistent images. Daniel, tell me what happened last night – Sky only gave me her interpretation."

I was growing weary of their privileged knowledge. "Tell me what you are thinking. If you really want to help me, tell me everything you know."

My mother reached out to grab my hand. "There was no photo shoot at the state capital. I left in order to give you some time to be honest with yourself and to meet Sky. It appears I made a mistake. I thought you would realize what was driving your spate of incarnations. Sky was incredibly candid with you about her incarnations, her experiences. Her pain. If that wasn't enough for you to admit the guilt, fear, and rage that is irrationally building up inside you, I don't know what will."

"Admit my guilt? You left me. How was that my fault?"

"This has nothing to do with me."

"Really? You lied to me. Now you're belittling me. Clearly it's all my fault. I'm such a horrible person."

My mother breathed deeply then spoke again with more composure. "You know what the answer is, Daniel."

I pulled my hand away from her before she could pat it. "Why do you enjoy taunting me with vague remarks?"

Sky pushed her chair away from the table and crossed her arms. "Just tell him." I tried not to show it, but Sky's support was wonderful.

My mother pulled her limbs closer to her body and bowed her head in a submissive posture. She spoke quietly, but resolutely. "Melinda. You refuse to let her go."

I snickered. "Is that your huge reveal? My enlightenment is complete."

"Melinda is the source of your incarnations and--"

"I'm not having incarnations of Melinda! The disgusting things I'm seeing are the exact opposite of Melinda."

"That's not true, Daniel."

My mother tried to reach out and touch me again. I pushed my chair away from her. Was she calling Melinda disgusting? Or did she know that I did have an incarnation of Melinda? I hadn't discussed the night Melinda died with her. I had not mentioned her gruesome representation with anyone. I had guarded it. Dismissed it. No longer thought about it.

My mother moved closer to me. "The hospital, Daniel. Remember?"

"No."

"The doctors couldn't calm you down. They started pumping you with sedatives."

"I don't remember."

"The meds were not enough. You kept screaming: *It's coming after me.* Over and over."

Despite my protestations, the charred memory reassembled in my mind.

I'm staring at blue snowflakes.

It's the pattern on my hospital gown. It reminds me of a Christmas card I had once bought for Melinda.

My eyes get heavy. No. I can't fall asleep.

Listen to me! It's coming after me!

Nothing is coming for you, sweetheart.

It's coming!

My back is itchy from stale sweat. Intolerable position caused by leather forcible restraints.

I need to move! I need to scratch! My back, my legs. My face! I need to scratch!

My mother asks someone to turn off the television – a baseball game is starting. A woman is signing the National Anthem. She's famous, but I can't think of her name.

The song cuts off. No one wants to sing for me.

Try to sleep, Daniel.

No! Don't leave! I think the words, but don't say them. My eyes have gone cold and they close.

No more talking, no more sound. I'm alone. Confined to a hot, sterile bed that sizzles against my skin.

No, someone remains. Someone is near me. I hear thick breathing. Rapid panting.

Sandy breath scrapes against my cheeks. Hair sticks against my forehead and nose. Steamy wet hair with a sweet and sour scent. It's not my hair. A strand tunnels its way into my ear. It tickles.

I open my eyes. Melinda's face is staring at me.

A runny, sallow, decomposing face.

And her eyes. Not her normal eyes, but two brilliant red dots, surrounded by a dozen little, black rings.

The eyes captivate me.

Melinda bends down to kiss me with scabby, cancerous lips.

Urine dribbles down my leg and I force my eyes shut.

It's coming after me! It's coming after me!

Racing footsteps clatter in the hallway and stomp into my room.

A hollow, synthetic voice speaks:

You're right, Danny. I am coming after you.

"That was fucking weird." Sky's voice shook my body, reeling my mind back into the break room.

I blasted my mother. "You had me tied down to a hospital bed!"

"I didn't know what else to do! It was only one night, Daniel. You were so sick and you wouldn't stop shouting or let the doctors help you. The following day your health improved, you calmed down, and you were untied. But you were frightened. You told me that Melinda had appeared at your bedside. An awful vision of her that sickened you to the core. You begged me to get you out of the hospital. I knew it was an incarnation so I immediately went to the doctors and persuaded them to release you. I took you to your apartment and you recovered. I thought you understood what had happened. Or so I had believed."

Salty phlegm coated my throat. Not all memories deserved to be resurrected. The voice I had heard coming out of Melinda's rotted face that night was the same voice I had heard from Mioten.

My mother was standing next to me. Holding my hands. I had no idea how long she had been touching me. "Please, Daniel. Let her go. Let Melinda go – she was not right for you. She was too much for you to take on."

I burst up from my seat, accidentally knocking my chair to the ground as I pulled away from my mother. "How can you say that? Don't tell me how I should feel about Melinda!" My shouts caused me to have another coughing fit.

Sky got up from her chair and stood next to my mother. "He sounds terrible. I think he needs a doctor."

My mother ignored her. "Melinda was far from perfect. She admitted to me that she conned you in helping her with her most difficult subject – Chemistry."

She stung me, injecting shame into my veins. "No. It was my decision to help her. You're wrong."

"Sky already had a Chemistry tutor. Some girl named Elsie. But she wanted you because you were better at the subject than anyone else. She wasn't like us, Daniel. She had a disorder. A clinical, mental disorder."

I was losing my anchor on what words I thought I could understand and trust. I started to shiver. "You're lying. You're a liar."

My comeback was weak. Was my mother a liar? I recalled Diana's remark at Melinda's sorority house. It was the end of Junior Year. Diana was one of Melinda's sorority sisters. She and Melinda had never gotten along, and I always thought it was due to a mix of conflicting egos and imagined jealousies. Diana was one of the reasons Melinda wanted to move out of the house for her senior year. It was an April night, and I was waiting in the lobby of the sorority house for Melinda to come down from her room. Diana sauntered past me. Raised her $7000 nose up to me and fluted out an offhand remark. *Everyone knows what Melinda did to you. How can you still be with her?*

I had dismissed her comment with an unwitty combo of an f-word and a b-word, but hadn't her ungainly question rattled me? Wasn't there something I could not accept?

I stifled my thoughts with another cough. "No. Melinda loved me."

"I'm not saying she didn't fall in love you which made her conceal her original intentions. Or hide the mistakes of her *cognitive* disorder. Her love for you made her death even more tragic."

"Stop lying to me! Melinda was perfect. Perfect for me."

"Really, Daniel?" Sky had asked that question. Her incredulous voice unsettled me. "No relationship is perfect. Or harmless. Alan had once been the sweetest person."

"Are you comparing Melinda to Alan? She was nowhere near my mother's age." I regretted my words immediately.

"Fuck you, Daniel! I was comparing Alan to you." Sky shoved her body away from the table and started pulling empty cardboard boxes down from the storage rack.

"Settle down, Daniel. Don't strike out at Sky."

"I didn't mean it, Sky. Sorry." She didn't look at me. She was breaking down the boxes into flat sheets.

My mother continued with her rebuke. "Your arrogance blinds you. You are wantonly conjuring up incarnations as a substitute for reality."

Sky finally perked her head up. "I think you're enjoying them."

I didn't want to repel Sky further but I couldn't help myself. "Actually, I love them! I love images of death and disembowelment. It makes me so happy to see myself as a decaying old man and an injured toddler. And it was so fucking great to finally get that chance to chat with Gayle a few minutes ago!"

"That's the problem, Daniel. Incarnations are usually consistent. For Sky, it was spiders. When I was younger, it was bees. As I got older, it became boys, probably in response to my guilt over leaving you when you were just twelve."

"Back to me? Back to blaming me for everything?"

"I'm not blaming you! Your incarnations have become random and erratic. I warned you, Daniel. You cannot allow them to spiral out of control."

"I love how the concept of an incarnation gets modified when the conditions vary! I was better at home with Dad. I've only gotten worse with you. I never--" I couldn't finish my sentence because a coughing fit had overtaken me again.

"You're making yourself sick, Daniel. You need to go to the hospital. Like before."

"No! I'm not sick!"

I looked at my hands which had been covering up my mouth. There were droplets of blood all over my palms. I quickly wiped them on my jeans, causing a violet streak on each leg.

"Just go see a doctor." Sky's fluttery voice signified concern, but it was drowned out by my mother.

"Your reluctance to let go of Melinda has completely subverted your mind. You've extended so much energy constructing walls around certain memories in order to protect yourself, but you've inadvertently made yourself worse. The gulf between your conscious and subconscious has become too great. The monsters have taken over your mind. And your body – you won't even accept that you've become physically ill again!"

"I'm not sick! It's not real!" I took a few steps away from the people whom I now considered traitors to the possible recovery of my life. My coughing resumed.

Sky's voice turned grim. "There's blood on your lips."

My mother took a few steps closer me. "Listen to me Daniel. Melinda's death was not your fault. It was her own doing. Caused by her own brain." My mother began to approach me.

"What?" I turned away as I began hacking up blood again.

"Please Daniel. You're coughing up blood. You need to go to the hospital."

"I won't go."

"I won't let you continue hurting yourself. I don't want you to end up like Melinda."

"You think I'm going to die?"

My mother reached for me. "No. Like you, I never would have believed that Melinda would lose complete control. I never believed that she would actually kill herself." My mother speared me with her last words.

Sky squealed at me. "Daniel! Did she? I didn't know that! I didn't know."

"Melinda died because of her medications! The Valerian root! Even the doctors said it was undetermined...."

"They had to list it as undetermined. Misdiagnosing her mental illness would've had severe repercussions--"

"She was not mentally ill!" My coughing intensified. "Why do you keep saying that?" Blood droplets shot out of my mouth.

"Because she wasn't like us, Daniel." My mother tried to grab me, but I pushed her away. I could taste my blood accumulating along the roof of my mouth. I was having an overstressed reaction to my mother's onslaught of lies.

"What have you done to me?"

I sped out of the storeroom. I didn't need a doctor. I needed to be alone. Away from my mother. Perhaps forever.

I stopped running when I reached the center of the store. Gayle was standing by the science book section. She was deliberately knocking books off the shelf, one by one, to the floor. She had transformed again, this time aging significantly. Her hair had turned completely ashen and her skin was charred, flakes of epidermis drifting off her face like burnt scraps of paper fluttering away from an open fire. Her dress barely clung to her morbidly underweight body. Words rattled out of her wilted mouth.

You're the blind one, Danny. These books won't help you. Nor will those bitches. They're only lost souls baffling you with bullshit. Do you understand what's happening?

It's coming. It's coming for you.

Shall I wait? Shall I dance? Dance with me Danny – I'm different like you!

Gayle eyes were inflamed, swollen orbs of brackish blood. Pink froth dribbled from her lips and was expelled by an onyx tongue. Gayle slinked over to the one of the couches and straddled the backrest, grinding her pelvis into the upholstery in a heinously seductive manner. Gayle moaned in disturbed pleasure.

Hurry up please its time!

My strength returned and my coughing abated. I took a bold step towards Gayle. Time to prove that this was just my abnormal brain chemistry toying with me and I could regain control.

"I'm fucking real. You're not."

Gayle vaulted off the couch and raced towards me. Even if she were merely a visualization, I held my ground and braced myself for impact.

Gayle's writhing face was the only thing I could see as she jumped on top of me, tackling me to the ground. Blood gushed from her eyes and chunks of flesh tore away from her cheeks and chin, exposing sinew and bone. She clawed and dug through my t-shirt with stake-like fingers and smothered my ears with lupine growls.

I tried to fight back but my flapping arms and legs only accelerated Gayle's assault. Her rancid teeth dug into the skin of my neck and I bleated like a calf being slaughtered. This was not an incarnation! This was real! My mind began to drift away, too shocked to process the severity, the certainty, of this attack. Gayle bit into me again, but this time I felt nothing. My pain and fear trickled away and I lapsed into unconsciousness.

When I regained my awareness, I found myself lying in a hospital bed, an IV attached to my right hand. I was dazed, still half-asleep and my entire body felt numb.

I wobbled my head back and forth. I was in a double bed patient room. The bed on my left was unoccupied. I wasn't sure of the time, but it was night and the television was on, volume muted, showing a news report.

I tried to sit up, but my legs wouldn't respond. I suppressed a momentary fear by confirming that I was not paralyzed. I could wiggle my fingers and toes, but the movements were modest and transitory.

I stared up at the TV. A weary-looking female news reporter in a flak jacket was giving a live broadcast from another conflict occurring in the Middle East. A village had been shelled by invading aircraft and the camera panned across a large swath of demolished brick and mortar homes. The news cast was such an exploitive circus as the live feed switched to an emotive news anchor and a bookworm analyst, each trying to appear more shocked than the other. Computerized graphics splashed theatrically across the screen, illustrating the extent of the carnage, and social media snippets in a never-ending bottom scroll highlighted the thrill-seeking audience's melodramatic approval. I'm sure in another instance I would have found a way to change the channel to something less sensationalized. But I continued to watch the high definition, highly demoralizing scenes. It helped keep my own torments in perspective.

A nurse entered the room, unsmiling, but showing some concern in her eyes. She had a fragile, unblemished face with olive skin and hair, possibly a Filipina. She looked barely eighteen years old, or more likely, blessed with youthful-looking genes.

"Hello, Danny. I'm Lorena, your nurse for this shift. How are you feeling?" Lorena approached my bed and began to diligently check my blood pressure and temperature.

It was a struggle at first to talk, but I managed to answer her with slurred, terse speech. "Why am I here?"

"Your mother brought you here because you had fainted. We think you have an infection, but your preliminary blood work was a bit inconclusive. Have you had flu symptoms?

"No. Just coughing."

"Your mother mentioned that. How long have you been coughing?"

"A few hours. I didn't feel sick."

"You might be suffering from exhaustion. We also took care of your bites."

"My what?"

"You have two large bite marks on your neck and a partial one on your shoulder. We bandaged them up and gave you a tetanus shot as a precaution."

I struggled to lift my left arm to my face. My fingertips still lacked sensation, but I could detect the cotton dressing on my neck. "I can't move."

"You were acting very restless so we gave you a strong sedative. You might feel groggy for a few more hours. Try to rest and get some sleep." Lorena shut off the TV with the remote attached to my bed.

"What time is it?"

"A little before midnight."

"My mother?"

"Your mother went home – she'll be back in the morning. Try to relax. You have this whole room to yourself. If you need anything you can call us with that button."

The nurse pointed to a blue button on the remote that had a white cross. She finally smiled at me then exited the room.

I wasn't tired. I reached for the remote and turned the TV back on. The screen showed only static even after I flipped through several different stations. I shut it back off and closed my eyes.

I wasn't trying to force myself to sleep but to think. What was happening to me? Was the attack real? Or was I getting worse? I thought I had been feeling better from my interaction with Sky, but she had turned on me and now I was lying in a hospital bed. My life had returned to its muddied and desperate condition.

No. It had been real. No self-made delusion, visualization, or incarnation could cause bite marks on my neck. The demon was real. My father had been correct all along.

I was being attacked by a demon that was beyond any form of logic. It was becoming more dangerous and unpredictable. And it wanted to devour me. Like it had Melinda. She had not committed suicide. She did not have a mental disorder. Why was my mother lying to me?

It didn't matter. I was approaching things in the wrong manner. I needed to stop my quest of finding a rational understanding, a fruitless probe for a scientific solution. I was in battle with an unrelenting evil. I needed to concentrate on finding a way to escape, to retreat to an ordinary existence where my greatest concern would be something trite like surviving commuter traffic or complaining about a supervisor at work. I needed to find a way to survive.

My prevaricating mother was right about only one thing. Melinda's death had overpowered my life and weakened me. My downfall, my pain, both physical and psychological, and the demon – all of it had been triggered after Melinda's death.

I missed her too much and it was killing me. I was giving the demon the exact conditions it wanted. I had to let her go.

I needed to focus on something else. Someone else.

Sky. She had upset me in her unwavering allegiance to my mother. But I couldn't ignore that my time alone with her had been when I felt the most capable and the most level-headed. It was only when Sky was with my mother that she failed me. Sky could never replace Melinda, but she was the only thing that could help me discover a new sense of normalcy and happiness.

I opened my eyes. From my peripheral vision, I saw a figure sitting on the bed next to me. I forced myself to turn my head to see who or what would be my next confrontation.

My heart rolled. It was Melinda. She was naked and stunning. Her bare skin stoked life into me and I was reacquainted with how tantalizingly rich and alluring she could be. Her skin was so vibrant it appeared to shimmer, as if her warm cells had transmuted into stars. She sat on the edge of the bed, her silky legs elegantly crossed, and her bare feet swaying in a playful, teasing motion. Her lusty smile submerged my pain with serene memories. Tears paraded down my cheeks as she spoke to me.

"Danny, I miss you so much. Maybe we can find a way to start over again? Get another chance? Let's go back to the University, back to Perkins Hall. I want to meet you again. Learn from you again. Fall in love again. I need that. I need you."

I tried to respond but I couldn't speak. I couldn't move. I hoped Melinda could recognize how I was staring at her. Perpetually content. Infinitely secure.

Her smile degraded and her feet stopped swaying. "Something's wrong, Danny. My head hurts. I'm getting cold. Please come hold me."

I tried moving my left arm. It edged only a fraction of inch on top of the bed sheet. I rocked my head back and forth, the only part of my body that I could budge.

"Danny, I'm shaking. What's happening? I'm scared." Melinda wrapped her arms around her own body as small tremors buffeted her body.

I was desperate to move and get words out of my mouth. Melinda deserved a response! My jaw began to quiver and saliva fizzed at my lips.

Melinda's extended one of her hands towards me, her fingers flexing, grasping for something other than air. "Don't you love me anymore?"

I shut my bleary eyes, focusing all my hope on my mouth, and finally my lips parted to allow one strained, shaky word vent out of me.

"YES!"

I reopened my eyes. Melinda was gone. My lungs deflated. I had been too slow to speak. She had left me again.

My heart skipped faster. I wanted it to stop beating. I needed her to return. I needed some form of consolation, otherwise my tentative existence was going to reach its ultimate tensile strength. I frantically pushed the button for the nurse. I could not be alone anymore.

A voice sounded from the speaker on the remote, "Yes, this is the nurse's station – do you need something?"

I let out a mournful howl. A few seconds later, Lorena stepped into the room. She gasped as she looked past me and stared over at the adjacent bed.

I followed her gaze. Sitting on the edge of the bed, much like Melinda had been doing, was me. Naked. My skin was jaundiced and scaly. My chest, arms and legs were bombarded with a motley of purple and black bruises. Gooey blood leached out of the uncovered bite marks on my neck as well as a fresh cut on the top of my right hand. This was no incarnation – Lorena could see it!

Lorena tried to cast an angry face, but her soft features made it appear disingenuous. "Get back into bed! Did you rip out your IV?" Lorena started coughing while my doppelganger began to snicker. Did she not see me? The real me, still lying in bed?

Lorena took a step forward, but her coughing grew more intense and she had to stop to compose herself. My doppelganger picked up the remote attached to the other bed and turned on the second television set in the room. The sitcom *Friends* crackled to life, with its signature theme song playing. Lorena tried to speak, but her words were blocked by her unrelenting coughs. The volume to the television grew louder, drowning out Lorena's soggy barks. She dropped to her knees and faced the floor, blood speckles spraying from her mouth and spotting the immaculate, white-tiled floor. The overly happy *Friends* melody jarred disturbingly with the scene of Lorena lurching over, coughing up blood.

From my own bed, I pushed the nurse call button repeatedly as the repulsive, naked version of me got off the bed and approached Lorena. It turned its head to me and uttered a few disturbing words.

I'll be there for you, Danny. Get it? Come on, let's get rid of this one.

It was the demon, pretending to be me. More distressing, it was going to attack an innocent stranger. I continued to rapidly press the nurse call button. The unfolding events were energizing me to the point where I could arc my neck and shoulders off the bed. Why wasn't anyone else responding? Couldn't they hear the alarm or the blaring television? Wasn't there anyone else in the hospital? We needed help!

Lorena looked up and stared directly at the demon. She tried to crawl away from it, but the demon reached out and grabbed a chunk of her hair. Lorena screamed and twisted herself away, leaving the demon with the clump of hair in its hand. With one final effort, Lorena, rose to her feet and scampered out the door.

The door to my room shut and the television turned off. The demon showed me the strands of Lorena's hair in its hand. It balled up the hair in a closed fist and when it reopened its hand, the hair had deteriorated into dust. The demon blew the dust off its hand and onto my bed.

I showed you a fool in a handful of dust. Aren't you proud of me?

In two inhumanly rapid steps, the demon slid over to me and thrust its hands on my shoulders, slamming my body back down.

*This will be our home. Our home of sickness and death.
Let's be good hosts and welcome it when it arrives. It's almost
here!*

My finger kept pressing the nurse call button as the
demon's icy fingers latched onto my upper arm. It lowered its
face closer to me, my own disfigured face, until its nose
touched my own. Our skin started to merge, its face bleeding
into my own. A deep, burning sensation pierced through my
arm where the demon's fingers were wrapped around me like
a tourniquet. It hissed a loathsome refrain into my ear.

*Until tomorrow...sleep with me. Sleep with me and dream,
my sweet.*

Sadly, my body complied. My heart rate and breathing
decelerated, and I drifted into sleep.

It was daylight when I reawakened. I was still in bed, in
the same hospital room, and I appeared to be alone. That is,
until my sluggish eyes regained enough focus to see my
mother standing in the doorway to my room, peering at me
with a timorous smile.

A fierce-looking nurse pushed past my mother. With a
bulbous frame and sagging hefty breasts, a face of ironed-on
wrinkles and hair packed with stony bristles, she appeared
both intimidating and overdue for retirement. My mother
followed the nurse into the room and they approached my bed
simultaneously.

My mother spoke first. "Good morning, Daniel. This is
Olivia – your nurse. She's not going to hurt you. There's no
reason to attack her."

I stared at the burly nurse as she attached a new bag to
the IV attached to me. "Why would I attack her? Where's
Lorena? Is it not her shift?"

The nurse snarled at me then spoke tersely to my mother.
"He should be in restraints – sedatives aren't enough. You're
lucky Lorena is one of the kindest and sweetest people alive.
She felt sorry for him." Olivia increased the drip flow of my
IV. "Sleep and dream, my sweet."

My mother tried to placate the scowling nurse with a nod
and gentle pat on the shoulder, but the act only made both of
them uneasy. Olivia exited, grumbling incoherently. My

mother extended her hand and rubbed her fingers through my hair. "It'll be OK, Daniel. You'll feel better soon."

I didn't believe her. This home of sickness and death was not where I needed to be. Olivia had spoken some of the same words as the demon had. Could Olivia be the demon? Could it appear as anyone? I didn't want to uncover the answer. I needed to get out of the hospital. I reached up with both my hands, grabbed my mother's shoulders, and begged her one last time for help – to be the mother who would never give up on her son.

"Please! Get me out of here!"

My mother ripped herself away from me as if she were repulsed by my request.

"I'm sorry, Daniel. I can't do that."

I sunk back into the hospital bed, the dank, white sheets welcoming me like the spumy, milk-tipped waves of an impending oceanic grave. It was over. My mother's second chance with me was over.

EIGHT

After my mother's damnable refusal, I was swallowed back
up by sleep, exploited by the sedative that Olivia had unfairly
injected into my IV. When I awoke, my mother, unfortunately,
was still in my room, sitting in one of the two orchid colored
urethane chairs the hospital had provided for guests. I tried
to take in a deep breath, but the air made me gag. It was
unctuous, acidic – the oxygen had double bonded with the
exfoliated carbon being shed from the dead and dying. I
didn't make eye contact with my mother, even after she stood
up from her chair and watched over my prone body like a
harebrained minister considering an opportune moment to
begin last rites.

When she decided to fling a few anointing words at me,
she said she was going to find my doctor and would return
soon with an update on my condition. Her words recoiled off
me and stuck up against the ceiling, a knobby surface of
ridged white rectangles, dotted with dozens of miniature
bumps and holes. Two grooved plastic panels broke up the
ceiling pattern, housing damp fluorescent light that floated
down into the room. I wanted to float too. Float up to the

ceiling, let my skin congeal with the panels, and allow my cells to dissolve into the patterned dots.

My mother trotted out of my sight and I reacquainted myself with my surroundings. The patient bed next to me was still empty. The two mounted television sets were turned off; the remote for mine had been placed out of my reach on a portable dining tray. Behind my head, against the wall, was an overhead reading light, and to the left, above a small storage cabinet, were several redundant connections, sockets for life-saving equipment, including my IV which was plugged into one of the open slots. A frosted window at the end of my room (similar to the one I had seen in the police interrogation, only twice as large), seemed to indicate that it was late afternoon. Verdant sun rays parsed through the frost, splitting open a pair of drab argent curtains, and consuming some of the fluorescent glow. No one (or nothing) entered my room, although it seemed extremely busy out in the hallway with dozens of people – nurses, doctors and other hospital employees – zooming past my open door. I heard multiple pages over the intercom system calling for certain staff and relaying various codes which were undecipherable to me, but from my perspective it appeared that the activity wasn't routine. Curiously, I hadn't seen any other patients or visitors amidst the swarm of activity in the hall. I was alone in this purgatory.

Minutes, perhaps an hour, passed before my mother stepped back into my room. She clasped her hands together and covered her mouth as if politely covering a yawn, or more likely, trying to obscure an exasperated groan over my condition. I remembered I didn't want to look at her so I cast my eyes back up to the ceiling. The panels appeared to swell and descend. I wouldn't have to float – the ceiling was coming down to me.

"Feeling better, Daniel?" My mother eased up to the side of my bed.

"Great." My eyes became listless, blubbery, as I tried to count the approaching dots in the ceiling. When would my mother realize I did not want to see her?

"I spoke to Dr. Molker, your attending physician. You have a serious infection in your lungs. Worse than last time. They want to increase your antibiotics and keep you under watch. They've scheduled you for an X-ray tomorrow."

"Great."

I hadn't coughed since Sky's bookstore. In fact, the only signs of sickness were coming from outside my room in the hallway. Barking coughs gushed from the swarming hospital staff like the exaggerated guffaws from a canned laugh track. I thought back to the nurse, Lorena, coughing as the demon began to attack her. Was this illness a product of the demon? Did it mean that the demon now had a greater effect on the external world? How far could it reach?

"You will get better, Daniel. You're going to recover and the hospital is exactly where you need to be."

The ceiling stopped moving, and snapped back to its original position. I forced myself to engage my mother. "Stop lying."

"I care about you, Daniel."

"I'm not sick. Sick is out there – can't you hear it?" I picked up my arm and pointed out into the hall. The huffs and wheezes that shot through the open door had to be battering my mother's ears as much as my own.

"You'll get the proper treatment here, Daniel. For everything. This is a teaching hospital and the doctors are among the best."

"You were never going to help me."

"I was selfish to think that I could help you alone. The things I did only made you worse."

"Uh-huh." I finally found something on which my mother and I could agree.

"I have another warning for you, Daniel. I think you need to hear that your friend Trent is back in the hospital."

"That's too bad."

"Your father told me that Trent had an aneurysm yesterday. His outlook isn't good."

"You spoke with Dad? I want to talk with him." The news about Trent was immaterial. How much were my parents still talking with each other? Why did they always keep me out of their loop?

"His death is going to look so inevitable in hindsight."

It was likely that death was what Trent wanted all along and it was better for everyone that he was gone.

The whirr of a running motor bellowed over my thoughts. At first, I thought it was a hospital janitor, operating a floor buffer, but as the sound intensified, I recognized it as the engine to a vacuum cleaner. I spotted it on the floor, next to the other bed, running by itself.

"What is that?"

"What is what, Daniel?"

I stared at the vacuum until the tiled floor turned into carpet, and the hospital room turned into my bedroom. I was back in my father's house, remembering everything that occurred between me and Trent. Between me and Talia.

Casting butterfly kisses against the Berber loops of the carpet in my bedroom. I was lying on my stomach, still drunk after passing out for some unguarded moment of time. I rolled over and stared up at the bare feet hanging off my bed. Talia's dirty, cracked, calloused feet. I could hear her humming the melody of an unfamiliar lullaby.

The fucking best!

The exclamation startled me. It had been voiced by a man, not Talia. Trent's face appeared, slithering in between Talia's feet. He kissed her toes and when his eyes caught mine, he smiled widely.

Having a good time, bro?

Trent belched and blew it in my direction. I fought off a queasy wave.

She was here for me.

Trent chuckled.

How generous do you think I am? Don't be a bitch – she's still my girl. Or wait...wait, did you think...did you fall for her?

Gutless laughter spewed from Talia and she slapped her feet against Trent's face. Another wave roiled my belly.

I don't want you here, Trent.

Fuck you, Danny. I'm done doing you favors. You want me to go? Fine. We're done here. Enjoy your sheets.

I gnashed my teeth together to remain silent. Trent's lumpy, over-nourished naked body bounced off the bed and he started putting on his clothes. Talia slid her cosmetically-enhanced nude body off the bed and stood over me. She spat out an order.

You can get back to cleaning now.

I swallowed down some regurgitated bile. I slinked away from Talia and crept into the hallway. I turned on the vacuum I had pushed out of my room. I waited a few seconds then turned it back off. Another two seconds and I turned it back on. I couldn't stop. Off. On. Off.

Fuck, stop!

Trent was fully dressed and he shook an empty bottle of whiskey at me like he wanted to throw it at my head.

Just stop it, Danny. Get it together. You're beyond help. I tried to make you happy, sharing my girl with you, but you rather be fucking miserable.

Talia, still naked, went down to the floor, onto her hands and knees. She crawled up to Trent, curled her back into his legs, and croaked out a meow.

She winked at me.

You tasted real good, Danny-boy. Really, you did.

Please leave.

I turned the vacuum back on.

Look, babe. All he wanted to do was show me these.

Talia grabbed my Physics notebook that was lying on the floor next to the bed and waved it at Trent.

So bored I made him call you.

She opened it up and rummaged through Melinda's heart notes.

My Melinda? Wasn't that her name?

I yanked the vacuum's plug out of the outlet and shouted at her.

Go! Get out of here!

Talia ignored my outburst and read one of the heart notes aloud. She feigned throwing up.

I shouted again.

Going!

Talia stuck the note she had read into her mouth and began crawling towards me.

Going!

She chewed the note with exaggerated gusto.

Going!

When she reached me, Talia opened up her mouth to confirm that she had swallowed it.

Gone. I just ate your girlfriend. She's gone, baby.

GET THE FUCK OUT OF HERE!

My effeminate scream shook tears out of my eyes despite my attempt to dam up my humiliation with my hands.

What's wrong? Don't you want to fuck me now?

Talia stuck her hands down into the crotch of my jeans.

Get away from me!

Trent shouted from the room.

Leave the kid alone! Don't touch him anymore.

Talia pulled her hand out of my pants and stuck a finger in her mouth.

I lied. You taste awful.

She wiped her wet finger across my forehead, cutting me with her jagged fake nail. She crawled over my body and continued down the hallway in an exaggerated naked cat crawl.

Put your damn clothes on!

Trent called out from inside my room as he bundled up Talia's clothes in his arms. I closed my eyes and wiped my tears away and for a hallowed moment, nothing existed.

When I heard Trent's voice, I reopened my eyes. He was standing over me, clutching Talia's clothes as well as the empty whiskey bottle.

Aw, I'm shit-full of sorry, bro. Another accidental civilian casualty. You know how it is. Let's forget all this shit. Get back to basics. I'm still down to grab some drinks. Lemme know, OK? Recycle?

Trent waved the bottle in my face.

I plugged the vacuum cleaner back into the socket and turned it on. Trent walked away from me shaking his head. I squirmed back into my room until my forehead hit the bottom corner of my bed frame. Blood dug its way out of my skin. I didn't care. I fell back onto my stomach. Let my face fall flat into the Berber loops. The autumn sun drifting into my room singed my skin, as a hollow voice, drenched in static, whispered into my ear:

Don't worry, Danny. I'll take care of them for you.

I smiled and started to laugh.

It hurt so much I couldn't stop laughing.

My mother had one hand in my hair, and another caressing my shoulder. Her hands dredged me out of my memories.

"Don't touch me, mother."

"You slipped away again."

I had imagined the demon attacking me, taking the form of Talia. Speaking with Melinda's voice. I had simply been too ashamed to admit what had actually occurred. But the

193

demon's presence had been with me, waiting until they had left to speak with me. Had the demon attacked Trent and Talia on my behalf? That didn't make any sense. I must have imagined the demon's voice too. Or maybe the whole thing really was an incarnation. I was flip-flopping on my beliefs in demons and incarnations and the equivocation was crucifying my brain. I had to stay focused. Focused on what I knew to be true.

"Trent was not my friend."

"Did you remember something about him?"

"Irrelevant."

My mother reclaimed her seat on one of the guest chairs. "I know how difficult it can be to open up and share certain things. Personal failures. Shameful events."

Her sympathy was a ruse. She no longer wanted to help me. "Irrelevant."

"I've tried to forget things myself. I tried to forget the first time I noticed you were an Incarnator."

"The day you left me and Dad."

"No, Daniel. Your first incarnation. Out on the beach. During your father's forty-sixth birthday. You were so afraid of the ocean."

"You upset Dad. There was no incarnation."

"Remember? Floating in the water?"

"No."

"Ducking your head into the ocean waves."

"I don't like the ocean."

"You never did. That's why your father became angry with me. He didn't want me to force you into the water, but I thought you'd be fine." My mother started blinking rapidly and I began counting the blinks.

"I was fine." *Three blinks.*

"Yes, you were! For a while, you were happy. Even held your breath for over ten seconds. Then you started splashing. Gulping seawater. Said you saw a snake. Floating next to you. Wrapping around your leg. You said it was an anaconda – your incarnations used to be so simple, based on silly movies. I didn't take them seriously. I calmed you down, helped you back to shore, and took your mind off it all by playing Frisbee golf with you." *Eleven blinks.*

"Your lies are repetitive." *Three blinks.*

194

"Why would I lie, Daniel? Don't you think I'd rather be the perfect mother?" *Five blinks.*

I shrugged my shoulders. *Two blinks.*

"I didn't tell your father about your incarnation. He said I was badgering you, acting like my mother. Your grandmother. I told him to stop acting like he knew who that woman was. I didn't even know her. She was dead and forgotten." *Nine blinks.*

"Shifting the blame onto another dead woman?" My mother closed her eyes and I stopped counting.

"Maturity and intelligence are not correlated, Daniel."

"For who?"

My mother stood up and started pacing. She was becoming blurry to me, like rediscovering a favorite childhood book and seeing nothing more than a myopic story.

"I overindulged you when you were younger. Slathered you with a multitude of intellectual stimuli. Downplayed your incarnations. I wanted you to be different. But nature trumps nurture."

"I am different. That's why you left."

"No! I left because I needed an answer! I was tired of trying to forget what had happened to me. I needed to know what being an Incarnator meant. And what it meant if you were becoming one too."

"You didn't figure anything out. We're not the same. I am not like you."

"I never wanted you to be." My mother slumped back down in the guest chair. She maintained one clear characteristic: the uneven wrinkles that lined her forehead. Crooked, aged lines that I had noticed before, but not fully appreciated. Those lines were the clearest things about her – her common, irregular imperfections. That was her legacy.

My mother continued. "I've always been tender with you. I've always accepted you. I never yanked your hair because you had turned on a curling iron. Slapped you across the mouth so hard your lipstick merged with your bleeding gums. Forced you to take scalding hot showers because you used too much perfume. Get laughed at continuously because you wouldn't stop talking about the bees – the bees on your armoire, the bees on your best dress, the bees on your bathroom mirror. Your grandmother was cruel, Daniel. Very cruel."

I was growing weary of her voice. "Can you hand me the TV remote?"

"I am not cruel! Despite everything she did to me, I am not my mother. I am not cruel. Do you know what it's like to be blamed for the crippling stomach pain that your grandmother ignored until it was too late? I would never be that cruel, Daniel."

My mother was trying to elicit empathy from me as if she were the one trapped in a hospital bed. "Interesting story. Is it true?"

My mother rose to her feet. Her eyes had become shrunken pits. Her mouth, a swollen pustule. "I never wanted to share my life with you. I want to change. I want to try and give you what I couldn't before."

"It doesn't matter."

"Please, Daniel. Let me try."

"You don't understand. I don't care about you anymore."

My mother's body was trembling. She turned as if to exit, but stopped. Stepped closer to me. Leaned into me, as close as possible without touching the bed, dropped a feathery kiss on my forehead, and darted out of my room without looking back. It was the first kiss I had received from her since I had arrived and it was a kiss that someone would give to a waxy body lying in state.

I still loved my mother, but I pitied her. My words were not meant to be mean. I wasn't cruel either. I had only wanted her to realize that she didn't have all the answers.

Her words did have an effect on me, though. She made me feel disconnected from the outside world's existence, as if the reality that guided most people's lives was an automatic program of a simple ruled algorithm, an artificial construct that ordered up two part laughs and one part tears, and the truth, my truth, lay in the complex, sullen and provincial cloud that both rotted and nourished my family. Maybe fear and anguish were the only honest rulers of my family's lives. I was beginning to accept the certainty of having a dismal fate, and my anxiety about the demon was replaced by a consoling sensation of placidity. I could grow accustomed to misfortune's smothering hands.

No. No, I would not succumb to quiet, mindless horror. I needed to reenter the naïve world inhabited by people who would rather accept boredom than wisdom. I needed to live in the fantasy of monotonous, predictable expectations that everyone else had no problem defining as real success. I needed to get out of the hospital and find a way to live a life no more exciting or grandiose than the chemical engineer career I had envisioned for myself. That would be the only way I could extricate myself from the malignant demon that was ruthlessly attacking me and everyone unfortunate enough to be near me.

It sounded like a good plan. But there was something I wanted more. I wanted to see Melinda again.

The beautiful vision of her, sitting naked in the adjacent bed, continued to reverberate inside me. Her face, her legs, her skin, all had been too wonderful to be associated with the demon. My mother had told me that Melinda hadn't been right for me. That she had a *disorder*, a mental disease, an incurable perversion that segregated her from the rest of us. I couldn't believe my mother had uttered those words. Melinda may not have been as perfect as the image shielded in my mind, but she was the most decent, miraculous thing to ever happen to me. She had made me happy. Why would I ever let that feeling go?

I tuned out my surroundings until the sunrays filtering through the window began to splinter and fade. Night was approaching. Night was confirmation that I would be staying in the hospital another day, and I needed a distraction. I stretched my body over the edge of my bed, and with the tips of my fingers, grabbed the remote control from the dining tray and turned on the television. The major channels were showing nothing but the grisly scenes of the Middle East conflict unfolding. This time it was too discomforting to watch. I kept changing the channels until I landed on *Friends* – fortunately, not while its opening theme song was playing. I shut the television back off. This wasn't the distraction I needed. I needed someone to talk to.

As if summoned by a vengeful god, Olivia thundered into my room. She was directing two male orderlies who were transporting a patient on a gurney. I was getting a roommate. An elderly man, wheezing loudly, with a shriveled head and a concave nose, his nostrils punctured by an oxygen tube. I asked Olivia what was wrong with him. She didn't answer

197

me. I followed up with a question about my own condition. She still ignored me.

As the orderlies wheeled the gurney past me, they smacked into the bottom of my bed, jarring my entire body. I expected an apology, but instead, one of the orderlies coughed on my bed without covering his mouth. The white sheet that draped over my feet was tagged with a few droplets of blood. This hospital was a sewage pit.

"What is wrong with all of you?" I didn't expect an answer and I didn't receive one.

They dumped the old man on the second bed and Olivia drew the privacy curtain completely around him. She and the two orderlies exited without even a casual glance at me.

Wind whistled from the elderly patient's mouth like a deflating balloon. If I didn't have a lung infection already, I would soon be getting one.

I needed to get myself discharged from the hospital. If I did have an infection, I could simply pop some antibiotic pills and be on my way. Sign any necessary paperwork and find a cab to take me back to my mother's apartment – just to collect my things since neither of us would be pleased to see each other. I would go back to my father's house. I had some money and I might be able to convince my father to buy me a bus ticket. It wasn't much of a plan, but I was pleased with the cogent line of thought. It was time to get moving.

I sat up in bed, energized by my new scheme. I pulled my legs out from underneath the covers and dangled them over the edge of the bed. The movement made me a little dizzy, and it also awakened my bladder – when was the last time I had used the bathroom? My first goal was to walk to the restroom.

I wheeled the IV stand closer to me. I had seen many movies characters yank their IV line out of their arms as they escaped out of a hospital, but I couldn't stomach that – it looked like a painful and messy process. Plus the needle had been inserted into a vein in my hand, an indelicate entry point. As soon as I found someone trustful and competent to assist me, I would get them to remove the IV. I took deliberative care to ensure the tubing wouldn't get entangled as my feet made their way to the floor.

My roommate started to retch and I thought about calling the nurse station to get someone back in the room to help

198

him. But the urge to relieve myself was growing. I downplayed his spurting, labored gasps; he could suffer for a few minutes.

When my feet hit the smooth, arid tile, I almost retched onto myself. I wasn't as strong as I thought. Weakness distorted my vision and the room began to spin. I almost teetered over, but managed to breathe slowly and take one step forward. The onrush of blood began to abate and I steadied myself. I tested out my injured ankle. It didn't hurt, and I was thankful at least something positive had carried over from Sky's bookstore. If I wanted to travel further than a few feet, I would have to take the IV pump with me. I grabbed the pump's electrical cord and started to tug, trying to remove the plug from the wall socket in a careless, impatient fashion, akin to a three-year-old brat. Each pull on the cord squeezed my bladder and squirts of urine shot into my hospital gown. Finally, I pulled the cord free and the IV pump beeped loudly as a sensor indicated that the machine was now using battery-power. I shuffled as quickly as I could to the restroom, dragging the IV stand behind me like a dog, heading to a hydrant, carrying its own leash. I closed the restroom door behind me when I realized I had to do more than pee.

Exiting the restroom, with patience and comfort reclaimed, I became unraveled by a chaotic scene that had ignited around my elderly roommate.

The privacy curtain had fallen to the floor. A Hispanic doctor sporting excessive makeup and ornately coiffed hair was performing resuscitative efforts on the old man, while a stoic Olivia and two stressed-out nurses (a pudgy man with a goatee and an Indian woman donning thick framed glasses) surrounded the bed, shouting out the patient's condition from the flashing digital readings of various medical devices. A gloomy African American teenage girl, dressed like one of the student volunteers I used to see at the University's hospital, was standing a few feet away from the bed, reading a passage from the Bible. This student's recitation jumbled incomprehensibly in my ears, until I recognized the words from the Nicene Creed. Only she was reading it in reverse.

"End no have will kingdom his and dead the and living the judge to glory in again come will he Father..."

The girl stopped praying. Actually, her mouth was still moving, only the sound of her voice had ceased. Had she uttered the words out of order or had she been praying in silence and my mind had reverted to its untrustworthy state? I snuck closer to girl. She took a step away from me. I was barging into a private crisis. I took a step back, but returned my attention the elderly man. A tube had been jammed down his throat. His chin, his neck, and the pearly white sheets that had been pulled to his feet were all splattered with blood. His prospects did not look good. I shouldn't have delayed contacting the nurse's station. The praying girl's voice returned, juddering my ears with her cranked up volume. She was completing the prayer, reciting it in its proper order.

"We look for the resurrection of the dead, and the life of the world to come. Amen."

The girl closed up the Bible and turned to me. "I said, Amen!"

I stared at her.

She pointed at the door. "Leave!"

I complied with her bizarre request because she had unnerved me. No matter. I needed to continue with my plan to leave the hospital. I would find someone unpreoccupied to help me with my discharge.

I slipped into the hospital hallway and tried to figure out a direction to take. My room number was 428. I assumed that meant I was on the fourth floor of the hospital. There was another patient room to my left and that had number 426. I opted to go left and follow the decreasing room numbers even though I was unsure where I needed to go to discharge myself.

As I made my way down the building wing, past the other patient rooms – 424, 422, and 420 – I heard a cacophony of hacks, coughs, and groans as if everyone were succumbing to the same chest-borne illness the elderly man had. Was there some sort of flu epidemic taking place? Why were there no other hospital staff parading down the hall? The hazy white sheen of the walls and floor, amplified by blaring ceiling lights made it feel as if I were walking through a giant PVC pipe, built to channel the flushed remains of human-sized effluvium.

I strolled past the nurse station. It was empty. Was the hospital short-staffed? Or were they all attending to critical patients like the sick man in my room? Across the station I could see another hallway, an exact match of the one I was on. It was occupied by another solitary walker – a janitor, pushing a trash cart and wearing a surgical mask and bulky blue rubber gloves. I recognized the symbol on his trash receptacle. It appeared he was stuck doing the lowly job of collecting bio-hazardous waste from the patient rooms.

A page went off on the intercom system. "Code blue. Dr. Panetti please report to four-two-eight. Code blue. Dr. Panetti: four-two-eight." Was that a phone extension or were they signaling my room number?

I spotted a sign indicating the elevator location. There might be someone to assist me down at the hospital lobby or admitting section, but since I was carting around an IV and wearing only a hospital gown, I thought it best to refrain from going to a less private, and less sterile, open area.

As I reached the end of the hallway, I saw that that my path would merely wrap around and I would be walking back up the second hallway. I wasn't accomplishing anything if I continued with this aimless journey. I needed to find someone who could help me. I decided to go back to my room to wait for the staff to finish with the old man. He didn't look like he was going to last very long. Before I could turn back, a female patient ambled around the curve of the hallway, heading directly to me, carting her own IV. She looked about seventy years old with rumpled, amber skin, indicative of either a lifetime of chronic smoking or ultraviolet radiation. Her greyish brown hair was half-flat, half-frazzled like she had just woken up from hours of sleep. As she plodded closer to me, the fuzzy pink slippers on her feet squeaked and squawked along the floor while her hospital gown kept parting open, revealing her tarry, flabby flesh. Each of her short, heavy steps caused her face to tighten and wince as if she was in significant pain.

She stopped in front of me with a growling remark. "What are you doing here?"

Her abrasive tone startled me. "Why do you care? I don't need this."

"You can't walk around like that!"

"Like what?"

She pointed down to my bare feet. "Against the rules!"

"Doesn't matter. I'm leaving."

"Why you pushing that around?" Her accusatory finger was now aimed at my IV stand.

"It needs to be removed."

The old woman scoffed. "What? It ain't attached to nothing!"

I looked at my right hand. It was puffy and a little bloody, covered by white netting that looked like a wrist glove, but she was correct. The IV was no longer attached to my vein and the strip of tape that had bound the IV tube to my arm was dangling loose. Had the needle fallen out of its own accord while I was walking?

As I followed the path of tubing from the IV to find the needle, the old woman coughed up a blackened piece of phlegm and spit it out on her patient gown. She smiled, exposing a missing front tooth.

"Extra chunky. Just for you."

She laughed for a second then started to cough. I spun away from the gross hag.

The old woman cast out a plea. "Don't you love me?"

I froze, remembering the words of Melinda from the night before. Coincidence or not, the words cut open my courage, and thwarted my confidence that I'd be able to leave the hospital. I pushed the worthless IV stand in front of me and began scooting my unsettled legs back to my room.

"Ooh! Sweetie's givin' me some ass!"

I glanced back at the old woman. She lifted up her gown, flashing her corpulent stomach and her gristly, stony haired pubis.

I scrambled back to my room, trying my best to keep my own gown closed and ignoring the repulsive mix of raspy laughs and wet coughs behind me.

When I reached my room, I couldn't get past the doorway. There were now twelve hospital employees, doctors, nurses, specialists, and who knows who else, barely distinguishable from one another since they all were wearing yellow surgical gowns, masks, and rubber gloves. The young girl who had been praying was now sitting on one of the visitor's chairs, her legs tucked into her chest, sobbing softly.

I edged inside the room, curious. Wary. The team of twelve were not moving as they surrounded the bed of the elderly patient. They were simply staring down at his still body, a body ravaged with blood painted tubes, bags, paddles, wires, and gauze – the clumsy, tortuous instruments used to sustain life. The old man had to be dead, but the calcified vigil over his body did not make any sense. I snuck up to the crying girl and spoke gently.

"What's going on?"

The twelve workers around the bed all snapped their heads at me. Their engorged eyes seemed to indicate I had interrupted something of serious intent. The young girl stopped crying. She got up from the chair and handed me the Bible.

"You shouldn't have come back."

The girl exited the room as one nurse pealed herself away from the group and approached me. It was Olivia. She slammed her face in front of mine and pulled down her surgical mask.

"What are you doing here?"

"I'm going to lie back down." I turned towards my bed.

"No, you're not."

"Is it not safe to be here?"

"Go back to your room. You don't belong here."

Before I could ask for clarification, Olivia grabbed my right arm with one of her blood-stained, gloved hands. The Bible I was still holding tumbled to the ground. "Did you pull out your IV again?"

"No. It fell out while I was walking."

Olivia located the needle at the end of the IV tube. "This isn't something to fool around with." She slid off the netting around my hand and buried the needle harshly back into another vein. I cried out from the ensuing pain.

I tucked my hand to my chest as if it had been broken. "What the hell? You can't just jab me like that!"

"I don't have time for you. Go back to your room."

"This is my room!"

Olivia forcibly began to escort me out the door. "This is room 428. Geriatrics. On the fourth floor. Your room is 328. I don't even know how you got up here. The security guard at the elevator should've stopped you."

Although I was confused and weakened, Olivia displayed unusual strength, pushing me easily back out into the hallway. She yanked me down the hall by my newly stuck arm, and I struggled to keep up with her pace. Blood droplets formed where she had callously reinserted the needle. My vain throbbed and I could see it rolling under my skin as I walked.

203

Olivia relinquished her vice grip on my arm when she stopped to deposit her soiled gloves into a bio-hazard waste container. My arm was smeared with blood – an unsanitary mixture of my own and the residue from Olivia's gloved hand. I hoped that whatever had killed the old man had not penetrated into my system as well.

"This hospital is making me sick!"

Olivia ignored my outburst and resumed propelling me forward, grasping my IV stand instead of my arm to goad me into compliance. There was still no one in the hallway – the janitor was gone and the deranged older woman had presumably returned to her rank bed. My sniveling moans protesting Olivia's behavior went unheard.

When we reached the elevator, a security guard was standing near the call buttons. He was a tall, reedy man whose brown uniform pants didn't adequately fit the length of his legs. His starchy, short-sleeved white shirt, garnished with a brown clip-on tie, showcased gangly arms that were out of proportion and bent forward as he rested his hands on his hips. His limbs looked like the lines of a rapidly drawn stick-figure. Short black hair saturated with jet black hair dye augmented his pasty complexion and the droopy cartilage that hung off his ears. He was comically ugly, and his protruding Adam's apple, tapered chin, and bullet-shaped nose all looked like embryonic horns that were ready to burst. But his eyes intimidated me. Yellow-brown irises that twinkled and winked at me like the thirsty eyes of a neglected lover. He didn't take his eyes off me even as Olivia barked out her order.

"Take him to room 328. Make sure he stays in bed. Restrain if necessary."

The guard nodded and stepped closer to me. I actually looked back at Olivia to plead for forgiveness and request another escort to my room. But she had begun to trot as if called to another emergency. The guard dropped his hand on my left shoulder, pressing down roughly like he was training an unruly mutt how to sit. I obediently lowered my head and let him usher me into the elevator as the doors opened.

The guard did not let go of my shoulder as the doors enclosed us inside the shiny cage, the stainless steel walls reflecting multiple, distorted images. The guard stood too close to me as if the surrounding reflections had cramped and trapped him as much as me.

He pressed the button for the third floor, but it didn't seem like we were moving. My shoulder burned from the guard's sweaty hand which manacled my movement. My own stifling sweat spiraled down my chest and back. I stared down at my bare feet which had become blackened from the grimy hospital floor.

The elevator shook, presumably beginning its descent, and the guard released me. He crouched his six and a half foot frame down so that his head became even with mine. I didn't turn to look into his elongated face, as he drew his nose closer to me, pausing only an inch away from my left cheek. Stagnant air blew out of his nostrils. I tried to move my head and body away from him, but my muscles wouldn't respond. A hoarse, static-filled voice that I had undeniably heard before, spewed out of his mouth, jettisoning words that crawled deep into my ear and squirmed their way into my brain.

I'm here, Daniel. I've finally come for you.

The demon. In its definitive form. Everything else had been a veiled representation, mimicking myself and my acquaintances. Heralds for this ultimate presence.

Were you trying to leave me?

I shook my head. It was the only movement my body allowed.

I think you were. It's very disappointing.

I shook my head again. I tried to speak, shout for help, but I could only stutter and gasp. The demon's calloused finger brushed against my left forearm, near my cigar burn scar.

Something wonderful marked you. You should be grateful for such a remembrance.

The demon dug its fingernail into my old wound. I squirmed but still could not speak. In my mind, I tried to recite my mantra. *You do not exist. I am fucking real. I am fucking real.*

No, Daniel. You are no Incarnator. I always exist. I am always fucking real.

Involuntarily, my head turned to face the demon. Its eyes had enlarged, the brown irises transforming into a dozen concentric rings. The rings seemed to spin, spiraling into an intensely red singularity that pulsed in sync with my heartbeat.

You can see me clearly now. It pleases me.

The demon brought my arm up to his mouth and he licked my scar with a crimson, icy tongue, corrugating my flesh like soaked newspaper.

I'm very busy, but I love you.

The opprobrious lick was enough to finally drive me out of my stupor and I found the will to jerk my arm away from the demon. The force necessary to free myself caused me to fall to the ground, and the IV needle tore out of its renewed connection, shooting a small jet of blood out into the air.

Both of my arms ached as if they had been mangled in a machine and I blurted out the only string of words that my mind could fashion together.

"I DON'T LOVE YOU! YOU DON'T EXIST!"

The demon's security guard persona, its humanity, dissolved in front of me – starting with its shoddy clothes, then its chalky skin, then its stringy muscles and tissue, continuing past its blackened bones – until only a shadow remained. The shadow of a raptor with two red, pinpoint eyes. Like wings, the shadow wrapped itself around the perimeter of the elevator, encircling me and eclipsing the interior light. I hunkered down on the floor, tucking my body into a wobbly ball of discombobulated flesh as the darkness enveloped me. The demon's vulturine voice hovered over me.

Soon you won't exist.

The elevator doors opened. The light returned. I lifted my head as Lorena and a male nurse reached down to pick me off the floor of the elevator. I failed to answer their concerned questions, but allowed them to treat my bleeding arm and transport my limp, damaged body back to my room.

I awoke, back in my hospital bed, lying in a half-reclined position, a single sheet covering my body. I didn't know how much time had passed, but my surroundings appeared normal. Bright sunlight easily pierced through the room window. My television set was turned on, showing the news. The bed next to me was clean and empty. But I wasn't alone. There was a woman sitting in the visitor's chair in my room, wearing a surgical mask.

It took me a moment, and an eye rub, to recognize Sky. Aside from the mask, she was dressed in the same attire as when I first met her: tights, the college sweatshirt, and flip-flops. She was reading a piece of notebook paper and wasn't looking at me. The mask unsettled me and I hesitated in trying to gain her attention.

I watched Sky for several seconds before I exhaled loudly, followed by a throat-clearing cough.

Sky stood up and put the paper down on her chair next to her red purse. I dribbled out a sigh. She cautiously approached my bed, her eyes narrowed as if unsure of what she was seeing. I tried to smile.

Sky pulled down her mask. "Fuck this thing. How are you feeling?"

I eked out a few words. "I don't know. Alive?"

Sky smiled warmly. "Yeah, you're alive. You were pretty sick. You've been sleeping a lot."

"For how long?"

"I don't know – that's just what I heard."

"No. How long have I been here?"

"Three nights. Since you crashed and burned at my bookstore."

Disappointment crept onto my face and Sky tried to reassure me. "You look better?"

"Really?"

"Well, you don't look worse. You had a severe lung infection – they thought it was TB, but your test was a false positive. Dr. Molker said you weren't contagious, but he still made me wear the mask. Power tripping. Can't stand it. Makes me feel like I'm recycling my own spit."

"Why are you here? Where's my mother?"

"Thought I'd check in on you. Still can't break the habit."

"My mother?"

It was Sky's turn to display disappointment. "Yeah, that's why I'm here. She left, Daniel."

"What do you mean?"

"I don't know. She left. Left town – packed up her shit and cleaned out her apartment. Didn't even tell me where she was going. I've got your bags in my Jeep."

Where had my mother gone? Had I offended her that much? Was I now beyond hope? How could she abandon me again?

My mind was bombarded by ions of anxiety and incredulity. I was not simply surviving the biggest, most challenging moment in my life – I was battling for my entire existence! I was physically and mentally ravaged. Struggling to recombine the pieces that comprised my puzzled sanity. And I was losing. Losing to the demon.

(Soon you won't exist.)

If I had to continue alone, the demon had augured the truth.

I shriveled up tightly in my bed, shivering under my flimsy cover. Entropy was increasing.

Sky steered the subject away from my mother. "Maybe you'll be released soon? Dr. Molker said the worst was over. Your fever's gone and they only need to run a few more tests. Heard you were very unsettled – kept climbing out of bed. One night they even found you in the elevator. Also ripped out your IV a few times. So gross."

My IV line had been switched from my right to my left hand. In the previous spot, a *Sesame Street* Band-Aid had been applied. *Elmo.* There was also one hiding my burn scar. *Big Bird.* A tiny chuckle wormed out of me, and I was unsure if it was due to the ridiculousness of this juvenile treatment or my inability to get past the hopelessness of my situation.

Sky was waiting for me to say something. I remained silent so she continued. "Did you really pull the hair of that Lorena nurse? She looks twelve years old. Could be considered child abuse."

"No."

"She looks scared every time she comes in here."

"Why would my mother leave me?"

Sky walked back to the visitor's chair and grabbed the piece of paper she had been reading.

"She left this for you. I couldn't help reading it. Not sure if I should give it to you."

I stretched out my child-bandaged right hand and Sky reluctantly handed me the letter. I read it three times.

Daniel, I'm sorry. You won't get better with me around. I thought I could force you to accept my help. To accept me. But your will is stronger than mine.

You're free to hate me. Curse me for all the failures I've made with you. It doesn't matter. My love for you will always

208

be the same. We will always be the same. You are my son and you are an Incarnator. Those are the things you have to accept for the rest of your life. I have no doubt Melinda was able to inhibit your incarnations – your father had a similar effect on me. But your memory "loss" and your refusal to work on controlling your incarnations are products of your own making.

There is another thing you have to accept. I know you blame yourself for Melinda's death. That she wouldn't have committed suicide if you had acted better, listened better, or communicated better. I know you wish you could've been someone different. But that's not possible. Melinda loved the person you are. She loved you so much she couldn't be honest with herself. Or honest with you.

Daniel, despite how much you cared for one another, you and Melinda were not meant to live the rest of your lives together.

A year ago last Christmas, when I took Melinda's photo, she mentioned that her relationship with you had grown problematic. How her disorder was causing her difficulties. She couldn't sleep. Couldn't do her schoolwork. And the other relationships in her life – her friends and family – were falling apart. She said it even affected her thoughts about the future. She never explicitly said it, but I believe Melinda wanted to break up with you. I didn't tell you because I wasn't sure.

My guess is that Melinda didn't go through with it because she didn't want to hurt you. It was a terrible decision. Her mental struggle over doing what was right vs. what was compassionate is revealed in the thirteen notes you brought. You know that Melinda expressed herself, and her emotions, through her writing. These notes are thirteen verses to a poem, although I'm not sure of their proper order. Melinda may not have believed you would completely understand the meaning behind her poem, but I think on some level you must have. That's why you saved these notes and brought them with you, is it not? Your father said he found dozens of other notes from Melinda in your bedroom trashcan. You didn't have to do that to concede the importance of these notes.

To me, her poem illustrates the struggle she had with her disorder and in trying to leave you. I only wish it had given some indication of why she had decided to give up on everything.

Melinda's Poem

1. Do you hear it? Its daunting voice makes me feel so strong, so radiant, like how I felt when you danced with me at the Moonlight Formal.

2. Swirling in my cerulean dress, I'm infused with knowledge, courage, and dreams of independence and fulfilment.

3. Must dreams stay united? Or must we accept our waking, hurtful truths?

4. Remember, it was you who said: mastery comes to those who believe in solitude.

5. An escape finally revealed itself to me, but tragically, I was consumed with doubt. Does your God create mazes?

6. Eyes shrieking, lips weeping, I filter my heart with sheets of isinglass.

7. My cells lyse and regenerate over and over and I can't stop laughing.

8. Sometimes the least painful choice is the most painful course of action.

9. Let's imagine I left my galvanized oasis for the unknown.

10. Walking alone, desert sand pelting my face, the devil-wind is trying to make me forget your name.

11. I never thought it would be easy, but an infatuated soul cannot be tricked by gifts of reason.

12. I awoke and found you. Lying on your bed of lovelorn dust, sealing my future with your sunfire eyes that blind me so sweetly.

13. Sunlight drips down your face each night, and with that, I find solace.

Melinda didn't have to die, Daniel. But it was her choice. It wasn't your fault.

Accepting that fact will enable you to control your incarnations. But that by itself, won't be enough. You need a doctor's help. Let the doctors at the hospital do what I cannot.

Goodbye, Daniel.

Mom

After the third reading, I stuck out the piece of paper as far away from me as I could hold it until Sky grabbed it.

"Do you know why Melinda committed suicide?"

I couldn't answer Sky's question. I couldn't answer it because it didn't happen. It was impossible. Impossible to believe. Despite the exceptions. Exceptions that could upend even the most beautifully pragmatic theory.

Exception 1. The day I took Melinda to the hospital, the doctors didn't find anything wrong.

Exception 2. Melinda had asked for a specific prescribed sedative that the doctor warned should only be taken if absolutely necessary.

Exception 3. Melinda knew she was allergic to Valerian and had told me she had thrown the supplements away.

It was my fault. My fault that I had taken her back to her apartment after the hospital. My fault that I had woken up and seen the open medicine cabinet as she stood in the bathroom, admitting that she had done something bad to herself. My fault that I did not want to see the impossible....

No, my brain couldn't process exceptions. There were only simple truths. My Melinda would never have killed herself. My Melinda would never have considered leaving me. I mounted one more defense of my newly formed beliefs.

"No! She didn't kill herself. The demon killed her."

Sky remained close to me, unflustered by my answer to her question. "Do you know why she wanted to break up with you?"

"Sky, it's not true! My mother is wrong." I started coughing.

"Yeah, I'm sorry. You're right. It doesn't make any sense. Your mother's not making sense." Sky poured me a glass of water and I drank it all in one gulp.

"She never made sense, Sky. I think there's something wrong with her."

Sky reached out and touched me. "This is a horrible letter to give someone. And your mother leaving – that's fucking unforgivable."

"Means nothing to me."

"Do you want me to throw it away?" She waved my mother's letter like it was a piece of used tissue.

"Yes." As Sky began crumpling up the letter, I changed my mind. "No. No, keep it. It's a reminder of what she did. Who she is."

Sky reopened the letter, folded it into quarters, and stuffed it into the red purse she had left on the visitor's chair. "I'll save it. And when you're ready to accept it, I'll give it back to you."

"Is that all you wanted to do? Give me the letter?"

"And your bags." Sky sat down. "No, that's not everything. Daniel, how did you get those bite marks on your neck?"

Did Sky really want to know the answer? I decided to keep quiet.

She continued. "Your mother blamed Mr. Rogers. That's bullshit! My dog doesn't bite! He can barely chew – he only eats mushy food."

"Your dog didn't touch me."

"I don't know what's happened to you. It's different – it's more than an incarnation. Your mother can't see that! She doesn't want to. It's something else and I don't know what it is."

"Are you worried about me?"

"A little. But you're not a monster."

"Thanks."

"Never thought your mother would disappoint me this much. I keep imagining how you feel."

"Does it matter?"

"Yes, it does! I changed my mind."

"About what?"

"In the worst ways, we're the same. We're alike."

Sky popped back up from her chair, walked over and grabbed my hand. She interlocked her fingers with mine and I understood the comfort that Melinda had been seeking in me in her final hours alive. During our entire relationship. That's what the thirteen notes were really about – pleas for help that I had ignorantly snubbed. Pleas for help against the demon. The demon that had killed her. Now Sky was helping me and my fight. And I didn't even have to ask.

"I feel better, Sky. But I need to get out of here."

Lorena entered my room. The young nurse appeared nervous, plastering a fake smile when she saw me. "Oh, you're awake."

"I'm feeling much better."

Lorena smiled like a supplicating coward. "I'm glad. You were very ill. It's OK – bad things can happen when we're sick."

Lorena bounced her eyes to the television set. A special report was showing a scene of unfolding pandemonium as the war had drifted into central Asia. Citizens were rioting against the state government and the defecting military was responding with unilateral artillery fire. The phrase *"Civil War or World War?"* was printed on the screen.

Lorena did the sign of the cross, and lowered her head. "So many innocent people." On television a despondent woman was holding a dead infant in her arms. One moment she was crying, cradling the lifeless, battered body in her arms and compulsively kissing his head. The next she was shouting and holding the baby up by his foot, sticking him in front of the camera as if he were contaminated garbage.

"No one needs to see that." Lorena reached down to the remote on my bed and turned the TV off. "I'll be back in a bit to check your vitals."

Sky stepped in front of the nurse. "When will my brother be able to leave?"

"Dr. Molker will let you know what to expect."

As Lorena exited, Sky turned back to me and answered my quizzical look. "They wouldn't tell me anything unless I was family. Your mother told them I was your sister before she left – surprised me, but I guess she could tell how pissed I was at her."

It didn't surprise me. It was probably my mother's plan all along to dump me at the hospital. She had never wanted to take care of me. Sky leaned against the bed and ran her hands through her hair. "No one knows what's going on."

"What do you mean?"

"Whole fucking world is falling apart and no one knows what they're doing. Everyone is either over or under."

"Huh?"

"Over-medicated or under-medicated. That's the battle. That's what's wrong with the world."

I nodded. The war-torn scene of the mother kissing her dead baby resonated with me – she didn't know whether to love it or let it go. Take her medicine or vomit it up. Maybe the entire world had a *disorder*. Everyone wanted to survive, but no one knew if the means of survival were actually worth it.

Did Melinda know?

I recalled the security guard or, more accurately, the demon licking the scar on my arm. It wanted to give me an easy answer, an easy way out. It wanted to *love* me. I heard its repulsive voice repeat inside my head.

(I'm very busy, but I love you.)

Sky snatched her body off the bed, and her head spun around the room.

"What's wrong?"

"Did you hear that? That fucking voice?"

I shook my head and hoped that she would blame her tense nerves for playing an aural illusion on her. A momentary incarnation caused by frazzled emotions and her severe disenchantment with my mother, Sky's surrogate mother. I needed Sky to stay with me, to keep holding my hand and maintain our connection. I had lost my mother, but I had gained a friend.

I stuck out my hand. She hesitated for a moment before retaking it. I tried to clear my mind. Remain positive. Regain my strength. If I allowed myself to be weak, the demon would continue with its cruel amusements. I needed to get out of the hospital and escape from the demon on my terms.

I detected Sky's excited pulse as I held her hand. I hoped my friend wouldn't hear the demon's voice again. I didn't know what I would do if the demon wanted to devour Sky too.

NINE

I began to indulge in micro-acts of normal behavior, and the world responded in kind. I ate a lunch of sliced turkey, mashed potatoes, and applesauce. While taking my vital signs, I complimented Lorena on the food and her kindness and she gave me another packet of applesauce and lessened the amount of fluid in my IV, pleased with my caloric intake. I turned the television back on and the news had switched to a story about another young celebrity having a meltdown, a moment of packaged Schadenfreude that I enjoyed with Sky. I was fortunate to have her company, and I thanked her for doing so much for me. Sky repeatedly hunted down Dr. Molker, asking when I would be able to leave. The physician's non-committal response (*Perhaps this evening with positive results*) got shorter (*Perhaps this evening*) after each of her requests (*Perhaps*). Soon Sky told me that she couldn't find the doctor anymore. But I remained positive. I was certain I would be able to get out of the hospital soon and figure out a way to permanently escape from the demon.

Sky informed me that my mother had assumed financial liability for my hospital stay. She had done the same during my hospital confinement after Melinda's death and at the time, I had appreciated it. Now I felt like an unsuspecting dupe who had been pawned off by an unscrupulous saleswoman. My earlier notions of her maternal abundance were a farce. All the money, gifts and educational benefits she had doled out to me in my life had not been done to maximize my abilities or potential for further accomplishment. They had been done to counteract or stave off her own failures – to silence a nagging conscience that wanted to assign genetic blame for producing another Incarnator. My success and health were merely remedies to absolve her own stained, narcissistic life.

However, her hypothesis was correct. I would be better off without her.

I only needed my father. I missed him terribly. I wanted to talk to him. Tell him that he'd been right all along about the demon. Tell him that he wasn't to blame for my mother's leaving him. Tell him that I loved him, that he had been my true parent and not my mother. Tell him that his house was where I belonged. It was my home. That would be my next step after I was discharged from the hospital – to go home.

Sky left around one-thirty to attend to her bookstore and promised to be back in a few hours. When I told her that after my discharge I wanted to go home, she backed my plan with her own elaborations: she would close the bookstore for the night, drop off Mr. Rogers with one of her apartment neighbors, and drive me at least halfway to my father's house. I told her my father could probably drive his truck to pick me up, but since I was unsure how far his recovery had come, I didn't know how long he could be on the road. She told me that we'd figure it out once I contacted my father. Sky hinted that she wouldn't mind driving me the entire way back home, but I told her it wouldn't be necessary – untrue since I wanted Sky to remain with me for as long as possible. I didn't think the demon was actually impeded by Sky's direct presence, but when she left the room, I started feeling the heart constricting precursors of an old, encroaching visitor – a panic attack.

My oncoming attack was luckily interrupted by a red bearded imp of a man who glided up to my bed. His hospital name badge indicated that he was Dr. Molker. He appeared no more than five feet tall and one hundred pounds, yet his frame was buoyed by a fluffy red afro, an oversized lab coat, baggy green corduroys, and thick soled loafers. He also donned wire framed circular bifocals and a paisley bow tie that matched his pants. Another cartoon attempting to demand my respect.

He grinned after a quick glance around the room. "Your sister leave? She's an ornery young lady."

"When will I be able to leave?"

Dr. Molker started flipping through a medical chart. "I have a few questions for you first, Daniel. If you don't mind."

"As long as it will get me away from you." It was a half-hearted attempt at humor, but Molker didn't buy it. He seemed offended and his smile vanished.

"How's your ankle? Your record shows you suffered a fracture about three weeks ago."

"It was minor. I can put my full weight on it."

"You should be careful with it. It usually takes about six weeks before it'd be strong enough for regular use. Aside from the ankle, how do you feel? Do you really feel better, Daniel?"

"I'm fine. And call me Danny."

"Not a problem. Your mother informed us that you had a bout with pneumonia earlier in the year that required hospitalization. Did you complete any necessary follow-ups?"

"Yes." I had no idea what he meant by follow-ups.

"Do you smoke?"

"No."

"Drink?"

"Occasionally."

"Drugs?"

"Never."

"A lot of stress in your life?"

"No. Nothing." There was absolutely no reason to share any of the events that had happened to me with this man who looked better suited to be a circus veterinarian.

"I don't think you're taking care of yourself, Danny. You're a young man who shouldn't be in the hospital twice in a year for a lung infection. External stressors have a way of manifesting themselves in your internal health. Your mother indicated that you've been having an extremely difficult time. Your sister was less forthcoming, but seemed to hint that something very traumatic happened to you."

"I said I was fine."

"Have you considered seeing a therapist or a psychiatrist? It's not something to be ashamed of. I had to see a therapist

217

myself when I was your age. I didn't think I had made the right decision to enter medical school and I was plagued with cluster headaches. But talking about my anxiety, openly sharing my frustration and fear with someone who would listen and provide guidance, enabled my health to improve far better than any medication could."

I was extremely annoyed with Molker's blithe manner. He was trying to bond with me. "I don't need a fucking therapist."

Dr. Molker looked away from me and buried his face in my medical chart. "I'm sorry you feel that way. But I'm going to agree with your mother and recommend that you get some form of counseling. We have someone on staff that I'd like you to see. I think he'll be able to meet with you around four-thirty this afternoon or perhaps tomorrow morning."

Molker wanted to delay my release. I decided to play the sycophant card and get him back on my side. "I think you've done an excellent job in taking care of me. You don't need to go any further out of your way. Except maybe a snack? My energy has returned and I'm hungry. Another good sign of health, right?"

Dr. Molker closed up my patient record. "I'm on your side, Danny. You're not as strong as you think."

Now he was trying to bait me, trying to reignite my anger to get another harsh, negative response out of me to prove his point. It wouldn't work. "Please, Dr. Molker. I only want to go home and see my father. He means everything to me."

The doctor released a smile that appeared to be forced. "OK, Danny. I'll make some calls and we'll see what we can do."

I cast my own feigned grin as he exited my room. I didn't need to be analyzed at this point. Once the demon was out of my life I'd happily see a therapist for the next twenty years.

Lorena reentered my room. She was holding a small cup of fruit and a jug of ice water. At least I was getting my snack.

Lorena put the snack down on my bed's food tray and began to disconnect my IV. Progress! Maybe my calm response had worked. My mind eased further and I hoped Sky would return sooner than expected. Lorena poured me a glass of water and handed me two small tablets. "Take these. They will help you relax."

"I don't need them. I feel fine."

"Would you rather have the IV?"

Lorena stared at me expectantly. I figured I needed to be a good patient for a little while longer so I downed the tablets with my water and tore into my fruit cup.

Dr. Molker returned as I was halfway through my snack. Both the nurse and doctor maintained a vigilant watch over me.

"What do you need?" I spoke with my mouth still full with bits of pears, pineapples and grapes.

Molker and Lorena continued staring at me as if impatiently waiting to hear the punchline of an overly setup joke. Was this another one of Molker's tests to generate an irrational response from me?

Or had I grown too relaxed, too careless? Forgotten the possibility that the demon could make an appearance at any time? Did I really need to be reminded on what little control I had of my situation?

As dispassionately as I could, I ignored Lorena and Dr. Molker and finished eating my fruit. They remained silent but kept exchanging wary glances. The instant I put the empty container down on the tray, Lorena scooped it up and sped out of my room with Dr. Molker trailing her like a spurned suitor. They looked like bit actors exiting their hometown stage, proud of their limited accomplishment.

I didn't know if I had passed their test or if the scene was merely a prelude to the demon's entrance. The fruit began to rumble in my stomach. A layer of clammy air congealed over my body and I had the urge to jump out of bed. I tried to remain stationary until the need to head into the bathroom overpowered me. I was going to be sick.

I skidded off the bed and when my sweaty bare feet touched the cool floor, a redox reaction occurred as electrolytes seeped out of my skin, generating a battery between the soles of my feet and the floor tile. A superheated impulse propagated through my entire body and I felt like I could run. Run out of my room, down the hallway and out of the hospital. Run all the way back to my father's house. But my nausea lingered. I hopped to the bathroom and flung open the door. As I stepped inside and flicked on the light, I caught my reflection in the small mirror mounted to the left of the sink.

I looked deranged.

Ragged, glaring eyes. Flaring, engorged nostrils. Caved in cheeks reminiscent of a starvation victim. And an ugly smile. I was casting a wide, warped grin, but I couldn't feel it – my facial muscles were not in my control and when I tried to frown my lips only parted wider.

What the hell was wrong with me? Was this why Lorena and Molker were concerned? I appeared to be in need of institutionalization, not therapy.

I tore myself away from the mirror and closed the door. I relieved myself and my sickness abated. I washed up, slathering my hands and face with the antiseptic foam soap, even dousing my hair as best I could. I hoped that my concerted cleaning effort would compose me, and reconcile my appearance with the ease I had felt before Sky had left.

I rechecked myself in the mirror. My slapdash washing and primping hadn't done a damn thing. I was still displaying a disgusting smile, and my damp, sloppy hair only amplified my psychotic appearance.

Was it time to accept that I had lost my mind? Or had the demon deteriorated my brain to such an extent that I couldn't even control my physical appearance? Was there a difference? I didn't want Sky to see me as a madman.

I scampered back into my bed. Maybe some further rest would erase my crudely expressive state and render me presentable. I did not want to remain in the hospital, or undergo a merry-go-round conversation with a psychiatrist.

I tugged the bed sheet up over my head, regressing to a five-year-old child, hiding myself to make the world disappear and return my perspective to a primordial state of bliss. I closed my eyes and for the first time since I had been a guileless kid who believed in ever-loving parents and an everlasting God, I recited the Lord's Prayer.

A high pitched cackle rang out in my room. It was a bitter sound, effused with contempt and ridicule. And I knew it was directed at me. I didn't care if I looked absurd. I kept the sheet over my head.

More laughter. Slower. Deeper. It was emanating from a man. Could it be Dr. Molker, chortling with smug satisfaction over his adult patient now cowering under the covers like a disturbed child? Was I confirming his expectations? I wanted to unleash a furious rebuke, boasting that I had endured hardships far greater than his trifling bout with MCAT jitters.

But I harnessed my tongue and remained covered. He would eventually have to attend to other patients and leave me alone.

The bed sheet was lifted up at my feet and yanked down, exposing the top of my head. I snatched the top edge of the sheet with both my hands and pulled back. The force tugging at the bottom of the sheet was stronger than me. More laughter. Repetitive and synthetic. The laughs sounded like a digital recording. They were not human, not from Dr. Molker. The sheet dropped below my forehead. My arm tendons bulged, fraying my connective tissue as I tried to hold onto the sheet, but its edge reached my eyes. This tug of war was over. I had to let go. The sheet flew off the bed exposing my entire body to whatever abysmal influence was awaiting me.

Standing at the end of my bed was a middle-aged man with tanned skin, shoulder length, wavy brown hair, a flush, neatly trimmed mustache and beard, and gentle hazel eyes that seemed to console as well as request comfort. He wore an unadorned, beige tunic with sleeves that hung loosely from his arms as he rested his hands on the footboard of my bed.

It was a preposterous sight. He looked exactly like the modern pictorial representation of Jesus Christ.

Who are you to pray to my father?

The voice was not kind. And I had heard it before. The familiarity was confirmed when the almond eyes of the ersatz Jesus blew up to owl-size orbs, exposing the concentric circles that lay within the sclera. The face of Jesus transformed into the slender, haunting disguise of the demon.

No one can hear a faithless prayer.

I muttered a response. "I still have faith."

Faith? Only buffoons like your father have faith. Prayer does not belong in an accidental universe built from a random assembly of secondhand atoms.

"I'm not afraid of you."

Oh, but you are.

"No! I am stronger than you!"

We're always afraid of the things we love.

I shut my eyes and shouted. There was no intensity to my voice. Words sputtered out of me, truncating into babbled nonsense. "Leave! Don't love...I don't. Don't...leaf turns to you...not afraid!"

"You're not making sense, Danny. We're only trying to help you."

I opened my eyes. Dr. Molker was standing at the side of my bed, his head askew and his bearded mouth partially covered by a medical chart. A couple feet behind him stood, Lorena, peering over the doctor's shoulder. The demon had vanished.

The fire I had intended to direct to the demon finally discharged, albeit unintentionally. "What are you doing? Get away from me! Back off, dwarf!"

The doctor shook his head and looked back at Lorena. "It's all a big joke to him."

My eyes shifted past the doctor as the bathroom door cracked open, revealing a sliver of absolute darkness that the interior room light could not penetrate. A void. An intriguing absence of matter.

Dr. Molker stepped out into the hallway with Lorena. I could hear the nurse's words despite her attempt to muffle her voice. "He was OK when his sister was here, but I think you're right. His condition's degrading. That smile – it's not normal. My shift's over, and I don't want to step in there anymore."

Apparently I was smiling sadistically again, without any awareness of it. I spoke out once more. "I'm not smiling at you!"

My loud, irate tone bewildered me, as if I were subconsciously trying to sabotage myself. I took a deep breath. I needed to speak slowly. Gently. Restrain my self-immolating outbursts.

The door to the bathroom opened wider, enlarging the blackness that dwelled inside. I needed confirmation from Dr. Molker that what I was witnessing truly did exist.

"I'm sorry, doctor. Come back. You need to see the darkness."

Dr. Molker stepped back into the room only to give me a momentary glance. It had been long enough for me to see the grave concern in his face. Or more accurately, grave fear. He and Lorena departed, vanishing from my view. I had lost any chance for redress.

The bathroom door swung completely open. The impenetrable darkness was actually a large humanoid shadow figure. The shadow figure was as tall and wide as the entire

222

bathroom. It was motionless. Staring at me with two pinpoint red eyes. The demon. It had never left me. Its voice turned maternal, yet it shook my body, and rattled my brain inside my skull.

I will take you now.

Sweat bubbled out of my skin, clogging my pores. My gaping mouth contained only a pocket of carbon dioxide. Unoxygenated blood turned to sludge in my veins. My brain rallied to buttress itself, desperate to evade my fate. Inaudible morphemes sputtered off my tongue.

"Not now. Not afraid. Not you."

You love me. You will never let me go.

The demon shadow stirred. It eased out of the bathroom like the crawling snake-tendrils of smoke from an arsonist's first flame. The door to my room closed and all the light inside my room deteriorated, including the strained sunlight coming through the frosted window. It was as if a column of cumulonimbus clouds had spontaneously condensed and descended over the hospital. My sweat dried up and I began to tremble. The room temperature dropped. The demon had extracted not only the illumination, but also the heat. It was ingesting all energy into its obsidian core.

The demon shadow began to sway in a measured manner, similar to the slowest tempo of a metronome. The red eyes of the demon became the nodes of an oscillating sine wave – its frequency long, its amplitude short – the first fundamental frequency of its continuous Fourier transform. I couldn't stop watching the hypnotic movements even though instinct was pounding my brain with one command:

Flee.

I couldn't move.

I'm inside you now.

The demon shadow stopped moving. And for a few seconds, the Universe froze along with us.

My eyes blinked. And blinked. And blinked. I couldn't stop blinking. I counted my blinks until I reached a thousand blinks.

The demon shadow exploded into the room, enveloping everything in total darkness – a vast, non-Euclidean manifold of unencumbered evil that consumed reality like a voracious python eating itself.

The demon had swallowed me up.

My ears clogged as if I had been submerged in water. An elephantine, invisible weight compressed my chest. Crushing my ribs. My lungs. My heart. I could barely hear the demon's voice over my agony.

This is how she died.

My struggling heart released a string of choppy, clipped beats until there was one final, elongated thump. Then nothing. No pulse. No pain. I allowed the emptiness and dissolution to enshroud me.

Was this death? Had I welcomed it?

"Daniel."

My eardrums popped. A torrent of blood rushed into my brain and out to my most distant capillaries. My heart restarted, pumping furiously, transmitting waves of life back to my extremities. The darkness was gone. I throttled my eyes wider as I caressed my sore chest. I was alive.

"Daniel."

I followed the voice – it was Sky. She was sitting once again on the visitor's chair. With a glowing smile that welcomed me back among the living.

I kicked off my bed sheet which was drenched with sweat and smiled back at her.

She erased her happiness. Stood up from the chair and glared at me as if I were pointing a gun at her face. Was it my appearance? Had I inadvertently shared my crazed, deviant grin with her?

A hollow baritone voice jumbled with static, reminiscent of the incongruent sound of an AM radio station, scratched itself out of Sky's mouth.

If you don't want it. She'll take it.

Sky's body collapsed to the floor and she began to shake. Blood streamed from her nose, ears and mouth. She was disassembling in the same way that Melinda had the moments before she died. Sky's head jerked to the left, snapping the vertebrae in her neck. Her movement ceased. Sky's head dangled away from her shoulders like a broken tree branch.

I screamed. "NO! SKY!"

This wasn't real. It was an incarnation induced by the demon itself. That wasn't Sky on the floor. She wasn't dead. Sky was alive. She had every reason to live. She needed to live.

The pungent odor of decay swept through my room, stinging my sinuses. I buried my distraught face into my pillow as the demon's voice, danced around me in a nonsensical Latin refrain.

Resurgere, daemon annuli!
Resurgere, daemon annuli!
Resurgere, daemon annuli!
Resurgere, daemon annuli!

A hand latched onto the back of my head. Fingers raked through my tangled hair. I spun around, primed to muster up one more fight against the demon. I formed a fist, and tried to focus my embalmed eyes on the entity next to my bed, crouching over me.

It was Sky. Alive and standing. Could I finally trust my eyes? Joyful confirmation came as she wiped her hand on her sweatshirt, muttering that I was in need of an entire bottle of shampoo.

Overwhelmed, I almost struck out and hit her, regardless. Sky grabbed my hand and I relaxed my fist.

"Whoa, picadillo. What the fuck?"

I closed my eyes and let her soothing touch comfort me. "I'm OK."

"Are you?"

"I thought you were something else." I couldn't tell Sky about the demon. I couldn't let her know that it wanted her. "Dr. Molker isn't going to let me leave."

Sky let go of my hand. "Shit. I thought that might happen. You look like hell, Daniel. Worse than this morning."

"This place is damaging me. I can't stay here. I need to go home."

"Not sure that's best."

"I need my father!"

"OK. Let me try talking to Molker again. Put yourself together. The best you can."

"OK." I wasn't at all certain I could do anything to improve my condition, but Sky gave me the will to try. I did not want to descend back into the void with the demon. Where I was dead. Where Sky was dead.

My friend hurried out of the room and I tried to keep myself from looking over at the partially open door to the bathroom. It was clear, but I craved something to settle my chaotic synapses and occlude the possibility of the demon's return. In middle school, after finally expunged the belief that my mother would return home, and realizing the world was only a series of hastily stitched together tatters, I used to perform a magic trick. Not the sleight-of-hand, masturbatory theatrics honed by other loners and unloved misfits. An illusion that enabled me to believe that the universe was grounded in structure, glued together by symmetrical, coherent patterns.

My magic was reciting the periodic table and the atomic orbitals. I had memorized the abbreviations and atomic weights when I was eight or nine years old, but by the time I was twelve, I had uncovered electron configurations and the Aufbau principle. The recitation became my sacramental partner, a sacrosanct guide leading me through the moments of collapsing solitude that had begun to foul up my life.

H. Hydrogen. $1s^1$. He. Helium. $1s^2$. Li. Lithium. $2s^1$. Be. Beryllium. $2s^2$.

I had reached bismuth *($4f^{14}$ $5d^{10}$ $6s^2$ $6p^2$)* when Sky returned. She was rubbing the back of her neck – not kneading her skin as if she were in pain or frustrated, but strumming her fingers absentmindedly. It gave her a reason to bow her head and limit her eye contact with me.

"You won't be released until you get a consult from one of their staff psychiatrists."

"Can they do that? Involuntarily?"

"If they think you are a danger to yourself or others. Your mother sold you out. Told them you were hallucinating – that you are the one who called them incarnations and she didn't know what crazy shit you were...."

I rolled over onto my side and disregarded the rest of Sky's words. I thought back to bismuth and how it was used in the generation of *Pepto-Bismol*. The element was actually radioactive, but its half-life was billions of years long. It was completely harmless. *Pepto-Bismol*: the only healing potion that would outlast us all.

The sound of cabinet drawers opening and closing recaptured my attention to external life. I sat up in bed and saw Sky rummaging through a six-drawer, white wood dresser below the mounted television set.

"What are you doing?"

226

"The clothes you were wearing. They're in here somewhere."

On the bottom drawer, Sky pulled out a blue plastic bag. She tossed it onto the bed next to me. "Get dressed."

"What?"

Sky walked away from me and stuck her head out the doorway. Her head popped back inside and she flung her arms wildly at me. "Hurry up! Don't you want to get the fuck out of here?"

Although I had no idea what Sky was thinking, I had no intention of disobeying the one person who wanted to help me. I swung myself out of bed (almost falling to my knees as my balance was again unsteady) while Sky stepped outside and closed the door. I emptied out the bag and began to get dressed. In addition to my clothes, the bag contained my wallet, my cell phone (I turned it on – 10% charge remained), the key to my father's house and thirty-three cents in change. My clothes were the same as I had worn at Sky's bookstore, and although they were a bit sullied, it felt wonderful to put them on.

I was slipping on my shoes when Sky reopened the door. "Good. Hurry."

She motioned for me to join her at the doorway. Before I could hobble up to her, Sky darted out of view.

At the door, I craned my head out into the hallway. Sky had intercepted Dr. Molker.

My friend was an inch or two taller than the doctor, and she was able to obscure his view as I slipped out of my room and went into the adjacent room, 326. Inside was a single, sleeping patient, a young Hispanic woman with an oxygen mask strapped to her mouth. I edged up to the woman and stared into her almond face. She was gorgeous. Peaceful. A Diego Rivera painted masterpiece. For all I knew, she may have been deeply ill, but I envied the depth of her serene presence.

As Dr. Molker and Sky walked past the doorway, I crouched down below the woman's bed. My reaction time had been slow and the doctor had probably noticed me. After a few seconds with no confrontation, I peered over the mattress. No one had joined me in the room. The Hispanic woman stirred. Her eyes were open and her tremulous forehead indicated that my presence was unwelcome.

227

I crept out from behind the woman's bed on my hands and knees and paused when I reached the door. I poked my nose into the hallway like a mischievous pet.

Standing next to the closed door of my room was Sky. Her arms were crossed and her back was leaning against the wall. She kept sniffing, wiping her nose, and her eyes were scrunched together as if she were hindered by the fluorescent glare ricocheting off the waxed floor.

I called out to Sky, aiming for a hushed but forceful tone. I had to call her name several times with increasing volume before I caught her attention. Her eyes jutted open and her back bounced off the wall.

"What? How did you?"

"I saw him coming. So I snuck over here."

I stood up and motioned for Sky to come to me. She hesitated. Looked back at the closed door of my former room. What was wrong with her?

"Come on, Sky. Let's go!"

"What are you doing?" A spiteful voice hit me in the back of my head.

I turned around. Olivia was standing behind me. Apparently, she had approached me while I was getting Sky's attention.

"Get out of that room! Have you no decency? Why are you dressed? You're not going anywhere."

I nodded and stepped out into the hall. Sky finally looked back in my direction.

Olivia berated Sky. "Did you help him leave his room?"

Before she could answer, the door to my room opened.

Dr. Molker stumbled out into the hall. He looked up and down the hallway as if checking for traffic before crossing a busy street. He took a step forward then dropped down to his knees. He took off his glasses, laid them on the floor, and began wiping his brow with the back of his left hand. The doctor glanced once at Sky then teetered to the left, falling head-first to the floor.

Olivia rushed to his aid, screaming Molker's name. For some reason, Sky was not looking at the doctor. She was transfixed by something, back inside my patient room.

"Sky!" My voice was weak against the roar of rising pandemonium within the hospital as more hospital staff

228

appeared, rushing to the fallen doctor. An intercom page blared.

"Code blue, third floor! Code blue, third floor!"

I shouted as loud as I could. "Sky! Come on!"

She finally turned away from my room and broke out into a sprint. Despite wearing flip-flops, Sky sped past me and I could only follow her with a gimpy trot. My ankle was flaring up again. I caught up to her as she stood by the elevator, slapping her hand against the call button, waiting for the doors to open.

"No, not there!"

Sky shook her head at me as the elevator doors opened. The demon in his security guard persona stepped out, his protruding tongue licking his chapped lips.

There's no reason to run! I'll gladly take you both where you're supposed to be.

I pushed Sky past the elevator and towards a door marked *STAIRS*. Laughter from the demon snapped at our backs.

Sky shoved open the door leading to the stairway and leaped down the steps. Again I tried to keep up, but my remaining strength began to elapse. My lungs felt like they had constricted to half their size. My ankle felt like a rabid animal had bit into me. Every step I took was a hard landing, causing one searing blade to slice into my chest while another punctured my leg. I had to slow down or I was going to tumble.

"Don't leave me, Sky."

Sky stopped. Turned around and stuck out her hand. Her distress saddened me. I caught up to her and connected with her open hand. As our fingers interlaced, I became recharged enough to catch my breath.

It didn't last. Sky pulled me down the stairs, forcing me to pick up my pace and fight through the pain. When we finally reached the first floor, my ankle stung so badly it felt like my entire leg needed amputation.

I compelled my body to move forward. I followed Sky as she sped through the hospital lobby, weaving around a variety of visitors, hospital staff and a few mobile patients, everyone staring at us like we were fugitives. But no one called out to us. No one tried to stop us. We hustled through the sliding glass doors of the main entrance and headed towards a parking structure bounded by a cross street. I fell to the ground. Sky barely looked at me.

"Fuck! My Jeep's on the third level! Stay here."

Sky pulled off her flip-flops – the thong straps had chewed into the skin between her toes – and zipped across the street and up the exposed stairwell of the parking garage. I managed to pick myself up and I drifted out into the street. There was not much traffic, but two drivers blared their horns at me. I ignored them as I limped into the garage and ducked in between the rows of cars, bystanders to my escape who silently disapproved of my action, goading me with a grisly thought: *Sky is going to leave without you.*

I shuffled past several luxury automobiles – a silver Audi A6, a white Infiniti Hybrid, a red BMW 5 Series. There was a Reserved Parking sign tacked to the wall of each high-end car's space, asserting that this particular row was exclusive to the hospital's doctors. I started reading the reserved signs, searching for Dr. Molker's name. What had happened to him? Had he been attacked by the demon? What had Sky seen inside my room that had mesmerized her?

As two cars entered the garage, searching for open, unreserved spaces, Sky's Jeep rolled down the exit ramp from the garage's second floor. Its engine revved and Sky accelerated past me. The double beep of a car being disarmed and unlocked hit my ears like a snotty girl mocking me with a high-pitched, *Told ya.* Sky had left me.

The Jeep skidded to a halt. It shifted into reverse and backtracked until it reached me. I saw my crutches, backpack and suitcase stashed in the back seat.

Sky stuck her head at the window. "I told you to wait!"

I struggled to circle around the Jeep and hoist myself into the passenger seat, my leg no longer needing amputation since it felt like it had fallen off. Before I could close the side door, Sky punched the vehicle forward.

I clung onto the interior grab handle with both hands as the Jeep blasted out of the parking garage and turned onto the side street, speeding away from the hospital. We had traveled perhaps a mile before Sky slowed the vehicle down and I could let go of the handle to address my unbuckled seatbelt. After securing myself, I pulled out my cell phone which I had stashed in my pocket and used the 5% remaining charge to call my father.

There was no answer. I left him a voicemail stating I needed to come back home and to call me immediately.

"Do you have a charger?"

Sky didn't answer me. I checked her glove compartment and found a compatible charger, next to an eyeglass case. I connected it to my phone and her cigarette lighter, noticing a couple of cigarette butts poking out of the ashtray.

"You smoke?

Still no answer. I turned on the radio and was greeted with the drone of an NPR news commentator. Sky slapped the radio off. We drove silently for a few more minutes before Sky finally said something.

"I saw you."

"What?"

"In the room."

"I don't understand."

"When Dr. Molker went into your room. You were sitting on the bed."

"You saw me in the next room."

"I saw you on the bed! Naked and smiling. I thought you had lost it."

"It wasn't me."

"It had to be an incarnation."

"It was the demon."

"But Dr. Molker *saw* you. He was talking to you. He was talking to you, and looking at me, and...."

The Jeep started accelerating again.

"Sky, slow down."

"You got up and closed the door. Molker looked so scared...his eyes were pleading with me as you closed the door...."

"Sky, please. Drive slower."

The Jeep veered up an onramp for the interstate highway.

"No! Fuck this! I saw nothing. Nothing."

"Do you mean darkness? Did you see darkness?"

Sky gripped the steering wheel tightly with both her hands and continued to speed up, winding around cars to pass them.

I had to try to calm her down. "We're safe, Sky. Everything will be OK."

Sky didn't slow the Jeep down nor did she look at me.

231

"Sky, you've done so much for me. I'm incredibly thankful. You're the only person who makes me feel better."

Sky glanced at me. A small improvement.

"Sky, you're going to be fine."

"Shit! It wasn't nothing! I saw you! I saw you in the room! The doctor saw you! We saw you!"

"I told you what it really was."

"When Molker stepped back out – you were still on the bed. You spoke to me. Explain that."

"Was it a deep, scratchy voice?"

"You said, *I still love you*. What the fuck?"

I couldn't compose a response. Did the demon appear as something different to everyone? Could the demon appear as anyone? What did it do to Dr. Molker?

Sky pounded on the steering wheel with her hands. "I'm in control! I did the right things! This isn't supposed to happen!"

I extended my hand to her shoulder, but Sky shrugged it off. I left my arm hanging in the air as if pulling it back would only admit defeat. On my forearm, the *Sesame Street* Band-Aid was still covering up my scar. I ripped it off.

Removing it was a mistake. My scar had changed. It had darkened significantly, turning into a charcoal stigma, resembling an oversized cancerous mole or a necrotic hole bored by a insatiable parasite. I tried to reapply the Band-Aid but it didn't stick so I crossed my arms on my chest. I didn't want Sky to see it.

"Fuck. Where does your father live?"

I told Sky the city and she slowed the Jeep down along with her voice. "About 500 miles away. I can do that. One stop and I could get there before midnight."

"Once my father calls me back, he should be able to pick me up. He's probably feeling better and if he's more mobile he can--"

"I'm taking you home."

"Thanks, Sky. I don't know what--"

"Enough! I'm only driving. I don't want to talk. I don't want to think. I just don't want to be alone."

I checked my cell phone even though I didn't hear it ring, to see if my father had called. He hadn't.

We continued down the highway for almost half an hour until we jounced over a pothole. A quarter mile later, the

232

rubber of the back left tire started flapping against the asphalt.

"Damn it!" Sky slowed the Jeep down and edged over onto the shoulder.

"Tires are only a year old – fucking nightmare inside a nightmare." Sky put the vehicle into park and opened her side door.

"Stay here. I got it."

I decided to step out anyways, even though I had never changed a flat in my life.

Cars chugged along the highway at a rate of three or four a minute. It was traffic suitable for the type of country the interstate was bisecting. Bumpkin-land. Sky's hometown was surrounded by miles of scrub-scape. It was unlikely any Good Samaritan would pause to assist us. Five cars had passed us since we pulled over (three in our direction, two in the opposing lanes), and not one had bothered to slow down. In fact, they had sped up. Sunset was less than an hour away and the drivers were simply passing through, on to more populated locales and more pressing duties: fighting with know-too-much, ADHD kids over iPad playing rights; channel-flipping on an overpriced cable box attached to an underpriced 50" HDTV; emptying a bladder bloated with cheap beer from a party-of-one at Applebee's happy-hour, or nuking a frozen dinner heated up by a wife who was too tired to cook, too tired to sign divorce papers.

Shadows from the rows of bristlecone pine trees that lined the highway pointed at us like a stream of rifle barrels hoisted by a mob of hunters. The trees were only a few rows deep, but it heightened the feeling of exclusion. We had become prey, wounded game, stranded along a sylvan path, desperate for camouflage, cheating death for as long as we could.

I inched over to Sky who had already removed the spare from the back the Jeep. She handed me a flashlight from the rear storage compartment.

"If you want to help, hold this while I jack it up." Sky squatted down and began to position a hand crank jack. My ankle started to quiver and I leaned against the side of the Jeep to give it a rest.

"Really? You're gonna put your weight on the car?"

I forced myself back onto my hurt ankle, trying to be a little more obedient to the only person who had a valid reason to ditch me and force me to fend for myself. I aimed the flashlight beam at Sky's hands while she turned the jack's handle. She was still barefoot, and her painted toes began to bury themselves into the shoulder's sandy gravel as her arms spun the handle.

"Point the light at the jack, please."

I kneeled to get in a better position for both the light and my ankle. It took Sky less than thirty seconds to get the tire off the ground. She forcibly moved the flashlight into another position before she began unscrewing the tire's lug nuts. Even if my ankle had been healthy, I would've been useless.

The temperature started to drop in tandem with the sun. I started to fidget, to preempt an involuntary shiver. I caught a glance of an object moving along the side of the road about a mile behind us. It looked like a car with its headlights off, trailing along the shoulder. My first thought was that it might be a police cruiser, but it was too tall, shaped more like a truck with a camper shell. Or maybe its height was exaggerated by my viewing angle and the setting sun. My shaking intensified. Sky berated me; I wasn't keeping the light steady. I made myself a mental note to pull out a sweater from my suitcase before we got going again. The Jeep's soft top had been zipped up, but air had whistled its way inside when we were flying down the road. Even with the heater on, the Jeep might still be an uncomfortably cold chamber, callously absorbing my limited warmth.

Sky popped off the deflated tire and put on the spare in almost a single motion. She moved so efficiently I doubted she had picked up this skill from a book in her store. There was a lot about Sky I didn't know, and I hoped that I would have a chance to find out in a calmer, trouble-free future. A future that I had to admit, was difficult to imagine.

My ears clogged up. Something was wrong. I spun back around – the dark object along the shoulder was now only a couple of hundred yards away. It wasn't another vehicle. It was a growing, amorphous shadow that extended across the width of the highway.

"Sky, we need to go."

"A few more minutes."

I maintained my gaze at the shadow as it came closer. If this was the demon, why didn't it just appear next to us? Why was it patiently approaching us like a confident and deliberate stalker? No cars had zoomed down the highway in the past few minutes and aside from Sky's work, our surroundings had become quietly numb.

"Sky, please hurry."

"What's the matter?"

I didn't want to alarm her, but I still needed to convey a sense of urgency. "Need to eat something. I'm not feeling well."

"OK. We'll stop at the next town. I think it's about ten minutes away."

The shadow was now less than a hundred yards away. The last few rays of sunlight were aimed directly at it, but the photons seemed to dissolve before they could come into contact – a miscarriage of the double-slit experiment. I aimed my flashlight at the shadow. The bulb dimmed and burned out. It was the demon and I couldn't stop staring at it. I no longer felt cold and my chest began to tighten.

"A little more light would help." Sky was oblivious to what was occurring.

My ears popped. I was able to look away from the demon and I rose to my feet. "We need to go now!"

Sky was lowering the tire back down with the jack. "I'm done. What's the problem?"

"It's here. It found us."

Sky didn't ask for an explanation. She grabbed the jack and flat tire and flung it into her back seat, smashing my suitcase. I tried not to look at the shadow (now fifty yards away!) and hopped back into the passenger seat, waving the dead flashlight around like a defective game controller. Sky slammed the Jeep's back door shut then paused. She was frozen. Staring at the oncoming shadow. I threw the broken flashlight at her. I purposely didn't hit her, striking the ground a full two feet behind her, but it was enough for Sky to pull her eyes off the demon and onto me, eyes that were clearly aggravated over my poor choice in attention getting. Sky walked up to the driver's side door while I slid into the passenger seat.

I buckled my seatbelt as Sky jumped in and started the engine. I couldn't help myself – I looked back. The obsidian demon was less than a hundred feet away and had swallowed the entire background. The Jeep pulled off the shoulder, as two red dots emerged within the shadow. The demon's eyes. I spun my head forward. It was only a half-second glimpse, but it had punished me with a blinding thought that split through my head. A premonition. Death was rapidly approaching us.

Sky punched the accelerator and we resumed our flight down the highway. My anxiety began to dissipate. How had we escaped from the demon so easily again? Thankfully, I didn't let the question linger nor the morbid warning of death.

"I didn't see anything." I couldn't tell if Sky was talking to me or simply thinking out loud. "I didn't see anything."

An SUV with its high-beams on, passed us going in the opposite direction on the highway. A few seconds later, I heard the sound of screeching tires. For the second time, I turned around. The SUV had skidded off to the side of the road, its taillights angled up as if it had dropped into a shallow ditch.

I turned to Sky. Her eyes were focused on the road in front of her. She had resumed her vice-grip on the steering wheel.

"Should I call 9-1-1?"

"What? Why?" Sky was in denial. Not a good sign.

"I'll call 9-1-1. You can keep going. You don't have to stop at the next town. I'm not hungry."

I dialed the emergency line and reported the accident. My message was vague and I didn't identify myself, although I'm sure they could look up my cell phone number. I convinced myself that whoever had been in the SUV were uninjured and help would arrive for them shortly.

"Hang up, Daniel. Nothing's wrong."

But I knew Sky had to have heard the scream. Even with our windows closed and our increasing distance from the accident, the frantic scream of a woman or a child was unmistakable. A primitive howl that shattered the frigid evening air.

We continued down the road as the final fingers of sunlight relinquished their grasp. I had forgotten to get my sweater, but I didn't feel the least bit chilled. I rolled down my window a few inches and leaned my head against the glass. My skin was burning up. Sweaty. I was feverish again.

Sky turned to look at me. "Why the hell are you smiling?"

I looked out the window to hide my face. The cold rush that caressed my flushed skin felt good, but I was worried. I couldn't be getting sick again, not around Sky. She was the only thing that had made me feel better. Something was wrong. Something had infected me again. Something had stirred up my blood, and was restless to escape.

TEN

We traveled approximately two hundred miles before Sky pulled the Jeep off the highway to stop for gas. My feverish state had become unbearable, but I did my best to try and hide it from Sky. Judging from her hawkish glances that constantly pecked at me, I didn't think I had been very successful. We drove into a well-lit and populated gas station based on Sky's assertion that it was the safest place. Her claim didn't really make sense since it was the most isolated building of the highway outpost (which housed three other gas stations, five fast food joints and two family restaurants), and she wouldn't acknowledge that the demon was physically pursuing us. Sky refused to talk about the demon despite my multiple attempts to garner her opinion.

Sky told me to wait in the Jeep while she went inside the gas station's mini-mart to pay for gas. I had very little money on me ($14.33 to be exact), but I still tried to hand a few bills to Sky; it felt like the honorable thing to do. She refused. I got out of the Jeep and told her I wouldn't mind keeping her company. She told me to get back into the Jeep.

"The demon, Sky. It's mimicking us. I don't think we should separate."

"It'll only be a few minutes."

"I need to use the restroom. Clean myself up. Wipe the cobwebs away."

Sky continued to the entrance of the mini-mart, not bothering to wait for me as I unhooked my phone from the charger and stuck it in my pocket. I didn't want to miss my father's call. I wasn't sure why he hadn't contacted me yet.

As I trailed behind Sky, new perspiration beads formed on my forehead, upper lip, and neck. My temperature was still elevated, localized around my head. Frankly, I was afraid to go to the bathroom. I didn't want to look in the mirror and receive a repetitive, disheartening confirmation that I had physically deteriorated, returning to the point where I appeared mentally unstable. I didn't want to verify that my smiling face was the cause of Sky's shrewish demeanor.

I yelled out to her. "In case we get separated, we should have a safe word. Like in a movie."

At the mini-mart doors, Sky turned around but didn't make eye contact. "What are you talking about?"

"Maybe an answer to a question. Like password security. Something the demon wouldn't know. So we know it's really us."

An elderly couple with their crooked, fossilized hips practically fused together trudged out of the store. They both gave me a sideways, suspicious leer. I limped past them and caught up to Sky.

"How about this: name someone you love?"

Sky turned to look through the glass doors. It was a conventional store with mummified aisles of stale crackers, broken cookies, decade-old beef jerky, and brain-dead magazines, surrounded by a bank of refrigerated cabinets stocked with watered-down beer, bottled-up tap water and diabetes-inducing soft drinks. There were half a dozen people inside, not counting the ditzy-face girl behind the register.

"Whatever." I couldn't tell if Sky agreed with me or was blowing me off.

"It's a question the demon wouldn't know how to answer."

"Yeah. Nothing evil could ever love someone."

For some reason her clarification made me giggle. Sky entered the store without holding the door open for me, cutting off my inane chuckles.

239

As I headed down a skinny hallway at the back of the store to locate the restroom, Sky started to meander around the aisles. Was she hungry? There was a McDonald's across the street from the gas station, but neither of us had mentioned the need to gorge ourselves on cheap burgers and fries. I wasn't hungry at all. Back at the hospital, Sky had mentioned that the meal I had eaten for lunch had made me feel better. She had actually said "look better," but "feel better" was how I chose to interpret her words. Maybe Sky was getting something to help me "feel better" once again.

The men's bathroom was single occupancy and the locked door informed me I would have to wait. My left ankle didn't hurt much. It felt like a weighty and thick stump, an engorged rock that had been calcified during my afternoon sprint to freedom, and my feverish state was likely cloaking any additional damage I was inflicting on myself. I watched Sky wander through the store, picking up some potato chips, looking over at me, putting the bag of chips down, reading the label on a package of jerky, looking at me again, walking to the refrigerated section, snagging a bottle of water, glancing at me once more and grabbing a second bottle of water. Her quick decision making on these minor food choices was similar to the rapid-fire judgment she had shown in sprinting me out of the hospital and driving me all the way to my father's house. I had to regain control of my body. I didn't want Sky to regret her impulsive nature. Funny how that characteristic endeared me to Sky, but provoked me with my mother.

In order to stand in the cashier line, Sky had to skid around two beefy, bearded men wearing flannel shirts and oil stained jeans, two flatheads who looked like Appalachian-bred truck drivers. They were blocking an entire aisle, taking their time, contemplating which brand of mints or chewing gum would conceal their possum breath. I hadn't seen any semis parked at the station, but it was possible they had wandered over here from the Golden Arches – looking for a breath saver to top off their gassy mix of carbohydrate and protein fuel. Even from my distance, I could see the trucker's doltish eyes trailing over Sky's behind as she merged into the queue, balancing two water bottles in her left hand like Lady Justice holding her scales, and I felt a barb of protectionism poke out of me. I was certain that Sky would be able to handle any of their unwanted advances, yet I had an almost irrepressible compulsion to pounce on the two flatheads, pluck out their eyes with my fingers, and end their lascivious gazing forever.

Sky stood behind a middle-aged, scrawny Asian couple who were rustling a couple of hyperactive boys, possible twins around six or seven years old. When the lion-eyed wife glanced at Sky, she whispered something to her trout-mouthed husband and they oddly steered themselves and their two brats out of line. We had apparently wandered into a mini-mart filled with obnoxious assholes.

An oily faced teenage boy, with a severe overbite and wearing a uniform touting the gas station's colors and name, exited the bathroom with the trailing odor of a cigarette. He sneered at me and gave me a slight jostle with his shoulder as he brushed past. The store's patrons weren't the only ones with behavior problems. No doubt the kid had been taking an unscheduled smoke break from a boss who would hopefully wise up and fire him, but since he looked older than the cashier, he probably was the station manager. Sky and I needed to leave this human dump soon, otherwise I was liable to test out my fury and annotate the consequences. I stomped into the bathroom, slapped on the ventilation fan, and locked the door.

There was no bathroom mirror so I had no idea how degraded I had become. I tried to tidy myself up as best I could by splashing cold water on my face, wetting a paper towel to dampen my neck and chest, and using my wet fingers to comb my wild hair. I think I did a better job of cleaning myself than my attempt in the hospital bathroom, and I felt cooler, but my stress level was still as high as it had been when Sky had driven the Jeep away from demon shadow on the road.

I tried some hokey deliberate breathing, inhaling and exhaling on a meditation-prescribed ten count, as I distractedly read some of the juvenile graffiti scrawled on the bathroom wall next to the toilet. There was a happy face smoking a joint, a large penis with hairy, jumbo testicles, and a swastika that looked more like the letter S crossed by a sideways number 5. There was also writing – a person's name (*Josue*), something illegible (*curlies bab*?), and a fairly long, ungrammatical inscription. A bungled requiem to a doomed relationship:

She a mutha fuckin liar!
Kink in the stink!
You anotha tea-baggin bitch!
so I guess we aint meant to be we

The disrespected lover seemed to have lost some of his steam as he wrote his final sentence. Likely zoomed past anger and went face-first into depression. Maybe he even regretted his words and had gotten back together with his Delilah as soon as he had left the bathroom. Must've been difficult to let go of a *tea-baggin bitch*. I managed another small chuckle which eased me a bit, realizing that upholding a shred of humor in bleak times was always considered a highly positive attribute.

However, my lightheartedness was choked into paranoia as my eyes drifted down a few tiles to another line of scribbled words.

Don't trust her, Daniel. Equilibrium is a dangerous place.

It could have been a message for anyone – my name was common enough. But what wall-tagging delinquent would write the word "equilibrium?" I started sweating again.

Don't trust her, Daniel.

Those words branded me as if they were the prescient advice of a close confidant. Who should I not trust? Sky? Ridiculous. I had no reason to worry about her. She had become a savior to me. Perhaps another meaningless incarnation. Or at the very least, a fever induced visual scourge.

I tried to regain some liveliness by rereading the previous disgruntled message. Instead, my eyes focused on the capitalized words. *She. Kink. You.* The first letter of each word spelled out S-K-Y. My mind would not step down from its vulgar role, acting as my worst enemy.

I drenched my face with more cold water, hoping it would permeate my skin and infiltrate my stewing bloodstream. I had to stop formulating absurd connections. I slurped water into my mouth, relieving my throat which had become parched and itchy. I would not get worse. I would regain dominion over my body and my mind. I would stop manufacturing messages where there were none. I would reclaim my composure, and return with Sky to the Jeep and give her no further cause for alarm. To hell with the etched advice on the wall – I needed to obtain equilibrium.

The sound of the toilet flushing startled me.

I stood up and the room began to bob and weave after I discovered what had triggered the automatic flush on the toilet. My head. Through some awful loss of awareness, I had somehow drifted away from the sink, kneeled over to the fecal speckled toilet bowl, and bathed my face in the toilet's foamy, bacterium-drenched water. Foulness that I had also generously lapped into my mouth.

I threw up until I could no longer summon any further contents from my stomach. I dragged myself back to the sink, wiped the excess froth from my mouth with a few paper towels, and scurried out of the restroom.

Like an intoxicated vagrant who had been denied his purchase of *Old English "800,"* I staggered out of the mini-mart, tripping over my own outrage and disgrace. I was scattered. Lost. I scanned the vehicles at the gas pumps. A black pickup. A silver sedan. Cars, trucks, SUVs – where was Sky's Jeep? Did she leave? No. She wouldn't. Had the demon returned? Attacked Sky? Or had something else happened to her?

Don't trust her, Daniel.

I looked back inside the mini-mart – was she still inside? Another pervy trucker stood at the checkout line. An overweight kid, hopped through the sugar carb aisles. A woman in a business suit burned her fingers as she served herself a coffee. No sign of Sky. Maybe she had gone to the restroom herself? But then where was her Jeep?

Don't trust her, Daniel. Don't trust her, Daniel.
Don't trust her, Daniel. Don't trust her, Daniel.
Don't trust her, Daniel. Don't trust her, Daniel.

I violently shook my head to obliterate the foreign, invading phrase that had been insidiously injected into me. I pulled my cell phone out of my pocket to check the time. 8:43 PM. And one missed call. My father. I hadn't heard my phone ring or felt it vibrate. I must have missed it while I was hunched over the toilet, purging away my latest lapse from objective reality.

There was no voice message from my father, so I quickly called him back. No answer. I left a brief second message on his voice mail, asking him to please try contacting me again as soon as possible. Even though I had missed speaking with him, I regained some confidence. My father would help me. I could take a seat and wait here for him, if needed. I could walk over to Mickey's and take two cheeseburgers, if needed.

(*Melinda, the prescription says: take two Ativan tablets (1 mg each) twice a day, IF NEEDED.*)

I scanned my surroundings with a half-cleaned head. I spotted Sky's Jeep at the parking lot of a family diner about two hundred yards away. Relief? Sky hadn't left me, but why did she move her vehicle without telling me?

I hustled over to the Jeep. Sky wasn't sitting inside. I tried the doors. Locked. Had she gone into the diner to get something to eat?

I scanned the restaurant. A poorly lit sign written with cheap, marquee lettering said the diner's name: *Ravie's*. And the special of the day: *BBQ Spaghetti*. Who would want to eat that? I peered through the diner's boxcar windows, skipping through the patrons searching for Sky. The Asian couple again with their twin terrors. A lithe blond woman eating alone; a stumpy brunette cozying up with a balding beau. An urbane fifty-something man sitting across from two preppy twenty-something guys, trading high fives.

I located Sky. She appeared near the entrance, closely following what looked like yet another truck driver. A slack-jawed, scrawny, middle-aged clod, wearing a forest green quilted vest and an avocado green knit skull cap. An unlit cigarette stuck limply out of his mouth. I could almost detect a pungent cloud of smoke emanating from this trucker, as if his entire body had turned into a Kafkaesque tobacco leaf.

Sky and the trucker tramped out of the diner. My loathing of the man intensified as he handed Sky a cigarette and lit it up for her before lighting his own. Once we were back on the road, I needed to find a way to delicately inform Sky that her secret habit was abhorrent to me.

Intentionally clenching my hands into fists, I marched over to Sky and her newfound smoking buddy. The trucker looked away when he saw me while Sky took a long drag on her cigarette before dropping it onto the ground. The trucker stomped out her barely smoked cig as Sky moved forward, flashing the palm of her hand at me like a traffic cop. I stopped walking, unsure as to what was disturbing her and concerned that my appearance still looked disheveled.

"Go wait by my Jeep."

"Why? What's wrong?"

I relaxed my fists and forced myself to ignore the trucker who continued to smoke his cigarette and stare at the ground, like a perturbed father pretending to be preoccupied as he waited for his daughter's date to leave.

Sky dropped her hand. "I'm tired."

"Do you want me to drive?"

"I want to go home."

What was wrong with Sky?

Don't trust her, Daniel.

"You want to leave me?"

(*Danny you are completely blind! Blind! Blind! Blind!*)

"No. I'll wait with you until your father calls...."

The trucker interrupted Sky and finally made eye contact with me. "The young lady should've left. You belong in a hospital. Crazy looking fuck." As he spoke, the veins on his forehead swelled up like suffocating worms tunneling out of inundated dirt.

My fury against the trucker flushed through my own blood, slicing through the epithelial walls of my veins and arteries. My cells were engorged with inflamed red cells and it felt good.

"You won't speak to me anymore."

My words had slithered out of my mouth and wrapped themselves around the trucker's neck. He bowed his head and kicked the toe of his Timberlands into the pebbly ground. I had scared him. Empowerment was always a noble goal. The night air whirled around my body, tickling each exposed layer of heated skin. Fever could be a gift.

Sky stepped in front of the trucker. "You need to relax. I'm going home."

"I'm sorry Sky, but you're acting irrationally." This time my words sounded patronizing and I knew I had made a mistake.

"What's happening to you?"

I needed to cajole logic out of her by keeping things simple. "Did you move the Jeep to get away from me? Is that why you're over here with him, smoking a cigarette?"

"You were in the fucking bathroom for over twenty minutes! I had the manager bang on the door to ask if you were all right – all you did was laugh!"

"I didn't hear anyone."

"I felt like a dumbshit waiting for you. So I drove over here. I stopped here. I could've kept going."

The trucker regained some courage. "Just let her be."

I laughed at him. He was nothing more than a meek, ignorant man, a waste of organic self-assembly and replication. I visualized myself slamming the trucker's head into the ground until his DNA denatured, smashed into crumbly oblivion. I took a few steps in his direction.

"Fuck this. Good luck, hon." The chicken-shit trucker tossed his cigarette to the ground with a fluttering hand, ducked past me, and trotted out to the diner's parking lot. Sky's eyes followed him for a moment. Her smoking buddy had acquiesced; I had won. My vehement blood no longer boiled and my hostile thoughts began to decompress.

"It'll be better now, Sky. Everything will be OK."

"Fuck you. I made a mistake. You should've stayed at the hospital."

Why was Sky challenging me? Had the demon affected her? *Infected* her?

"Who do you love?"

"What?"

"Password security – remember? Who do you love?"

"I'm not playing around."

"This is serious, Sky. Please answer."

"Fine. My bookstore." Sky brushed past me, heading to the parking lot.

"Nope. Has to be a person."

"Oh my God! Fuck off!"

"Please, Sky."

"No one, Daniel. Fucking no one."

I smiled brightly at her to try and alleviate some of her unfounded distress. "That's how I used to feel."

"So what? I'm the fucking idiot." Sky picked up her pace; she was heading to her Jeep. I began to follow, and my hurt ankle came back to life. For some reason, Sky didn't trust me.

(*Don't trust her, Daniel.*)

I had done something wrong.

(*I'm shit-full of sorry, bro.*)

"We need to stick together, Sky. I promise everything will be OK."

246

"You promise? You don't even know me! And I don't fucking know you!"

Sky was crashing, much like I had when challenged with something so incomprehensible, so mentally destructive, as the demon. I could easily empathize with how overwhelming the day must have been for her. How confusion and fear could occlude any semblance of reality, or rational awareness. Sky needed to regain her sense of self.

"You're fucking real."

"I'm going home." Sky was a few yards away from the Jeep. For a moment, I considered letting her go. My health had improved. My fever was under control. I was under control. All I needed to do was grab my things out of her car and wait for my father to call again. Tell him to pick me up underneath the BBQ Spaghetti sign.

But that would be an egregious mistake. Leaving Sky was exactly what the demon wanted from me. It wanted me to submit to the same selfish urges I displayed the night Melinda died. To cast off Sky so she could succumb to the same miserable fate.

I would not allow that to happen.

"Wait!" I shouted out as Sky reached the driver's side door.

Sky opened her door. "You can grab your shit or I can throw it out of my car."

"Wait." I repeated. Softer.

I would not allow my life to be an imperfect replay of a Platonic form, a rerun of an unearned, unsolvable tragedy. I needed to progress, chart a linear, or better, an exponential path away from past errors and shortcomings. That was the path that would take me away from the demon. That was the path I could only achieve with Sky. There was absolutely no way I would surmount the demon's cavernous shadow if Sky wasn't with me.

"Wait." It was my weakest utterance of the night.

"Wait for what?" Sky opened up the Jeep's rear hatch.

I tapped into every bit of energy inside my body, even harnessing the sparks from the tiniest biochemical reactions occurring in the least consequential cells. I stoked the remaining embers of my compassion, and let the past melt away as a preternatural speech poured out of my mouth.

"I despise everything that has happened to you because of me. I never wanted you to experience the confusion and insanity that I've endured. I didn't want to compound any pain and torment that still afflicts you. The demon that haunts me is something that is impossible to comprehend, much less accept without incurring immense negative consequences. It shatters every logical, natural thought, every assumed concept of reality, and you begin to lose trust in everything. And everyone. But I am alive. I am alive, Sky! And it's because of you. You have helped me so damn much. I only want to help you in return. I want to be your friend. If you need to leave me in order to ensure your own sanity and survival, I will accept that. I can accept my fate, and I will obtain happiness knowing that you will live and live well. I'm so sorry that you had to be with me during these brief and endless moments in my life that have imprisoned you in a random and Godless universe of my own making."

Sky closed the hatch. She approached me in silence, and stood in front of me. I had never spoken so eloquently in my life. Sky probably thought I had turned into the demon. I nervously awaited her response.

"I can drive you back to the hospital. Is that what you want?"

"Yes."

"I really want to trust you. In order for me to stay with you, I really need to be able to do that."

"I understand. You can trust me, Sky."

"Why do you look so fucked up?"

"Blame my mother."

A tentative grin slipped out of Sky. I had finally reached her. Sky's next words fumbled out of her, exhausted and fragile. "Your universe isn't completely random. Or Godless. There are good people."

My nose began to run, but I was at ease. My mind was calm. I had reached equilibrium and it was not a dangerous place.

Sky reached out and rubbed my shoulder. It was a substantial moment and my arms sprung out and wrapped around her, squeezing her tightly. Sky's body became rigid and she didn't reciprocate the hug. It didn't matter. We would remain together and I would continue to be her protector.

248

"Please let me go."

I complied and wiped my nose clear. "I'm sorry. Thank you, Sky."

Sky nodded and gave me a half-hearted smile. "Let's go before it gets any colder." Did she still have misgivings?

(*Don't trust her, Daniel.*)

The night hadn't gotten that much cooler.

(*Metaphor, motherfucker!*)

I needed to stop being ridiculous. I would never stop trusting Sky.

Never.

As Sky reopened the door the Jeep, I made a request. "Can I drive?" I was so energized I wouldn't be able to sit still in the passenger seat. "You look tired and it'll help take my mind off things. I've always wanted a Jeep and since it's an automatic it's in my skill range."

Sky climbed into the driver's seat and I thought I had been rebuffed, but she shimmied over the center console to the passenger seat. I followed her inside and jumped into the driver's seat. Sky handed me the keys. "I only need a little rest. Thirty minutes tops."

I started the engine as Sky slumped in her seat. It was as if we had not only exchanged roles within the Jeep, but also states of alertness. I had renewed my strength. Sky had become lethargic. I pulled the Jeep out of the parking lot as my phone vibrated in my pocket. I couldn't answer it. I couldn't tell my dad I wasn't coming.

"The left onramp, not the right."

I took the highway onramp going away from my father's house. I was content to take Sky home. No matter what happened, I would not let anything hurt her. I would not make the same mistake with Sky that I had committed with Melinda.

As I rolled the Jeep smoothly onto the two lane road, Sky kicked off her flip-flops and turned up the heater. After a few miles, she shut her eyes. My lips curled up into a smile, a real smile. I had regained her trust.

We had been driving for about thirty minutes when I thought I heard a groan squeak out of Sky.

"Are you OK?"

She didn't respond. She looked asleep. I wanted to extend my hand out to her and give her a reassuring touch, but I didn't want to wake her.

I let my eyes bounce back and forth from Sky and the road. The smooth, straight highway was fairly empty and if I wasn't so wide awake the monotony of staying in between the dotted white lines would be coma-inducing. Sky was definitely asleep. The logo emblem on her sweatshirt slowly heaved, up and down with automatic, effortless breaths. Stray strands of her curly brown hair had fallen onto her legs and appeared to glow orange from the combination of the Jeep's interior lights and the blackness of her tights. The soles of her bare feet were tarnished with dirt from all the commotion of the day. Sky was not a beauty like Melinda, but she was a molecular wonder. And together we had achieved maximum covalency.

My unhurried, appreciative mind sifted through desiccated memories, distilling one pure, poignant moment. A moment that I revived despite my body's parasympathetic efforts to suffocate it.

How original.

Melinda was sitting in the passenger seat of a rental car, a taxi cab yellow Ford Focus with an interior that had been lathered with lemon-lime Fabreeze. I was driving the car on the Interstate. It was after ten, at night. Junior Year. Memorial Day weekend.

What?

I said, how original. You heard me, Danny.

We were halfway through a road trip to the coast to stay at the beach house of Melinda's cousin Jess. The beach house wasn't really a house, but a thirty-year-old rental shack jammed next to a trashy beach that would be teeming with vacationing lemmings over the holiday – mainly twenty-year-old drunks, desperate for a budget remedy to boredom. Jess was giving up drunk days on the beach for drunk days in the mountains so we would have the place to ourselves.

We were stuck on a glacier of traffic, having left at the wrong time. I had suggested that we should give up our fight with the highway rats, and find an inexpensive hotel to crash for the night. Head over to her cousin's place in the morning. Melinda had vetoed my idea apparently on its lack of novelty.

But we're just sitting here. I'm going to take the next exit.

I took her silence as acquiescence, and forced a path off the Interstate, choosing to exit into an isolated agricultural town surrounded by cabbage and tomato fields. I made my decision to enter the boondocks not on familiarity with the undeveloped surroundings (in fact, persisting on the road a little while longer would have taken us to a much larger and amenity-laden city), but on impertinence. I wanted to throw some bitter scenery onto Melinda's sour face.

She had been excited when we started the trip. The weather was balmy and Melinda couldn't wait to tickle her feet against the sandy, iridescent pebbles and numb her lips against the cool, briny water. For the ride, she had even opted to wear the cover up dress that she would put on over her bikini, unconcerned that wearing the gossamer, peach fabric over her underwear revealed every stitched outline of her Victoria's Secret navy colored bra and thong.

I turned right on the exit and down the main thoroughfare of the farm town, passing a large shopping center anchored by a graffiti tagged Safeway, a taqueria and a Taco Bell, a few shoebox homes (irregularly packed together like a kicked-over pile of Legos), and empty lots pockmarked by overgrown crabgrass, witch grass and palm trees. I only saw two hotels. One looked abandoned and the other was a Super 8. Melinda remained gratingly silent during the drive through town until I pulled into the Super 8 parking lot and shut off the engine.

What's wrong with you? Are you doing this on purpose? I'm staying in the car.

Beach house is probably as dirty as this place.

I tried to laugh, but Melinda continued with her onslaught.

This isn't spontaneous, Danny. It's a waste of time. How can you not know the difference?

I had never seen Melinda so upset over what I believed to be a minor disagreement, or at worst, a superfluous lack of tact on my part. All I wanted to do was make a calm, rational decision to make our travel easier. She was lobbing irrelevant criticisms at me as if she wanted a war. I chose to remain neutral.

No response? Perfect. Just take me home, Danny. I'd rather go home.

What did she expect from me?

It's a joke, Melinda. There are more hotels in the next town.

I restarted the engine.

Oh, God! Is that what you think I want? Boldness, Danny. I needed you to be bold. Not blind.

Melinda let loose with a fake series of laughs.

I don't know what you want, Melinda.

I wanted to go to the beach.

We're still going! In the morning.

Too late, Danny. I wanted this to be different!

Nothing Melinda was saying made sense to me and I struggled to pull the car out of the lot and back onto the main road.

Do you want to go to the beach or not? It was your idea.

Exactly.

This is impossible. I'm trying, Melinda. Can't you see I'm trying?

I had turned the wrong way on the road, and had to make a U-turn in order to head to the Interstate.

Stop the car if you can't drive and talk.

What? I'm almost back on the highway.

Pull the car over, Danny.

Why?

Over there.

Melinda pointed to any empty parking lot next to a closed Hispanic grocery store. I decided to oblige her. I parked the car in a spot that was farthest from the road and faced a three foot retaining wall that supported a weedy, rocky slope. I turned the car off, but left the headlights on. I stared at the beams as they lit up the cracked cinderblock wall, highlighting a few powdery pieces of cement breaking free.

You're trying too hard.

That isn't my fault.

And you're going to kill the battery.

Melinda reached over me and flipped off the headlights.

If you didn't want to go the beach, you could've just said so.

I wanted to go.

You said you hated the ocean.

No, I said I wanted to go with you.

A foggy minute passed before Melina responded. In that time, my eyes had adjusted to the limited light and I noticed a

252

violet hyacinth plant that had managed to take root on the slope. An elegant flower that didn't belong on a craggy pile of dirt.

You're better than this, Danny.

I've been the same since you met me. Since Perkins.

I know.

Our Senior Year will be better. It'll be the best. I'll be getting my own place. You'll be out of the sorority house.

I'm sorry I made you put up with that place.

My mouth dried up and the air around me grew heavy like a forsaken specter had crept into the car with us, demanding attention.

What do you want to do? Just tell me.

I don't know, Danny.

We sat in painful silence for another minute until Melinda turned the ignition key and flipped on the radio. She fumbled through the meager sampling of local stations. Tejano music. Static. Hip-Hop. More Spanish music. More static. Top 40. Country tunes. Finally she stopped on an 80's flashback. The song playing was "Like the Weather" by 10,000 Maniacs – one of Melinda's favorites. She let the song run through the chorus then turned the radio off.

Melinda looked out her side window.

It's been almost three months.

I'm not keeping track.

You always count the days and hours. You can't stop counting time. It's like you're always waiting for something.

It doesn't matter. No need to keep track.

Why? It does to me.

I stretched over the center armrest and began peppering Melinda's shoulder and neck with kisses.

No, Danny.

I told you. It doesn't matter.

It should.

She closed her eyes.

Is this really what you want?

Yes. Don't you?

You should hate me. He danced and danced and danced with me.

I'll never hate you. I still love you.

Melinda laughed.

253

The world is dancing around us. See the flowers? Look – they're dancing!

I only see shadows.

We're the shadows, Danny.

Dance with me, Melinda. Now.

I jerked the driver's seat back to its fully reclined position.

We had never had sex in a car before. I had convinced myself that it would be too cumbersome and too adolescent, as if I had actually experienced bumbling, backseat car sex in high school and wanted to distance myself from it. Neither Melinda nor I had a car so it had never really been an option for one of our liaisons. We had kept things conventional; our biggest stray from a bed occurred on top of a sleeping bag at an overnight camping trip in the hills above the University.

After Melinda ran her fingers through her hair several times as if it had become severely matted, she climbed over the center armrest and straddled me, kneeing me in the thigh. As she shifted her weight to counter her mistake, her forearm slid off my chest and jammed me in my throat. She didn't apologize. I told her again that I loved her.

Melinda unzipped my pants and moved fast. Inadvertently bumped the car horn a couple of times when she tried to lean into me. Dug one of her fingernails into my neck when I tried to thrust. A small trickle of blood that ran to my shoulder blade felt like a tuft of melting snow.

We finished before the windows even had a chance to fog up. Melinda rolled off me and resumed staring out the side window. I zipped up my pants, and focused on the hyacinth flowers. They did appear to be dancing, trying to break free from their soiled prison. Finally I spoke.

Who was he? Do I know him?

Melinda turned away from the window. She stared at the cut on my neck.

I hurt you.

It doesn't hurt.

I think the beach might be too crowded.

I think it'll be fine.

It'll be too windy. Sand will hit my face.

It'll be fine. There will only be sunlight on your face. It'll drip off your face.

Are you sure?

No.

I want to be sure.

I don't know how to do that.

Don't stop dancing, Danny. Don't stop dancing, or else....

I started up the car to get back onto the Interstate. As I reversed, the car lights hit the hyacinth plant and I realized the flowers weren't violet, but red. Blood red as if they had exsanguinated me with their beauty. The headlights created shadows against the hill and wall, shadows that were dancing madly as we drove away.

Once on the highway, the traffic was so familiar it became easy to pretend Melinda and I had never taken the exit. The accidental detour. We completed our weekend trip with no mention of our conversation, our parking lot liaison, and no further arguments, plastering ourselves with thoughtless play and automatic kisses, topping it all off with Melinda's Instagram post of my serenely content face cast against a purple ocean sunset – a waxed and buffered photo that had been processed with the most self-aggrandizing filter available. It got over 100 likes.

I had to pull Sky's Jeep over to the side of the road. An acute, distressing realization had seized me.

In an ideal, just world, Melinda would've never been the perfect woman for me.

My jaw clenched. Every muscle in my back and legs shortened, ready to jettison my body into an unforgiving windshield. I looked over at Sky.

She was awake. Her sweatshirt was off, exposing a black lace bra. Her feet were on top the dashboard, her legs splayed apart, and her right hand buried underneath the waistband of her tights. Her left hand reached out to me as a shy grin heated her face.

"Is this what you want, Danny?"

As alluring as Sky was, her seductive actions were too overt, too outlandish. Too manipulative.

I grumbled. "I don't trust you."

"How can you not trust me? I finally trusted you."

The plush voice slipping out of Sky was purposefully unthreaded to entice me. This wasn't Sky next to me. This was the demon, capitalizing on my pained remembrance of Melinda. Somehow all the righteous anger I had accumulated moments earlier had transformed into fragile impulses of frustration and disillusionment. My chest quivered as if I were about to cry.

"Come closer, Danny." Sky lifted up her bra.

I needed to maintain control over my reptilian brain. "No. I don't trust you."

But I couldn't take my eyes off Sky and I couldn't stop myself from obeying. I dragged my body over to her seat, and crawled on top of her. I nuzzled her neck and breasts with my nose and lips while she ran her fingers through my hair. Her salty skin tingled my tongue. I let my hand swoop and caress her thighs and slip in between her legs. Sky leaned into me, and I unzipped my pants, rapidly pulling them down along with my underwear. My eyes began to water, upset that I couldn't resist.

A powerful slap ran across my face, splitting my lip and stunning my nose. It took my brain a maladjusted second to process the entirely new scene in front of my eyes.

Sky was fully dressed, disgust and revulsion marring her face. I hovered over her, dumbfounded, my pants and briefs down to my knees and my erect penis sticking out like an unexpected prosthetic limb.

"Get the fuck off me!"

Sky kneed me in the groin, sending me back down into the driver's seat, gasping for air. She reached for her side door and started fumbling with the door handle to leave, apparently too shaken to notice that she needed to undo her seatbelt first. She screamed at me without looking at me.

"Fucking asshole! God damn you!"

Sky's words slurred from the frantic weeping she was trying to suppress. I found it incongruously humorous that she couldn't figure out she needed to get out of her own seatbelt.

I tried to calmly explain the situation. That either I had been dreaming or this was a manufactured ploy by the demon to destroy us. I started the engine to Sky's Jeep and told her that everything would be fine once we got going once again.

Sky finally released her belt and popped the door open. But before she could step outside, I screamed.

"This was your idea, Melinda!"

I said Melinda even though I was completely aware I was talking to Sky. It was simply a last ditch effort to distract her from leaving.

Sky twisted her head to face me. "God help me. Not again."

Unlike her earlier inflamed barks, these words tumbled out of Sky like a forfeiting whimper. Surprisingly, Sky didn't bolt out of the Jeep. She sat still and silent, her mouth half open, her eyes glazed.

"It's the demon, Sky. Give me a chance to explain."

My friend wasn't moving. She had become alarmingly inert, essentially paralyzed.

"Sky?" I repeated her name several times before I realized that her eyes were not fixated on me. They were looking past my face, staring blankly at something directly behind me. I swiveled around.

Well done. I knew we'd be together.

The demon's lanky security guard persona had returned. The demon was standing outside my closed side window, its face pressing against the glass. The circles within its eyes swirled around their red prisms as he cast a lecherous grin.

Let's finish her. Together.

I raised my arm to shield myself from the abomination and was blind-sided by the bleakness surrounding my burn scar. The skin on my arm appeared to be hideously burned, bubbling amber blisters puckered my skin, thinning it so it appeared translucent. Through the blisters I could see my muscle fibers twitching, stretched red tubules bundled in a lacy web of capillaries, and nerve cords vibrating as if attacked by a fusillade of electric shocks. But my burn scar was unscathed. Against my wounded, scarlet skin it had become dark matter, an impenetrable mass that refracted any trace of light away from it. My eyes widened and drifted into the darkness.

I was evolving.

My mind welcomed disorder.

Complex adaptive systems sometime lose the ability for self-organization.

A multitude of interactions does not lead to causation, only an emergence of patterns with irreducible properties.

Equilibrium is dangerous. Equilibrium is death.

A few fractured photons of light, minute pieces of reality, staggered randomly in the darkness until a few landed on the rod receptors on my retina. The Jeep's dashboard was lit up. The engine was running. I couldn't give up. Not yet.

I dropped my foot onto the gas pedal, roaring the engine. The sound enabled me to regain some measure of control and I shifted myself forward in my seat, and popped the gear shift into drive.

The Jeep clumsily jerked forward, its tires scrapping against the soft highway shoulder as it dug its way back onto the asphalt. I kept my foot down on the gas pedal, driving faster, speeding faster, over reflective lines and reflective bumpers, chasing distant tail lights, breathing faster, seeing faster, feeling the glimmer of starlight racing above me against my face. Until I turned my head to look at Sky.

Her body was flaccid. Blood was trickling out of her nose. And she was precariously close to tumbling out of the Jeep from the side door which was still wide open.

I braked. Pulled back over to the side of the highway. I leaned over and lugged Sky's unresponsive body back into the seat, and struggled to reach for the side door. It took me several tries before I could grab the handle, and in the meantime, a large swath of blackness, the undying demon shadow spanned across the highway in front of me.

With one final, extenuated lunge, I grabbed the handle and slammed the door shut. The shadow began to obscure the interior of the Jeep. It had penetrated the vehicle, and was penetrating Sky. I pulled the Jeep back onto the highway and drove over the dirt and brush covered median, flipping a U-turn away from the shadow, and almost colliding with the one sedan travelling in my new direction. I regained my speed, but kept track of the speedometer, leveling out when it read 90 MPH. I glanced through the rear view mirror – no sign of the shadow. No sign of the demon.

I checked Sky, hoping for a positive sign. A lot of blood had seeped out of her nose; some of it had gotten on the back of my hand, apparently when I leaned over her to close the door. Maybe she was just unconscious. Her mind only taking a quick respite from the shock she had experienced. But I couldn't detect if she was still breathing. Should I risk taking her to the hospital? Call 9-1-1? What would I say? How could I explain anything?

I was asking pointless questions. I couldn't stop. If Sky had any remaining capacity for survival, stopping would only give the demon a chance to catch up and finish us.

Sky had to be OK. She had to survive! I had saved her by driving away. I had done the right thing. I needed to live up to my promise that everything would be OK.

But what if I had been too late? What if I had failed again?

Sky was grey and lifeless. She looked like Melinda, in her final moments, lying on the floor of her apartment. I wanted to cry but I couldn't manufacture a single tear. Grief swathed me with stillness.

I continued speeding down the highway, now heading towards my father's house, but it didn't matter. My arms were abandoning me. Although my skin no longer appeared burned, my muscles had turned to slush. I started to lose control of the steering wheel. The Jeep drifted erratically, skidding up against the dirt median, swerving across the pavement, drifting onto the shoulder, swerving back onto the highway. I couldn't keep my mind steady much longer.

I shouldn't have driven away. I should have conceded everything to the demon.

Because if Sky were dead, it no longer mattered if I were dead too.

ELEVEN

My reckless path on the highway continued until a coupe on my left blared its horn at me and squirreled out of my way. The near-miss made me cognizant that the two lane highway had grown to four and that I was heading directly into an impassable juncture.

Two lines of cars at a standstill. A traffic jam. There was no way I could maintain my accelerated state without plowing into every vehicle in front of me. Instead of a recovered memory, I was cowered by my brain's instant review of a probable outcome.

A Mercedes GLK-Class. In the front, two young parents with matching Brooks Brothers' outfits and laser bleached teeth. In the back, their daughter, all blond, all curls, seven or eight years old, engrossed with a cartoon game app on her mother's passé cell phone. And their son, an infant, barely over nine months old, asleep with a binky in a luxurious leather car seat.

The impact unfolds in slow motion. Sky's Jeep crushes through the entire rear cargo space of the SUV. The parents last moment, a hushed, dirty joke, is shattered as their necks whip forward and their heads slam into their respective, *exploding airbags, bashing their faces into a pulpy mess. The daughter is strangled by her seatbelt as her tiny, frail body flounders wildly in the back seat, her arms dislocating from her shoulder sockets as she incomprehensibly tries to hold onto her mother's phone. The $900.00 car seat fails. Its polished, emblazoned buckles break loose and the baby flies up into the air, an angelic soul in weightless flight, still asleep and floating, until his soft head careens into the back of his mother's seat.*

My suicidal inclinations abruptly terminated. I would not inflict disaster on any innocent people around me and bestow a greater, more ruinous victory for the demon. I took my foot off the gas pedal and slammed on the brakes.

The Jeep jolted to a stop, and I thought I heard a slight gasp leak out of Sky. I stared over at her – her listless body was still slumped on the passenger seat like an unloved, partially crafted *American Girl* doll. The blood from her nose had begun to dry on her pale cheeks and lips.

Are the ones least equipped to handle tragedy, doomed to inflict further tragedy on those they care about the most?

I yelled out to the body next to me. "Can you hear me? Can you move? Answer me!" My words spit out like cement chips flying away from a construction jackhammer.

No response from Sky.

Another car horn. This one from a black BMW behind the Jeep. I needed to move forward as the line of traffic had rolled ahead a few yards. As I eased my foot of the brake and let the vehicle drift up, my gutted mind was filled by a sympathetic voice. Melinda's voice.

Danny, what did you do?

I answered out loud. "Nothing. I didn't do anything!"

Stop. It's over.

"No. It's different – I'm different!"

It's OK. I still love you. Please stop.

"It's not my fault!"

It's too late. Doesn't matter who's at fault.

"It's not too late. Leave me alone."

I can't, Danny. I'm dead. You're the one who has to stop.

"Go away!"

I'm sorry, Danny. I can't do that.

The BMW's horn sounded again as I had failed to keep pace with the Buick in front of me. I purposefully lagged in moving forward. My anger was returning. I scratched away another harmful itch: to jump out of the Jeep, march over to the driver behind me, and strangle the impatience out of him.

I glanced back at Sky. A human body was never meant to be so inert. Evolution had instilled survival purpose within her layered complexity, florid movement and detailed expression. Sky had lost her purpose, and it sickened me that the demon had regressed her to such an unnatural state. I wanted to prop her back up in her seat, smooth out her hair and clothes and breathe color back into her skin. If given the chance, I could nurture her back to health. My will could be strong enough. My actions could be benevolent.

Incredibly, my intentions seemed to be making an impact. A few flat drops of sweat appeared on her neck. Was it possible? Or was my manufactured perception continuing to cloud my judgment?

"Sky? Can you hear me?"

No response.

A third honk from the BMW. The black car cut into the patch of tar between the left lane and the median (which was now a three foot tall cement barrier) in an attempt to pass me. I closed the gap between the Jeep and the vehicle in front of me, thwarting the BMW's efforts.

I returned my attention to Sky to see if the earlier, life-affirming sign had only been a mirage. I didn't detect any more perspiration, but her face had become flushed. This had to be real – Sky was alive! Interestingly, her right hand which had been limp across her right leg had moved, ever so slightly, from her lap to the edge of the passenger door.

"Sky." I purposely extended the vowel sound in her name to elicit a response. "Say something if you can."

Again, no reply and no further movement. But I was certain she was alive. Did she not have the strength yet to respond? My undulations of joy were tempered by the sensation that something was awry. The demon could've inflicted serious harm on my friend. I had to remain prudent.

I lifted my foot off the brake pedal to continue our slow procession and gazed at the people in the BMW from my rear view mirror. At first, I thought the driver was a woman with wrap-around almond eyes, a long angled nose and a pristine helmet cut of black hair. Or a mediocre drag queen, failing with his imitation of Cleopatra. But as he scrunched his face into a pointy prune, exasperated by his BMW's lack of mobility, clumps of an emerging goat beard came into view. The ugly twit was also wearing a formal black coat along with a skinny, dark blue tie.

His companion in the passenger seat was an entirely different human. She was an artistic beauty, despite her bored appearance and the fact that her attractiveness was easily amplified in comparison to the driver. Wavy, brown hair coiffed by Rodin. Titian painted eyes. Etruscan nose. Watercolor ruby lips, washed into a pout that drew attention to tanned cleavage, lifted by a low-cut blue gown. It was difficult to look away from her. She also looked familiar.

My eyes drifted back to Sky. Her chest was rising and falling. She was breathing. Rapidly. Aggressively, like a common animal. There was even a slight curl in her upper lip as if she were about to snarl. It was unsettling. Was she hurting? Or was it the demon's influence? Could it have infected her like it had me? Did she have a fever?

I braked hard. The car in front had stopped abruptly. About a mile or so up ahead I saw a barrage of flashing lights on both sides of the cement median: one set from a departing ambulance, another from a parked police car, a third from a tow truck, and a final set from an idle police motorcycle. The ambulance indicated that there had been an accident a bit more injurious than a routine fender-bender. As a precaution, I merged into the slow lane. The shoulder would give me a quick exit, an alternative for my unfocused, uninsured attention.

The BMW spurted forward, taking my vacated spot in the left lane. As we moved in parallel, I glanced over at the striking woman. She was starting at me, possibly with the same hint of recognition that I had. She mouthed out a couple of words, either "slow down" or "be slow." I shook my head, indicating my confusion. As I approached the traffic accident, the left lane was closed off by a series of road flares. The two lanes were merging. Was that what she was trying to tell me?

Gesticulating wildly, the woman continued to command my attention. She kept mouthing out the same words to me. Did she think I was oblivious to the upcoming merge? Or maybe she was voicing some sort of displeasure over my earlier driving which had annoyed her companion. But the irascible driver was ignoring his passenger's antics.

The woman lowered her window and I did the same. She pointed a finger at me and shouted out her message.

"She knows! She knows!"

My ignorance of the message was superseded by my recognition of what was familiar about the woman. It wasn't her face. It was her dress. It was the same dark blue dress Melinda had worn. Senior Year. At the Moonlight Formal.

The woman began to laugh, sticking her lathery tongue out at me and I rolled my window up. It was the demon. Playing the fool. I wasn't intimidated anymore. I checked on Sky.

Droplets of sweat had reappeared on her neck. Her cheeks twitched several times in a row. Had she become incapacitated by the demon? Was she trapped within the confines of an overwrought, paralyzed body, desperately trying to speak to me, to let me know how terrified she was? Knowing Sky, she was fighting, struggling to escape the prison the demon had encased her body in – that would explain her minute facial movements and her sweating. Sky was exerting all the remaining strength inside her to break free. It was admirable. Courageous.

"Are you trying to fight back, Sky? Is that what you're doing?"

My eyes bounced over to the BMW. The woman was no longer looking at me. She had returned to her blank, bored appearance.

(*She knows! She knows!*)

What was the demon doing? It had been a weak interaction – maybe things had changed? Maybe I had changed? Maybe I had beaten it?

My cell phone vibrated in my pocket, interrupting my unanswered questions. I pulled it out. It was my father.

"Dad? I've finally reached you!" My voice was high, full of longing. I needed to see my father so badly.

"What have you done, Danny?" My father's own hurried voice rippled through me, a rip current that ran against my inbounding exuberance.

"I'm coming to see you. I need to see you!"

At the first road flare, a police officer was standing next to his motorcycle directing traffic. I graciously allowed the BMW to cut in front of the Jeep.

"Don't come here." My father's voice turned flat and my enthusiasm began to ebb.

"What's wrong, Dad?"

"I've talked with your mother. You should be in the hospital."

"Mom abandoned me. Her advice is worthless."

"Your mother has nothing to do with this."

"With what? The demon? Dad, I think we can beat it! I think it's getting weaker!"

I looked over at Sky. Her closed eyelids tightened. It had been subtle, as quick as an eye blink, but I believe her eyes had been open, shutting as soon as I had turned my head to look at her.

"No. Not anymore. You need help that we cannot provide."

"What's wrong? I've got a friend with me – she's helped me so much. Her name is Sky and I want you to meet her."

I had reached the accident scene. Although there were only two cars in front of me – the black BMW and a silver Honda Accord – before the Jeep and Sky and I would be in the clear, progress had ended. The tow truck was now blocking both lanes of the highway as it positioned itself to remove a rusty brown Mazda pickup truck in the left lane that had smashed into the center divider resulting in a demolished front end, a flat left tire and a windshield that had crumpled into a kaleidoscope of misfortune.

"Stop being stupid, Danny!" My father sounded edgy, unsure of his words.

"You're not making any sense, Dad. I'm coming home."

I checked on Sky again. Her right hand had traveled to the door's armrest, her fingers gently touching the door handle. She was getting stronger! I quickly reached over and grabbed Sky's left hand, but my over ebullience caused her to tense up and her right hand fell away from the door. I gently relinquished my grip. I couldn't force Sky's recovery. She needed to regain her stamina at her own pace.

"I'm praying for you, Danny. I'm praying that God can help you."

"Why do you sound nervous? You don't have to worry. I'll be home soon."

My father began to mutter as if he were talking to someone in the background. "If I have to, I'll call the police." He sounded dejected. Pathetic.

"Dad, I'll see you at home."

My father's voice began to fade. "Please don't make me do this."

"I'll see you at home." I hung up on my father before he could muster another nonsensical reply. I chucked my cell into one of the Jeep's cup holders. He wasn't himself and I was worried that the demon had managed to corrupt him too, turning his amorphous, fearful thoughts into binding ropes of insecurity. He sounded as if he had given up.

I couldn't accept that. I needed to get home as quickly as possible. I tried to calculate how much of a delay this accident would cause in my arrival time at my father's house. The math wouldn't coalesce in my head. I tried to perform my magic trick to recalibrate my brain.

H. Hydrogen. $1s^1$. He. Helium. $1s^2$. Li. Lithium. $2s^1$.

I couldn't remember anything after Lithium. What the hell was wrong with my father? What the hell was wrong with me? I thought the world was finally acquiescing, coming under my control?

The two cars in front of the Jeep were still not moving. Two cars! I was two cars away from freedom. The tow truck operator, a rickety man with a pancake face and a pumpkin body, seemed to be taking an inordinate amount of time securing the wreckage. From the side mirror, I could see that the motorcycle cop, his hands on his hips, no longer directing traffic, also appeared annoyed by the slow moving operator. A police cruiser was parked on the other side of the center divider. Inside was a stony officer, sitting arrogantly in the driver's seat, and maintaining a surface vigilance over the scene. I couldn't believe my father said he would call the police. If these civil servants were baffled by a relatively minor car crash, how could they deal with the onslaught of a demon?

I observed Sky out of the corner of my eyes. Her eyelids were fluttering as her right hand began to inch towards the door's armrest.

I tried to engage her again. "Sky. I think you can hear me."

Sky's hand stopped moving.

I needed to let my friend know I understood her plight, but it was imperative that I remained calm. I was racing with delight over her well-being, but I didn't want to overexcite her, or worse, let her know that I thought she had been dead. I didn't want to undermine her growing strength and confidence; I wanted her to continue her recovery with one methodical, sustainable movement at a time.

"It'll be OK, Sky. No need to struggle. I'm not going anywhere. I can take care of you and everything will be back to normal soon."

I thought I heard another gasp leach out of her, but I didn't see Sky's mouth move. I continued soothing her with my words, letting her know that I would do anything to abate her concerns.

"You are a strong woman, Sky. Amazingly strong. And I'm strong too. But we will only survive if we stay together."

I reached out and clasped my fingers around her left arm. It shuddered in my grasp. If only she could touch me back! Hold hands like we had done before, imparting reassurance and compassion to each other through the gradual and gentle interlocking of our fingers. I lovingly stroked her arm. I had no doubt that Sky would fully recover – she only needed a little more time. And it was up to me to elude whatever nefarious act the demon would fling at us so Sky could get that time. Once we reached my home, we would join my father and find a way to vanquish the evil forever. That was the final version of my plan.

I patted Sky's arm before putting my hand back on the steering wheel. The next words I said to her were meant to encourage me as much as her.

"It'll be great for you to meet my father. That will be our goal."

I returned my attention to the ineptitude of the tow truck operator. He didn't know where to attach the winch in order to haul the pickup into the tow truck's flatbed tilt-tray. This delay had explicit intent: to keep me from getting home. The demon's manipulation was weak, but pervasive. It would be careless for me not to keep an eye out for another possible sighting of the demon. I understood how the demon thrived on vulnerability, but I also believed it emerged whenever I had grown complacent.

I needed a careful balance of optimism and caution, a proper mix of deliberate self-control and instinctual action. I needed to tap into the cosmological constant that maintained the pure density of the universe and everything contained within it, including me.

I rolled my head back to Sky, and saw that her hand had returned to the arm rest. It made me giddy to witness Sky's recovery and I had to release some nervous energy. I began to compulsively lock and unlock the Jeep's doors with the master button on my door. This time Sky's hand jumped (expanding energy, a mini Big Bang!), but she kept it on the arm rest. I stopped fooling with the lock and turned on the radio. I spun the tuner off the NPR radio station and through meaningless blather until I landed on the opening chords of a Beatles' song, "Do You Want to Know a Secret?" Unintentionally, I began to hum with the melody. The insipid song was strangely relaxing.

My eyes started to water and I stopped humming. My happiness waned. I felt drugged as if I were back in the hospital bed. I became despondent. Indolent. Apathetic to everything including my drastically slowed breathing. I only wanted to cry myself to sleep. What was causing my sudden shift in emotion?

I picked up my drooping head as the passenger door popped open. I blinked my eyes clear, but only caught a snapshot of Sky launching herself out of the Jeep, leaving her flip-flops on the passenger seat floor.

My fatigue had been a warning. Operant conditioning. Despite the progress I had achieved against the demon, I was still susceptible to the strumming of its pernicious fingers. It was also a precursor, an alarm, to an upcoming chain of events. I was imparted with the knowledge that a horde of flippant minds were about to fracture. Brownian motion was about to be amplified on a neurochemical level, diffusing the coherent thoughts and behavior of the people surrounding me into erratic, detrimental results.

I propped myself up in my seat in time to see Sky tumble to the ground, falling face first into the rocky gravel that blanketed the right-hand shoulder of the highway. Her legs were still not strong enough to hold up her body. Cruelly, I began to snicker at her, even though it saddened me to see her indisposed condition. An empathetic migraine began to oscillate inside my head. What was she trying to do? Where was she going? Did she even realize where she was?

I had to help my friend. I reignited my body. I put the Jeep into park, left the engine running, and hopped outside to pursue her. My primary concern was her health and I didn't want her to reinjure herself or inadvertently hurt someone else. She was horror-struck, like I had been before we had reached the backlog of cars. It would be unjust if one of our blameless, fellow night travelers were harmed simply because they had chosen an inopportune time and place to drive in the vicinity of us. I had to try and preclude any ill event.

As my tired feet and spent ankle hit the rigid surface of the highway, I thankfully regained my keen focus. In fact, my perception blossomed and my senses became engorged with external stimuli as if I had been granted temporary omniscience. I could perceive every minute detail of the events occurring around me – even those actions I was not directly viewing. I could sense the events about to unfold, in parallel and in succession, and time seemed to dilate and protract in conjunction with my own relative motion. It was an overwhelming, fantastical experience, an unexpected gift that I couldn't help but admire. Yet my awe did not keep me from realizing what was going to occur.

A symphony of mandated chaos.

With a migraine still twisting inside me, my starchy brain managed to deliver the proper impulses to instruct my legs to move towards Sky. She was still on the ground, lying on her stomach, using her elbows to hoist herself up.

The motorcycle cop, standing a few yards behind me, shouted for me to get back inside my vehicle. I acknowledged him with a light nod and continued towards Sky. The cop took no action and he simply stared at me, hands on hips, boots pointed in a V.

Sky stretched her hands up in the air as if she were a toddler desperately trying to grasp onto the hands and fingers of a distracted mother.

One step closer to Sky. A tittering of car horns signaled a Greek chorus' disapproval over Sky's infantile conduct.

Two steps closer to Sky, about to cross the front of the Jeep. The woman, or demon, wearing Melinda's dark blue dress stepped out of the black BMW in front of me. She chucked a hateful frown in my direction before approaching

269

Sky with a disingenuous smile. The demon was closer to Sky and it would easily reach her before me. I had to pick up my pace before it had a chance to inflict any further damage on my friend.

Three steps closer. Sky gave up trying to stand and began a belly crawl, inching along the dirt ground dotted with cigarette butts, weeds and rubber shards excreted from tires. Whelps of "help" spluttered out of her mouth.

Four steps closer. A cascade of collapsing aluminum and glass silenced the chorus of honks. The totaled pickup truck had broken free from the tow truck's winch and had slammed back into the center divider. The pickup's rear axle (which had apparently been used as the connection point for the winch) remained inside the tow truck's flatbed, still clinging to the crane hooks, dangling in the air like a plucked fishbone.

The motorcycle cop nearly fell to the ground from an exaggerated recoil caused by the rancorous clatter of the fallen wreckage.

The driver of the silver Accord at the head of the queue, evidently spooked by the loose pickup, bolted his car into reverse. The Accord banged directly into the BMW, smashing the luxury vehicle's front bumper and pushing the car back in my direction.

I quickly sidestepped the BMW before it pinned me against the front of Sky's Jeep. The BMW barely scratched the Jeep, but the chain reaction damaged Sky's determination. She let out a startled squeal and huddled herself down against the ground, while the demon who had adroitly sidestepped away from the moving BMW, simply shook its head, straightened out its blue dress, and let out a self-satisfied cackle.

The male driver of the BMW jumped out of his car, his androgynous helmet hair still unadulterated, and marched up to the closed driver's side window of the Accord.

The demon crept over to Sky's clustered up body. The sensual feminine beauty in the BMW that it had invaded began to dematerialize. Its face eroded and cratered as ulcers and pustules dotted its skin, and its hair, once flowing lustfully and abundantly, became a nest of crooked, knotty twigs.

My sense of urgency heightened and I galloped towards Sky to save her from whatever misery the demon had planned.

Back at the Accord, the BMW driver began to pound both of his fists against the glass of the driver's side window. He cursed madly and screeched at the driver, commanding her to step outside.

The motorcycle cop finally reacted, and he ran to the BMW driver to halt his ensuing road rage. The second policeman on the scene continued to sit in his squad car, indefensibly failing to come to his colleague's aid. His worthless, dumbfounded stare at the unfolding action was compounded by his refusal to answer an incoming call on his radio, requesting an update.

The flustered tow truck operator, trying to locate an appropriate area to reconnect the wreck to his winch, crouched down near the front tires of the practically unrecognizable pickup. The ground next to the center barrier was saturated with strewn metal fragments, bits of polyvinyl chloride, flakes of polyethylene, and a viscous mix of gasoline, grease and radiator fluid. As he placed his hand on the ground to balance his globular body, it landed in a small pool of liquid that coated his fingers with a sticky sheen. The consistency of the gooey liquid took a moment to travel from his tactile nerve skin cells to his muddled brain, but once it registered, his agitated state switched to revulsion. He lifted up his hand realizing that it had been doused in blood that had seeped out from the bottom of the pickup's side door.

Sky had risen to her knees as the demon squatted down to make direct eye contact her. An earnest plea for comfort and safety began to formulate out of Sky's mouth until her eyes recognized that something was disturbingly wrong with her rescuer. The demon extended one of its decaying hands to touch Sky shoulder and let its elongated black tongue sweep across its lips as if eager to taste Sky's swelling uncertainty.

Sky pushed herself away from the demon, falling hard onto her back. The demon mocked her.

Clumsy girl. Always falling for the wrong things.

Her deflated lungs gulping for oxygen, Sky had to abort a scream. She flipped herself over and began to scamper away from the demon. I was only a few feet away from my Sky when the demon reached out and snatched the back of her left leg, tearing a hole in her tights.

Back at the wreckage, the tow truck operator stood up with a rattle and a jiggle, vigorously wiping his blood-soaked hand on his pants. His eyes followed the trail of blood to its source and carefully he began to pry open the pickup's side door.

The still enraged BMW driver ignored the motorcycle cop's direct order to move away from the Accord and end his tirade. He continued his onslaught, slapping his hands on the hood of the car and screaming, "Get out!" repeatedly. The motorcycle cop unsnapped his gun from its holster.

The squad car officer finally reacted. He shouted out a request for additional help on his radio, leapt out of his cruiser, and hurdled the center divider. He ignored the tow truck operator and sprinted to assist his colleague.

I finally reached Sky as the demon was clawing Sky's leg, pulling her body back into its arms. I latched onto one of the demon's shriveled arms with both of my hands and tried to pry it off of Sky. The demon spat into my face.

No! You had your chance!

I relinquished my grip on the demon in order to punch its heartless body. My blitz distracted the demon enough for Sky to twist her torso in an attempt to break loose. She pushed off her free, right leg to try and lift herself off the ground. It didn't work. Sky fell solidly back down on the ground and the demon held onto her left leg.

At the median, the tow truck operator cracked open the mangled side door of the pickup. Spilling out onto the ground were the remains of a black and brown Boston terrier, its torso split open on one side. Its internal organs had liquefied, splattering onto the shoes of the operator. The stunned man wheeled his body away from the wreck, and let out a meek, convulsive yell. He tried to shake loose the offal stuck to his work boots, but his repugnant, bungled state caused him to amusingly dance away from the pickup until his stomach collided with the center divider and he threw up on himself.

The two police officers commanded the vehement driver of the BMW to back away from the Accord. Their furious chant finally resonated with the livid man and he stopped hitting the hood of the car. He spun around and faced the two officers, snapping at them in a surprisingly masculine voice.

"Bacon and sausage. Sausage and bacon. I'm not in the mood for breakfast, boys."

The motorcycle cop pulled out his gun and pointed it at the BMW driver. He barked out another order. "Put your hands on top of your head! Now!"

The BMW driver snorted and didn't comply. The squad car officer unsnapped his weapon from its holster.

I was failing with Sky. Her writhing body could not break free from the demon's grasp. Her swirling, distraught eyes volleyed between me and the demon, unable to ascertain who was helping or hurting her. Sky raised up her right leg and began to sweep and kick at both of us indiscriminately, stomping her foot at anything she could make contact with. She connected with my lower jaw. I tumbled back, allowing the demon to grab Sky's ankles, one bare foot in each of its hands.

With two Glocks aimed directly at his chest, the BMW driver reluctantly placed his hands on top of his head. The squad car officer ordered the driver to turn around. Before complying, the BMW driver puckered his lips and smacked a kiss to each policeman.

The squad car officer secured his gun, rushed up to the BMW driver, and kicked the back of the driver's left knee. The driver moaned and as his body buckled, the officer slammed the recalcitrant man's body to the ground. The officer rolled the driver onto his stomach, rammed a knee into his groin and began to handcuff the driver who was now wiggling and hollering like a molested cat. The motorcycle cop put his gun back in its holster and assisted his fellow officer by throttling the back of the driver's neck with his hands, shoving the arrested man's mouth into the pavement to try and silence him.

Rubbing my jaw, I bounced back up and resumed my counterattack, yanking the demon's hair and poking my thumb in its throat. It was dragging Sky along the ground by her feet and sweeping her body across the dirt. I landed a closed fist against the demon's right ear and it finally let Sky go, distracted more by the screaming BMW driver being arrested than my efforts.

Sky bear-crawled away from both of us, along the highway shoulder and towards a cement drainage ditch. The demon spat at me again and swiped its disfigured fingers at my face. I dodged its attack, but the demon wasn't concerned with me.

273

It leapfrogged past my body and began to chase Sky. Once again, I rumbled after them.

The two policemen had to struggle in order to get the BMW driver to submit. For such a fragile-looking man, he put up a surprisingly strong fight. As the BMW driver was hoisted up to his feet, the Accord driver stepped out of the vehicle. She was a middle-aged woman, permed brown hair shaped into a deflated mushroom cap, with a head and body that was better suited for a preteen boy. Fresh teardrops and mucous glazed the diminutive woman's cheeks and chin, and she gawked up at the sky as if to thank God. However, instead of uttering a hushed, reverent prayer, she unleashed a torrential shriek that exploded from her lungs.

The tow truck operator was taking off his vomit soaked jacket and watching the police officers subdue the BMW driver. He had apparently been unfazed by the drawn guns and the vicious arrest, but once the woman from the Accord let out her cry, he bobbled over to his tow truck, hoisted himself inside, and locked the door.

Two more highway denizens, a male college student, dressed to play a pickup basketball game, and a husky thirty-something woman in a grocery store uniform, stepped out of their respective cars (a 4Runner and a Civic) as concerned citizens, searching for a way to assist and quell the ensuing disorder.

A Mini Cooper, three spaces behind Sky's Jeep, broke away from the stacked line of cars, seeking a path around the madness. It traveled along the highway shoulder, kicking up a buttery cloud of dust. The Cooper had almost cleared the scene until Sky crawled into its path. The toy car turned sharply to the right to avoid hitting Sky – luckily the brake control kept the car from driving straight into the drainage ditch. The Cooper's driver, a humming bird-sized Vietnamese woman who appeared mini even inside the Mini, rolled down her window and shouted at Sky.

"What are you doing? What's wrong with you?"

With lattice-marked hands and abraded tights, both shredded by the gravel littering the dirt shoulder, Sky climbed up to the Cooper's open window, gasping and mewling at the Vietnamese woman like a newborn kitten. The tiny driver covered her ears and bowed her head like a laboratory rabbit, and began rolling up her window.

A fifty-year-old man with a grey pompadour and matching mustache, exited the silver Accord and tried to comfort his hysterical, still wailing female driver. He wrapped one arm around her waist and with the other, held out a striped straw tote bag the size of a picnic basket in front of her face. The woman quieted down and shook her companion's arm off her while snatching the tote and cuddling it in her arms like she had rediscovered her childhood Teddy. The formerly distraught woman began to laugh, but it transformed into coughs and hacks, feral wheezes from a throat that had turned raw. The man rubbed his mustache vigorously, belched out a string of apologies, and turned around and walked away from the woman. He continued past the tow truck and down the empty, darkened lanes of the highway like a tomcat deserting its owner's home in the middle of the night.

As Sky slapped her scratched hands against the closed driver's side window of the Mini Cooper, a white GMC Yukon barreled up the shoulder, trying to duplicate the Cooper's route. Its excessive speed and lack of brake control foiled an abrupt stop, and the heavyweight SUV veered violently to the right to avoid slamming into Sky and the Cooper. The Yukon slid across the dirt until it toppled, headfirst, into the drainage ditch.

The demon caught up to Sky, jumping onto the hood of the Mini Cooper and perching itself like a carrion crow staring down my distressed friend. I had almost reached Sky when the demon frightened the Vietnamese woman into kinetic energy and she put the Cooper into reverse. As the demon clung to the shortened hood over the engine, the Cooper flew in reverse a couple of yards, braked hard then went forward again in the same line, stopping before it fell into the drainage ditch next to the Yukon.

In the back seat of the Mini Cooper, a ten-year-old boy who looked like the driver's son, banged his baseball cap covered head against the side window. His broken state was captured in the words that kept repeating out of his mouth. "I just wanna go home. I just wanna go home." For a moment I felt sympathy for him.

And in that one moment, one discontinuous instant of time, I caught a flash of the demon reverting to its former self, the gorgeous, seductive woman in Melinda's blue dress, frantically holding onto the hood of the Cooper with strained, nervy arms and a horrified, disheartened face that said *I don't understand what's happening to me.*

The Cooper's tires chirped as the car punched back into reverse. The car traveled in a semicircle around Sky to avoid hitting her, and stopped when it was pointed in the opposite direction of traffic. During the car's counter-clockwise swirl, the demon clung to the Cooper, squealing in delight, seemingly enjoying the rudderless ride.

After witnessing the erratic mess occurring on the highway shoulder, the two police officers separated. The squad car officer dragged the handcuffed BMW driver (his chin and lip busted, his helmet hair cracked open, and his resistance splintered) towards the center divider and his police cruiser. The motorcycle cop trotted toward the demon on the Cooper.

Before the Cooper had positioned itself in its new direction, I had reached Sky. She was sitting down, her left leg straight and right leg bent, in a hurdler's stretch, and her arms drooped down at her sides. She looked defeated. I got down on my knees, laid my hands on her left foot and beseeched her to come back to the Jeep with me. Sky was on the verge of accepting my help when the demon leaped from the hood of the Mini Cooper and landed directly behind Sky. It wrapped its arms completely around her chest. Sky's eyes flared and her body began to shake as I sprayed the demon with curses and demands to let her go.

The motorcycle cop, the athletic college student and the grocery store clerk converged on Sky, as a few more drivers and passengers popped their heads out of their cars. A few were filming the action with their cell phones.

Inside the Mini Cooper, the Vietnamese woman was consoling her boy in the backseat, pulling him away from the side window which was blotted with crimson sweat from the boy's self-battered forehead.

Inside the Yukon, which hung in the drainage ditch like an uprooted tree, a nineteen-year-old roughneck with a mullet of red hair and wearing a wife beater stained yellow from sweat and beer, let his intoxicated body flop out from the driver's seat.

On the other side of the highway divider, the squad car cop was about to forcibly shove the BMW driver into the backseat of his cruiser when another ear-draining scream split the air.

It was Sky. The demon had bit down onto Sky's shoulder, piercing through her sweatshirt.

Pulsing and boiling with unvented malice, I sprung back up to my feet. But the college student-athlete had arrived and he laid into me with a forearm, dropping me back down to the ground and berating me with a *Get the fuck away from her!*

The college student launched himself at the mordacious demon, attempting to rip the demon's arms off of Sky. At first, the demon disregarded his efforts, but it soon allowed Sky's flaccid body to slump out of its embrace and it lashed out at the college boy, jamming one of its fanged fingers into the college student's right eye. The hapless hero moaned in agony and scurried off, covering his injured eye with both hands and pleading for someone to rescue him.

Sky was lying on the ground, on her right side, her knees angled towards her chest as if conceding her body to a victorious gladiator. The demon didn't touch her. It stood over her body in a haughty posture that showcased its dominion over its surroundings. It bent down at the waist at a precise ninety degree angle, and unleashed a serpentine string of scorched words into Sky's ear.

You deserve this. You deserve everything that has happened to you!

Sky's eyes welled up with inconsolable, silent tears.

The motorcycle cop arrived and he faced the demon. "Back away from the girl. I don't want to hurt you."

The demon laughed.

How can you – a common queer – hurt me?

The motorcycle cop let the fingers of his right hand graze the top of his Glock before reaching with his other hand to unclip a small black can of pepper spray off his belt.

The grocery store clerk (who had momentarily tried to aid the injured college student) plunked her gut in front of my face, and began to crowd into me, keeping me down on the ground. She raised a finger and wagged it across my nose. "The police will handle this. You stay down. They will clean up this mess."

Back at the police cruiser, the BMW driver spotted the demon, his former lovely female companion, in a standoff with the other officer. His fight returned. Writhing in the officer's arm lock, he shouted. "Leave her alone! Leave the beautiful people alone!"

The demon snapped its attention away from the motorcycle cop, searching for the source of a recognized voice. When it spied the BMW driver being thrown into the back seat with a sucker punch to the gut, the demon let out a buzzard call and took a vaulting step in the direction of the police cruiser.

The motorcycle cop snagged the demon's wrist. He yanked on her arm as he spoke to her. "Settle down! You're not going anywhere!"

The demon took a swing at the motorcycle cop's head with its free arm. He ducked it while simultaneously dousing the demon's face with his pepper spray.

Caterwauls spewed out of the demon. A hyperkinetic chain of spasms shook the demon's body and each paroxysm rolled into the motorcycle cop who dropped to his knees but did not relinquish his grip on the demon. Instead, he blasted the demon with another round from his spray can.

The drunk Yukon driver had crawled out of the drainage ditch and was now approaching the motorcycle cop and the demon. His face skewed and puckered as he cursed the officer. "What the fuck are you doing to her? Fucking pig! Let her go! Fucking pig bitch! Let her go!"

The grocery store clerk was still in my face but when I tried to push her away, not only didn't she budge, she flung out her hands and plastered them to the sides of my head, squashing my ears into my skull, and digging her acrylic fingernails into my scalp.

You had your chance, Danny-boy! Sky doesn't want to play with you!

Did the demon jump into this woman like an exorcised spirit? Incensed, I mimicked my assailant's tactic, pounding my own hands into the sides of the podgy head that had been commandeered by the demon. I imagined my hands turning into the parallel jaws of a vise, gradually coming together to collapse this cranium and pulverize its contents into mashed, raw mulch. I could feel the palms of my hands sinking into the *dura mater*, and the demon let out an excruciating wail. It abandoned its own two-handed grip on my head and the assailed body in front of me reverted to its former self, a lonely woman who had sought to elevate her image above her

278

grocery store uniform. I easily cast her aside and resumed my attempt to safeguard Sky.

With the BMW driver safely incapacitated inside the cruiser's back seat, the squad car officer jumped back over the center divider and sprinted to his colleague who was still down on his knees, and latched onto the demon's arm. The motorcycle cop had dropped the pepper spray can and was now holding on to the demon with both of his hands. Their battle had dragged both of their bodies closer to the tow truck, causing the operator still sitting inside to duck his head and erase himself out of this night's existence.

About a mile or so away, on the opposing lanes of the highway, a contingent of flashing police lights approached the still uncontrolled scene.

The drunk Yukon driver continued his curses at the motorcycle cop until the thrashing demon twisted itself in a complete circle and its arm popped with a sickening crack. The demon had broken its ulna, and a shard of bone had burst through its skin. Blinded by alcohol-induced righteousness, the drunk driver ran up to the motorcycle cop, swinging his left arm and hand as if batting away a horsefly, and kicked him solidly in the stomach.

The squad car officer arrived with his gun drawn and he blasted a shot at the drunk driver. The bullet missed its target, somehow squeezing through the pocket of air between the drunk driver's flapping arm and his waist, but its aftereffect was profoundly surprising.

Surprise number one. The Yukon driver belly flopped onto the ground, pleading "Don't kill me!" He voluntarily placed his hands behind his head and spread his legs open.

Surprise number two. The demon stopped its bizarre growls and ceased all movement. It conceded the fight and it crumbled down to its knees and began to sob. It transformed back into the woman in the blue dress, but her beauty was destroyed from her ruptured arm and psyche.

Surprise number three. The motorcycle cop, still hanging onto the demon's arm, and the squad car officer, still pointing the gun at the empty spot where the drunk driver had been standing, stared at each other as if they did not recognize their respective faces and had just woken up from a bout of sleepwalking.

Surprise number four. The college student and the grocery store clerk were huddled together, heading back to their vehicles, commiserating over the pain from their individual injuries and the fact that no one had bothered to come to their aid.

Not a surprise: the individuals who had been craning their heads and necks out of their vehicles, recording the scene with their phones, rapidly retracted into their cars and rolled up their windows like dutiful, dependent children.

I used everyone's confounded and compliant behavior to my advantage. With adrenaline swaddling my exhausted body and sore ankle, I ran up to Sky, her body still lying on its side in a tender pose, and lifted her into my arms. She didn't say a word or resist my efforts as I cradled her back and legs, and raced back to the Jeep.

Sense and purpose returned to the squad car officer. He holstered his weapon and carefully approached the drunk Yukon driver. The motorcycle cop also reacted and he let go of the woman's arm, but forced her trembling, broken body to remain prostrate on the ground.

When I reached the Jeep, the sirens of the oncoming police cars grew louder. Simultaneously, the Mini Cooper weaved itself along the shoulder, in reverse, until it cleared the tow truck. It spun itself around and sped away, zipping down the open highway.

I gently placed Sky into the passenger seat and I hopped back behind the wheel. I put the Jeep in drive and followed a gold Mercedes as it charted the same weaving path the Mini Cooper had created on the shoulder. As the Jeep rolled past the two officers, the motorcycle cop stared directly at me. I returned his gaze until he looked away and returned to the damaged woman in the blue dress. Along with the last remnant of my migraine, I felt my meta-perception slipping away like a waning hangover as the Jeep cleared the scene and Sky and I were back flying down the highway to my father's house.

I looked in the rear view mirror and saw another motorcycle cop rolling up along the shoulder. For a moment I thought it was pursuing us, but it stopped and blocked the path of other vehicles that were trying to flee the surreal accident scene in the same manner that we had.

As four police cruisers blew past us on the other side of the center divider, I looked over at Sky. Her eyes were open, scattershot and vacant, but her breathing was normal and I didn't see any additional, significant physical injury on her. It was clear Sky had succumbed to another wave of shock, but she had been successfully rescued.

I had defeated the demon once again and I allowed a smile of mirthful satisfaction to take over my face.

My glee abated when I realized that strangely, the radio was broadcasting the closing lyrics of the same Beatles song that had been playing before Sky had jumped out of the Jeep.

The song couldn't have been more than two minutes long and although I didn't know how long it took me to recover Sky, it had to have been much longer than a couple of minutes. Or had it? It was possible the song was either stuck on replay because of an obtuse radio deejay or due to some unheralded George Harrison tribute. Or maybe time really had slowed down, not only in my own relative space-time configuration, but in the entire closed system of the so-called Universe?

A *Geico* commercial began to play and I shut the radio back off. Time was an unreliable illusion. Outside my window, I spotted the man from the silver Accord before I drove past him. He was still walking along the highway, tracking next to the center divider, and had made significant progress despite his sluggish pace. His head appeared to be pointed up, resplendently, at the night sky.

"I'm trapped...my mind hates me...." Sky's trailing voice startled me and it took a moment for her words to register any coherent meaning in my head. Sky didn't know that she was safe.

"No, Sky. We did it. We beat the demon and now everything will be better."

Sky's head turned to face the side window.

My cell phone began to vibrate, shaking against the cup holder where I had left it. I picked it up – it was my father again.

"Hello, father."

"I'm sorry. I had to call."

"What?"

"It's like a fire. You have to know."

"What do you mean?"

281

"The failure. It hurts. Understand?"

"No. Not making any sense. What's wrong? Is it the demon?"

"Always comes back to me. I can't keep doing this. Expects too much...I'm sorry...."

"Dad! I'm on my way! I can help you!"

My father hung up the phone. Any lingering joviality had been snuffed out. My father had to be under severe duress. The demon couldn't take me or Sky, so it was going after my father!

I tried calling him back. It kicked directly into his voicemail. I shouted out a recorded message.

"I'll be home soon, Dad! Please hold on! Please! I love you."

I threw my phone against the dashboard, cracking its glass screen. I needed to reach him. I needed to reach him now!

I increased my speed until I passed the Mercedes that had also fled the demon-generated mass psychosis. I wanted to go faster, but I couldn't risk losing control or encountering any other police officers who would only delay my reaching my father.

"Don't hurt me." Sky's head still faced the window. A spider trickled down the glass and passed in front of her face.

"Nothing will hurt you. Not now."

Her words offended me. Had she not just witnessed the extent of my goodwill? That I would do anything to help her?

(*Don't trust her, Daniel.*)

I was unable to shake off my misgivings. Regardless of what I had achieved, doubts continued to infiltrate my convictions. Was it possible to care so much about someone yet still feel like they were an unwelcome stranger?

Maybe Sky didn't realize the extent of what had occurred or the depth of what she meant to me. Maybe I could harness a bit more patience. I wouldn't let it bother me that I could detect her restrained hand movements, little finger sweeps that were trying to discreetly wipe away the mute tears that had started flowing down her cheeks again.

Sky hadn't yet received the insight that there was only one enduring, sacred pathway in life. One that took time to discover. She didn't understand that lonely, victimized sobs were immoral, and had to be disposed, renounced, and forgotten.

TWELVE

Two hours. Twenty-three minutes. Fifteen seconds. Or
three hours. Thirty-two minutes. Fifty one seconds. One
was the correct amount of time it took to reach my hometown.
I had checked the clock on the Jeep's radio as well as my cell
phone, but I was unclear on how much time had elapsed. I
hadn't lost track of time like my previous overwhelming
experiences – I simply lost track of the numbers. I blamed a
lingering state of blurred anxiety for clouding my eyes. I
hadn't been able to stop thinking about my father and my
friend. After her sobs had dried up, Sky hadn't uttered
another sound. She had barely shifted her head, continuing
to face the window and the glassy darkness that zipped past
us on the highway.

I was worried that it had taken too long for me to get
home. My father's weakened physical condition had
undoubtedly made him highly susceptible to the demon's
attack. I had called him several more times, but never
connected with him and I didn't bother leaving any additional
messages. While driving, I had tried to pacify my mind by
humming additional tracks from the Beatles, but an arresting,

merciless scene of what the demon might be doing to my father kept flashing in front of me.

The demon, in the form of my father's paramour, enters his bedroom while he's asleep. She slips off her black slacks and straddles my father in his bed. His eyes flare open as the demon transforms into a gelatinous corpse. My father writhes to escape, but the demon shoves its rotting, left hand through my father's chest and wraps its flesh-stripped fingers around his heart. With its other hand, the demon digs into his scalp, scraping away his hair, skin and bone. My father's useless, hoarse screams go unheard as the demon squeezes his heart, keeping his blood flowing and his mind half-alive. The inhuman creature starts ingesting scooped out chunks of my father's veiny brain tissue. My father flashes his teeth, his once-in-a-decade smile, hopeless in his unrecognition of his impending death.

I turned onto the street of my father's house. My self-protection mechanism kicked in and the images of the demon attacking my father vanished. I latched onto a syrupy fog of forgetfulness with its accustomed, enchanting taste. My internal homunculus rollicked in the sweetness and I started to shed memories, systematically deleting all the events that had occurred after Sky and I had left the gas station. It was surprisingly easy. Sky continued her listless gaze out the window, looking at the suburban homes that dotted the neighborhood as if she hadn't realized we had left the brush covered highway.

"We're here, Sky."

No response.

As I neared my father's house, a disheartening sight crystalized into view. My mother's Prius. Parked in the driveway. What the fuck was she doing here? Sky finally made a noise that sounded like a baby's coo. My foot edged back on the accelerator. I wanted to keep driving. I didn't know where I could go, but I didn't want to see that woman.

Still, my father needed me and I had exceeded my selfishness quota for the night by driving Sky's Jeep. I pulled the vehicle up to the curb and shut the engine off. I stared at my mother's car and wondered if my father had called her for help or if her arrival was of her own volition. Either way I wasn't prepared to see her. I rested my head on top of the steering wheel and played with the Jeep's key that was still stuck in the ignition.

"Is it worth it? Is it worthwhile?"

Sky remained silent. She had to have noticed my mother's car.

"Do you want to go inside with me?"

Sky's first conspicuous movement. She gently shook her head.

"I understand. I don't want to see her either. I'm not sure I can face her. But I can't just sit out here in the Jeep."

I stared at my father's house. The front lawn was cropped short, brown and yellow, blemished with random pimples of dirt and mud that were sprouting dandelions and pigweed. Like the rest of the house, the grass displayed a mix of dormancy and neglect. My father always took better care of the community college landscape than his own home, particularly in winter. Leaves and bark from the neighbor's overgrown sycamore tree cluttered the rain gutters on the roof. An outlawed plastic bag clung to an untrimmed boxwood hedgerow. Even the overextended glow from a corner street lamp was enough to highlight shingled sidewalls and crosshatched windows that were mottled from month old dust and rain. In each of the street facing windows of the house, the Roman shades were closed with no signs of light or life inside.

Measured movement from Mrs. Gualia's home next door caught my eye. A parting curtain. A crowning face. Mrs. Gualia was peeking through the floral drapes of her living room's bay window. I waved to her. Her turtle head retreated and the drapes snapped shut. A few seconds later, the light shining over her porch turned off.

Sky shifted in her seat as the front door of my father's house cracked open. Someone was waiting for me.

It was time to act. I opened the side door and stepped outside. "I'll go first. If it's OK, I'll come back and get you."

Sky's head bobbed, almost imperceptible against the rigors of my excited atomic state. I closed the Jeep door and started up the walkway to the open front door. My ankle tingled like a static charge primed for release.

I examined my mother's Prius. It was covered with a fresh layer of condensation. No boxes or bags inside. How long had she been here? Had she come straight to my father's house after moving out of her apartment? If so, where were her personal, albeit meagre, belongings? On the walkway, my feet crunched against the ground like I was traversing a frozen snowpack. The crunch was from several trampled snails that had unfortunately strayed into my path. I paused and listened. I heard my molars clapping, grinding. My stone-cutting breaths and snorts. A yipping, nipping dog, three houses down. A revving motorcycle, drifting past the audible horizon. But not one sound leaked out of my father's house.

At the doorway, I wiped the snail guts off my soles on the polypropylene "Welcome!" doormat, and pushed the door fully open. No one was around to greet me. This wasn't my home. This was nothing but a murky, sour house.

As I stepped inside, the Jeep's engine turned over. I flipped around in time to catch a glimpse of Sky's enraged face as she put the Jeep into drive and sped away.

I held onto the open front door. Why would she leave me? I had left the key in the Jeep's ignition – maybe I had subconsciously wanted her to get away? Get away from me? Or get away from my mother? Yes, that was the reason. Sky left because of my mother – it was her fault. My mother would never stop adding to her list of transgressions.

"Mom – where are you? Do you know what you've done?"

The house answered me with booming, black silence. Why were there no lights turned on?

"Dad? Are you up?"

I let go of the front door, leaving it wide open, and wandered inside. I passed the dining table – there was a dirty dish and fork on one of the place settings, a book (Gaiman's *American Gods*) and a half-empty bottle of Shiraz on another. What was going on? I drifted into the kitchen, flipping on the recessed lights. There was a chocolate frosted cake on the island countertop with a one-eighth piece missing. Sitting next to the cake, was a flat, finely serrated knife, stained with icing and sprinkled with dark crumbs. In the sink, unwashed, were a mixing bowl, utensils and a round cake pan. Did my mother bake a dessert for my father like a well-oiled homemaker? Feed him a slice and top it off with several glasses of wine? Auditioning for the role of unruffled, devoted wife returning from self-imposed exile? What was she doing here? Why would my father be so obtuse as to let her into the house?

287

A crumpled moan escaped from the living room. I slinked out of the kitchen until I faced the back of the leather sofa. A figure sat at one end, one spindly arm leaning on the armrest, and the other bent in the air so its hand and fingers could run through its long slats of hair. It wasn't my mother. I crept closer. Plain yellow blouse. Black pants. Legs crossed modestly at the ankles. It was my father's paramour. My father's banshee.

The woman turned her head to face me. Her eyes were gone, cleanly gouged out, like my incarnation of the predatory Talia. Only I didn't harbor an ounce of fear. I refused to think of her as the demon.

"You don't matter anymore. I don't see you. I only see defeated, forgotten dust."

You're free to believe anything you'd like.

"I am free."

Really? Your mother's a bitch to get rid of.

"Yes, she is."

I was having fun with your father. Until she interrupted me.

"What did you do to him?

A nibble here, a nibble there. Nothing you haven't already done to a couple of prize winning tarts.

"I don't want you here. Get out." I turned on the bronze shaded lamp on the end table next to the couch. The woman stood up, revealing a body ravaged by two vicious stab wounds. Pink blood bubbled through a hole near her breast pocket while maroon blood seeped from a jagged gash across her stomach.

This is what you need to do to her. It's all her fault.

"You don't belong here." I marched away from her and back into the dining room. The woman followed me, sliding into the kitchen with feline stealth.

Patty cake, patty cake, baker's man.

Take this with you as fast as you can.

She picked up the knife and licked it roughly, slicing open her bottom lip. I continued into the hallway leading to the bedrooms.

Quo vadis?

The door to my father's room was closed. The door to *de facto* storage room was open. Inside, I spied a few of my mother's photographs stacked atop a cardboard box. I continued walking. The master bedroom door was closed, but my bedroom door was open, a lamp turned on inside.

The woman snuck up next to me. A bedraggled hand caressed my shoulder. Wounded lips nestled up to my ear.

Three is the cruelest number. Let her know that.

I ignored the woman even as she began to rake the cake knife along the patterned wall between the storage room and my bedroom. I stopped only when I reached my open doorway.

Sitting on the edge of my bed, her face staring at the floor, was my mother. She was crying. Melinda's heart notes were scattered across the comforter. Not the thirteen I had given my mother, but the others that I thought I had lost. She lifted her head as she spoke to me.

"Is this why you threw them away? Because the handwriting is different? The ones you gave me – they were written by you? You wrote them, didn't you?"

Out in the hallway, the woman clapped the knife against my father's closed bedroom door. I berated her, weary of her provocations.

"You will leave. You don't belong here. I don't want you here!"

My mother continued to reproach me as the woman in the hallway crouched, her torso undulating and writhing like a stalking eel.

"Quiet, Daniel! I heard you. Let your father sleep. He's not as strong as you think. You haven't shown him any consideration since you arrived

I returned my attention to my mother. "What are you doing in my room?"

"This is no longer yours."

I had been oblivious to the condition of my bedroom. The posters, including the Einstein that everyone loved, had been taken off my wall. My books had been placed into unsealed boxes. My clothes had been taken out of the closet and dumped into a pile near the bed.

"Why are you moving my things?"

"Your father and I have made some incredibly difficult decisions."

"Over wine and cake?"

I looked back into the hall. The woman was clinging to the ceiling like a spider, poised above the entrance to my father's room. She scraped the knife against the ceiling's drywall, cutting a swaying, chipped fresco of judgmental ire.

I took a step inside my bedroom. My mother began stacking Melinda's notes into an ordered pile.

"We decided to put your belongings into storage. While you get treatment."

"Treatment? I'm the one least in need of treatment!"

"Where's Sky, Daniel?"

"In the Jeep. I should've stayed with her."

"Is she outside? Oh, Daniel. What did you do to her?"

"I rescued her."

"Where is she?"

"Gone. You scared her away. She drove off."

"Oh my God. I pray nothing bad happened to her."

"Pray? You're an atheist!"

My mother shook her head. "The police are on their way. I called them as soon as you stepped inside."

"What? Are you in danger?"

From my peripheral vision, I saw the woman plastered against the wall next to my bedroom door, her mouth gaped open as she pierced the end of the knife up through her lip and cheek.

"You are not an Incarnator. You have the archetype, but not the phenotype. Your behavior is atypical. I didn't know that my techniques would be so grossly insufficient. You are *different*. You've become a danger."

"Everything about you is bullshit! I don't need this. I need to talk to Dad." I took a step back out of my room.

"Let him be. He explicitly told me he was done speaking with you."

I looked into the hallway. The woman was gone. But the knife was sitting on the floor in the middle of the hallway. Waiting.

My mother stood up from my bed. Two rosettes formed on her blouse. One near her heart. Another across her stomach. Melinda's voice swam through the air.

I'm leaving you, Danny. It's final. I can't stop dancing. There's nothing else left to say. I'll be busy the rest of the day so I'll stop by later for my things....

I shook her words out of my head until they were drowned by the depths of my ignominy.

"I am a ruin because of you."

290

My mother took a few steps away from me, a cerise bouquet splashed on the front of her blouse.

"No, Daniel! You've ruined me! My life! I'm moving back with your father. We both need support. We need to be together. It's the only way we can get through this!"

I was the reason my family was a farce. I had always been the reason. My mother had left my father because of me, and now she was returning because of me. I was the inconvenience. I was the mistake. I was *different*.

(*You're giving me more meds, Danny? I thought I already took my dose?*)

I was the monster.

(*Melinda, the prescription says: take two Ativan tablets (1 mg each) twice a day, IF NEEDED. You need it.*)

I dropped down to the ground and sat in the hallway like a dejected puppet who realized his strings were not illusory. The stain on my mother's blouse disappeared.

"I love you, Daniel. Your father loves you. And loving you is the hardest thing we have ever done."

There was a knock on the front door, followed by a stout, "Hello?" My mother didn't move. Tears pinched off the corners of her eyes.

"Stand up, Daniel."

I remained sitting. My life was rolling back into itself. The universe was collapsing and I was the focal point of the Big Crunch. A weak graviton surrounded by a dense cloud of dark energy as creation swarmed out of existence.

My mother wiped her tears, doing her best to compose herself. I shifted my head slightly as a tall, uniformed man turned into the hallway.

"Hello? Is everything OK?"

My mother wasn't OK. She was having enormous difficulty putting on her mask of self-control. She truly was in pain by what she had to do, by what she had to do to me.

The uniform stepped around me, and paused at the doorway to my bedroom. I buried my head into my chest.

My mother begged with me. "Daniel, please. Stand up."

He won't stand for you, my dear.

My head jolted up at the sound of the hollow, static filled voice. Standing in front of me wasn't a police uniform, but a hospital security guard uniform. The demon. Returning for one final attack. The cake knife was in its hand. My mother was blind to the severity of the threat.

"Is that my knife? What are you doing? Put that down!"

You know what I am. I am his Alpha. And your Omega.

"Stop it! Don't do this to me!" My mother was befuddled by the demon and beginning to fade. Her meekness elicited the repressed emotion inside me. I still loved her. I still loved her. I would always love her. She was my mother.

I jumped to my feet to intercede. I had one more moment of redemption.

My mother's brilliant voice had dimmed. "Where are the police...they're supposed to be...."

"Mom, don't talk to it! Move away!"

The problem with neuronal chemistry is that we never really know when the reaction ends and reality begins.

As the demon raised its arm holding the knife, I grabbed onto it with both hands. I tore into its ear.

"YOU WILL LEAVE!"

With an insignificant flick of its arm, the demon threw my body halfway down the hall.

I'm sorry, Daniel. I can't do that.

The demon walked into my bedroom and the door thundered shut behind it.

I ran back down the hall and tried to force my bedroom door open. The knob wouldn't budge. I pounded my entire body against the door, kicking, hitting, beating, blaring my mother's name, cursing the demon, but I could not get inside. My mother began to scream.

Help! I needed help! I ran to my father's room and burst through his closed door with ease.

My father was lying in bed, eyes closed. The lamp on his nightstand was on, casting a watery glow. How could he still be asleep?

I called his name as I leapt over to his bedside. I shook his arm. No response. His arm was limp and cold.

I shook his shoulder. I shook his chest. I shook him harder and harder and my father would not respond. I continued to shake him as I dropped to my knees.

"Dad? I need you! Mom needs you!"

The skin in my father's face had an ethereal blue tinge. I called his name one more time, but I knew it was pointless.

On the floor, next to a torn, tattered Bible, was an open prescription bottle. It was empty. I picked it up. *Demerol.* The prescription read: *take one tablet (50 mg) every twelve hours, AS NEEDED.*

I slumped against his bed and began talking to my father. I told him that I loved him. That he was right about the demon, right about everything. That I wished I had been the son he had deserved and needed. I told him about Sky. I told him everything was going to be OK.

I kept talking as my mother moaned from my bedroom. I kept talking as multiple footsteps and shouts entered the house. Kept talking as two police officers, guns raised, entered my father's bedroom. I kept talking to my dad, irrespective of the officers' questions, their calls and actions around my father's body and around the rest of the house. I only stopped talking when one of the officers broke through my bedroom door and let out a subhuman gasp that shattered the parochial walls of an average town that would never be my home.

I spent the next four days back inside a hospital room, recovering from the shock of my parents' deaths. Detective Gutierrez visited me eight times. Each time, he had asked me the same questions over and over: *How did you get to your house? Why did you go there? What time did you arrive? Who did you talk to first? What did you talk about? Why did your mother call the police on you? Why was she in your room? What were you doing in your father's room? Why were you in the hospital? Why did you leave? Where is Sky?* It was a complete reversal from the answer dominated performance he gave me in the interrogation room months ago. Gutierrez was excessively frustrated with me and I found it infuriating that over the entire questioning and accusing period, the eleven-fingered Walrus had the temerity to describe my mourning as superficial. He never once offered his condolences to me.

I guess it should've been expected since I never gave him any credible, consistent answers. It wasn't intentional – I could barely formulate any cognitive thoughts in my brain, much less produce a consistent explanation of the demon's attack. Despite my uncooperative mind, the detective and his cohort constructed a scenario of events that the press deemed "uncomfortably neat" and "plausible, pending further evidence."

The news reports said that my mother had died from "self-inflicted" knife wounds to her stomach and chest. She had been alive when the police officers had arrived, but bled out by the time she reached the hospital. The written articles put "self-inflicted" in editorial quotes even though the only fingerprints found on the knife were her own, the placement of her body and the knife were consistent with her own efforts, and there were no defensive wounds on her body. But they suspected, as I knew, that she never would have died at her own hands.

According to the idiotic medical examiner's report, my father could've passed away before I had even reached the house – there was a margin of error of about three hours for his time of death. Since my arrival was pegged at 11:30 PM (a compromise between the time my answers had settled on and the time my mother had placed her call to the police), it was possible he had overdosed on his medication hours earlier, likely after his last phone call with me. The report labeled his death as a suicide, but Detective Gutierrez believed someone had assisted with his actions. Of course there was no evidence indicating my mother's culpability, and Detective Gutierrez said that unless there was an admission of guilt, it would be impossible to prove any case of assisted suicide. He shared this fact with me during one of his visits, and he had lingered on the word "guilt." He said it was unsettling how much my father's death resembled Melinda's. I told him that he would never know what really happened.

He'd have to accept the official scenario because it made sense to him and his CSI-conditioned cronies. I couldn't tell him that it was all nonsense. I couldn't tell him that I knew what killed them. The demon had murdered my parents. Just as it had murdered Melinda. And had almost murdered Sky.

Because of my mental purging efforts prior to reaching my father's house, I had successfully forgotten about Sky's close call with death and the turbulent events on the highway. My memory only coalesced when I read an online article about an affluent couple (a quant bond trader and his part-time model girlfriend) who had generated havoc during an otherwise routine traffic accident. The couple were depicted as over-privileged snobs who were hooked on NightSpice – the drug described by Detective Gutierrez, the black powdery substance I had once ingested with Talia. The article had only piqued my curiosity because the author had done some research on the drug's chemical structure (benzene reduced to cyclohexane coupled with a synthesis of an aryl compound on a cyclohexylamine) and researchers were having difficulty reproducing its complicated and unstable nature. The author speculated that the drug might have been developed by a rogue government or possibly a *Breaking Bad*-type genius. The author clearly displayed admiration for whatever brilliantly warped mind had manufactured the drug and I couldn't help but share the sentiment.

At any rate, the crux of the newspaper article was to highlight the drug's ill effects: the fearless rage, illusion of omnipotence, and other alleged observable signs. It went into detail about the couple's antics on the interstate highway and it was that visual description which managed to dig out my memories. The gorgeous female in the BMW wearing Melinda's blue dress. Her possession by the demon and its pursuit of Sky. The article even linked to a YouTube video, taken by one of the stalled highway drivers who had witnessed the couple's hysteria.

I watched the cell phone video about fifty times. I was barely visible, a bit player in the background, always out of focus. The three minute, nineteen second video only showed eleven seconds of me, walking around in a disjointed loop. One moment I'm in front of Sky's Jeep, waving my right hand languidly in the air as insouciantly swatting a fly (an act I still had no recollection of ever doing), and the next moment, I'm carrying Sky in my arms, plopping her back into the Jeep.

I could only assume the inept, amateur videographer had been too entranced by the demon and had disregarded how relevant Sky and I were to the situation.

I was released from the hospital after I passed a routine physical examination. But due to the non-routine nature of my previous hospital stay (based on the notes of Dr. Molker who had unfortunately succumbed to a stroke) and the vague concerns expressed by my parents to the police, I was mandated to go to outpatient psychiatric care. I had to undergo twice a week visits with a sympathy-averse doctor until it was deemed unnecessary. I accepted without protest.

I was certain I could figure out a way to minimize my therapy since I hadn't seen or heard the demon since its appearance at my father's house. It wouldn't be difficult to avoid mentioning the free radical in a rotten chain reaction if I pretended cancer didn't exist.

Before I left the hospital, I paid a quick visit to Trent who was still clinging to life after his aneurysm. I couldn't believe no one had pulled the plug on him. I let him know that I was sorry for what happened to him, even though I felt no residual blame and my words were as torpid and rank as his fuzzed-over, waxed-up ears.

My parents' funeral occurred on a bastardly sunny day, too hot for January, a day better suited for a climate change infomercial. It was a short ceremony with few guests (I passed on the Jesus-Loves-Me Episcopalian service that some of my relatives wanted) and they were buried together in the double plot they had purchased over a decade earlier. My mother's eviscerated body had been given several large bouquets, wreaths of roses and chrysanthemums and carnations, tagged with pruned sympathies, but my father had been given only a token bucket of lilies. After everyone had left, and the bodies interred, I moved most of my mother's flowers onto my father's grave. I tried to recite a prayer, but gave up after realizing I looked foolish.

My mother and father's wills (written, unbeknownst to me, at the same time of their plot purchase) had both designated me as their secondary beneficiary. From my father I received the house, and from my mother, an unbelievable amount of money – she had an overseas account that was worth almost twice the value of the house. I digested my inherited legacy poorly and dedicated myself to utilize this blood wealth with astute parsimony on behalf of their memory. I missed my father deeply, but one of my first orders of business was to sell the house and everything contained within. I didn't want to retain any tangible aspect of a family that never existed.

My next step was to find Sky. Gutierrez was continuing to pester me about her, wanting to perform his due diligence and ask her his litany of follow-up questions, but she had disappeared. According to Gayle (or rather, according to a conversation I overheard at the hospital between Gutierrez and a fellow detective), Sky had shown up to work at the bookstore the day after my parents' death, acting as if nothing were out of the ordinary, though complaining of sleep-deprivation and an emerging cold. Sky had broken for lunch (and to check in on Mr. Rogers) and had never returned. Her Jeep was found parked behind the bookstore, my bags and crutches still inside, my meagre belongings smashed underneath a flat tire. Mr. Rogers was found later in the care of her neighbor. Sky had apparently deserted everything, her parents, her beloved bookstore and pet, and her town without any obvious trace.

Detective Gutierrez held onto my bags for some reason – saying he would keep them until he met with Sky. Although I wanted my books back, I didn't complain and told him he could keep my stuff, including the crutches which were no longer needed because my ankle had fully healed.

The only explanation I could derive about Sky was that she was on the run. Fleeing the demon. It had likely moved on to her since I had not seen the demon and it probably considered her unfinished business. She had to have heard about my parents' deaths as it was on all the major news networks and had even preempted news of a UN peace accord – the public couldn't be bothered with scenes of humanity's goodwill. Her abrupt departure worried me. Although I strongly believed Sky would be able to outrun and outwit the demon, she was undoubtedly wracked with fear.

I tried not to worry about her, but it was impossible. The demon had destroyed the magnificent lives of those I had loved and it wouldn't stop until it claimed the last love in my life.

Yes, I did love Sky. If she could somehow hear my beloved words, my cherished thoughts, I knew they would give her renewed strength and resolve in her fight with the demon.

If I could speak to Sky I would tell her to hold on. I simply needed time. Once I jettisoned my father's house, once I finagled the psychiatrist to shorten our meetings to at most once a month, once I convinced Detective Gutierrez that I was the victim, and once I became bland enough for the news reporters to move past my story and onto more titillating, yellow lies, I would have the time to resurrect my freedom and begin my new, normal life.

(Resurgere tento! Resurgere, Daniel!)

A life dedicated to the memory of Melinda. Dedicated to the memory of my parents.

A life dedicated to finding and helping Sky.

So don't worry, Sky. Rest and be patient. Once I find a way to wrap my ordinary, reassuring arms around the extraordinary, indifferent universe....

I'm coming after you next.

www.ingramcontent.com/pod-product-compliance
Lightning Source LLC
Chambersburg PA
CBHW032154190626
46814CB00005BA/1985